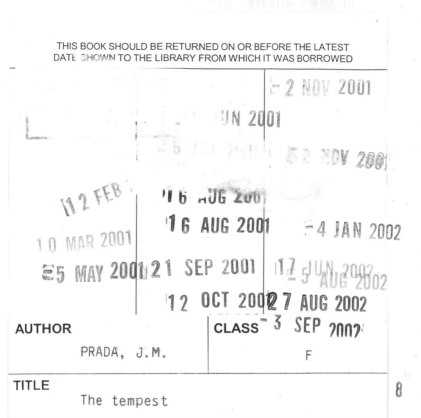

D0353651

THIS BOOK SHOULD BE RETURNED ON OR BEFORE THE LATEST
DATE SHOWN TO THE LIBRARY FROM WHICH IT WAS BORROWED

- 2 NOV 2001

JN 2001

NOV 2001

12 FEB

16 AUG 2001

10 MAR 2001

16 AUG 2001   - 4 JAN 2002

5 MAY 2001 21 SEP 2001   17 JUN 2002
                                    AUG 2002

12 OCT 2002 7 AUG 2002

AUTHOR   **CLASS** - 3 SEP 2002

PRADA, J.M.   F

TITLE   8

The tempest

Juan Manuel de Prada was born in Baracaldo in Spain in 1970 and brought up in Zamora. Although he graduated in Law he devoted himself to literature from an early age, at 25 being hailed by critics as a leading writer of his generation on publication in the same year of *Coños*, a series of meditations, and a collection of short stories, *El Silencio del Patinador*. This was followed by his first novel, the prize-winning *Las Máscaras del Héroe* and, in 1997, *The Tempest*, which won the prestigious Planeta Prize and has since sold over 300,000 copies in its Spanish edition alone. A regular contributor to several leading Spanish newspapers and magazines, de Prada's latest novel, *Las esquinas del aire*, has recently been published in Spain.

THE TEMPEST

Juan Manuel de Prada

Translated by Paul Antill

SCEPTRE

082313002

First published as *La Tempestad* in 1997 by Planeta, Spain
This English translation first published in Great Britain in 2000
by Hodder and Stoughton
A division of Hodder Headline
A Sceptre Paperback

10 9 8 7 6 5 4 3 2 1

A CIP catalogue record for this title is available from the British Library.

ISBN 0 340 75023 5

Typeset by Palimpsest Book Production Limited,
Polmont, Stirlingshire
Printed and bound in Great Britain by
Clays Ltd, St Ives plc

Hodder and Stoughton
A division of Hodder Headline
338 Euston Road
London NW1 3BH

To my mother,
So that she may no longer feel bereft of a son.

Someone should write a novel that has the
consistency of a nightmare. A novel in
which elapsing time is plastic, and oppressive
as it is in dreams. Or maybe it does not
even elapse.

André Pieyre de Mandiargues

Joyful form that flows between my hands,
beloved face in which I view the world,
it mirrors the flight of graceful birds,
who fly to the land of the unforgotten.

Vicente Aleixandre

The most pathetic error of an art critic is
not that he is wrong or that he fails to understand,
but that he *understands* a work of art
for which he has no true feeling.

Ramón Gaya

ONE

It is hard, despicable even, to avert your eyes from those of a man who is bleeding to death; but it is even harder to hold his gaze while trying to delve into the maelstrom of confused passions and deathbed secrets racing across his retinas. It is hard, and painful, having to witness the last agony of a man you do not know, in a city where you are a stranger, and when the darkness of the night has attained that degree of malevolent foreboding that makes the matter of death irrevocable. It is hard, and distressing, to watch a man bleed profusely in a deserted snow-clad street, and to try to grasp the sense of imprecations spoken in a foreign language, without knowing how muddled or meaningful they are when mumbled in the last seconds before death. It is hard, and futile, observing the flow of blood from his chest, with no dressing to hand with which to staunch it, and without even knowing the right words to soothe him, or to help him on his way; and not even having the presence of mind to call for help or inform the police. It is hard, and hopeless, hearing the death rattle of a man beside the sluggishly drifting water of a canal that looks like an open coffin, and to be unable to rouse the neighbourhood to summon assistance, or worse, to try to rouse it and be met by a hostile silence that seems to reverberate from every stone. It is hard, and inauspicious, stumbling across a murder committed in a city abandoned by God and man, and to find yourself caught up in its resolution when you have travelled there with the sole intention of elucidating mysteries of a far more pleasant kind. It only needed this man to die in my arms for me to begin to suspect that other calamities lay in wait for me. Until then, Venice had simply been the landscape of my midnight studies, but I was soon to be overwhelmed by a series of misfortunes: and to the phenomenon of death there would be added the sudden onset of love – that even greater cataclysm! I was soon to learn, during my first police interrogation, that the man's name was Fabio Valenzin, an art dealer and expert forger.

I had travelled to Venice to seek out a painting which I knew from photographic reproductions and the extensive bibliography of specialists who, for hundreds of years, have attempted to explain its meaning. I had squandered most of my student years on a similar task; I had immersed myself in the study of those enigmatic figures, and after exhaustive enquiries and investigations had endowed posterity with a weighty tome, or doctoral thesis, in which I outlined one more interpretation to add to all the others. This painting to which I had dedicated so many sleepless nights is called *The Tempest*. It was painted by Giorgione – assuming that Giorgione really existed and was not just an amalgam of phantoms like Homer – in the later years of his life, about 1505. It may be superfluous to describe *The Tempest* in all its detail because the iconographic literature has done it repeatedly – indeed to excess.

Against the background of a city that preserves the fantastical style of architecture which is the stuff of dreams, and in the midst of a wooded landscape, we see, on the right, a nude woman (a shrub mitigates the blatant spectacle of naked flesh) suckling her child. She does so with an air of sensual sadness and indifference to her surroundings, whereas on the left, a man attired in the fashion of the time and carrying a pilgrim's staff has the air of an intruder on the scene, but one who, nevertheless, may once have known the woman, and may even have enjoyed her favours. We do not know whether the woman is patrician or plebeian (naked flesh is a great equaliser), we do not know if the man is guarding her or spying on her or simply passing by, but we do know, because the composition suggests it, that there hangs over them an atmosphere of disapproval of their lack of communication, the stigma of a silence possibly more eloquent than reproaches or excuses. At their feet a murmuring stream flows beneath a wooden bridge, and there are also stone ruins that stand conspicuous amid the undergrowth like symbols of a dead love, and trees that shake and quiver, rippled by a breeze that portends bad weather. Dominating the picture we see a baleful sky, oppressive and overcast, dense with static clouds through which there suddenly appears, like a scar, a streak of lightning that heralds the gathering storm, a storm as shocking as the memory of a crime committed, or the remains of a passion reduced to ashes.

In *The Tempest*, for the first time in the history of painting, landscape ceases to be purely ornamental, and becomes a symbol, or pictorial representation, of the turmoil of passions in the heart of man. Specialists (of whom I am one) have endeavoured to decipher the theme of the painting – which may be excessively cryptic or convoluted – by reference to classical mythology and allegorical allusions, or to the inexhaustible inspiration of the lives of the saints or episodes from the Bible: there are those who have claimed that the painting represents Moses rescued from the waters of the Nile, others have affirmed that it is the young Paris nurtured by a bear in the shape of a woman (in this theory, the lightning and the ruins are a forewarning of the destruction of Troy); there is also an interpretation with widespread currency that it represents St Joseph and the Virgin resting during their flight to Egypt. These more or less convincing hypotheses fail to refute the suspicion that Giorgione's intention was to disguise the non-existence of a specific theme through misleading equivocation, or possibly that he was simply alluding to the storms which rage in the obscure landscapes of the heart. I had succumbed, like many others, to the fascination of this picture, and had fused it with the febrile mass of my own obsessions.

After wasting nearly five years studying Giorgione I felt the need to visit Venice, in order to be sure that the search for a meaning was worth the trouble. I was travelling with that eagerness lovers have when they embark on marriage – although I had ruled out thoughts of marital delights for myself – but with that edgy feeling of unease that disturbs the desecrators of holy places. I was travelling, drawn by the secret avidity which the imminent solution of a mystery produces in us, and which subjects us to unspeakable hardships from which we emerge prematurely aged. I was travelling to Venice with the barely admitted hope that the experience would rekindle the ashes of my youth. It is said that although all our journeys are undertaken in search of lost youth, all we reap in the end is old age, disillusion, and more troubles than we deserve.

January was setting in like an opiate; cold and harsh, but with a measure of serenity. The outlines of Venice were just visible in the distance beneath a protective shield of snow held in a precarious balance, which seemed to augur its destruction. A clammy mist over the lagoon clung limpet-like to the stone, blurring its contours and bestowing on the palaces lining the

Grand Canal the appearance of closed and shuttered factories, on which the chipped masonry of the façades resembled sores on the body of a leper. Venice possessed something of a leper who persists in remaining upright even after the verdict of dissolution has been decreed; Venice possessed something redolent of death, and nothing could conceal the onset of decay. From the streetlamps illuminating at intervals the Riva degli Schiavoni traces of light melted into the mist like the pale slime of snails while the *vaporetto* cut through the waters of the Grand Canal with a noise like the rattle of an old cart, which *vaporetti* make in winter when ice collects in the engines and makes them judder. The *vaporetto* from Marco Polo airport carried only half a dozen lonely and sleepy tourists who had given up talking to each other, thereby making their weary journey seem even longer; or possibly they were affected by that inexorable and mute dejection that characterises cities on the point of foundering – for Venice was foundering: the water of the lagoon had risen above the level of the *rive*, invading the halls of palaces and the porticoes of churches, and spreading its infestation of mud and lapping waves up to the mosaics of the Basilica of St Mark, which stood out in the background like a mammoth resigned to its fate, its foundations weakened by the damp, and its cupolas, belly upwards, breathing the corrosive night air.

I had stationed myself in the prow of the *vaporetto*, abandoning the passenger cabin to the tourists, and I leant over the forward rail of the boat to cool down in the rush of air that smelled of frozen seaweed. I defied the cold with blithe arrogance, as if the city were offering itself to me alone. We had passed the island of Murano at an exasperatingly slow speed and with muffled splashes, as if the crew of the *vaporetto* sought to pay tribute to its decrepit appearance: six black gondolas were moored to its quayside, swaying and banging in the swell like funeral biers teetering against each other; and the buildings on the island, probably glass factories, had the appearance of plebeian mausoleums – if the paradox may be permitted – where the corpses are piled following a catastrophic epidemic. The headlight of the *vaporetto* pierced the murk, cutting through the dank haze, with the temerity of a diver plunging into a sea thick with weed.

Then, almost imperceptibly at first, but with increasing intensity, it began to snow. It settled on the lagoon instantly, as if falling on dry land, and I watched this phenomenon, which seemed to defy the laws of physics, with the same grateful wonder with which the Jews must have received the fall of manna in the middle of their exodus: I did not know that snow fell on cities beside the sea – as a true provincial I thought that snow was the prerogative of mountain country – I did not know that snow could settle on the sea without melting. In less than five minutes, the swirl had become dense and the lagoon was carpeted with an unblemished whiteness that the *vaporetto* defiled with its bows as it made its way through it. Behind us, we left a wash of black, churning water over whose scars the snow quietly laid its blessed mantle. I had never experienced such a heavy snowstorm, never had I witnessed such a wild scene of nature, which violated its own laws and drew us into a world of unreality. It was snowing over the lagoon, it was snowing over Venice, and it was snowing on me.

It was snowing with that obstinacy the heavens reserve for cities they have determined to erase from the map, and it was the first real sign of discouragement that Venice gave me, the first hint of the vicissitudes that awaited me in its streets, vicissitudes that would multiply like a creeping malediction. Its persistence contained a threat, or premonition of a fate which, at the time, I failed to understand.

I should have sensed the disasters lying in wait for me, but whether from obtuseness or lack of experience, I failed to interpret this warning from above. I did not know I was to be a witness to a murder, nor that I was to become involved in a criminal investigation; nor did I know that I would fall in love with the wrong woman – although we do not choose when or with whom we fall in love, because love is governed by a celestial mechanism beyond our control – even less did I know that this sudden falling in love and this inexplicable murder would finish off for ever the man that I had been and replace him with another – possibly more adult, but deeply troubled and disillusioned: growing up is a process of decline. I thought naïvely that foreign cities, and other people's lives, pass through our experience without imprinting themselves on our memories, like water which trickles harmlessly away, leaving our skin with a fleeting sensation of coolness or, at most, a shiver. Venice disproved this belief. Nobody changes his habits with impunity; nobody meddles in the lives of others without suffering an incurable sickness; nobody bestows on others his hatred or his friendship without receiving in return a weight of responsibility, unwanted confidences, and tears choked back.

Hours later, while I was supporting the inanimate body of Fabio Valenzin, while I listened to the exhalation from his wound and observed the fine plume of steam welling up from the breach in which the bullet had lodged itself, while I watched helplessly as he bled to death, that same snow absorbed his blood and made it disappear, like a cautious criminal removing the traces of his crime; and it was only then that I realised that Venice was bringing down on my head the curse she reserves for intruders. Until that moment, I had been unaware that I was trespassing on territory that was no concern of mine. For now I confined myself to watching with dazzled delight the snow falling over the city, floating down like particles of soot from a conflagration which, having destroyed the city, was falling back, converted into ash. Venice seemed a city wasted by a thousand fires, both real and symbolic.

On my left, just before entering the Grand Canal, I thought I saw the island of San Giorgio Maggiore with the church of Andrea Palladio, its *campanile* rising above the flood like a mast that senses shipwreck.

'San Marco,' announced one of the crew, in order to rouse the disheartened and drowsy tourists.

Near the landing stage, two monolithic columns rose straight out of the water because the flood had taken possession of the most famous square in the world, that priceless location which, winter after winter, blends into the lagoon and threatens to surrender to it like the island of Atlantis hesitating to take the final plunge. On top of those columns reposed bronze casts of the wingèd lion of St Mark and the statue of St Theodore, ostentatious symbols of a primacy lost centuries ago. The *acqua alta* swamped the landing stage made of sagging planks and sought shelter in the Palace of the Doges, under the columned archways that form a filigree of stone. From the mooring place as far as the Mercerie a long duckboard pontoon allowed recent arrivals to keep their feet dry as they crossed that scene which the combination of snow and flood had transformed into an underwater dream world. The crew of the *vaporetto* said goodbye to us in an impenetrable language, a mixture of Venetian dialect and macaronic English, and they watched us go with a resigned and funereal compassion such as would be aroused by condemned exiles when abandoned to their fate on the beach of an island frequented only by wild beasts and mariners who have lost their bearings.

I refused to allow myself to be cast down by any sense of exclusion, in spite of the fact that the welcome extended by the drowned city did not inspire me with enthusiasm. I advanced cautiously across the pontoon; the snow cushioned my steps and scrunched beneath my feet with a sort of crackling sound, like an invertebrate animal that dares not protest as it is squashed – but snow recovers from footfalls, just as it does from blood spilled on its white surface, as, a short time later, I should have the opportunity to confirm – and it made me sense the remorse a man must feel after violating the virginity of a young girl, or abusing an innocent person. The square of St Mark's, overrun by filth swept in by the floodwaters, had the despoiled and distressed atmosphere of a dance hall at the end of a party where the guests have drunk themselves sick, and have strewn the floor with broken bottles. The water invaded the arcades, forcing its way into the shops, spoiling the goods in the windows, and claiming right of entry into the more exclusive cafés – those with pianos and rococo mouldings, which certain cosmopolitan and literary individuals have taken it upon themselves to denigrate. The shopkeepers and waiters – the latter with a reluctance becoming their superior station – prolonged their working day mopping up, but they did so with the grudging discontent of those performing a formal duty or suffering from a biblical curse. They were the only people in the square, and their air of impassive resignation added to its desolate appearance. The sense of desolation was contagious: a sour welcome, enough to discourage any traveller from pursuing his quest.

I was arriving in Venice with a very modest grant from my university, and with no other surety than the address of a cheap but respectable hotel – if by respectable one means clean sheets and a lavatory shared by not too many people – and a letter of introduction which, supposedly, would ensure the hospitality of Gilberto Gabetti, the director of the Accademia, the gallery which houses *The Tempest* of Giorgione, and who is perhaps the most distinguished authority on Venetian art from Bellini to Tintoretto. In any case, I preferred the indifferent hospitality of an unknown to the ignominious treatment inflicted on me during my five years at university, where I had had to act as virtual errand boy for Professor Mendoza, to kowtow to him uncomplainingly, to listen to accounts of his amorous exploits, to swallow my pride and lick his arse in order to keep in his good books, all because my remaining in the academic world depended upon him. Professor Mendoza, who had directed the work on my thesis and was a rigorous observer of the privileges granted to those higher up the promotion ladder, never missed an opportunity to entrust me with demeaning chores designed to destroy my self-respect: it was my job to prevent the more boisterous and bumptious of the students from bursting into his study; it was my job to attend to their most trivial requests; it was my job to read them the unsatisfactory reports on their tests, which I myself had corrected. Very infrequently, Professor Mendoza, by way of encouragement, would call me into his study and ask routine questions about the progress of my researches; and before I could mumble my routine response he would lumber me with a number of modifications. Professor Mendoza travelled frequently to Madrid to attend conferences, to intrigue in the centres of power, and to divide his time amongst a legion of insatiable lady friends; this nomadic propensity of his distanced him more and more from his teaching duties. For years, as I say, I suffered the despotism of Professor Mendoza with the remote consolation that one day he would do me the favour of promoting me, of recommending me to a college, or of placing me in charge of an examination board. It was vital for me to have a clear aim. For this reason, I was not too concerned if I met with hostility from Gilberto Gabetti, just as I was not too bothered by Venice's disagreeable welcome.

The pontoon ended suddenly when it reached the Mercerie, a labyrinth of tiny streets where a bazaar-like infinity of smart boutiques exists cheek by jowl with souvenir shops, second-hand bookshops, and banks. The pontoon ended, but the floodwaters did not, so I resigned myself to proceeding to my hotel through water made mushy by the snow melting under my feet. My trousers were wet to the knee, the tails of my raincoat were soaked, and I ruined for ever a pair of shoes not designed for paddling through rivers – even though I walked on tiptoe, trying to keep my balance as I juggled my luggage. It was both pathetic and ridiculous appearing in such a state in a foreign city, but, as I knew from experience, physical humiliation is never as bad as moral servitude.

In Venice, the number system does not go by individual streets, but extends to all the streets that make up a district. There are six districts in the city, and I was still in that of St Mark's, turning corners at random and having constantly to retrace my steps: even in its organisation, Venice must be as exceptional as it is in its location, and in the almost excessive richness of its beauty. The snow had become lighter and was turning to sleet when, at last, I chanced upon the entrance to the Albergo Cusmano, which was sheltered by a porch that looked like a tunnel on the point of collapse; above the lintel there was a fluorescent sign that emitted an irritating hum, and the walls of the porch, crumbling with damp, had a reptilian feel to them that would have horrified a traveller less forbearing than I.

'Good evening,' I mumbled, uncertain whether I was saying something inappropriate.

The woman in the lobby turned her head, her attention drawn more by the bell that sounded when I pushed open the door than by my hoarse greeting in indifferent Italian. There was something haughty in the way she looked up, her dark and very large eyes resembling the stones in a Byzantine mosaic; her features were unusual, both ardent and stern, but the shape of her breasts inside the black sweater could by no means be described as severe. She was sloppily dressed, and yet there seemed to be something premeditated in her sloppiness, for she wore high-heeled shoes and lipstick. Although she must have been forty she retained that ripe maturity which easily assimilates a few wrinkles without appearing blemished. I had expected to be met by a less distinguished type of landlady, possibly with curlers in her hair and an apron round her waist, and I allowed myself to be stirred by an irrational spasm of desire – a partial erection in fact.

'What a night!' she said, and glanced with sympathy, not unmixed with distaste, at my dripping clothes.

'I have a room reserved in the name of Alejandro Ballesteros.'

I stammered this out in the rudimentary and rusty Italian of my school visits, back in the days of my adolescence. Either from antipathy, or a desire to keep her distance, she resorted to English.

'Let me see . . .'

The hall carpet retained the tiny horseshoe imprints of her heels which somehow served to intensify my erection. Seen from behind she revealed a bottom just on the acceptable side of plump: her skirt was disgracefully tight over her hips and highly constricting round her buttocks which I fancied were slightly asymmetrical and, of course, soft. I confess that I like soft and asymmetrical bottoms.

'Yes, here you are. Your room is number 107. Can I have your passport, please?'

Behind the counter there was a heater turned up to its maximum. My ears were burning with the sudden change of temperature, and I feared that they would soon be covered in chilblains.

'Spanish,' she stated, with a smile which did nothing to diminish her air of severity.

She spoke the word in Castilian, but in that silky Italian way as if to tease me, and she had shrugged her shoulders (her breasts quivered inside her jumper as she did so – possibly they too were soft and asymmetrical), all of which made me feel even more foolish and inferior, as if it was not enough to be guilty of having soaking wet clothes and a secret erection in the corner of my underpants.

'Follow me, please.'

The hotel did not have a lift – in Venice, both cars and lifts are banned – and the staircase, which was so narrow that there was scarcely room for my luggage, was carpeted like the floor of the entrance hall: the landlady dug her heels into it without concern, but the carpet neither scrunched nor crackled, unlike the snow I had trodden down on my way there, perhaps because it no longer had a virginity to violate, nor an innocence to abuse. She made her way up the stairs with scarcely any movement of her hips due to her constricting skirt, and her calves flexed, making her ankles look slender, but also emphasising the backs of her knees where the flesh was dimpled – similar to those other dimples she must have had where her back met her buttocks. I also noticed the hollow in the nape of her neck which her hair, gathered up in a complicated chignon, left exposed. The danger in making these detailed observations is that one ends up with a kind of handbook of anatomy, but my profession, which consists largely of scrutinising paintings for hours on end, makes me a keen observer of such things.

'Just across there you have the bathroom. In your room you'll find a wash-basin and a telephone.' She gave me this information much like a museum guide. 'Just take a look to see that it suits you.'

It might not have suited a distinguished visitor, but it served the modest needs of a not so fussy junior lecturer. The mirror over the wash-basin was small and had lost some of its silvering, and the mattress on the bed sagged from long use – and by no means gentle use at that. On the other hand, the window provided a view over a small, secluded square meanly lit by one small lamp that accommodated a mortuary of dead insects. The canal which bounded the square had not risen above its banks, and its waters possessed the enduring sadness of caged animals. Just behind the square rose the bell tower of the church of San Stefano, leaning to the right like a lighthouse yielding to the surf breaking below it.

'Excuse me, what is your name?' I asked abruptly, yet keeping to our diplomatic and standoffish English.

The half-light of the room emphasised the lines at the corners of her mouth, and added a few more crow's-feet round her eyes, which I did not find at all displeasing.

'Dina Cusmano,' she replied, either taken aback, or flattered that I should ask. 'But I don't see—'

I interrupted her to prevent any possible reproach for my temerity.

'Sorry,' I said. 'I just thought it would simplify our relations.'

A moment later, I regretted having used the word *relations* which might have suggested certain physical intentions. Clearly she forgave me, because she added a slightly more personal touch to our conversation.

'If you go out at night, this is the front door key.' She indicated one which was bigger and shinier than my room key. 'I usually close about now because I am alone, and I don't wait up.'

She spurned English, and now spoke in the Venetian dialect which, on her lips, sounded less coarse, reminding me vaguely of Catalan.

'I sleep in the room just above yours. If you like I could make you some coffee.'

Maybe she was the bold one, and I was just a shy man overcome by the audacity that can affect you at the end of a long journey. I withdrew like a snail into my shell.

'Don't worry ... Thank you very much ... I am very tired ... Perhaps tomorrow ...'

She left the room without turning round, denying me another glimpse of her bottom, but whether this was due to discretion or disappointment, I cannot say. I think I desired Dina Cusmano just as I might desire any woman, with that indiscriminate lust that is the bane of the excessively sensitive amongst us. I heard the muffled sound of her heels as she went up another flight of stairs and then down a passage, also carpeted, to her own apartments, while I removed my shoes which oozed water and bits of weed, my wet socks, and my trousers whose condition gave me the shudders. Now I could hear Dina's footsteps just above my head where there was no carpet, but my erection had subsided because suddenly my feet had begun to stiffen painfully, and I amused myself by putting them up against the radiator to feel the pleasant tingling as the warmth penetrated my toes. I could hear the clatter of her heels on a tiled floor – Dina had her own bathroom – and the squeak of a tap, and that distinctive sound that water makes when it splashes against the porcelain of a lavatory. It was disturbing, but also pleasant, to know that Dina was urinating, but even more disturbing to suspect that she knew that the sound carried through the walls. She urinated with relief, or possibly from great need, slowly finishing off just a moment before I heard the thunderous noise of the cistern. Through the window I could see the leaning tower of San Stefano, and also the hieroglyphic shapes of the snowflakes, a monotonous and italicised alphabet that helped to distract my attention. I remembered then – it was not yet midnight – that I had promised to phone Gabetti to let him know I had arrived. I dialled the number that I knew by heart and counted five rings before I heard a hesitant and rather worried voice at the other end of the line.

'Excuse me, am I speaking to Gilberto Gabetti? This is Alejandro Ballesteros – from Spain.'

The line crackled for a second or so. When he spoke, Gabetti's voice was affected by the interference which made every word sound like a careless footstep in the snow that blanketed Venice.

'At last, Ballesteros! I wondered whether your damned plane had turned back halfway through the flight. So you got here safe and sound?'

His Spanish was impeccable and upper-class, with a diction that sounded as if it had been learned in a school of oratory.

'Yes, sir, the flight was only half an hour late. I hope I didn't wake you up—'

'Not at all, not at all, my dear friend.' I detected a note of false familiarity in his voice. 'I am reading the last chapters of your thesis at this very moment. By the way, where are you staying?'

I knew that my landlady had lain down because the springs of her bed received the weight of her body with a mildly protesting groan, like a cast-off lover who does not dare to reject the untimely visit of the woman who is unfaithful to him. I also collapsed on to my bed (or into the hollow of the mattress to be precise), which roused identical protestations from its springs. From that position, with my head resting on the pillow, all I could see through the window was a rectangle of sky and the bell tower of San Stefano in the background.

'The place is called the Albergo Cusmano in the district of St Mark's, but I can't give you its exact location. Venice is such a labyrinth.'

I could guess at Gabetti's forced and condescending smile; I was conscious of having broached a tricky subject.

'All right. Now what can you see through the window?'

For a few seconds I had allowed my attention to wander and I was gazing at the ceiling, staring at the damp stains in the whitewash that spread like a fantastical map with a very broken outline.

'A leaning tower – that is what I can see.'

But I had closed my eyes, the better to imagine Dina lying naked on her own bed, also examining the damp stains on her ceiling. Possibly she had removed the skirt that so cruelly constricted her behind and the black sweater that scarcely managed to confine her breasts, and also her bra and panties, which would leave the pale impression of their elastic on her skin. Possibly she was feeling pleasantly aroused, stimulated by the thought that a man was thinking of her naked body – with all the darkness of the night centred on her pubis.

'A leaning tower?' repeated Gabetti after a pause, but with

a brusqueness that gave an edge to his words. 'The bell tower of the church of San Stefano!' Suddenly, he changed the course of the conversation: 'Did I tell you I am enjoying your thesis very much?'

'That is very kind of you,' I replied, heartened by the praise.

'Not at all, kindness has no place in my book. I call a spade a spade – just like you Spaniards.' I attributed his volubility to enthusiasm. 'I don't agree with any of your conclusions, but the work you have done seems to me superb!'

Gilberto Gabetti was one of the most respected experts on Venetian art, but the respect, awe even, in which he was held by fellow students in the profession was based more on the prestige of his lectures and verbal pronouncements than on specific achievements in research. The vast talent of Gabetti had never been committed to writing – he despised analytical studies, or what he described as documentary waffle that buries art and turns it into a dead discipline – and his claim to scholarliness derived from having immersed himself in the works themselves of the great painters. He had managed the Accademia for twenty-five years without contributing anything of academic merit or ideological conviction, and although a few envious individuals with a taste for long-gone history charged him with having flirted with fascism in the days of his youth, he had managed to maintain his prestige in spite of all accusations and insults, with that proud indifference which men of the world have at their command.

'I have already declared that I am against those who persist in bringing out new interpretations of *The Tempest*,' he said severely. This bewildered me and caused me to doubt the sincerity of his original judgement, because the whole structure of my doctoral thesis was predicated on an attempt to provide an interpretation. 'Giorgione was the first modern artist, he painted in accordance with the emotions that his state of mind enjoined without being tied down by a predetermined theme. Remember the words of Vasari who was almost his contemporary: *Giorgione worked with no other inspiration than his own vision.* I cannot see any reason to slog away searching for symbols and allegories in his pictures.'

Although he expressed these views in civil terms which moderated their harshness, their shocking message left no room for doubt: my ideas were, as far as he was concerned, either crass or superfluous. I felt suddenly overcome by the fatigue of the journey. That was when I heard the shot.

'What was that?' I exclaimed, sitting up in the bed.

'What did you say?'

I leaned out of the window as far as the length of the telephone wire allowed. Opposite the hotel was one of those big, rambling old houses, or palaces, that preserve their imposing appearance in spite of the neglect of their owners; the façade was lined by an arched balcony with alabaster pilasters. Startled by the shot, a number of pigeons flew out of the run-down building which they had obviously made their home and burst into the icy air in a flutter of confused and drowsy wings like moths dazzled by a blaze of light. Several of them collided, their wings frantically entangled, and an occasional feather fell away from them, descending slowly to become camouflaged in the snow.

'Hey, Ballesteros – what the devil's happening?' Gabetti was indignant at the sudden interruption in our conversation.

From inside the palace, someone threw a round and shiny object – possibly a coin, or a ring, or an earring – which traced an eccentric arc like an expiring meteorite, before dropping into the motionless water of the canal, and sinking into the weeds and slime at the bottom that would swallow it for ever.

'Listen, Ballesteros . . . Can you hear me?' Gabetti repeated, his tone veering from exasperation to supplication.

'Christ, yes, I can hear you only too well!' I shocked myself by the sharpness of my reply. 'But I think something extraordinary has happened.'

'Where? What have you seen?'

'I can't say that I have actually seen anything,' I lied, perfidiously omitting to mention that fleeting tell-tale object that left its sparkle in my memory, 'but I thought I heard a shot.'

It had stopped snowing, and the darkness of the night was lessening above the rooftops of the palaces, as if by magic, or as if it was retreating from what was about to happen. A distant bell began to strike twelve.

'A shot? Are you sure?'

The door of the abandoned building, also framed in an alabaster arch, opened slowly, with that apparent reticence of doors reluctant to release their secrets. On the threshold appeared an individual, his face haggard and as pale as parchment. His look evinced terror. He staggered as if dazed or drunk. When I discerned the red stain spreading across the front of his shirt and smearing the lapels of his jacket I knew that he had been the target of the shot that still echoed loudly in my ears. He pressed one hand against the wound in his chest and this immediately became soaked in the blood which pulsed between his fingers as he walked. He stuck close to the wall of the house on the narrow bank which separated the building from the canal. He soon slipped on the snow, and fell on his face with a thud.

'We'll talk again later, Gabetti,' I said, without replacing the phone properly.

I charged out of the room, and as I ran down the stairs, feeling the velvety carpet beneath my feet, I realised I was barefoot and wearing only my underpants. The temperature in the lobby was like an oven, but in the cold of the street my breath turned to mist, and the snow stung my feet. The mouth of the unknown man on the other side of the canal was open and gorged with the blood gushing up his throat, and a fine plume of steam oozed from his wound like the wraith of his departing spirit.

'Wait – I'm coming,' I shouted absurdly, before plunging into the foul water of the canal which came up to the level of my chest, making my nipples stiffen.

It was much easier to wade through the water without shoes, socks or trousers, but the slime at the bottom and the marine plant life which wrapped its rotting tendrils round my legs felt disgusting. I was across in a matter of seconds, but the loathsome sensation remained on my skin for days, impervious to soaping and scrubbing. The unknown man had fallen with the side of his face in the pool of blood which the snow was diligently trying to absorb, and he stared up at me with a look of wonder or amazement, or that gratitude full of anguish with which one would look at the Samaritan who has arrived too late. I raised him a few inches off the ground, cradling his head so that he should not choke on his own blood. He had a long thin face, and its pallor made it appear even thinner, almost translucent. He wore expensive clothes – too expensive to be wasted shrouding a dead man. I talked without stopping. I whispered to him in the way a nanny comforts a sleepless child, or one soothes with lies and prevarications the suspicions of a lover. I talked to calm my own agitation, and he looked up at me with a fixed blue stare; I watched his pupils glaze over, foreshadowing the *rigor* that would shortly grip him.

'We're going to call the police. We're going to call the police and an ambulance.'

I talked for the sake of talking. I could think of no way of calling the police other than by yelling at the top of my voice, always supposing that the Venetian police patrol the canals – which was assuming a lot. The unknown man tore his shirt open – his fingers were stiffening, and the pattern of his veins stood out beneath the parchment of his skin – to reveal the breach made by the bullet that had been fired at point-blank range, maybe even with the pistol pressed against his chest. The wound seemed to breathe like a second mouth – its breath also turned to steam – as it pumped out gobbets of blood with every beat of his ruptured heart.

'Oh, Christ,' I said. My words poured out as uncontrollably as the blood from the wounded man. 'Oh, shit! Fucking hell! What in God's name am I going to do?'

The lamp cast its unwavering light on the canal, the canal cast its quivering amber reflection on the façade of the palace and over the latticed windows on the ground floor. Suddenly, I caught a brief glimpse of a horrible white face at one of these. It had hollow eyes and a nose like the beak of a huge bird. It enveloped itself in a cape, before disappearing into the darkness. It was an unearthly sight which bore no possible resemblance to a human being, unless the walls of that big old building hid one of the monsters of mythology. As recklessness does not feature among my virtues I rejected the idea of pursuing it, although I could clearly hear it running away through the back of the building; I heard its footsteps, a remorseless flight across the virgin snow, and shouted in order to relieve my own distress.

'Dina, wake up! You must call the police!'

The blood that now oozed out of the man was thick and tar-like, plumbing the last residues in his body. He gripped me fiercely, digging his fingernails into my arms, bruising and gashing them with the strength of this last convulsion. I was deeply distressed by a situation to which I saw no end.

'Dina, wake up!' My voice was hoarse. 'And you – tell me who it was.'

I shook him pitilessly, but all that emerged from his lips was a series of blasphemies mixed with clots of blood. Dina had switched on the light in her room and pushed back the wooden shutters that had prevented her from seeing what was happening; like the pigeons startled by the shot, she was still gripped by the remnants of a dream that clouded her understanding. The dying man raised his right hand to within inches of my face (the veins no longer stood out, and had turned a greenish colour), and he separated his fingers as widely as he could: on the second finger there remained a pale circle, the mark of a ring that somebody had wrenched off. The hole in his chest had ceased to exhale, and his body – his corpse, rather – sagged, all resistance ended. Only his eyes retained their steely gaze.

'Shall I call the police?'

Dina was virtually on the sill of her window. She awaited my instructions, bewildered by the horror of the scene and on the point of bursting into tears. The thin material of her nightdress barely concealed her shivering body.

'There's no longer any hurry,' I said, wiping the stranger's blood on my shirt. His blood was still warm, and it worked like a salve on my numbed fingers.

TWO

The jangle of church bells penetrated deep inside the police station, as they competed with each other to strike the correct time and to summon the non-existent faithful to prayer; non-existent, because in Venice there remained only corpses and the shades of future corpses, apart from the tourists, who understood no liturgy other than that of herding together. It was a brazen prayer of thanks that celebrated the retreat of the water and welcomed the advent of a morning during which the sun might succeed in breaking through like a dirty copper coin between the drifts of snow. Every time a new bell joined in the jubilation my head throbbed, as if pierced by a splinter of metal. Inspector Nicolussi was probably quite as tired as I was, but either his respect for the letter of the law, or loyalty to his masochistic principles, prevented him from halting the interrogation. He was a man worn down by late nights, with a villainous beard that grew thickly over his cheeks, his chin, and down his throat. The contrast with his head was remarkable because he was bald, except for some hair over his temples and the back of his neck. His lips were dry and cracked and with no other lustre than that provided by his cigarette (he had got through a full packet in just three hours). By contrast, his eyes were bright and moist because of a persistent discharge from the tear ducts. His face, and the rest of his anatomy, seemed to have been shaped by the tensions between opposing forces. Inspector Nicolussi was both thin and pudgy, possibly because his work gave him frequent sleepless nights, combined with a sedentary lifestyle. They had just given him a first draft of the forensic report.

'Valenzin died at about twelve o'clock,' he said.

His glance encompassed both Dina and me; besides being bright, his eyes crossed, and seemed to function independently of each other.

'Now do you believe I'm not lying? I've been telling you that for hours.'

In Nicolussi's office, apart from the subordinate who had typed out our statements, there was an interpreter whose interventions were futile because I understood Nicolussi's Italian – he spoke an exuberant, southern dialect – and I suspect that he also understood my Spanish. Dina's lips shaped a weary smile; like me she had been up all night answering routine questions, and her version of events was exactly the same as mine. It was she who had notified the police of Valenzin's murder, and had attended the removal of the corpse with greater fortitude than I. The impulsive desire I had felt for her when I first arrived at the hotel had diminished as the hours went by, and had changed to a vague sentiment combining admiration, gratitude, complicity, and also fear.

Once the police launches arrived they cordoned off the little square, took the first photographs of Valenzin, and the forensic surgeon examined the mess the bullet had made of him, while Dina and I were made to remain in the lobby of the hotel under the eye of a youthful policeman who must have mistaken us for a pair of adulterers, judging by the severe way he looked us over, keeping one hand on the butt of his pistol. As if with the reverberations of a nightmare, I was assailed by images of a crime that did not concern me, but of which I had been the sole witness: Valenzin's steely gaze, the figure glimpsed inside the building, and the shiny round object which had fallen into the canal and now lay at the bottom, waiting for someone to reclaim it from the mud. Dina had wrapped me in a blanket, had moved the heater near my feet, and had placed a sympathetic hand on my knee to help calm my agitation. I should have liked to reciprocate her gesture but my hands were coated in Valenzin's blood which was drying to a sticky crust, and they gave off a cloying, sour smell, like badly-aired bedclothes. In the little square outside, Inspector Nicolussi was giving out orders and sending messages to his subordinates. Although they all wore gum boots quite a few slipped over, and in different circumstances this would have been amusing. 'I must look terrible,' said Dina, and she was right. Her hair was in rats' tails and she wore a garish dressing-gown which hid her legs and just revealed her shabby, well-worn slippers, her small toes protruding through the broken seams. She put them so close to the heater – 'to help the circulation,' she explained – that the rubber soles were in danger of catching fire. I gazed with unashamed deliberation at the way her toes twitched, threatening to burst completely through the seams. I also looked at her fragile ankles, and her heels which had lost their curvature, flattened by too much walking. 'Now comes the worst of it,' she warned me. 'They're going to torture us with a thousand and one questions – and our answers had better be convincing.' I tried to defuse this menace. 'As long as they limit their tortures to questions we're sitting pretty.' I remember I used this homely expression although it was obviously incomprehensible to her, so I changed it to: 'What I mean is, we shall be all right provided they don't use more forceful methods.' Dina bit her lip, and for a moment or two I could see the marks of her teeth, which faded as she spoke again. I have already mentioned that her lips were severe – possibly because they were bereft of other lips to relieve their loneliness. 'Don't worry,' she said, 'the police here aren't violent; at the worst they'll be a bit rude.' The young policeman who had been put in charge of us gave a snort to express either self-importance or irritation, because we seemed to be ignoring his presence. I felt slightly uncomfortable and tried to divert the conversation to more inconsequential matters, but I soon realised that it was too late: Dina had started off down the path that leads to the easing of a burden of guilt. I should have preferred not to be the repository of her confessions (how many sins of other people was I going to be saddled with in one night!), but there was no stopping her, and she spoke without self-pity: 'This isn't the first time I've had dealings with the police. I had to put up with them when I killed my husband.' The heater was drying my socks and toasting my toes that were still numb with cold. I attempted a response which would combine self-possession and sympathy in equal proportions, but was unable to hide either my astonishment, or the dread I felt at having landed in a city in which murder was an everyday affair. Dina again placed her hand on my knee, as if to forgive my weakness: 'Don't be upset, I had no regrets about killing him. In fact I shouldn't have left it so long. The very first day after our wedding I knew I'd made a mistake. But when you are young you do lots of foolish things.' I nodded to show that I understood, although, in fact, my youth had been devoid of foolishness, and I gave her a glance, to warn her that she ought to be cautious about what she said, to avoid creating any further suspicion in the mind of the policeman who was watching us carefully from the shadows, where he stood like a statue, or a mannequin. 'Oh, I'm sure he knows the whole story. He was probably there with a bunch of his cronies when they got drunk one night, and sang filthy songs outside the door of the hotel.' She spoke with weary resignation, as if such outrages were run-of-the-mill affairs, not worth making a fuss about. 'Here in Venice everybody knows everything about everybody: as neighbours, we are models of malice, and we're all as bad as each other. They call me the Black Widow, and avoid me like the plague.' A shadow crossed her face, and deepened the little wrinkles that had kindled my devotion; her eyelids drooped, and I wondered what memories were flickering at that moment across those Byzantine eyes that I should have loved to anoint with my kisses, if only to defend them against the past. 'I was just twenty when I married. At that age we are all rebels with a cause, we want to run away without knowing exactly what we are running away from – possibly, from the fate that others have mapped out for us. My parents worked in a flour mill on Giudecca island. The mill went bankrupt, and they saw nothing wrong in my marrying the lawyer who was negotiating the terms of their dismissal. If he was going to be their saviour, he might as well become their son-in-law. In the end, the compensation granted by the judge wasn't enough for them to live on, and as for my marriage, well, that was a disaster. My husband, Carlo, had an office in Mestre at the other end of the Ponte della Libertà, on dry land, three kilometres north of this city which has always been my prison. So there was no good reason *not* to marry him. But as I said, I knew the very next day I had made a mistake. Our engagement was short. It was just a charade in which both of us were on our best behaviour. Carlo was a boorish, ill-mannered individual, but when it suited him he could hide his bad manners behind the sort of lively good humour that makes men popular, and this won him a lot of clients. But at home his behaviour was appalling, and he behaved in the

29

same way with anyone who dared to cross him.' She paused and frowned, with an expression of reluctant exasperation. 'No, I can't complain that he ill-treated or hit me – it's easy to get used to physical violence. It is much worse having to learn how to live silently with failure, waking up each morning knowing there is someone there beside you who hates you unremittingly, and for no reason – or for reasons which you can't begin to guess. There was a time when I did all I could to find ways of putting up with his hatred; I even thought that having a baby might give me some semblance of happiness.'

I had no difficulty imagining her, fifteen or twenty years younger, having to submit to that silent and disdainful man's breath on her face, her cheeks scratched by a badly shaven beard, her body smeared and besmirched by his sweat and saliva. I had no difficulty either in imagining her feelings of alienation, the unconquerable disgust that churned in her stomach every day that hostile body penetrated and thrust inside her with the loathsome depravity of a rapist, depositing its barren seed in a recess of her body, before withdrawing with an oath or a reproach. I had no difficulty imagining her stretched out across the bed, the dampness between her legs caused by the viscous substance that had soiled her most intimate parts, like a noxious flow of lava which continues to do its damage even after it has cooled. I had no difficulty imagining her eyes swollen through lack of sleep – the closed lids would have hidden the full extent of the horror – as she recalled the sordid touch of hands squeezing her breasts, the pain of his teeth biting her nipples, and the slimy feel of a phallus retracting after having injected its poison. 'I smothered him with the pillow,' she said, with deep solemnity. 'I pressed his head down with the pillow, and then pressed the pillow down with my whole body – just as he had oppressed me with his hatred. I did it without premeditation; but even today I'm frightened to think I had the strength to overcome his resistance.'

It all flooded back into her mind with the same lucidity she must have possessed when she decided to squeeze the breath out of the man, and to listen for the signs of suffocation beneath the pillow stifling his cries for help. Nor did I find it difficult to visualise her in the very act, sitting astride the man who had been her husband and her bane, curbing, with all the strength in her thighs, the flailing of his arms in the final throes of death. 'It was a ten minute battle . . .' She told the story as if she had not been personally involved, or as if remorse, and perhaps the satisfaction of having gained her revenge, had both wasted away, leaving only indifference. 'His body was already pale and stiff, but his limbs were still twitching. He had stopped breathing, but his fingers still clawed at the sheets with the same fury with which they had clawed at me.' She spoke as if trying to shake off a remote but confused sensation. After her trial, a number of psychiatrists agreed she had suffered a temporary fit of insanity, and in consequence her sentence was reduced. 'I got twelve years, but I was only in prison for three,' she quickly summed up, because Inspector Nicolussi pushed open the door of the hotel at that moment – the bell announced his arrival – and he entered, preceded by the lighted tip of his cigarette. The young policeman sprang dutifully to attention, and a cold blast of icy air stabbed through the lobby like an open knife.

'We meet again, Dina,' said the Inspector, with that mixture of surprise and acerbity which we feel when we bump into a dissolute relation who we thought had turned over a new leaf.

'Yes, once again, Inspector. What are we going to do about it?' replied Dina, her face expressing mock contrition.

Now, Dina lit the cigarette offered her by Inspector Nicolussi, and gave a jaded smile caused by exhaustion, or by the thought of having to go through the same tedious formalities all over again. She had swathed herself once more in the black sweater which a few hours before I had registered as a sign of mourning but which now was explicable simply as a mark of indifference. The early morning light and lack of make-up accentuated the vicissitudes of her life apparent in her face, but revealed a frailty more attributable to fatigue than to age. Nicolussi's office combined that anonymous, aseptic air of deserted dwelling-places and efficient hospitals, which greatly increased my feeling of helplessness, and of having got myself involved in a nightmare from which there was no escape. A fluorescent tube hummed above our heads.

'So, you are a lecturer in the history of art,' Nicolussi muttered, after glancing cursorily through my personal documents.

His desk was becoming littered with badly-typed reports covered in handwritten comments.

'I'm a specialist in Renaissance painting. Gilberto Gabetti, the Director of the Accademia, will be able to confirm this.'

'Gabetti has been informed. He's on his way.' Nicolussi stifled a yawn between his dry, cracked lips, which puckered oddly; his eyes were becoming encrusted as the involuntary secretions from the tear ducts began to harden. 'So, as a specialist in art history—' he repeated, sarcastically '—you would have known Fabio Valenzin.'

This time I jumped in before the interpreter, with a promptness that probably betrayed my sudden anger.

'Just a minute – what are you insinuating? I hadn't seen the man before in all my bloody life.'

I recalled Valenzin's face, haggard, the colour of parchment, like that of a cardsharp who for many years has hidden away from the sun; I also recalled his unwavering and compelling gaze that seemed to harbour a terror which dared not speak its name.

'I'm not insinuating anything. Valenzin's business was trafficking in works of art and in fake copies. His name is registered with Interpol, so don't talk rubbish.'

Irritation led him to puff even more heavily at his cigarette, with long drags which made the end glow red. The smoke became so dense round his face that I could not read the expression on his lips. This time, I was grateful for the intervention of the interpreter.

'I hadn't the slightest idea.'

My dismay came through clearly in my tone. I should have preferred to have been well out of it, and not to have known what I was just beginning to learn; I should have preferred to have had a dispensation absolving me from matters which were no concern of mine, but it was too late to back out. Dina cut in on my behalf, although I was not sure that her intervention was to my advantage, given what I knew of her past history.

'The young man's telling the truth. What's the point in trying to muddle him?'

I should have liked to protest at the improperly maternal tone in which she referred to me, but Nicolussi jumped in first.

'Let the young man speak for himself,' he said, adding in a curt and depressed voice: 'We have to go over your statement, Ballesteros.'

The clerk, whose job it had been to transcribe what I had said during my preliminary questioning, had interpolated so many *non sequiturs* and errors of syntax that he had turned my statement into a gibberish which baffled even Nicolussi, who lost himself completely in the muddle of subordinate clauses, intermediate phrases, and those which simply ended nowhere.

'God alone knows what all this means,' he said bitterly to the clerk, before starting to question me. 'You were talking to Gilberto Gabetti on the phone when you heard the shot. What made you think it came from the palace opposite the hotel?'

The church bells had begun to ring again with an even more exuberant series of peals which reverberated painfully through my head. The sky over Venice was heavy and menacing, like a sewer which has had no fresh air through it for months.

'Because it frightened a number of pigeons. They were sleeping there, and the shot woke them up.'

From sheer perversity, I shied away from making any mention of that shiny object – almost certainly Valenzin's ring – which an unknown hand had thrown into the canal. I knew I was committing an offence by omission, but I also knew that the unlikely story would only serve to tangle the investigation further, and would also prejudice my innocence; but what prevailed with me was the avarice of one who possesses something precious he wants to keep for himself.

'Nothing else? Couldn't you see the murderer?'

I was unhappy about indulging in guesswork.

'Later, while I was trying to help Valenzin I thought I got a glimpse of someone. It was human . . . or vaguely human. It was utterly monstrous . . . utterly . . . *protervous*—' I hesitated over the choice of this unusual adjective which was bound to make the interpreter's task difficult. 'But I can't be really certain of my own evidence: I was jumpy, and this could have led me to believe I saw something that wasn't there. I also thought I heard somebody running away in the distance, but my impressions are confused, so don't take all this too seriously.'

The interpreter superimposed his version over mine like a

feeble echo, adding a further level of obfuscation to what was already unclear. Nicolussi expelled a mouthful of smoke which settled round the top of his head like a saintly halo; his eyes battled their way through the jumbled text of my statement.

'And then?'

'Then Valenzin died. I didn't manage to get anything out of him.'

I did not mention that Valenzin, before expiring, had raised his right hand in front of my eyes so that I could see the well-defined mark of the ring which he had been wearing on the second finger until just a few minutes before – a gesture more eloquent than words.

'It's not surprising,' observed Nicolussi, scratching his rampant beard. 'The bullet had gone through the trachea.'

Another police officer came in after receiving permission; prim but eloquent, he was clearly practised in the use of officialese.

'As we feared, there's nobody in the palace,' he said. 'The Department of Artistic and Historic Properties sold it at a bargain price to a millionaire from Illinois, subject to the condition that he would restore it and live in it for at least two months a year. The American has failed to comply with that undertaking, but he did instal a caretaker, one Vittorio Tedeschi, to look after it.' The officer hesitated, and blinked, as he tried to gauge whether or not to introduce matters of a moral nature into his report. 'This Tedeschi is an individual who leads a dissolute life, sir. He often abandons his post at night and frequents the brothels in Mestre.' To make matters quite clear, either from prudery or malice, he added: 'Very sordid brothels indeed, sir.'

Nicolussi licked his lips to disguise his impatience.

'So what are you waiting for? Pick him up!'

'We're working on that, sir.' The officer lowered his voice to little more than a whisper, as if he were in a confessional. 'At the same time, we don't want to make too much of a fuss — you know how furious those whores get when we raid their houses.'

This little speech, midway between that of a pettifogging lawyer and a pious bigot, seemed to get on Nicolussi's nerves, and he dismissed the officer with a wave of his hand, which could have been interpreted as a benediction. The big windows behind him began to vibrate as if a tidal wave were imminent, but it was a minor one, caused by the propellers of a police launch. Nicolussi sat back in his chair. 'That's Gabetti at last.' He spoke into his interphone. 'Gabetti's arriving. Prepare the body for identification.' Before stubbing his cigarette out in the ash-tray, he finished it off with a powerful drag which scorched the filter. 'Come with me, Ballesteros.'

Dina gave me a nod to express acquiescence. It was her ritual, or superstitious way of imbuing me with the confidence that comes only from personal experience. I followed Nicolussi down corridors which echoed with the clatter of a typewriter, the sound of our footsteps, and the dripping of water that penetrated and stained the ceiling. Nicolussi had a way of walking sideways as if he offered less resistance to the air that way, and he looked at me out of the corner of his eye as if hoping to discover in my demeanour some sign of irresolution.

We received Gilberto Gabetti in the forecourt of the police station under the shelter of an arch which gave a solemn echo to our greetings. He was a man getting on for seventy, but was well preserved. His hair was white, as if dusted with snow, and cut very short; his face was blotched by vitiligo, although the features themselves had a refined elegance – slightly Jewish-looking – and were unimpaired by age. He disembarked from the launch before any of the police officers who accompanied him, taking for granted his right of precedence. His manner, as he walked, was arrogant, and he did not even notice the snow which absorbed his footsteps, just as earlier it had absorbed the blood of Valenzin.

'This is an honour, Mr Gabetti,' I said, extending a limp hand which he grasped warmly.

'Don't exaggerate, my dear friend, don't exaggerate. There's nothing very honourable about me!'

He was both formal and austere. I noticed that his hands, although blotched with vitiligo like his face, looked as if they would excel at sensual caresses, but might also be adroit where theft was concerned; they were bony and emaciated as if by a lifetime of mysticism such as El Greco might have painted. There was also something in his look that combined the affectionate and the criminal, as if behind those blue eyes there co-existed kindness and cruelty, dark depths and a deep calm.

'Follow me, please,' said Nicolussi, who would undoubtedly have overlooked these subtleties.

Amongst its other facilities, the police station held a small morgue, its walls clad with tiles. The gaps between them were thick with dirt. Face up on a stretcher, his arms hanging over the sides like strips of meat, lay the dead body of Fabio Valenzin. There was no sheet to hide his wound, and nothing to cover his penis, its veins the colour of tar; and his testicles hung like empty pouches, suggesting a not very potent virility. Valenzin (I mean his corpse) still retained the frozen and compelling stare of his death throes, and his cheeks, which I remembered having been clean-shaven, were turning blue with a post-mortem growth of beard. His nostrils were blocked with congealed blood, and a row of stitches stretched from his chest to his navel.

'They had to carry out an autopsy, as you can imagine.' Nicolussi spoke apologetically to Gabetti.

Valenzin's stomach had collapsed as if they had removed the viscera, and the projection of the chest cage jutted out, the ribs resembling the strings of a harp. The monotonous drone of a cooling unit smothered the sound of our breathing.

'I always knew you'd finish badly, Fabio,' Gabetti said at last, his words directed at no one in particular. 'Remember, I warned you.'

He extended a hand to blot out the fixed stare of the dead man; the eyelids fell unresistingly, just as they do when drooping with sleep. Having done this, he took a handkerchief from a pocket of his jacket and spread it over the genitals.

'Were you friendly with Valenzin?' asked Nicolussi, with more awkwardness than malice in his tone.

'Let's say we had known each other for a long time.' He allowed no concession to nostalgia to colour this reply. 'When Fabio began his career I was working as an auctioneer's valuer. He was only twenty, or twenty-two or so, but his fakes were already creating problems for the experts. Later, he became a virtuoso swindler, but eventually he tired of his own virtuosity. As you no doubt know, getting away with crime can become boring, so the criminal always leaves some clue or other so that he can gloat over the frustration he is causing, and play hide-and-seek with his pursuers. Quite apart from the fact that the quality of his work was irreproachable, he was very prolific. It has been reckoned that he managed to fake more than a thousand works by Picasso and Modigliani, Matisse and Renoir, Van Gogh and Cézanne, always going for the artist with the highest prices who happened to be most fashionable at the time. Nowadays, these paintings of his are scattered throughout the private collections of half the world. But what he most enjoyed was imitating the Surrealists, because there is nothing more gratifying than faking the fakers.' He spoke with sardonic nonchalance. 'Did you know I once had some business dealings with him?'

He gave the sort of forced smile that might have expressed either candour or bad faith, like a child caught in a mischievous prank. Nicolussi and I both shook our heads with growing curiosity. It was inappropriate to carry on a conversation of this nature in a mortuary, but Gabetti held us enthralled with his smooth, beguiling voice.

'It happened in the spring of 1962. I remember it clearly because an auction house in Rome had just fired me – or had decided to dispense with my further services – because Fabio Valenzin had foisted on me a consignment of fake Modiglianis. I wanted to meet the author of my misfortune so I went up to Milan where he was living at that time. I was staggered by how young he was, by his self-assurance, and by his intolerable intelligence. To compensate for having made me lose my job, he invited me out to dinner, and we made a night of it in a most luxurious brothel, of the sort which exists mainly for government ministers and fashion tycoons, if you follow me. The girls in the brothel served us whisky in a pretty little garden with stucco columns artistically placed between shrubs of ivy and acanthus. As the girls were aloof and unfriendly – I believe the speciality of the house was masochism – and they wandered around amongst the columns like sleepwalkers, wearing only their bras and panties, Fabio mentioned the paintings of the Belgian artist, Paul Delvaux. I was drunk and in a reminiscent mood, and I recalled the fact that in my late childhood, or early adolescence, I had known

Delvaux and had even worked for him during his short stay in Venice, mixing his colours and carrying his easel. In 1939, Delvaux travelled all round Italy studying classical architecture which he would later use as background in his paintings. "In his early years, Delvaux's work was much more salacious – his women didn't just wander around like sleepwalkers, he had them masturbating in bizarre ways, and being sodomised by statues. But all the paintings of that period were lost during the upheavals of the war," I told Fabio, who could not contain his delight. "In other words, they were pretty hot stuff," he said, his eyes shining with lust. "Yes, pretty hot," I smiled. "At least, those first sketches that I saw were. Delvaux made his models try out the most revealing contortions." Fabio became thoughtful, as if he was already assessing the enormity of the swindle that was taking shape in his mind. "What would you say if we put together an exhibition of those paintings? All you would have to do would be to lend it your professional authority by writing a pretentious article for the catalogue," he suggested.'

It is possible that Gabetti was embroidering the truth with details and anecdotes to make it a better story, but Valenzin was in no position to speak out and contradict him.

'And you agreed? Come off it!' declared Nicolussi, with that disguised veneration that the police harbour for the perfect criminal.

'Well, at first I refused; but I hadn't a lira to my name. I was destitute.' He gave a spiteful laugh. 'In the space of a couple of months, Fabio perpetrated thirty fake Delvaux pictures, both sketches and finished canvases. Every one of them surpassed in pornographic audacity the originals, or at least the dim memory I had of them. There were lesbian scenes with the genitals openly displayed, and I believe there was even a scene of coprophilia. We announced the exhibition with heavy publicity which was enough to draw the attention of the most pathological collectors – all collectors, in other words. But, what happened? Suddenly, on the very opening day, the newspapers announced that Delvaux himself was coming to Milan.'

'So you were caught,' interrupted Nicolussi, privately disappointed, although he feigned relief.

'Wait, wait, don't jump ahead.' Gabetti was revelling in these preliminaries. 'It was too late to cancel the exhibition, so Fabio, who was a most resourceful fellow, suggested we visit Delvaux in his hotel. I can still see him today, calm, but quite unscrupulous, as he faced that old wreck of a Surrealist. "Look, sir, we are on the point of inaugurating an exhibition of some of your work produced many years ago, but we have heard rumours to the effect that there could be one or two fakes among them. We wonder whether you would be so kind as to come with us to the gallery and examine the paintings? There is no more reliable judgement than that of the artist himself." Delvaux, who, between ourselves, was a long-haired, conceited ass, came to the gallery, examined the pictures with the rapture of a true narcissist, and after going round three or four times, put aside a pair of canvases and one drawing that was particularly obscene – possibly it reflected his own fantasies rather too closely. All the others seemed to him authentic, and he congratulated us most warmly on having recovered works which he had believed to be lost for ever.'

He gave a long and affectionate look at the corpse of Valenzin, and sighed. 'That was Fabio, the rogue, he could have hoodwinked the devil himself.'

There was an awkward silence broken only by the cooling unit which continued to emit its funereal drone, a mechanical death rattle, suggesting that it was time to pension it off, or scrap it. The body of Fabio Valenzin seemed quite unperturbed in the face of Gabetti's encomium, and was slowly beginning to take on the coarse appearance that precedes decay. Inspector Nicolussi felt in the pockets of his overcoat, ready to break the rules and to cloud the clean air of the morgue with his cigarette smoke. It was hardly fifteen minutes since his last one, but he could not stand being deprived for so long.

'I imagine you know that apart from all that jiggery-pokery, he is believed to have stolen many of our national treasures and sold them abroad,' he said.

'I have already told you that Fabio was unwilling to believe he would get away with his crimes.' With these words, Gabetti abandoned his frivolous tone, but a certain worldly sophistication prevented him from being wholly serious. 'He got tired of contriving elaborate swindles, and began to loot churches. It is just possible he was responsible for one or two spectacular thefts from foreign art galleries, none of which has been cleared up. But there was never any conclusive proof against him. He was meticulous, he never bungled, and he left no clues. I always warned him: "so long as you don't touch the Accademia — for me that would be like attacking the Louvre."'

He referred to the Accademia in a highly possessive way, like a sultan who forbids anyone to enter his harem, although he tolerates and even approves of promiscuity and adultery between strangers. Nicolussi was about to reproach him for something he had said, but stopped short when he noticed Gabetti's disarming smile which seemed to mask an Olympian disdain.

'Has he any family?' he asked instead, with a resentful gesture.

'If he had, he must have disowned them because he never

mentioned anybody. He spent his childhood in a wretched orphanage, like so many other children in the war. He lived for long periods in Venice, but was so incompetent where domestic matters were concerned that he rented hotel rooms for much of the time. He used to stay at the Danieli, regardless of the cost.'

'Well, if nobody claims him he'll have to be buried in the common grave,' said Nicolussi brutally.

'Fabio in a common grave?' Gabetti was scandalised. 'In his lifetime he was an aristocrat among artists. Although he may have used his talents in a perverse way, in the final analysis he was an aristocrat. I shall not permit his death to reduce him to the condition of a pauper.'

He struck an angry pose, reaching to his full height, and not without a disdainful sneer.

'You take care of finding out who killed him,' he said, turning to Nicolussi, with all the hauteur with which a marquis would treat a manservant. 'And I shall take care of the costs.'

In the milky light of the fluorescent tube, the colour of Fabio Valenzin's corpse was fading towards marble or granite; the network of veins was mottled and the bruises and abrasions were beginning to look like chalky encrustations on his skin.

The prim but eloquent police officer who had come into Nicolussi's office earlier appeared in the doorway of the morgue.

'Can I come in, sir?'

His face was radiant with a triumph which dispelled his habitual bureaucratic demeneanour. Nicolussi gave his assent with a snort, or a rasping sound, which came all the way up from the nicotine deposits in his lungs.

'We have captured the aforementioned Tedeschi.'

Vittorio Tedeschi was dragged in by two youngsters who looked as if they had only recently joined the force: there was a clumsy synchronism in their manner and movements, characteristic of those who still respect the balletic rituals which have been drilled into them in their training school. Tedeschi could not have been over thirty-five, but he looked more like fifty. The slovenliness of his clothing – his corduroy trousers were worn at the knee, his fisherman's boots were coated with mud, and his sheepskin jacket had acquired a dark sheen of dirt – was made worse by the filthy state of his face, and through his clenched and rapacious teeth he was spitting with rage. He had an angular skull, and his hair was greasy and flattened, as if it had been licked by a cow. He remonstrated in Venetian dialect, but with a harshness which rasped his throat and grated on the ear of all those present. His tongue was still thickly furred, the sign of a drunken binge.

'Just as we thought, we caught him sleeping off a hang-over—' the officer, overjoyed that his prediction had turned out to be true, could not resist emphasising the fact '—in one of the more sordid brothels.'

Tedeschi squirmed with difficulty. Apart from the fact that the two novice policemen gripped his arms tightly, his hands were restrained by handcuffs which produced white pressure marks on his wrists. His captors almost lifted him off the floor, and he tried to break away by lashing out in the cold air, which very soon was thick with the stench of rancid sweat, the reek of wine-induced sexual excitement, and the sour smell of vomit and semen ejected during the past months. I cannot say I was sorry for him, but I did feel a slight twinge of conscience: they hadn't yanked me out of somebody else's bed, nor had they handcuffed me, nor had they dragged me all the way to the police station. Inspector Nicolussi was unable to resist any longer the need for smoke to leach his lungs with, and he took out another cigarette.

'Do you know him?' he asked, without looking at Tedeschi, who was suddenly quelled by the sight of the naked body on the stretcher.

'Of course I know him. It's Fabio Valenzin. Is there anybody in Venice who doesn't know him? But I could never have done that.' Tedeschi made a vague gesture with his manacled hands; it was not clear whether he was referring to the death of the other man, his nakedness barely concealed by Gabetti's handkerchief, or the mutilation of his body by the autopsy. 'In any case, I've got an alibi. I can tell you what I've been doing every minute of my time.'

He stopped at this point as he realised that his consumption of alcohol combined with the ecstasies of commercial copulation created blanks in the scenario of a night during which delirium might have led him unconsciously to an act of folly.

'To start with, you were doing what you're not supposed to do,' Nicolussi cautioned him. 'You're paid to look after that palace, and not to slope off and go chasing whores.'

'They pay me a pittance, believe me,' Tedeschi spat out, in a sudden fit of class consciousness.

'And you made up your income with the tips that Valenzin gave you on the side, isn't that right?'

Tedeschi's face went white, and then bilious, as he was thrown off balance. I too was surprised by the police inspector's shrewdness.

'I promise you that nothing you say in this room will appear in any indictment.'

Nicolussi's men meekly took in their superior's unorthodox methods, and Gabetti cleared his throat, pretending not to have heard.

'I did a few jobs for him, I don't deny,' Tedeschi admitted in a contrite, almost sepulchral voice. 'Climbing up the front of a church doesn't scare me.'

'And making off with a painting from inside it? That doesn't scare you either?' Nicolussi set his traps without tempering his sarcasm. 'I warn you that a robbery committed on holy ground is not only a crime, it's a mortal sin. What's it called? Sacrilege?'

The prim but eloquent young officer, who was obviously knowledgeable in the field of religious canons, nodded vigorously. The dead body of Fabio Valenzin was beginning to turn my stomach with its resemblance to a hibernating reptile, and my sense of smell was offended by its odour of cold meat. Tedeschi had relapsed into a hopeless silence.

'I think a couple of days in prison will make you more talkative, my friend,' concluded Nicolussi. 'And, by the way, it will also help you sort yourself out. You're a mess.'

'You can't arrest me without a warrant,' said Tedeschi, but he was begging, not insisting. 'Anyway, I'm innocent.'

Inspector Nicolussi allowed the smoke to anaesthetise his throat and bronchial tubes; by the time he blew it out he seemed to have reached nirvana.

'We've got seventy-two hours to decide whether you're guilty or not. In the meantime, you'll behave yourself in jail.'

They dragged Tedeschi out much as they had brought him in, and as they led him down the corridor towards the cells he let rip a whole arsenal of curses and profanities. I felt something approaching embarrassment (but also a shamefaced relief) that I had been given favourable treatment just because I was a foreigner in a city that worships money. Nicolussi bit pieces of skin off his dry lips.

'And you, Ballesteros, you have to sign your statement

before you go,' he said. 'The only condition I make is that you don't leave Venice.'

How could I leave a city in which everything was conspiring against me? How could I escape from Venice when winter had closed in on its canals and immured its streets and its inhabitants in a curse of oblivion? How could I break through the siege of a city which was sinking and dragging us all down in its ruin? Gabetti set himself up as my protector.

'I shall answer for him, Nicolussi, don't worry. He'll stay with me and I'll keep him under strict observation.' Then he added, with malice: 'And now I'm going to take him for a ride in a gondola down the Grand Canal, so that he has one pleasant memory of his stay here.'

We returned to the inspector's office where Dina was still waiting for us, with that look of quiet despair that girlfriends have as they wait alone on the platform of a railway station. She too was allowed to go, after signing her own statement. As she leaned over the desk, her breasts hung heavily inside the black sweater which squeezed and compressed them, just as once upon a time they had been squeezed and compressed by the hands of a husband who left them bruised and sweaty. I recall that when she heard I was moving into Gabetti's house, she looked me over with that unconcealed anger which seizes us when we are about to be abandoned. I managed only to whisper – cowardice prevented me from saying more – that I would return to the hotel to pick up my luggage.

THREE

'Of course, I have read your doctoral thesis, and found it very profitable,' Gabetti began. I had not had the courage to raise the subject myself at this untimely moment. 'There is a basic aspect to it that you will allow me to disagree with: you profess to be able to explain the enigma of *The Tempest* by intellectual means, and you take it for granted that Giorgione achieved his pictorial representations as a result of hard mental exertion. You hold the view that Giorgione aspired to create art which would be accessible only to a few initiates who dedicate their energies to interpreting cryptograms rather than studying painting. It is true that we know little of his life, but Vasari, who was almost a contemporary, tells us that "he drew with great delight", that he liked to play the lute during courtly revels, and – note this – "he never ceased enjoying the pleasures of love". He was so deeply in love, in fact, that he continued having sex with the lady who had yielded to his blandishments even when she caught the plague, and knowing that he was likely to catch the disease through intercourse with her. Can you really believe that a man who goes all out to commit suicide by inhaling the last breath of the woman he loves so that they can descend to Hades together – because Giorgione's love was illicit, and almost certainly adulterous – do you really believe that a man like him could coolly pick up his brushes and paint, simply to obey the commands of his intellect? No, my friend, Giorgione only acted when gripped by passion, or when tortured by grief, by the bitter aftertaste of lust, or the exultation we feel when we succeed at last with the woman we desire. Don't look for symbols or mysticism or complicated mythological meanings in his paintings. Moreover, in your professional work, give free rein to your own emotions, and that will enable you to come closer to what we mean by sensitivity towards art. What you, and so many other bookish students, call the enigma of this painting is nothing other than the artist giving shape to an emotion. Complex, incoherent, imprecise, inexplicable if you like, but are these really emotions that lend themselves to explanation? Make no mistake, *The Tempest* represents a state of mind, a deeply personal passion entering into spiritual communion with the landscape. Giorgione was the first Romantic, possibly even the last, because those who came later were a bunch of idiots.'

I understood why Gabetti had chosen a gondola as the scene of our first dialectic confrontation – our telephone conversation, aborted by the death of Valenzin, had been nothing more than a prelude or preliminary trial. Now, he wanted to make me feel uncomfortable and ridiculous. He had perched himself near the prow of the boat with his back to me, thereby preventing me from responding, and reducing me to a mere passive listener. As the gondola pitched from side to side, he made a play of maintaining his balance, by a slight flexing of the knees. From time to time, pieces of frozen seaweed floated by on the surface of the water, raising their stiff tendrils, images of supplication or farewell, like the hands of a drowned man whose fingers retain their rigidity. As he veered to the right, the gondolier emitted a guttural noise, a strangely pathetic sound, which penetrated the fog and was answered by a chorus of squawking gulls. We emerged on to the Grand Canal, flanked on either side by palaces which the snow, by softening their lines and edges, had converted into vast reefs of coral. Although the level of the water had fallen compared with the night before, it still reached up to the porticoed entrances, and created a curious optical illusion as if the columns were sunk into liquid cement.

'Apart from that, there is a technical aspect to Giorgione's painting that you have skilfully overlooked.' There was no bitterness in the way Gabetti scolded me – as one might scold a pardonable sinner. 'An aspect that X-rays of his pictures have confirmed: he was the first artist to paint directly on to the canvas with no preparatory, underlying drawing, and this meant that he had to make frequent corrections. If he had really thought out the composition of *The Tempest* in advance, if, as you maintain, he had wanted to represent a subject whose meaning would be accessible only to enlightened souls capable of understanding his allegories, don't you think he would have done a charcoal underdrawing first? An artist who meticulously plots out his compositions, like the thief who plans to rob a bank, must establish his route, or layout, almost to a fraction of an inch. Giorgione was an intuitive painter – let us say, a thief who acts on impulse. He adjusted as he went along. I don't have to remind you, you rascal, that in *The Tempest*, in the place where today we have the man with the staff, Giorgione had first painted a nude woman bathing in the stream, and he overpainted this in the final version. That completely demolishes any notion of a preconceived theme, don't you think?'

He turned round with an agility inappropriate to his age,

almost like a cat, in order to take me unawares and ensure that I was thoroughly discomfited. The wind blowing down the Grand Canal had undone the knot in his bandanna, revealing a long, scraggy neck, much like that of a chicken.

'I suppose you are right,' I admitted.

The spontaneity of my admission earned me a grateful look.

'Do you know why I have always avoided writing about matters of art? I can't stand the charlatanism of art critics, I cannot stand that pretentious jargon they use when analysing a painting, which simply buries it under a mountain of empty verbiage, to the point where you no longer derive any enjoyment from it. D'Annunzio used to say that criticism should be "the art of enjoying art", but the pedantry of experts has turned it into the art of sheer waffle. The devil take all that rubbish!'

He allowed himself to be carried away by a state of passion, or euphoria, that turned to gloom as the gondola headed past the Accademia: a depth of greenish water had taken possession of the little square that served as a forecourt to the building, and was seeping into its porous walls.

'We have had to close the museum to the public,' he grumbled. 'The whole of the ground floor is swamped. But that isn't the worst of it. The water will soon go down, but the moisture will remain, soaked into the stone for all eternity. You can't imagine the problem we have with humidity.'

'But I can imagine it,' I retorted, somewhat aggrieved.

'Nonsense, nonsense. Humidity in Venice is like gangrene. In any other city the stone would act as a barrier, but here stone is its principal ally, its natural habitat. In the summer, instead of diminishing, it gets worse: in the stinking heat, fungus grows on the oil paintings, and there are swarms of insects like woodlice with soft shells that are resistant to all insecticides. More than half our budget gets eaten up on conservation work.'

His voice, like the stones of Venice, became softer and distressed as he described the symptoms of this 'gangrene'. He sat down in front of me on one of those dreadful seats upholstered in velvet, which the gondoliers provide for the backsides of the more snobbish, or inexperienced, tourists. The hull of the gondola slid through the water with the bloodless ease of a dagger penetrating flesh without touching bone, propelled by an oar used like a pole, which sank into the mud at the bottom and from time to time got caught in patches of sand or excrement. My eyes grew wearied by the unending spectacle of palaces and marble façades covered in moss, by pointed arches with their alabaster crenellations and richly carved stone, wearied by such an accumulation of beauty; and only the blurring effect of the fog and the whiteness of the snow on the roofs and chimneys, the cornices and mouldings, made this architectural extravagance acceptable. The gulls broke the silence with the flapping of their wings as they escorted the boats carrying provisions, in the hope that one of the sailors would throw them a piece of rotted food as a reward for their perseverance. When we arrived at the Rialto Bridge, our course became darker and drearier because there, under its great marble span, the water shimmered, and the light – the dim morning light – sketched a flickering reflection in the gloom, and our respiration, barely audible before, took on a deep resonance which sounded like the breathing of a Cyclops. I had the sensation that my life also was entering a deep cavern in which the play of light, the vibration of footsteps, and the echo of voices would distort the outlines of reality; a cave that would grow longer and longer like a tunnel, and would lead me to regions on the borders of hell, waste lands where madness and sleeplessness make their home, shifting ground which would swallow me up for evermore.

'Take us to the church of the Madonna dell' Orto,' Gabetti instructed the gondolier. Politely, he informed me: 'It's a church near my house. Chiara is working there, restoring a Tintoretto.'

'Who is Chiara?'

He was slow to reply, as if he had to calculate their precise relationship, or possibly as if the mere mention of her name produced in him a feeling of great joy.

'My daughter, my daughter Chiara. The prop of my old age,' he said at last, with an emphasis that was not devoid of irony.

The Grand Canal was broadening out into a wide curve which created the illusion of the estuary of a river. The gondola made a sudden turn – I had to clutch the velvet cushion in order not to lose my balance – and took us into the district of Cannaregio where the city quickly lost its showcase appearance and became decidedly shabby. Pigeons wheeled over the labyrinth of canals and defecated in unison, leaving stalactites of shit on the sills of windows. The water was smoother here and its corrosive tongue licked the corners of the buildings; it flowed lazily through the canted bridges, leaving heaps of rubbish in the doorways of houses. There were shops which set out their wares for apparently non-existent customers: vegetables which seemed to shiver with the cold; fruit obtained from some inaccessible orchard; fish still breathing through their gills, with one eye staring upwards as they expired. In the distance I could make out the island of San Michele, the citadel of Venice's dead; but before entering the lagoon, the gondolier turned off to the left and penetrated a run-down, dilapidated area resembling the waterfront of a dockyard, stacked with bits of iron and scrap metal. A feeble sun had begun to shine through the fog and gleams of light were reflected from the rusty surfaces, adding to the air of abandonment.

'We disembark here,' said Gabetti, pointing out a flight of steps, of which two rungs only extended above the level of the water.

The gondolier pocketed the bundle of notes that Gabetti handed him, and moved off without a word, heading in the direction of the Grand Canal.

'Chiara doesn't know yet that Fabio is dead. Let us hope she isn't too upset by it.'

'Did they know each other?'

Gabetti shrugged. Possibly it was owing to a weak constitution that he wore a heavy overcoat to pad out his frail physique.

'To talk about knowing someone doesn't mean very much in Venice; we all know each other to some degree or other.' He said it as if excessive familiarity bothered him. 'Let's say they were good friends. Fabio taught her a few tricks which you don't learn at art school.'

'Tricks? What sort of tricks?'

I startled myself by the abruptness of my question, which he may have found irritatingly inquisitive, or more impertinent than is usual in polite behaviour. However, Gabetti forgave my indiscretion.

'Tricks used in restoring paintings, my friend, don't get the idea that they worked together. When you repair a picture and restore it to its original condition, there are not always well-defined limits between preservation and renovation. For example, colours can fade, the oil used by the artist can darken, creating those imperfections which some greenhorns confuse with *tenebrismo*, and these problems have to be treated with care. Fabio instructed her in his own meticulous methods.'

We had entered the church of the Madonna dell' Orto and were walking down the nave, dodging the puddles that had collected in the gaps between the flagstones. Gabetti explained to me that underneath the church there were vaults, or catacombs, that flooded in winter and leaked a rust-coloured water. Every side chapel held an example of Venetian painting, but the combination of gloom and neglect coated them with a patina (that false *tenebrismo* to which Gabetti had alluded) that made them impossible to see clearly. Only one chapel had been pillaged, and a sign drew attention to this. It indicated that – until some thief had decided on another home for it – a *Madonna and Child* by Giovanni Bellini had hung there. Between the central arches of the apse, there were five paintings which depicted the cardinal, or theological, virtues. All these manifested the lively technique and the almost clumsy brushwork of Tintoretto, as did the two vast canvases covering the side walls of the apse, with their exuberant sense of drama, dizzying in their use of light and contrast. One of these represented the *Adoration of the Golden Calf*, and the other the *Last Judgement*, a favourite subject of that dedicated artist.

Perched on a scaffold and working with a lamp which illuminated the semi-darkness of the place, there was a woman who was no longer young, but who retained her smooth, youthful skin and firm features. She was tall, with a delicacy which went with her slim figure – although later, with greater familiarity, I was to find that her apparent slimness was misleading. The floodlight would have engulfed less memorable features, but not hers: they were profiled with absolute precision against the crowd of figures that Tintoretto had painted. They also etched themselves on my memory, which is why I want to dwell on them here: her light brown hair was drawn back in a ponytail, her ears were like shells (or hieroglyphs), with lobes set close to the start of the jaw line; her chin seemed slightly pointed, but in fact was gently rounded, and her neck looked as if it were made for kisses; her lips were contemplative, and she moistened them with her tongue to prevent them splitting; her nose was aquiline and slightly biased to one side – the asymmetry did not in the least detract from her beauty; she had high cheek-bones, and a forehead that was equally noble, but her eyes, on the other hand, were the eyes of a peasant girl, although they nevertheless reflected a deep sorrow. They were chestnut eyes that seemed small in relation to her other features. Although she was olive-skinned, her bearing was almost Germanic.

'Let me introduce you to Alejandro Ballesteros, the Spanish professor I told you about,' said Gabetti, exaggerating my status in the academic hierarchy. 'He's a specialist on Giorgione, so I'm sure you'll have a lot in common.'

Chiara stopped working, turned round, and made no attempt to hide her genuine pleasure. Foolishly, because my infatuation was far too hasty, I recalled those lines:

> 'beloved face in which I view the world
> it mirrors the flight of graceful birds
> who fly to the land of the unforgotten . . .'

'I am very pleased to meet you,' she said, in Spanish, out of politeness.

She left her brushes and the rest of her professional gear on a shelf of the scaffolding, turned off the floodlight, and wiped her hands on a piece of rag sprinkled with turpentine. She wore a track suit, and over that she had a man's loose pullover, possibly Gabetti's, which hid her breasts and all the other curves of her figure from the waist up. The track-suit trousers, however, gave a clear outline of a well-rounded bottom, and thighs which were the very opposite of bony.

'You'll kill yourself one day if you're not more careful,' Gabetti warned her, perturbed by her contortions as she worked her way down the scaffolding.

I observed – it was an unthinking observation and not in the least lascivious – that as she clambered down, her panties became trapped between her buttocks, allowing them to move and wobble freely. With a jump, Chiara landed next to us. Above us there remained, like implacable witnesses, the figures that Tintoretto had painted in a jumble of violent colours and impossible perspectives, dominated by a Christ who was administering justice, supported by the Virgin Mary and St John the Baptist.

'What a girl! She'll break her neck one day,' grumbled Gabetti once more.

'Well, she looks extremely agile to me.'

I voiced this silly little compliment as I shook her hand – it had a slightly rough feel to it, as if the turpentine had irritated the skin. With an equally stupid complacency I noticed that the smell of turpentine passed from her hand to mine, so I kept it in the pocket of my raincoat with a delight which was positively fetishistic.

'Gilberto likes to believe that just because he suffers from stiff joints, the rest of us ought to as well,' said Chiara, with a gently malicious flirtatiousness. 'Just so that you know, I keep myself in good shape.'

'How could you do otherwise, getting up so early to go jogging every morning. The only problem is that when you come back with a stitch, I am the one who has to put up with the complaints,' disclosed Gabetti, and then, in a theatrical voice, he declaimed: 'Oh, sport, you pernicious heritage of Hellas!'

Chiara put one hand on his shoulder and gave a loud chuckle. She had a hearty and delightfully broad laugh which clearly displayed her perfect teeth, as if they offered themselves for inspection. Once again, I recalled the poet:

> 'the inscrutable call of thy lovely mouth
> that draws me to its intimacy . . .'

'The fact is, cellulite is unforgiving,' she said, patting her hips.

'Cellulite, indeed. You exaggerate. Come off it — if you don't want the gods to punish you.'

I was of the same opinion as Gabetti, but I thought it better not to express my opinion, in order not to sound too fulsome or presumptuous. Alongside the scaffolding lay a big basket in which Chiara kept her tubes of oil colour, her brushes, and various gadgets which would have been as useful for surgical purposes as for restoring paintings, or so it would have seemed to a layman. On top of this hotch-potch, wrapped in brown paper, was a rather sad, yellow sole, with gills the colour of clay.

'How's the Tintoretto going?' Gabetti was anxious to put off the reason for his presence there.

'A mass of cracks. I've never seen anything like it.' Chiara reverted to her own language to describe the technical details of her work. 'The damp has altered the chemical composition of the oil, and some of the colours are beyond repair. I'll have to see how I can stop further oxidation.' Before turning to me she paused as even the best linguists must. 'Do you like Tintoretto?'

'Let's say that I'm not mad about him. His work seems to me rather too luxuriant and vigorous.'

I was trying not to seem either rigid or insensitive, but Gabetti did not pass up the opportunity to attack me.

'Our friend is one of those who still believe that the greatness of art derives from the intellect of the artist.'

'So we shall have to convert him to our religion of feeling and emotion. Won't we, Gilberto?'

She spoke as if to him, although her message was really directed at me, to my delight. Never before had I felt so willing to be influenced by an unknown religion. I was getting ready to reveal this willingness, when Gabetti, in a voice that was at once dejected and formal, announced the death of Fabio Valenzin.

'Ballesteros witnessed it,' he concluded. 'At the very moment we were talking on the phone. You were asleep, and I didn't want to wake you.'

Chiara remained silent, her peasant-girl eyes seeming to shrink. A few wisps of hair had escaped from her ponytail and she brushed them away from her face with a mechanical gesture, pushing them back behind her ears, but they continued to rebel until she blew them aside. Her high spirits had disappeared in an instant, but her sadness did not diminish her beauty, just as the slight bias in the shape of her nose did nothing to impair it.

'Do they know who did it?' she asked, in a low, dejected tone.

'Who can say? Fabio had some dangerous friends. Disreputable ruffians who helped him in his dealings, not to mention *mafioso* customers who don't forgive trickery. And Fabio was a great one for playing tricks.'

'He was also a very good friend of mine.'

Chiara spoke with a shyness or regret which I found upsetting and made me jealous – a jealousy that was absurd and unjustified. Gabetti passed his hand over her face to wipe away the tears that had gathered in the corners of her eyes, just as a few hours earlier he had effaced Valenzin's frozen stare. She gave a sob.

'He taught me my job. It was he who taught me how to handle a brush, how to examine a picture, and how to distinguish between normal deterioration caused by ageing, and other more harmful types.'

Instinctively, she looked down at the front of her jersey that was many sizes too big for her and was coated in a thousand and one spots and streaks of oil, with the same frightened bewilderment with which a girl finds her sheets stained by her first period. My jealousy grew as I thought that perhaps Valenzin had lent it to her. I would not have considered him a suitable art teacher, but I accepted that the instruction he had given her did not extend to the other irregularities in his life. Somewhere deep inside the church, water dripped slowly down, like water seeping into a cave.

'You'll have to pull yourself together,' said Gabetti. 'We always knew that Fabio was walking a tightrope.'

He evidently found it exceedingly hard to act as the bearer of bad news, possibly because it was not in his nature to be solemn, and his irritation, or awkwardness, made him seem much older. He pressed Chiara's arm, but his effort to console her was impaired by his haste to get away, and it was not at all convincing.

'I have to speak to the undertaker and arrange the funeral. I also have to go the Accademia to see whether they've got rid of the water. You, Ballesteros, must be exhausted.' The paternal concern in his voice also sounded false. 'We have more than enough bedrooms at home so you can rest there. You'll have plenty of time later on to examine *The Tempest* in peace.'

I felt rather bad, and disloyal to my profession, for relegating the main reason for being in Venice to the status of a mission deferred, but nothing attracted me less than the study of art when life itself was offering me so many other inducements. We watched Gabetti walk off down the nave splashing through the puddles, and listened to the sharp beat of his footsteps reverberating in the domed ceiling and the vaulted niches which held the images of less popular saints. Chiara turned to me, and hiding her face against my chest, gave way to the tears she had held back in the presence of her father. They fell on the lapels of my raincoat like a shower of warm rain, and when they dried, they were to leave behind traces of salt as visible evidence of her grief. I plucked up the courage to caress the line of her jaw, and gently touched her throat where I could sense the onset of her sobs. Anyone less timid than I would have kissed her neck, and still lower, the place where a woman's collar bones almost meet but leave a hollow made to cup the lips of the man who worships her, and tempts his tongue to offer its libation of love and adoration. It was both pleasing and rewarding being able to assuage Chiara's tears, even though some of her oil paint stained my raincoat; it was pleasing to discover that she was not really flat-chested, and that beneath the baggy, male pullover I could feel the rise and fall of breasts, which were certainly not large, but sufficient to indulge a loving hand; it was pleasing to breathe the smell of turpentine that caught the back of my nose, and then unhurriedly, as that abated, to breathe the unalloyed perfume of a friendly body.

'I'm sorry. I must seem silly,' she said, springing back as if I had thrust her away. The wisps of hair which had rebelled against the ponytail and hung across her face were gathered into a forelock. 'Do you mind if I light a candle before we go?'

She picked up the basket in which she kept her tools, as well as the sole which may already have begun to go off. Although she had by no means recovered, she assumed a self-possession which gave her an air of quiet mystery.

'Are you a believer?' I blurted out, but immediately regretted the question because it sounded improper and out of place in the circumstances.

'That depends upon what you mean.' She gave another of her hearty laughs, but this time it was designed to raise our spirits. 'I told you a little while ago that I was thinking of converting you to our religion of feeling and emotion. Don't you remember? But don't worry. The candle isn't for a saint, it's for Tintoretto.'

Next to the sacristy, on a side altar, lay the bones – probably spurious, like most relics – of Jacopo Robusti, nicknamed Tintoretto, whose dedication to painting had been like an all-consuming and protracted illness. Chiara stole a votive lamp from a nearby chapel and placed it on the epitaph which commemorated the life and generous deeds of the artist. In the thin, flickering light of the lamp, her face took on a bronze cast, and the shadows thrown on it emphasised its angularities. She squatted on the marble stone, and spoke in a remote voice.

'My first memories go back to the winter of 1966, when the water in the lagoon rose nearly two metres, and everyone in Venice was preparing to evacuate the city. Both the Catholics, and even the less convinced atheists, prayed for a miracle, and they carried the images of the Virgin and the saints in procession through the streets that had turned into rivers. For someone like me, a little girl of four who had no idea how to pray, and knew nothing about the heavenly hierarchies because nobody had ever taught me, the sensation of disaster was doubly distressing.' Her eyes grew misty from the smoke of the lamp; misty and veiled. 'I wanted to invoke the help of somebody and pray to him for my salvation and that of Gilberto, but the list of Catholic saints was unfamiliar to me, besides which I wanted to commend myself to one exclusive protector, to whom I would reveal my troubles, because I thought that to share him with others would reduce the efficacy of his assistance. I lived, and still live, in a house that, according to tradition, Tintoretto lived in. I also knew that, according to tradition, he was buried in this church. Like coincidences, children are ruled by mechanisms and impulses which adults don't understand, so I decided that from then on, the painter Tintoretto would be my guardian angel. I persuaded Gilberto to come with me in a gondola to this church. I remember the canals were carrying off chairs and cupboards, and all sorts of domestic utensils, as well as dead animals, and lots of papers which were illegible because the ink had been smudged. We came into the church, still in the gondola. It was like going into a navigable cavern with paintings on its walls. The central aisle was completely flooded, but the water respected the tomb of Tintoretto and only just touched it with its waves, which were little more than ripples. Gilberto lifted me up, and put me on the stone over this tomb so that I shouldn't get wet. In those days he was strong, or at least I admired his strength. I lit a lamp and stayed there for a long time reading in its flame the words which my guardian angel dictated to me. I hadn't yet learned the alphabet, but I was able to decipher the message in the flame of the lamp, like a fortune-teller. "The waters are about to go down," I exclaimed, and Gilberto gave me a good-natured smile. Later, when my prediction came true, he began to look at me with alarm and respect.'

I too looked at her with alarm and respect; I gazed raptly at her profile, which would have inspired Giorgione himself, and was captivated by the movement of her lips; in the light of the lamp they gleamed so brightly that they seemed almost incandescent. I should have liked to have felt her scorching breath, and to have tasted the sweetness of her mouth; I should have liked to have expressed my feelings for her words – she spoke a fantastical Spanish, injected with some Italian, and even a little English – but as I have already said, I am a coward.

'In other words, it was you who saved Venice.' I said this to divert attention from the embarrassment that my faintheartedness produced.

'That is what I believed when I was young. But nobody can save Venice; nobody can avert the punishment to which the city has been condemned ever since the day it was founded.' Her fatalism made her compress her lips. 'Every winter the sea makes the canals overflow to remind us of this punishment. Venice is sinking, inch by inch, in a slow and magnificent agony. Chemical waste from the factories is poisoning the lagoon, the boreholes they are drilling in the search for drinking water have pierced the foundations of the city, and nobody bothers to dredge and cleanse the canals properly. One day we shall cease to be a city and become an underwater cemetery, with palaces as mausoleums, and large squares where the dead can walk, but it is our duty to stay here until the cataclysm overtakes us; our duty is to die in the city which chose us for sacrifice. To desert it is forbidden.'

Her fatalism had drifted towards an intransigence that frightened me. Although I was not personally involved in the curse – I was a stranger in Venice, just one more amongst the millions of anonymous tourists who come and go, breathing in its history, without ever being part of it – I would willingly have believed that it was incumbent on me to remain at her side. It was a choice that went against all reason, but it was not for nothing that I was being initiated into the religion of feeling and emotion.

'You're too young to be thinking about death.'

Chiara shook her head. In her peasant eyes was the foresight possessed only by visionaries.

'There is nothing more natural or pleasant than to plan your own death. It is much more painful being present at the death of a friend who goes too soon to meet his fate.' She was referring to Fabio Valenzin. 'Not so much for the friend who dies, but for oneself. When we talk about a dead friend, we are talking about our own death, or that part of ourselves that the other has taken with him, and which dies with him. We don't cry for our friend, but for that part of ourselves that our friend has taken from us. The dead feed on the deaths of the living.'

The lamp wick threw out flecks which, in contact with the oil, spluttered and emitted a soothing and soporific smell. Chiara had stood up – I heard the faint movement of her knees – and was walking in the direction of the main door in the aggrieved manner of a convalescent from whom an organ has been removed while it was still performing its natural function. Stupidly, I tried to cross myself, but stopped when I realised that the sign would invoke a God who was nothing to do with me. Like Chiara, I too would have to acquire a guardian angel.

'The dead feed on the deaths of the living,' Chiara had whispered to me in the half-light of the church of the Madonna dell' Orto. It was a paradox that gained credibility in Venice, which survives at the expense of its inhabitants, permeating their dreams and disturbing their nights, like the humidity that permeates the stone and makes the imperfections of a painting worse. Tourists are immune to this gangrene, because they look at Venice from the outside of the shop window and are not drawn in, but there are some unwary foreigners, like me, who pass through the window, and suddenly find themselves trapped by the spell of a city that is a law unto itself, and they experience a transformation of reality, a sickness of the senses, which distorts their perception of the world and instils in them a state of unease in which premonitions seem more worthy of belief than the evidence of their senses.

Chiara and Gabetti lived on the Fondamenta della Sensa, near the Madonna dell' Orto – although in Venice, proximity has its own degrees of complication – in a house the colour of pale cinnamon, on the façade of which was a medallion with the head of Tintoretto, and a plaque attesting that he had lived there during the years of his greatest creativity. Like so many other buildings in Venice, its fanciful architecture combined Gothic and Arabic elements along with links to later styles. The balcony on the main floor had a Gothic arcade decorated with pendant mouldings, but the windows of the upper floor were protected by those watermelon-green shutters which constitute the universal, and distinctive, protective barrier of a city that lives on the defensive. Where the cinnamon colour of the paintwork had chipped away, parts of the brickwork could be seen, and there were numerous patches of cement that had been applied in a vain attempt to conceal the cracks and fissures in the wall. The house was reached by a pontoon that ran along the *riva*, or pavement, but its hallway was flooded to the height of a hand.

'You'd better take your shoes off and roll up your trousers,' said Chiara.

I took her advice, more and more resigned to an amphibian existence. We went up a flight of stairs which were uneven and felt spongy, caused probably by cats' urine, and possibly also that of passers-by who found themselves in difficulty. The walls, streaked with saltpetre, betrayed the ravages caused by the *acqua alta*. To amuse myself as we went up, I did what I always do when a woman goes first, as I had done the previous night when Dina was showing me up to my room: I looked closely at her bottom and indulged in lyrical speculations on the subject of its proportions. Chiara's bottom was slender at its base, but the width of her hips made it seem both soft and generously shaped higher up, and also made it distinctly separate from her thighs. As the seat of her track suit, as well as her panties, was now trapped in the cleft between her buttocks, I was able to assess its precise dimensions. In my assessment – and this began to worry me, as being more appropriate to a eunuch – there was no hint of lust.

'Tintoretto's workshops were on this floor,' she informed me. 'The Department of Historic Properties requires us to keep it in good condition, and in return they let us have the house rent-free.'

The light brought life to these rooms, and banished germs, whereas the number of big windows encouraged draughts – and pneumonia.

'You must be starving.' Chiara turned round, displaying signs of alarm or modesty, as if she suspected my scrutiny. 'I'll warm something up for you.'

She went up another flight of stairs. This time she moved fast, having pulled the track suit from between her buttocks. Gilberto Gabetti's apartment was of such ample size that it easily allowed for space to be left unused. Its occupants had put up unnecessary, or decorative, partitions, that did not even reach the ceiling – they stopped short by at least two metres, and simply presented obstacles that had to be negotiated. The corridor was dotted with a series of alcoves, and gaps had been opened up in the main walls, like proscenium arches in a theatre. I was disconcerted by the absence of pictures. To reach the kitchen you had to play hide-and-seek.

'You'll find it a bit confusing at first,' Chiara admitted. 'But you'll get used to it.'

I was overcome by a feeling of lassitude which I compared to the moral exhaustion that parish priests must feel – those few who remain – on the eve of Easter and other important dates in the church calendar, when all their parishioners demand absolution and overflow the confessional with an outpouring of sins which go well beyond the Mosaic catalogue: from appalling sins that are quite unmentionable to peccadilloes so insignificant that they are a trouble only to the excessively pious; sins of prurience and sins of cold inhumanity; sins that give pleasure to the teller as he recounts them in all their scabrous detail, and sins which do not lend themselves to succinct explanation; sins that admit of extenuating circumstances, and sins about which it would be better to remain quiet; mortal sins, and sins which are no more than a joke. A whole inventory of other people's sins that prevent us from confessing our own, and besides impose on us a vow of silence.

'You're very quiet.'

Chiara put next to me a cup of milk that she had warmed on the stove, and a packet of biscuits which I found dry and tasteless. While waiting for my reply she took the brown paper package out of her basket, and gave the sole a pitying look as she held it up by its tail.

'The fact is I feel completely out of my depth,' I began. 'I came here to satisfy a harmless obsession, nothing more nor less than to look at a painting, and I find myself caught up in a horrible tangle. I came to rest my eyes, and even before I can settle in I am made to be a witness to a murder, I am made to make a statement to the police, and I am made to listen to the most terrible secrets . . .'

I was unable to suppress an angry gesture, and this seemed to scare Chiara.

'I'm sorry if *I* have bothered you,' she said, in a whisper which made her sound genuinely distressed. 'I don't know what has happened to me since I met you. I've been rambling on and on . . . I'm usually much more reserved.'

However, the mildness of her words was belied, or at least made up for, by the force she unleashed on the sole with a heavy knife, to cut off its fins. Her unruly hair, which she no longer tried to blow away from her face, added the tousled impression of a maenad to her appearance.

'No, don't misunderstand me; I am actually very proud that you feel able to confide in me.' Although the fact that I blushed flustered me, her words encouraged me to continue. 'I wasn't referring to you; I meant some of the people I met earlier.' I remembered I would have to go back to Dina's hotel to pick up my luggage, but was strongly tempted to put off this and other obligations. 'If the truth be told, I am probably upset because I'm apprehensive – the fact is, I was the only person to witness the outcome of the murder, but not the murder itself. It is true that none of the statements incriminate me – quite the opposite; and it is also true that if I don't want to share other people's secrets, all I have to do is stay out of trouble and keep my distance . . . At the same time, I can't help having a presentiment of catastrophe.'

Chiara was scraping away at the gills of the sole to remove any chemical residues – and any premonition of asphyxia that the fish may have felt – and then she cut it up the middle.

'From now on I'll have nothing more to do with it. I'll

simply concentrate on my own job – which is *The Tempest*,'
I finished off.

I could not help shuddering as Chiara put her hand inside
the belly of the fish, pulled its guts out, and held them up in
the air like battle trophies.

'But it is Venice itself that causes your feelings of apprehension. That is the mystery of Venice – here, everything seems to
be going to happen that doesn't actually happen.' She went over
to the sink, and offered her hand covered in blood and entrails
to the impious attention of the cold water tap. She spoke as if
lost in thought. It was perhaps at that moment that I sensed
she was a woman rather too dependent on portents, with just
a hint of madness or instability. 'And that lack of something
happening, which makes you feel anxious, you will also find in
The Tempest: in that picture too, there is an event that doesn't
quite happen, a threat hanging in the air, a flash of lightning
that doesn't bring on the rain. The individuals in *The Tempest*
don't seem startled, nothing affects their indifference, nothing
disturbs them. In *The Tempest*, as in Venice, catastrophes do
not actually occur, life hangs by a thread defying the laws of
physics, and it is the threat of what might happen, but doesn't,
that makes us anxious and apprehensive.'

Her words also caused me anxiety and apprehension, and
that feeling of alienation that clairvoyance produces. I had
spent five years trying to solve the enigma of *The Tempest*,
experimenting with all manner of arguments and interpretations, and it had never occurred to me to think that in fact it
represented the spirit of Venice, of the Venice that is immune to
the trivialisation of tourism, of the Venice that is ruled by laws
which differ from the laws of nature. Chiara was changing the
sheets on a bed which was too big for one person. She smoothed
the turndown of the sheet with hands that smelled of fish and

turpentine, fluffed up the pillow, and lent me a pair of pyjamas which had the initials of Gilberto Gabetti embroidered on the chest in a style of lettering that was intricate, medieval, and hopelessly anachronistic.

'If you need anything, just give me a call.'

What I needed more than anything was for her to watch over me as I slept and to assuage my uneasiness; what I needed was the unbroken, lulling effect of her breath on my chest, like an oracle of good omen, or a balm to allay my fear of the future; what I needed was the soothing touch of her body next to mine, for us to warm each other, putting chastity to the test; what I needed was to feel her breath mingling with mine; but there are needs that cannot be defined. When Chiara returned to the kitchen and left me alone, I was more conscious than ever of my sense of desolation, of the thick web that Venice had spun around me, and of the limited hopes I had of escaping from its snare. A flickering light reflected by the canal filtered through the bedroom window which led out on to the balcony at the front of the house, and lit the walls with a tremulous scrawl like wriggling worms. I closed the melon-green shutters, and the darkness drew me into bed. I slept for many hours with the heavy stupor of a drunk, or of sick people emerging from an operating theatre, still under the anaesthetic. My sleep was broken, and I was half-conscious of fantastic fragments of a nightmare scene which I could not quite recall: I saw a ring being recovered from the water, and my hands coated in blood; I saw Dina shaping a weary smile; I saw the smoke rising from Inspector Nicolussi's cigarettes and hanging in the air, like fog over the canals of Venice; I saw the unmelted snow on the lagoon and Gabetti spreading a handkerchief over the genitals of a corpse. Then, these visions dispersed, and the scene of *The Tempest* appeared: the city, its colours blanched by distance, and the wooden bridge over the stream, the willows, their dark and feathery leaves fluttering, and the broken columns worn down by weather. I was the pilgrim in the picture. I crossed the bridge, and my footsteps raised a groan in every plank; I watched the progress of the clouds, or their reflection in the stream; I watched also the swaying of the willows – each leaf moving separately as the wind caught it, showing me its dark face or its silvery underside – and I penetrated the undergrowth, noting as I went the harmless brushing of the ferns against my legs, and the springy resilience of the grass beneath my feet. Then, I came up against the woman in the picture suckling her little son, but unlike in the scene in Giorgione's painting she had her back to me. I dreamed of every detail of that woman, of the intricate fashion of her hair – of every single hair, one by one – I dreamed of the slope of her neck, the smooth arch of her back, the foreshortening of her thigh, the curve of her groin. I also dreamed of the soft feel of that groin, the trusting feel of the thigh, and the elusive feel of her shoulder, the barely noticeable sweat on her neck, and her light brown hair, spread like the frayed strings of a violin. The pilgrim – myself, in other words – as he drew near her, trod on a dry twig which disclosed his presence – although, in the dream, there was no sound – but the woman gave a start, and turned. It was Chiara.

I could not tell whether she was looking at me with hostility or anger or mute reproach, because suddenly I woke up with the desperation of a diver choking on his first mouthful of air after a long period under water which has nearly destroyed his lungs. In order that mine should recover from drowning, I turned the catch which held the window shut, went out barefoot on to the balcony which extended just three feet beyond the wall of the building, and leaned on the balustrade. It was already night. I was horrified at first to realise that so many hours had passed, horrified by the time lost, horrified to calculate how many events might have occurred while I remained shut away in the bedroom, but I calmed down when I remembered that Venice postpones events, slows down time, suspends it, and turns it into a flexible substance, like dreams. There was a light dew – or possibly the condensation of the humidity in the air – which produced a disagreeable sensation as it settled on my face. I fell back against the wall, and then discovered that the balcony extended past other rooms whose windows were in a line on my left, like yawning arches, shielding the mystery of their occupants, or that even emptier mystery that is solitude.

By night, Venice – and even more particularly the district of Cannaregio – loses its rich patina, and takes on the unostentatious appearance of a peaceful, lakeside city, medieval and unsophisticated. I tried to look towards the horizon and the open sea, but the mass of roofs and the darkness of the night falling like a funereal curtain of ink prevented this. I walked up and down the short length of the balcony to stretch my legs, and to get rid of the tiresome pins and needles that had started up like a tenacious sequel to my dream. Nobody had taken the trouble to close the shutters on the window next to mine, and the glass absorbed that inky blackness which my eyes could not penetrate. I used the glass as a mirror, and was able to make out my own features, at first with difficulty and surprise, and then with that grateful vanity which we feel when we see ourselves clearly, and recognise the perfect coincidence with the image we have of ourselves. It took me some minutes to get used to the blackness of the glass and another minute to be able to distinguish what lay behind the glass: a bedroom identical to mine, with the same furnishings reduced to the bare minimum, and the same enormous bed. With difficulty, I managed to stop seeing my own reflection, and to notice only the outlines of the room. It was not easy because, due to a curious optical effect, the glass revealed to me two images occupying the same space, two images which did not touch, and yet superimposed themselves one on the other to form a perfect whole. On one side there was myself, in pyjamas, leaning against the balustrade of the balcony; on the other were the walls of a bedroom next to mine; and between these walls a bed, whose sheets seemed to bulge as they shielded the body of another person. With the same care with which the man in my dream had approached the woman in the painting, I stepped closer to the glass, and established that the body I could see was Chiara's. She was sleeping diagonally across the bed as if wanting to keep all of it for herself, and she did so, totally relaxed, her back towards me, her hair resembling the frayed strings of a violin spread out across the pillow and swirling round her neck which seemed to be damp with sweat. The sheets covered her nakedness, but not the shape of her body which I was able to guess at with lingering enjoyment: the smooth arch of her back, the foreshortening of her thigh, the curve of the groin. I spied with impunity for nearly half an hour – but time in Venice is a flexible substance – and then I felt the need to complete my scrutiny with touch. As the glass continued to act jointly as window and mirror, I played at extending my hand and making its reflection coincide with the silhouette of Chiara. Tenderness – the feeling which consists of a desire to fuse one's own being with another's – came to me in the form of a pleasant tingling sensation, as if I really were able to feel the elusive touch of her shoulder, the trusting feel of her thigh, the harsher feel of her foot: and my tenderness was answered by her, because the illusion of my hand caressing her led Chiara to stir beneath the sheets, like a puppy stretching, roused by a secret joy. She turned over, and now offered for my continuing exploration her noble forehead and high cheek-bones, and her ears like shells, or hieroglyphs – it was agreeable, and also disturbing, to place the tips of my fingers over their firm surfaces – with the lobe of her ear so close to the start of the jaw, the aquiline profile of her nose and the contemplative lips, and the chin which shaped itself to the hollow of my hand in the way that breasts or ripe fruits do. I prolonged the magic for another whole half-hour, allowing the reflection of my hand in the glass to rest on her cheeks without actually touching them, but I knew that Chiara continued to sense my presence, in spite of the barriers of glass and sleep.

Only at the end did I lean forward to anoint her with a kiss on her forehead, near the line of her hair; only at the end did I dare extend the reflection of my mouth as well as my hand into the darkness of the room, so that my lips would earn the reward of carrying away a few beads of her perspiration.

I was about to withdraw when I noticed another figure in the room: it was Gabetti. He was leaning against the wall and watching over Chiara as she slept, with the same tender rapture as I had, except that in his case there was no glass interposed between them. Shivering, giddy, and guilty, I slipped away.

FOUR

For one-tenth of a second, or even less, our eyes met in the darkness, like thieves pillaging the same church. Gabetti caught me in the act of spying at the same moment that I glimpsed him – admittedly, his presence there may have been with her consent, or even her encouragement, as against mine – but that fraction of a second established a mutual awareness, combining something between a threat and a demarcation of territory, a sizing-up of relative strengths, that was resolved by my retreat. We were both prowlers, prying into the privacy of a person to which neither of us had a right, although Gabetti's relationship to her made his presence more or less legitimate, whereas mine could not be interpreted as anything other than an intrusion, an act of impertinence that turned a guest into a marauder. I left the balcony with a strong feeling of guilt which, although it did not turn into remorse, was to leave me anxious and shamefaced during what remained of the night, like a sinner who submits to a penance without quite knowing what sin he has committed. Concern about my misconduct still lingered in the tips of my fingers, because fantasies, like thoughts, can also commit offences, such as the slow caressing of a body I had wanted to defile and possess by abolishing that glass barrier; but the condemnatory look that Gabetti had given me was stamped indelibly on my memory. Although my host was not a man to show his feelings, the vivid impression that was to remain with me after the episode on the balcony was wholly unambiguous: Gabetti would not excuse my intrusion, nor the fact that I had betrayed his hospitality.

The night stretched out like a waste land, encouraging the growth of suspicion. It was not unreasonable to ask what obscure and unaccountable motives had led Gabetti to go into Chiara's room and to maintain his vigil there; but my sense of justice made me first analyse my own reasons, which were neither clear nor explicable. Desire rarely lends itself to rational explanation; it seizes us with a sort of irresponsible joy which does not turn to repentance until it has worked itself out, by which time the very idea of an explanation has become redundant. I spent the remaining hours until dawn in these and similar forms of self-torture, with that almost masochistic satisfaction that forces us to relive the most shaming details of our behaviour, like the criminal who gloats over the details of his misdeeds, blending in his mind an intention to go straight with a certain satisfied pride in his work. I was worried by the knowledge that I had been caught in the middle of an act that an impartial observer would describe as improper – although Gabetti was not an impartial observer – and yet, at the same time, I consoled myself with the thought that there was no trace of impropriety in my veneration of Chiara. I could not disown an act done without evil intention, just as I could not eliminate the feel of Chiara which remained on the tips of my fingers: the fleeting touch of her shoulder, the trusting touch of her thigh – as soft as tissue near the groin, and slightly less smooth down towards her knee – the rougher touch of her heel, the arch of her foot and its five toes; and finally, the most delicate touch of all, the curve of her groin. I closed my eyes to bring these memories back to life.

It was a long time before I heard Gabetti go out into the passage. Although he tried to cover his withdrawal with all the stealth that his accurate knowledge of the house made possible, it was not lost on me. I guessed at his dejection as he went, as if remorse at having been seen by me afflicted him as well. He paused in front of my door. I imagined him with his hand extended, wondering whether to knock or not, but after a moment – possibly feeling even more embarrassed than I did – he moved off towards his own room where he would give full rein to thoughts about his own predicament, as I had been doing for the past few hours. Dawn broke slowly, and the bells began to call to prayer parishioners who would certainly not obey the summons. That morning, the peal of bronze held a mournful resonance as if to commemorate the death of Fabio Valenzin, who had surely been the most assiduous frequenter of the holy places that Venice had ever known, although his visits had not been dictated by piety. While I dressed in the same clothes I had worn the previous day, and that had already been soaked several times over, I heard Chiara moving in the room next to mine, turning over in the bed as she had done earlier when she sensed the closeness of a hand reflected in her window. I also heard – or thought I heard – sobs being stifled in her pillow, and the sound of laboured breathing. I began again to feel that retrospective jealousy which had afflicted me in the Madonna dell' Orto when Gabetti told Chiara about the murder of Fabio Valenzin.

'How did you sleep, Ballesteros?'

Gabetti's voice startled me, but what startled me even more was that he sounded cheerful, and spoke without a trace of irony. I had gone out into the passage trying not to make any noise, almost on tiptoe to avoid his vigilance, but my precautions were useless. He was still in his pyjamas – a pair identical to the ones Chiara had lent me, with his initials embroidered on the chest in that intricate, medieval lettering. His smile was friendly, revealing his recently brushed teeth, as if the events of the night had happened only in my imagination. It was plain to me that he was astute, very subtle and astute.

'Well . . . Quite well, I think,' I muttered, ducking my head to avoid having to look him in the eye.

'You don't say! You slept like a log for more than twenty hours. You must let me know the secret because I am incapable of anything of the kind. I'd have to take a whole box of sleeping pills first, and I take enough pills already for all my other problems. Do you take sleeping pills?'

He had hidden his hands in his pyjama pockets, as if anxious to prevent me seeing any sign of them trembling, or of his fingers tensing, which might distract attention from the smile on his face.

'Not usually.'

'Of course not, of course not. What a fool I am. When you are young you don't need pills to help you sleep,' he said, hiding his malice in ingenuousness. 'At your age, I didn't need them either. But as you get older, when you go to bed your mind is full of worries and burdens. Do you know what I do to combat insomnia?'

His voice was dejected, and he spoke as if he really meant to take me into his confidence, so I judged it inappropriate to smile – but Gabetti had not given up his cynicism.

'What do you do?' I asked, hoping to be let in on his secret.

'I count sheep,' he said, to humiliate me. Then he gave a loud laugh, which made me start. 'It's the classic method, isn't it?'

I agreed. Gabetti patted me on the back; it was a gesture expressing indulgence, or paternalism, and this added to my discomfort.

'And now, I think the best thing would be a good shower to wake you up.' He hesitated, pretending to be perplexed. 'But now I come to think of it, you don't have a change of clothing with you. I would lend you one of my suits, but I don't want to make you look ridiculous. Anybody can use a pair of borrowed pyjamas, but a suit is another matter. Besides which, mine are made to measure. I can't stand the plebeian vulgarity of *prêt-à-porter* clothes.'

I could see he was drunk with victory. He had managed to instil in me a sense of guilt; he had given me a caution without alluding to my misdemeanour; he had established an unbridgeable gap between us; and all without needing to spell it out. Gabetti knew my secret, just as I knew his, but he preferred to suppress any degree of complicity by pretending to ignore it, the usual technique of a man who is expert at maintaining an element of tension in his dealings with people around him. An unspoken secret is like an unconfessed sin. It grows and festers inside us, and can only be sustained by even more secrets.

'Don't worry, Gabetti, I'll go and pick up my luggage from the hotel,' I said, in an attempt to rise to his level of rudeness. 'I've got clothes there, and all I need to clean myself up.'

'I would happily go with you, but I still have to work on certain papers and telephone the police station: the bureaucracy of death, if you follow me.' He took one hand out of his pyjama pocket to smooth his close-trimmed, white hair. 'We are burying Fabio in the San Michele cemetery on the dot of eleven. I hope you will be there.'

We heard the stifled sound of weeping from the room

next door. Gabetti and I both maintained a contrite and respectful silence.

'Chiara is the one who is suffering most in this affair,' he said, shaking his head. 'I'd have preferred to keep her out of it.'

'Sooner or later she'd have had to learn what happened. It was better for her to hear it from you.'

Chiara sat up in bed, the springs in her mattress betraying her movements; she was trying also to suppress her sobs. She choked back her tears, and breathed deeply, as if she were exercising.

'And with everything turned upside-down, you still haven't seen *The Tempest*,' said Gabetti, with surly civility – if the paradox is acceptable. 'Let us see if we can organise a visit this evening. It isn't possible to get in there now – the main entrance is still flooded.'

'I'll be sure to be free.'

Before leaving to collect my luggage, I had an opportunity to see Chiara, who was up, but pretending to be half-asleep. Her nightdress made her seem slimmer, and she looked like a sleepwalker. Her hair, which barely reached her shoulders, was tousled; this spoiled her appearance, and made her face look thinner. I was able to make out the pores in her skin which I had not noticed before, but possibly these were due to fatigue.

'I was telling Ballesteros that we might take him to the Accademia tonight.' Gabetti did his best to sound cheerful, but his voice hid a degree of unease. 'Did you have a good rest?'

Chiara made a face, implying uncertainty.

'All right, I suppose. What else can you do when you sleep on your own, except rest . . .'

She looked at us with that pitying malice that women adopt towards their more persistent admirers. I knew then that she was aware of my having spied on her, and this made me blush. The light shone through her nightdress, outlining the darker area of her body. She still had the stomach of a young girl, and at the point where they reached her groin, her soft thighs were slightly concave, leaving a tiny space that allowed the light to peer through.

'Is there any more news about the death of Fabio?' she asked, pushing her hair back, with the mechanical gesture that was natural to her.

'Very little,' murmured Gabetti. 'I called the police to get them to release the body to the undertaker. That Inspector Nicolussi sounded furious – he's a thoroughly ill-tempered individual. Apparently, the main suspect, Vittorio Tedeschi, a rogue who was supposed to be taking care of the palace, has a perfect alibi. It seems he had gone on a binge in a brothel in Mestre. The whores never forget a regular customer, especially one who is free with his money.' Gabetti softened the salaciousness of his account with sarcasm, but this did not detract one jot from its thoroughness. 'He managed to pleasure himself with three different girls in less than two hours, knocking back huge quantities of alcohol in the process. Somebody ought to make a study of the physiological stamina of the lower classes.' He laughed to express an upper class detachment, but at bottom he was disguising his irritation, or envy, faced with exploits which would never feature in his own life's curriculum. 'Nicolussi is very suspicious about a caretaker finding the money for that sort of orgy, but Tedeschi refuses to declare where his money comes from. "Get the tax authorities to investigate my affairs if you like," he said. "But don't lock me up for a crime I didn't commit." Very unwillingly, Nicolussi has had to let him go, for lack of evidence.'

Chiara seemed deep in a trance. She nodded to express

satisfaction at the more than adequate information Gabetti had provided, but she was staring in a way that was not only fixed, it seemed petrified. Her collar bones were exposed, and these gave the impression of being the main bulwark of her body; the light behind her revealed what the material of her nightdress tried to hide. Her breasts were small, and had lost some of their firmness. The way they gave shape to the nightdress made me think of the curled leaves of an open book. I may appear to digress when I describe Chiara in such detail, but beauty inevitably leads to digression.

'Have they checked Fabio's room at the Danieli?' She still looked absent-minded, but had not entirely lost her mental alertness.

'Emptier than a collection plate,' responded Gabetti, using a religious metaphor which in my country would have sounded anachronistic, and almost certainly was in his as well. 'All they found was a couple of suits, washing gear, a few items of clothing, but nothing to provide a lead; not even a diary or a notebook which might have given details of meetings. The hotel receptionist remembers vaguely that Fabio had arranged with a removal company to take away his luggage. Nicolussi has had a check made of the invoices of all such companies covering the last fortnight, but the name Fabio Valenzin doesn't appear anywhere. He probably bribed the carriers not to register it. But what I don't understand is why he went to so much trouble.'

Overcoming my shyness, I interrupted him.

'He was probably planning a job, and didn't want to have to bother with luggage when the time came to make his getaway. There's nothing more natural than wanting to travel light.'

Gabetti blinked, disturbed by ideas which his own normal shrewdness had not come up with.

'But I would have known . . .'

He fell silent, as if regretting having mentioned activities which were not in keeping with his professional position, activities which did not square with the honesty everyone assumes in a man who has lived through the caprices of official appointments and the dismissals of political protectors. He tried to correct the impression given by his words, but did so unconvincingly, because corrections of this kind need to be brief, and he delivered a speech.

'Fabio kept no secrets from me. When he was up to something new, he was irrepressible, ostentatiously cheerful, as if to hide any sign of tension. Normally, he was taciturn, and he never joked; by nature he was inclined to misanthropy. Most people had no experience of the depressed and misanthropic Fabio because they only rubbed shoulders with him when he was in the mood to be sociable, and then he would plague them with a spate of jokes in doubtful taste. But this overwrought side of him was largely assumed. The real Fabio was known only to a very few among us who had had dealings with him during periods of drought, that is to say, when his clients didn't commission impossible jobs, and the police lost interest in his activities.'

Gabetti adopted an air of wounded dignity. He pursed his lips, which had the effect of accentuating his Jewish-looking profile. The marks of vitiligo that blotched his face seemed to herald the start of physical decline. Chiara remained absorbed in her own thoughts, and inaccessible – even to my desire for her – just as the woman in *The Tempest* keeps herself inaccessible to the lust of the pilgrim who witnesses her nakedness from the other side of the stream.

'Don't be so sure, Gilberto,' she said. 'Fabio was too complex a character even for you to psychoanalyse.'

She spoke with the gravity of a sphinx, a precocious gravity that seemed to unsettle her both physically and mentally, and distanced her from me, like a painting that distances itself from onlookers by its display of hidden themes, or abstruse allegories, or perspectives that defy reality.

'I'm going to have a shower, to see if that wakes me up,' she said.

She walked barefoot across the tiles which, for a few seconds, retained the trace of footprints made by the warmth of her feet, in the way that glass captures and retains the mist of one's breath. Gradually, the marks became attenuated as they lost her warmth; they shrank until their outlines were indiscernible. It was a hypnotic sensation, watching their impression slowly dissipate as she moved away. A sensation as hypnotic as following a track that one believes to be trustworthy, but which turns out to be a mirage.

I was mildly fearful about tracks being able to turn into mirages. I say only mildly fearful, because a transmutation of this kind would not have upset me greatly, indeed I think it would have inspired in me that sense of freedom which we feel when we divulge a secret, or when we take advantage of someone prepared to listen to us, such as a priest, a psychoanalyst, or a friend we catch unawares, and on whom we unload a weight of guilt. I was mildly fearful, thinking that my perceptions were unreliable and failed to accord with reality; I was also mildly fearful that, because of the influence of Venice, my senses had lost their sharpness, and in consequence their evidence lacked truth. Just as, with the help of my sense of touch I had played at abolishing the divide between two different worlds separated by a pane of glass, it was not stupid to suspect that my eyesight may also have betrayed me and had added a degree of illusion or distortion to the images I had been registering since my arrival in the city. Who was there to assure me that the fleeting glimpse of a ring falling into a canal had not been a figment of an overactive imagination? There was another powerful reason why I was inclined to have a poor opinion of my perceptions: I am a person who has made passivity a norm of conduct. It is true that passivity can make us subject to petty tyrannies and compels us to be deferential — my academic career has made me put up with this meekly; it is true that it earns for us a reputation for being pusillanimous or submissive and leads us to put up with injustice; but it is also true that it helps us to keep out of serious difficulties. Why rebel against things which are beyond us, if all we get in return is dissatisfaction?

Although Gabetti had given me a plan of Venice and a pair of boots — we took the same size in footwear as in pyjamas, but that is the extent of the similarities between us — I did not succeed in reaching my destination without getting my socks wet and losing my way at least a dozen times. Finding your way round Venice, outside the busy routes signposted by the municipal authorities for guiding the herds of tourists, demands from the stranger in the city a high level of patience and a sense of direction which borders on the gift of divination. Only when the leaning tower of San Stefano loomed above the roof-tops could I be sure of my route, although I still had to backtrack along several minor streets which led nowhere. In the little square that had been the setting for the last moments in Fabio Valenzin's life, there remained just a few heaps of snow, here and there, like pale patches of vomit on the stone; but of the blood that had been spilled there was no trace. Night had taken care to make it disappear, as if it had been washed away by the waters of oblivion. The palace, which from my hotel room had so startled me, was just one of many Venetian buildings on the verge of collapse. The police had closed off access to it with wooden planks, and had bordered its façade with a yellow tape proclaiming the penalties which would face anyone who dared go through it. There were pigeons in the eaves and cornices as well as on the balustrade of the balcony, but the calm way in which they strutted about showed that they had reverted to their usual habits. The porch that protected the entrance to the Albergo Cusmano still seemed on the point of collapse, and its walls still had their reptilian feel. I pressed myself against one of these because I heard the voice of Inspector Nicolussi.

'You have to put yourself in my place, Dina. I can't conceal evidence. It's called perversion of justice.'

He spoke with the same southern accent that had been apparent during our interrogation in the police station, but now it no longer had the severity expected from officers of the law. On the contrary, it had become much milder, and was almost plaintive, as if he was about to give way on something. Dina's voice, by contrast, sounded strong and almost masculine.

'You did plenty of *perverting the course of justice* on my behalf in the past. I don't see why you're so fussy now.'

Dina had forgotten to switch off the neon sign bearing the name of the hotel, and its humming noise drowned the sound of my breathing. Nicolussi's words reached me clearly – much more clearly than in his office at the police station, where the interpreter's translations and repetitions had got in the way – though their force was blunted by some sort of conflict, or moral scruple.

'We'll say you knew nothing at all about Valenzin. As far as you are concerned, he was just a tourist like so many others.'

'Like so many others?' Dina spat the words out angrily, as if she were being made both the perpetrator and the butt of a bad joke. 'We all knew Valenzin. Besides, you know perfectly well I don't get many guests in this hotel; only occasionally, some poor devil who has lost his way, like that Spanish lad, Ballesteros. It must have been someone with a distorted sense of humour who told him to stay here.'

Feeling deeply embarrassed, I remembered that the address and phone number of the hotel had been given to me by Professor Mendoza, the supervisor of my thesis, who frequently visited Venice for purposes of intrigue or pleasure, whenever the scope for home-grown intrigue and pleasure became sparse. Somebody must have told him about Dina's earlier life, and Mendoza, who had treated me to so many other humiliations at the university, had been unable to resist treating me to even more from a distance.

'I assure you the judges won't suspect anything. You know from your own experience they don't conduct investigations personally; they always delegate to me.' Nicolussi was unable to repress a note of vanity. 'They delegated to me when your husband died, and they'll delegate to me on this occasion. As far as they are concerned, so long as I let them have a two- or three-hundred-page statement, they'll be delighted. But, you have to understand this, Dina. I can't go and simply say that there is no trace of Valenzin's luggage, or that he sent it off somewhere, but we don't know where. They'll have me go through every single receipt and voucher issued in the last few months by every single transport company. There are some types of evidence you can't hide.'

I wondered whether Dina had not mistaken her true calling, whether she would not have been better off running a left-luggage office for travellers in transit – to another city, or to somewhere beyond the grave – for strangers who wished to off-load something from their past, and to get rid of those objects belonging to it, or for drifting criminals who needed somewhere to leave the tools of their trade, or the loot they regarded as an investment for their retirement. Dina spoke again, less severely this time, but still with grim conviction.

'So what are we going to say? I don't want to admit that Valenzin had his hiding-place here.'

I pictured her resting against the desk in the hall of the hotel, leaning towards Nicolussi, and I pictured him looking subdued and passive – passivity can lead to a disregard for the law – staring at those breasts which possibly he too had crushed in his hands. I pictured Dina's big, Byzantine eyes, gazing unremittingly – like a river in full flood – into Nicolussi's eyes which, no doubt, would have lost their sparkle, but would glow with the ignoble flame of humility. Finally, it was not difficult to guess what these two had got up to, years before, in order to weaken the very serious charge of murdering her husband. There is evidence you cannot hide, and murder is irrefutable evidence, but you can falsify the circumstances: death by asphyxiation may conceal death by poisoning, just as snow conceals the obscenity of spilled blood. All you need is to have the autopsy carried out by a lazy pathologist, and to hand over the results of this autopsy to a negligent judge – or to one who believes in devolving responsibilities . . .

'I shall order a routine search of the hotel.' Nicolussi spoke in a cool matter-of-fact way, with that superstitious reluctance that prevents cardsharpers from cheerfully explaining their tricks. 'Any excuse will do. For example, because I want to make sure the Spaniard's room does look out on the palace, and to establish exactly what can be seen from there.'

'Don't get the Spaniard into even more trouble,' Dina interrupted. I was grateful for her concern. 'The poor boy isn't responsible for anything.'

Her tone was disapproving at first, then it sounded maternal, but not without a hint of sarcasm. Nicolussi lit a cigarette – I heard the scrape and flaring of the match – and he was silent while he took the first few puffs. I also heard another, quieter scraping sound, as if he was stroking his beard. Probably he had not had time to shave, or possibly it grew very quickly, particularly in his sleep, as happens with dead men.

'That poor devil has come out of it better than you or I, Dina,' he said. 'Gabetti's protecting him. To hell with the man! You should have been there when he made a sort of funeral oration for Valenzin, and shot us a line about the things they'd got up to together. It didn't really surprise me. They both came from the same mould.'

'Gabetti can be much more seductive.' Dina disagreed with him. 'He can turn any woman on.'

'Of course he's a seducer. Of minors, in the main!' Nicolussi laughed at his own joke, the significance of which escaped me. He had the laugh of a ventriloquist, and it grated with the bitterness of his words. 'We know quite well he is a criminal and a menace to society, but he gets away with his crimes while others get it in the neck.'

I assumed he was referring to Dina, but using the indirect form of speech in order to scare away the ghost of the crime that linked them. There were too many underlying meanings in their conversation, too many collusive silences and veiled allusions to leave any doubt about that link.

'But coming back to what concerns us now,' continued Nicolussi. 'I shall order a search, and then, quite by chance, one of the greenhorns who works for me will come across Valenzin's luggage. You will say that a gondolier left it with you in reception a few days ago, assuring you that its owner would soon arrive but that he had stopped to take some photographs of the Grand Canal. I suppose it hasn't occurred to you to open it?'

'I would never be so crazy,' replied Dina sharply, with the energy of one who pronounces an anathema. 'Valenzin arranged with me to look after his effects while he sounded out his clients. In return, he insisted on absolute discretion on my part and, above all, honesty. He paid promptly and generously, so much so there were times when I suspected that he wasn't just paying for a service, he was overpaying to ensure I would never let my curiosity get the better of me. Naturally, he succeeded completely: any curiosity I had to find out what was in his luggage was far weaker than my greed for the money.' She stopped for a moment, as if she had shocked herself by the ruthlessness of this admission. 'It never went through my head to go rummaging through his belongings, and even if I had wanted to I couldn't have done: Valenzin had made his case impossible to open. He had fitted security locks and gadgets that open only if you know the right combination. It is really more like a treasure chest than a suitcase. It weighs a ton. My guess is that it's armour-plated and has a special lining to protect it from scanners. And inside, it must be like a conjuror's box of tricks, with secret drawers, and a false bottom. I remember on one occasion he opened it in front of me because he hadn't got enough money in his pocket to pay me, so he had to get out the reserve he hid in the chest. I've never seen so many notes all together like that.' I imagined the mint feel of those notes, the embossed impressions of the numbers and the portraits, the sinuous indentations of the engraved paper. 'There was a lot of talk on the radio and in the newspapers about the robbery in the church of the Madonna dell' Orto, a forced entry, they said, and I expected to see chalices and monstrances, or that famous picture by Bellini, the *Madonna and Child*, but all I could see were dirty shirts and filthy, screwed up underpants, quite disgusting. You bachelors are a disgrace!'

There was an uncomfortable silence that was very wounding to Nicolussi and to me, because we were both bachelors and we stored up our filthy underpants until we had enough to justify the expense of a laundry. The unmarried man may seem more or less well-dressed, he may be vain, but behind the façade there is a back room full of dirty underpants – not to mention those nights of yearning when the bedsheets become an empty desert, our eyes remain mercilessly open, black nights, nights of refined cruelty which torment and demean us with the mortifying absence of a woman who exists only in our imagination. I pressed even closer into the wall of the porch where there was a niche for my celibate flank, my unscathed flank, from which no god had deigned to extract a rib.

'I don't understand why you had to have any dealings at all with that character,' said Nicolussi at last, in an oddly spiteful tone.

'And what was I going to live on if I didn't?' Dina was no longer just severe; genuine anger rose to her lips like a rush of blood. 'You know perfectly well that with the hotel I can't even cover my costs.'

There was a bitterness in her words that had fermented in loneliness; and she spat them out contemptuously at Nicolussi. They spattered him like tar or pitch; and internally, they obliged him to reflect on his own faintheartedness.

'The fact is, Valenzin has snuffed it, so there's no point arguing about the past,' he said, and his words had the effect of making his cowardice even more obvious. The past encourages argument, it burdens us with a load of unsettled accounts, and its legacy is crushing. 'We've got to clear this matter up quickly, because the press are hounding me and looking for blood. What do you think is hidden in the chest?'

'How do you expect me to know?' Dina still sounded annoyed. 'It must be something very big since it cost him his life.'

It was something so big that Nicolussi preferred to put off its examination until he could count on having subordinates with him, in order to share with them a find that his sense of duty advised him not to make on his own – his celibate shoulders were reluctant to carry the responsibility alone. Venice encourages collusion in crime, as well as the sharing of guilt. Dina herself had warned me that Venetians, like all deeply inbred people, practise a poisonous kind of closeness which enables each of them to know the sins of all the others. Now, I was to discover that this closeness does not stop at infringing personal privacy, it also comprises conspiracies and alliances, making for an extraordinary type of freemasonry with codes far too subtle for a novice like me to break. Possibly because my profession consists in looking at pictures, which are enclosed spaces in which reality is intangible, or because, like a picture, there have been so many intangibles in my life, I was baffled by these tangled and shifting relationships, which were initially invisible.

'The burial is at eleven. As you know, we mustn't be seen together,' said Nicolussi, as he put his hand on the door to leave.

The sound of the bell prevented me from hearing Dina's words of farewell, assuming she said anything at all. Nicolussi, preceded as always by the tip of his cigarette, moved off with that sideways walk of his which made him look as if he were on his guard against enemies waiting to ambush him. From my hiding-place in the porch, I watched him go, fearful that he might turn his head, or retrace his steps to warn Dina of some other detail that had slipped his mind, or to kiss her severe lips, mastering his timidity at last. The skirts of his raincoat clung to him like shabby rags, and he walked clumsily, almost like a duck.

The fluorescent sign ceased humming, and this interrupted my train of thought. Dina had switched it off from inside the hall, and was getting ready to leave the hotel which had no guests in it – or only inanimate guests: my luggage and Fabio Valenzin's armour-plated suitcase or 'treasure chest'. The bell which announced Dina's departure made less noise than usual, or possibly I was prepared for it, and for this reason it startled me less. Before locking the door she checked that she had not left any lights on. Even for going to the cemetery, she did not change out of her high-heeled shoes – she would leave those same tiny marks in the paths of the cemetery that she had imprinted on the hotel carpet. They were the most unsuitable type of footwear for a city full of bridges, most of which are stepped, but they made her ankles look slimmer, and they brought out the best in her legs – especially the muscles which had developed as a result of so much walking, and which had gripped her husband so tightly between them while he suffocated to death. She lifted her coat and her skirt in order to adjust her stockings, and for a second I caught a glimpse of her thighs sheathed in nylon. They were very white and fleshy – more cellulite – and I guessed that they rubbed against each other where they met in her groin. I imagined them having a texture similar to that of warm and slightly lumpy dough. I closed my eyes, so as not to get carried away by lustful thoughts, and also out of loyalty to Dina who did not deserve to be the victim of this stolen moment.

Nobody deserves to have moments like this one stolen from

them, when they believe themselves to be out of sight of other
people and immune from lustful or accusatory looks; nobody
deserves to be robbed of one moment of their innocence,
which is simply transmuted into an instant of lechery on the
part of the person spying; but since arriving in Venice I had
done nothing other than commit larceny with my eyes, my
hands, and my hearing, stealing instants that did not belong
to me, conversations that were no concern of mine, and crimes
that did not need my participation. Perhaps it was this newly
acquired practice of thieving that was blunting my sensibilities,
a sublimated habit of kleptomania that drove me on to a more
extreme form, overcoming my normally passive disposition.
I listened to the sound of Dina's footsteps fading into the
distance, tapping their way down tiny streets that are not
marked on any plan of the city, and it was only when I could
no longer hear them that I emerged from my hiding-place and
felt in my trouser pocket for my key. I believe I did not even
tremble as I put it in the lock and turned it twice, not because
of firmness of mind, but because I was stiff from having
remained stationary for so long. Inevitably, the bell rang,
and the lobby loomed in front of me, with its appearance of a
plebeian mausoleum, and its womb-like temperature created by
the heater that Dina had switched on the night I arrived. Behind
the reception desk, hanging from a hook there was a bunch of
keys which I seized – but now, yes, with a hand that shook and
was wet with sweat. I went up the narrow staircase that led to
the bedrooms, the same narrow staircase that I had climbed,
weighed down by my luggage, and preceded by Dina who had
presented me with a view of her bottom, cruelly constricted by
her skirt: her soft and asymmetric bottom. I crossed the first
landing, lined with the doors of guest bedrooms, all equally
empty, and went up to the top floor where Dina had made her

home. I still remembered the drumming of her footsteps above my ceiling, and the splashing of a stream of urine against the porcelain of her lavatory. All I had to do was find the door which corresponded with that of my room on the floor below. It was much harder, and more irritating, trying to find the right key for the lock. While I worked away at this, I thought I heard the sustained buzz of the fluorescent sign start up again: there was no doubt about it, my nervous system was playing me up. The corridor seemed to resound like a sea shell when you hold it to your ear.

The shutters were so tightly closed that no light penetrated between them. I found the light switch by feeling around blindly on the walls of the room, which differed little from other rooms, where life is nothing more than a fixed series of routines. Scattered and screwed up on the coverlet of the bed where Dina slept – lying on her back, naked, and with all the darkness of the night centred on her pubis! – there were various garments which, from affectation or modesty, we call *intimate*, like Fabio Valenzin's underwear, except that hers were not filthy: black tights to relieve the whiteness of her thighs that resembled dough; a bra of baroque construction with much lace and trimmings, designed to bear the burden of her breasts; and much plainer panties made to moderate the secret summons of her pubis.

There, between the wall and the wardrobe, in a recess that had something of a lair or burrow about it, was Fabio Valenzin's chest. Flat on the floor, armour-plated, but covered in a greenish hide, it might have been confused with a giant tortoise that had withdrawn into its shell. Just as Dina had said, it weighed a ton, although most of its weight seemed to be in the framework of the chest itself, and not in its contents. When I shook it, I had the impression that it might even be empty. I threw it on the bed – the panties, bra, and tights were transformed by proximity into bits and pieces that had been left out of someone's luggage – and I tried to poke around in its locks with the keys I had picked up in the hall.

Frustration led me to try to complete a task I should never have begun. I had taken a vow of passivity, and in no time at all I was trampling all over it; on top of that, I was getting involved in an illegal activity which needed greater care and daring than any of my normal daily activities. I wrestled with the locks, pushed hairpins that I borrowed from the bathroom into them, and worked away so hard that I broke several of my fingernails in the process. In the end, I lost all discretion, and like those destructive burglars who vent their spite on the furniture when the pickings are small, I smashed the chest against the floor, stamped on it, and spat. I also swore at it, but nothing I did would make it give up its secrets.

I decided to carry it away, and put off the moment when I would force it open – because I was determined that I would force it, even if I had to use dynamite.

However, it needed only the fresh morning air to cool my ardour and tame my impetuosity. Valenzin's chest weighed as heavy as a corpse that collapses into our arms without warning, already stiff with rigor mortis, and determined at all costs to obey the law of gravity, even if by doing so it tears our arms out of their sockets. I dragged the chest across the little square. The metal rivets at its corners caught in the gaps between the flagstones with which it was paved, and made the removal even more laborious. I was seized by a conviction that every second the chest remained in my possession multiplied the risk of arrest, from which even Gabetti's intercession would not release me. Water, which was blind, deaf, and mute, and which digested uncomplainingly all the rubbish, dead animals, and rings that polluted it, flowed slowly into the canal from the drains and gutters. I came very near to getting rid of the chest by hurling it into the canal, until I thought of the palace, its frontage bound in yellow tape and its doorways obstructed by wooden planks.

I convinced myself that this would be the safest hiding-place for the chest, precisely because it was the most obvious and inappropriate: when Inspector Nicolussi and his greenhorns undertook their search — and possibly they would not be the only ones anxious to get it back — they would concentrate on locations more elaborately obscure, and never the place where Valenzin had met his assassin. The planks had been nailed up in a slapdash way, and I had no difficulty in pulling them apart, particularly when compared with the excessive efforts I had expended on getting the chest that far. Once inside the palace, I was greeted by the pigeons that nested between the mouldings on the walls. As they flew around, they fanned the thick dust on the curtains which fell on me like a shower of ash. The hall was carpeted with their excrement, some of it quite recent, but much of it dried out, and of almost archaeological interest. There were coats of arms crowning the lintels of the doors, eaten away by neglect, and busts that wept tears of shit from the relentless attentions of the pigeons. The smooth ceiling was decorated with frescoes by one or other of Tiepolo's lesser followers. These celebrated the ancient triumphs of the family that had inhabited the palace long ago. Where the painter had run out of triumphs to celebrate he had had recourse to a banal arrangement of *putti* who flew aimlessly around, wearing crowns of laurel leaves. The colours of the frescoes were indistinguishable, and where chips and flakes had fallen away, the narrative of ancient triumphs was interrupted by their leprous gaps.

I went up the staircase leading to the *piano nobile*, or main floor. The metal corner pieces of the chest banged on every step, and these thuds reverberated round the domed ceiling where the *putti* painted in the fresco were supplanted by stucco *putti* which were even more chubby, cheerful, and repellent. The appearance of the wall was made ever more dreary by the mirrors hung at intervals along it, their mottled wooden frames overloaded with cornucopias. To my relief, I could not see myself in any of these mirrors, because the silvering was in such bad condition and the layers of dust on their glasses were uniformly thick. They were mirrors in which only the dead were reflected, they were mirrors which had retired from duty, and they slept the sleep of centuries.

'Is anyone there?' I shouted, as a shiver ran down my spine.

The *piano nobile* opened out into a vista of intercommunicating rooms. The door of each framed the door of the next one, and so on, through a vast succession of rooms that got progressively smaller and smaller. The only response to my call was the flapping of pigeons' wings, like a pulsation which disturbed the semi-darkness. I had the disagreeable sensation of walking through the slimy stomach of a whale; and every time a tapestry, or a curtain, brushed against my skin it felt like the kiss of a bat.

'That's what I should be asking.'

The silhouette of a man was outlined against the very end of the suite of rooms that diminished progressively in size like a set of Russian dolls. It belonged to a man whose clothing and physical appearance were equally slovenly, the latter prematurely aged by sleepless nights, and by that remarkable 'physiological stamina of the lower classes', to which Gabetti had enviously referred. I began to recognise the rapacious teeth, the angular skull, and the greasy, flattened hair, which made up the figure of Vittorio Tedeschi. He was armed with an ancient carbine that was more laughable than menacing, and probably dated from the wars of Garibaldi.

'I was expecting you,' he said in his coarse dialect, and with a conviction that struck me as unfounded.

'What do you mean, you were expecting me? As far as I am aware we hadn't planned to meet.'

'From the moment I saw you in the police station I knew we'd meet again,' he affirmed, not aggressively, but without relaxing his morose manner. 'Let me help you.'

He had the sinewy hands of a predatory animal, and he lifted the chest and carried it as far as the last room which he had made his billet. He slept in a stately bed, a four-poster, that in the past would have had a canopy over it. Although the sheets were made of fine linen they looked like sackcloth, for such was the crust of filth and urine stains that decorated it. Tedeschi slid the chest under the bed next to a chamberpot heaped with several days' deposits, and a small stove in which he cooked his unvarying meals. The smell of burnt meat, and the proliferation of feathers on the floor, reminded me that pigeons were always used for sacrifices in Latium. Worse, however, than the stink of burnt meat, worse even than the stench of excrement, was the lack of oxygen.

'It wouldn't do any harm to let a little air in here,' I said.

Tedeschi agreed mechanically, and took advantage of his stroll across to the window to empty the chamberpot into the canal. My face must have expressed my repugnance.

'No need to be so finicky. You don't look as if you're on your way to your first communion either!'

I had not washed or changed my clothes since leaving Spain, and the grime of the journey was compounded by the damage done by sleepless nights, several drenchings, and smears of dirt picked up in the palace where the dense dust had acquired the consistency of soot.

'Why were you so sure we would meet again?' I asked, in an attempt to get on friendly terms with him.

'In Venice you *always* meet up again with someone who's once crossed your path. And you and I have a good reason for doing so: we're the only ones who want the truth to come out.'

The sole remarkable feature of that room was the filth. Tedeschi sat on a corner of the bed and picked up a bottle of cheap wine which he kept hidden behind it. He offered it to me half-heartedly, before putting the neck of the bottle to his mouth.

'Where did you get hold of that chest? You must have sharp eyes.'

'I found out by chance that Valenzin had his hiding-place in the Albergo Cusmano,' I said, without claiming much merit for my find. 'But I'm sure you already knew that. All that's missing now are the keys to open it. This chest is as strong as a blockhouse, and there's no way of forcing it.' I made a gesture expressing both dismay and exhaustion, and tried to sound more friendly. 'You don't happen to have the keys, do you?'

Tedeschi knocked back more of his wine with an air of unhurried anxiety – if the contradiction in terms may be permitted. With the last gulp he rinsed his mouth and gums, and then gargled with it. His Adam's apple projected so sharply that it looked likely to pierce the skin of his neck.

'Take it easy, you're going too fast. Do you imagine that

if I had the keys I'd be sitting here, as large as life, chatting with you? Valenzin was bumped off because of this chest. He never let the keys out of his sight. The bastard who shot him pinched them, and before he went off he went all round the palace looking for it, the son of a bitch.'

It seemed to me that it would have been a ghastly and monstrous task to search all through a building in the appalling and chaotic state that this one was in, and liable to collapse at any moment, but not so ghastly or monstrous as the fantastic figure that had appeared at the window for a second while I was attending to Valenzin in his death throes: the horribly white and barely human face, with its hollow eyes, and a nose like the beak of a huge bird.

'And what's in the chest?' I was urged on by that zeal dogs have who sniff their prey but cannot see it. 'From what Inspector Nicolussi said in the police station you were Valenzin's best mate.'

Tedeschi stood up, and stalked a pigeon that was pecking at crumbs on the floor; as it tried to fly off he sprang on it. He held the body of the pigeon in his lethal hands to prevent it moving its wings while he felt under its feathers for the neck, which he then proceeded to wring. The pigeon died without a sound, and with one ineffective flutter – more of a posthumous convulsion than a sign of resistance. It had the slender grace of a ballet dancer who collapses in the middle of an exercise, and its broken neck had a ruff of iridescent, reddish-grey feathers.

'That's my dinner for today,' he said. I closed my eyes, declining an invitation to join him before he even proposed it. 'Not a close friend. Valenzin was a gentleman, who only wanted servants – lackeys to act as underlings in his less important jobs: climbing into a vestry, pinching a few candlesticks, or stealing the jewellery of some old Marchesa with Alzheimer's.' He sounded contrite as he enumerated his small-time assignments. 'He worked alone on his really big jobs; he got as much of a kick out of that as in fucking a good-looking married woman – and he wasn't prepared to share that with the skivvies.'

'Well, it looks on this occasion as if the husband got really annoyed.'

It was a poor joke, but even a professor of art history needs these occasional lapses into vulgarity. Tedeschi tapped his knuckles on the lid of the chest which I had jumped on earlier without inflicting a single dent on it. Its rough exterior still preserved its silent secrets, and it sounded hollow like the shell of a tortoise who has abandoned it while he goes off for a stroll.

'The husband may have avenged his honour, but he hasn't got his wife back,' said Tedeschi, making even more of our joke. 'We're the ones who've kidnapped her.'

Again I was beset by a feeling of indefinable alarm, the knowledge that I was mixed up in a family affair that was no concern of mine: there are still families today who will not put up with intrusions into their inbred way of life, families who resent the arrival of an outsider, families who rule their lives in accordance with codes that are indifferent to the laws of other men, and families who take it into their own hands to seek revenge and to eliminate the stranger who tries to insinuate himself into their genealogical tree. Venice was one of those families, totally absorbed in itself, and I was the stranger breaking their laws, the outsider who taints their blood and intrudes on their rites, and departs marked by a stigma which never fades. Venice was one of those families who take to crime in order to safeguard their crumbling integrity. I felt a compelling need to communicate my alarm to someone, although perhaps Tedeschi was not the best person.

'And the cuckolded husband will do everything possible to get her back,' he said, while I walked up and down the room like a caged animal. 'He'll answer the call all right.'

'Listen, Tedeschi, can you keep a secret?'

He was still holding the dead pigeon in his hands which looked like talons while he was strangling it, and now resembled more than anything a pair of gloves.

'All we have to do is to wait patiently. He'll end up answering the call.'

It exasperated me that he should have been the one to set himself up as the apostle of passiveness and calm, when both passiveness and calm were obsolete weapons, as obsolete as his old carbine, puny weapons compared with the wrath of a family that is preparing to avenge an affront. Tedeschi continued to outline his useless plan, like a strategist who still believes in hand-to-hand combat, and is ignorant of the progress made in modern weaponry.

'I asked you if you would keep a secret.'

'Well, yes, if I've got to.'

His look was passive and evasive, because nobody likes being burdened with another man's secrets, but when he noticed the expression on my face which must have been contorted, threatening an attack of hysteria, it became more decisive. Words came to me in a mad torrent; they poured out incoherently, because the rush of relief they gave me left no time for deliberation.

'I don't know why I've chosen you, and I don't know what it is that ties me to this place, in fact I don't know anything; I can't understand why I'm getting myself into so many difficulties, because my life used to be peaceful and well organised.' This was a lie: peace has no system, and is ultimately spurious. I was also lying when I said I was free from ties. I was drawn to a painting, and I was drawn to Chiara. 'I don't know why I didn't tell the whole truth to Nicolussi, possibly because I've always liked playing at being a detective, and when I'm trying to find out about an artist I pretend I'm the hero in a crime novel, so you can see how stupid I can be. But no, I don't think it was to play at being a detective, I was afraid to tell the full truth because truth can lead to disaster: it's like a button you push and – blow me down – the next thing you know is, everything's crashing about your head. So the best thing you can do is keep your trap shut.'

I had recourse to these obsolete and colloquial expressions – mixing words from my own language, some of them grotesquely Italianised – because the rush of relief I felt in talking left no time for deliberation, and it needed an extra effort of will to translate my thoughts into a semblance of Italian. Tedeschi, who only spoke the Venetian dialect, understood nothing of this mish-mash, but that did not make him less well-disposed.

'Come on, calm down, and have a drink.'

He passed me the wine bottle, the neck of which was thick with his germs and saliva, but the transmission of germs is a form of sincere comradeship, and I had no right to be squeamish.

'Come on, Ballesteros, what did you hide from Nicolussi?'

The wine was very potent, and it inflamed my guts without stopping in my empty stomach. I collapsed on to the mattress that was covered in sheets of fine linen – or sackcloth – before my drunken faint made me fall over even more spectacularly. With an effort this time to make my explanations less muddled and polyglot, I recounted the whole sequence of events from the moment I heard the shot until Fabio Valenzin died in my arms, without leaving out the fleeting glimpse of the ring, nor of the pale band that Valenzin drew my attention to on his second finger, nor even the predatory and fantastic apparition in one of the windows of the palace. Tedeschi nodded appreciatively, as if every nod was a bow expressing amazement – or an absolution of my crimes. The mattress sagged under the weight of our two backsides, and rested on the chest, which seemed to transmit an incandescent heat, as if the monster concealed inside had woken from his long sleep.

'We'll get the ring out of the canal later,' he said. 'But now, we must go to the cemetery, or we'll be late.'

FIVE

As it irrupted into the lagoon after leaving the Arsenal Bridge, the *vaporetto* described a broad arc, like the first flourish a torero makes with his cape to excite the applause of a public hungering for sensation. There were a few early tourists on board who were anticipating the beginning of carnival by wearing silly hats topped with little bells. They looked, and sounded, very pleased with themselves, and failed to understand the insults that Tedeschi hurled at them in his broad Venetian dialect. As he accompanied his insults with exaggerated gestures, the tourists assumed he was welcoming them to Venice, and they responded by bowing obsequiously, making the little bells on their hats ring as they did so.

'Look at that bunch of mental defectives. You'd think somebody had shoved hot chillies up their arses ...' He laughed, showing his teeth which were as rapacious as ever, and which looked dull beside those of the grinning Japanese. 'Fucking imbeciles!'

The air over the lagoon was cold and salty. It brushed my cheeks with such a refreshing sensation that I was overwhelmed by a feeling of intense joy and exhilaration, like a man who returns to the normality of domestic life after struggling through nightmares that seem to make sense while they last, but appear absurd and the result of a fever when he wakes up. Venice possessed the absurdity and terrors of a city under siege. Everything relating to it was absurd: the ties that bound its inhabitants, my distorted perceptions of them, my absurd and ingenuous conclusions which stemmed from increasing openmindedness, allied to natural caution. For the first time in those two days I did not feel myself beset by portents and threats; for the first time I felt able to laugh at Tedeschi's xenophobic broadsides. The lagoon was free of the snow that had greeted my arrival, but there were numerous lumps of ice floating on it which the *vaporetto* steered round or, occasionally, crashed into. Once he had unburdened himself of his animosity towards the tourists, Tedeschi joined me in the prow of the boat. His breath knocked me back because it smelled like a cellar in which wines of the poorest imaginable quality have fermented, but together with this awful smell there emanated from him an honest and homely warmth, in which prevailed the oldest and most universal of human emotions. It dawned on me that I had at last made a friend. Tedeschi told me how he had worked in coastal fishing before he began his career of caretaking pillaged palaces – and in pillaging palaces which did not have caretakers. He was still a fisherman, he made clear, because there are certain vocations which shape you, vocations which you accept because there is nothing better for you to do, or because of family tradition, although he should really have given it up when the fish gave up and left the lagoon – having had enough of dodging motor launches and breathing industrial waste through their gills. All that was left to him now was the rather masochistic consolation of going on a *vaporetto* in order to feel again the shifting green surface of the water beneath his feet, the same water that had provided a livelihood in his youth. Although he did not allow nostalgia to blur his recollections, they obviously made him very depressed. Looking at the lagoon divided up by buoys and cut across by the foaming wakes of water taxis, it was as painful for him as it must be for a deposed monarch to contemplate a kingdom that had once belonged to him and his ancestors – even commoners have ancestries – before being sacrificed to progress. I agreed with what he said and put up with his bad breath; I approved of the honest warmth of his regrets.

The island of San Michele was a walled cemetery, and at first sight it looked impregnable, like a fortress that has risen unexpectedly from the sea. Its sheer walls acted as a sort of dyke, and above them appeared the tops of cypresses, like spikes on a railing. For centuries the Venetian Republic had practised a form of segregation of its sick inhabitants, believing that this would keep the city pure and uncontaminated: the dead on San Michele, lunatics on San Servolo, lepers on San Lazzaro degli Armeni, Jews on the Giudecca. In this way, they created an archipelago of the marginalised, which failed however to protect them from miscegenation or leprosy, from madness or death, or from any other malady or blight.

The *vaporetto* tied up alongside a landing stage constructed for the loading and unloading of coffins, next to the funerary gondola that had brought over the body of Fabio Valenzin, the velvet of its seats covered in black crape. Tedeschi and I were the only ones to get off at that stop: the ridiculous tourists were going on to Murano, or Burano, in order to buy up glass vases and lace tablecloths for friends at home.

'Goodbye, you cretins, you bunch of stupid mother-fuckers.' With these words, Tedeschi bade farewell to the tourists, waving gaily at them, a gesture which they reciprocated, grateful for such warm expressions of hospitality.

When they choose to do so, the Venetians, who are accustomed to living in a city of great beauty, are nevertheless capable of closing their eyes to that and of allowing themselves to be drawn towards a blatant vulgarity that verges on the pretentious, and is in extremely bad taste. What they do not reject is class pride. If the city is split up into districts that maintain the distinctions between those of high and those of low estate, the cemetery is divided into sectors, each of which has its own particular style: pantheons hung with ivy for the more aristocratic families; whitewashed tombs for nuns and monks; lofty tombs for the more valiant of their military heroes; shaded tombs for practitioners of lesser religions; and niches for the plebs. The tombs of the bourgeoisie are the most consummately vulgar of them all: on the headstones of marble, or some marble substitute, there are epitaphs with photographs of the deceased, smiling, their white teeth becoming ever whiter as the years go by, since all the other colours are washed out by the weather. Some of these portraits look like X-rays of ectoplasm.

'Look, there they are,' Tedeschi pointed out. He threaded his way more skilfully than I through the multitudinous rows of graves.

The Venetians seem to harbour a peculiar grudge against their dead. They mock and humiliate them by decorating their graves with bunches of artificial flowers, which degrade the place. Morning light filtered through the sombre foliage of the cypresses, and fell about my shoulders. The tomb that had been assigned to Fabio Valenzin was not without its own floral tribute and identifying photograph. The priest had just sprinkled holy water on the grave, and the gravediggers were struggling with the gravestone, with the vigour characteristic of removal men. I noticed Inspector Nicolussi standing discreetly to one side, leaning against the trunk of a cypress; the worried expression on his face made it look as if he was trying to prevent it falling down. Not even his presence on holy ground could make him give up his cigarettes: they were the drug that helped him both to breathe and to remain awake. He was taking great care not to look at Dina, and she was taking equal care not to look at him. It was a sort of pantomime that obliged them to look very solemn and deeply absorbed in the prospect of the hundreds of crosses in the distance. The priest muttered his prayers without a trace of enthusiasm, as if convinced that he was presiding over the descent of a soul into the infernal regions.

'If we have died with Christ, we believe that we shall live with Him; for we know that Christ, who was raised from the dead, does not die, that death hath no power over Him. For in dying, He died for our sins, once and for all; but living, He lives in God. So, know then that ye die for your sins, but ye shall live in God and in Jesus Christ.'

Valenzin was commencing his journey to decay or towards God-in-Jesus-Christ without a single relative to weep at his departure, and with no messages of condolence or hypocritical lamentations. Chiara was the only one who seemed at all moved by the disappearance of a friend; she was the only one whose sorrow did not seem a mere formality. Although her eyes were shielded by sunglasses, I knew she had noticed me, and that my presence gave her a sense of relief. The realisation of this made me feel important. She had raised her coat collar, probably to protect her neck, which is the zone that feels most vividly the cold wind of death, and her hair, with its shades of a cool autumn day, blew about her face, more dishevelled than ever.

'Let us pray. Lend, Oh Lord, Thine ear to our supplication;

we implore Thee to be merciful in order that Thou may place on the altar of peace and of light the soul of Thy servant, Fabio, who by Thy command has left this world. For our Lord Jesus Christ's sake.'

'Amen.'

It was a very weak 'amen', neither spoken in unison, nor with great conviction, but this may have been due more to reluctance than agnosticism. Gilberto Gabetti, in spite of having borne the cost of the funeral service, seemed the most reluctant of all, the most disbelieving, and the most anxious for the ceremony to end. He had dressed with great care, and he looked at me with disapproval and annoyance when he saw that I had not changed my clothes, and had not even made an attempt to clean myself up. Tedeschi whispered in my ear.

'Look over there, that's Gabetti's ex-wife. A right poisonous old bird!'

He pointed out a very slim woman whose beauty had not been allowed to surrender to the years, although it was of a kind that tends to be mounted on a pedestal, protected by a veneer of disdain; one of those beauties that inspire awe and subservience, but never respect, or any other egalitarian sentiment. She wore a mink coat — in Venice, wealthy women are lavish with their money — and under it, by contrast, a pair of jeans, as if she wanted to emphasise her youthful figure, when in fact it was decades since her youth had deserted her.

'She's called Giovanna Zanon,' continued Tedeschi. 'She's married now to the owner of a big chain of hotels, one of the richest men in Italy.'

As if she guessed we were talking about her, Giovanna Zanon gave an inscrutable smile, like that of a Roman high priestess plotting the sacrifice of all the vestal virgins in her service. She smiled, trying not to relax the muscles of her face, in order to maintain her dignified expression, but she could not avoid deepening the wrinkles in the corners of her mouth, which made the skin there look like flaky pastry. It was the sort of smile that made me feel nervous, yet at the same time it held a compelling fascination.

'Bad luck, lad, she's noticed you. Bad luck!' Tedeschi clicked his tongue. 'But don't let her get near you.'

'Why do you say that?'

'She's a right cow!'

I resisted the idea of including her in the category of farmyard animals; it was enough for me that she was Chiara's mother for her arrogance to seem less offensive. Love is a volatile thing; apart from creating an irrational state of mind, its existence can lead us to embrace within its scope all the relations of the person we love. Giovanna Zanon was staring at me through half-closed eyes, with that effort that short-sighted people make when they don't want to demean themselves by wearing glasses. It was a gaze that intensified her air of insolence, as well as her impossibly statuesque beauty. The priest raised his voice, not best pleased with our whispering.

'Release, Oh Lord, the soul of Thy servant Fabio from all trace of sin in order that he may be raised to live joyfully in eternal glory amongst Thy Saints and Chosen. For the sake of our Lord Jesus Christ.'

'Amen.'

It needed a powerful dose of hypocrisy, or optimism, to imagine Valenzin taking his place in such blessed company.

The gathering at the funeral would have been reduced to an indecently small number if the friends of Valenzin had not been augmented by a group of journalists. They carried notebooks, and even a few tape-recorders. Giovanna Zanon turned towards them, possibly tired of being harassed, and began, very quietly, to give them a lecture. She pointed me out with the same shameless impudence with which Tedeschi had pointed her out to me.

'She's setting the dogs on you.'

Failing to understand, I looked at Tedeschi with bewilderment.

'What did you say?'

'The journalists. She's read the papers, so she's explaining who you are, or who she thinks you are.' Tedeschi nodded to express his admiration for the malevolence of the woman. 'They mentioned a Spaniard who had been present at the murder in their local news reports. They'll pester the bloody life out of you now.'

I trembled at the prospect of another interrogation that would be quite as exhausting, and much more discourteous, than the one conducted by Nicolussi in the police station. The priest was making crucifying motions in the air to signal the end of the service, when they shoved the first tape-recorder in my face.

'Are you the Spaniard who was with Valenzin when he died?'

I refused to answer in case my accent betrayed me, but they interpreted my silence as an indication that I was trying to avoid telling what I knew, so they bombarded me with even more questions.

'How long do you expect to be in Venice?'

'Is it true you're staying with Gilberto Gabetti?'

'Did you know anything about Fabio Valenzin before you came here?'

I tried to plot my flight along the gravel paths that opened up between the rows of tombs, but the journalists, who were either more athletic or more irreverent than I, jumped over the tombstones, leaned on the epitaphs, and trampled underfoot the flowers made of rag and plastic, in front of the faded smiles of the deceased. There were times when a cypress got in my way, and made me dodge to one side in a game of hide-and-seek, which made me feel thoroughly ridiculous. They had also approached Tedeschi, and he agreed willingly to their requests and answered their questions with lies grandiloquently phrased, breathing heavily into their tape-recorders in such a way as to soak them with his saliva.

When I reached the central alley, I broke into a run until I came up against a wall full of niches, the marble of which oozed a sort of green scum. Behind me I could hear the breaking of waves like repeated distant roars that matched the beating of my heart.

'That's enough now. Stop bullying him. Can't you see the gentleman is terrified?'

Giovanna Zanon's voice was both spiteful and caressing, like velvet secretly concealing a venom that is poisonous to the touch. When she took my arm I was buffeted by the first whiff of her perfume, a perfume which smelled strongly of lavender. The touch of her mink was pleasant and slightly sexy.

'Now that's enough. Go away before I get angry.'

The reporters scattered and moved on. It was a display of docility that left me astonished. Maybe they were specialists in society news and Giovanna Zanon was one of their key sources – both of news and bribes. I cursed myself mentally for having allowed myself to be rescued and for having displayed my vulnerability in front of her, and I persuaded myself that I would remain on my guard as long as I had any dealings with her. Giovanna Zanon waited until she was sure the reporters had retreated, crestfallen, and discomfited by the authority in her voice, like circus animals who, after being admonished by their trainer, abandon their hope of breakfasting on human flesh, and console themselves with the vegetarian diet she imposes, a diet that leaves them with rotted gums and teeth originally made sharp for the very purpose of tearing their prey apart. Possibly, Giovanna Zanon's nails were just as sharp, but I was unable to be certain of this because they were sheathed, like the rest of her hands, in gloves made from such fine suede that they revealed the shape of her knuckles and the pattern of her veins. Possibly her teeth had been capped and rectified by orthodontic treatment, but they retained a certain carnivorous threat when she showed them briefly as she smiled – which again made the skin round her mouth look like flaky pastry. Even so, Giovanna Zanon took good care when she smiled not to destroy all the handiwork that had gone into preserving her face.

'You see what these newspaper people are like,' she said. 'They have no respect for anybody.'

She spoke in a tediously affected voice, as if an operation had been performed on her vocal cords to eliminate all traces of a plebeian accent. I noticed that her neck, below the line reached by her hydrating creams, was not just wrinkled, it was deeply furrowed. The reporters, deprived of my testimony, began to battle with other people present at the interment, but these either gave vague replies or hid behind a forbidding silence. Chiara and Gabetti marched past me without stopping, and without even a smile. They looked straight ahead as if I had become invisible or at least semi-transparent, or as if the animosity they felt for Giovanna Zanon encompassed anyone who had recourse to her protection. Tedeschi also passed by, but in his case without embarrassment or indifference. He gave me a wink as he went, the significance of which I failed to interpret immediately – or, more correctly, my interpretation of it caused me considerable alarm. It was the sort of wink that combines the amused with the salacious, such as an elder brother directs at the Benjamin of the family, to give him courage as he is on the point of losing his virginity. Seized by a sudden aversion, I tried to escape from Giovanna Zanon, but she resisted, and refused to let go of my arm.

'Since when does a gentleman refuse to support a lady who has just come to his rescue?' she said, scornfully.

Inspector Nicolussi had taken Dina furtively by the arm and, behind a box hedge, appeared to be lecturing her in their private language of equivocation and reticence. Giovanna Zanon quickly carried me off: as well as being high and mighty in her behaviour, she also had very long legs – even without high heels – and as she walked she made an odd swerving movement as if she was anxious not to swing her hips, and at the same time to hide a slight limp. For her journeys round the lagoon she had at her disposal a motor launch driven by a young man who looked like a cabin boy, but was far too good-looking for me not to suppose that he was employed for other specific tasks as well – although his uniform conferred on him an element of respectability.

'Please be my guest,' she said, inviting me to precede her into the cabin of the launch.

It was a small cabin, but with many windows, and its tiny door made it necessary to bend almost double. The floor was carpeted all over, and instead of benches without backs, there were sofas covered in a burgundy-coloured velvet. I could not make up my mind whether the decorations were inspired by the palace of Versailles, or a high-class brothel. A Siamese cat lay stretched out on a cushion and it licked its whiskers with a tongue like that of a hummingbird, very long and fluttery. It saluted its mistress with a miaow, and climbed up her mink coat.

'Down, pussykins, or you'll leave me without any clothes.'

Giovanna Zanon removed her coat with many contortions, because the small dimensions of the cabin did not allow for normal manoeuvres. Beneath it, she wore a very constricting, strapless bodice of black silk, adorned with sequins and stones. I guessed that the stones were artificial because I could not imagine that, however rich her millionaire, hotel-owning husband was, he would have run to that sort of extravagance – although you never know. The bodice was tight round her waist and pushed her breasts up high, quite unnecessarily, because their implants of silicone had turned them into swollen protuberances. The skin in the hollow between them, by contrast, was mottled and withered. A double string of pearls, which I presumed to be real, distracted attention from her cleavage. Giovanna Zanon signalled to the boatman or chauffeur, and the motor started up with a noisy vibration that reverberated through the cabin, and obliged us to shout at each other.

'And what sort of work do you do?'

She had taken a good look at my dishevelled clothing, and had almost certainly assumed I had some sort of employment which, if not manual, was certainly pedestrian. The prow of the launch bounced across the lagoon with a jolt at every wave. We left all the others behind on the San Michele quay because none of them had private transport.

'I am a university professor,' I exaggerated. 'I specialise in Renaissance painting.'

Giovanna Zanon smiled approvingly while she scratched the neck of the Siamese cat, without removing her gloves – possibly in order not to pick up a host of fleas under her fingernails. The launch left a gash of foam in its wake, and water splashed against the cabin windows like shrapnel.

'Marvellous, how absolutely marvellous,' said Giovanna Zanon, clapping her hands with delight. 'We have a little Renaissance painting at home, but we are not sure of its authenticity. Would it be too much to ask you to give us your expert opinion? Obviously, we would pay you for it . . .'

She proclaimed the fact that there would be a pecuniary award as if she were offering charity or a tip. I searched her face for features which would resemble, or in any way remind me of, Chiara. I looked for recollections of Chiara in Giovanna Zanon, and vice versa – a vague physical likeness, or just the quiver of a muscle, of the sort that carries through from one generation to another, and allows us to pin down a relationship, just as the brushwork of an artist and his use of *sfumatura* allows us to make a confident attribution of a picture. But the search turned out to be fruitless.

'Don't worry, I'll do it for nothing,' I said, and immediately regretted my generous proposal, which would merely discredit me in her eyes.

'You can't know how grateful I am. One is always at the mercy of crooks like Valenzin.'

She had removed her shoes and was rubbing her toes as if they were sore, but her shoes could not have pinched them or hurt them, because they were flat and not at all narrow. Her gesture was as false as the stones on her bodice.

'I thought Valenzin was a family friend.' I was hesitant about whether to link her with Chiara and Gabetti. 'Your previous family, I mean.'

Giovanna Zanon got rid of the Siamese cat by giving it a firm pat on its behind. She stretched out her long legs and held them suspended in the air at the level of my knees, as if she was working on an exercise for her stomach muscles, or was offering me her feet for admiration, or expecting me to wash them. Through her stockings I counted ten toes, their nails varnished in a shade that matched the velvet of the sofas. She was asking me for an expert opinion, and a foot massage as well.

'Go on, what are you waiting for?'

Her feet also smelled of lavender. They had the feel of cold, smooth marble, a feel that was by no means soft, and was very different from the memory that stayed on my hands after caressing Chiara's feet through her window. I withstood Giovanna Zanon's look, not out of insolence or a desire to issue a challenge, but because I was bewildered by her disdain. Her eyes were liquid, and their colour was that of mature vinegar which distils its poison very slowly, eyes that you never meet in a small village, or in a country girl – quite different from Chiara's. The lips were no longer smiling, mainly in order not to distort the tight skin of her cheeks.

'But your daughter was very upset by his death,' I dared to murmur.

I thought the noise of the engine would have drowned my words, but Giovanna Zanon had vigilant hearing – I am not sure if that expression is permissible – or maybe she was able to guess other people's thoughts just as Chiara guessed at the rise and fall of the tides and the spying of strangers. I noticed her fingers, curling up like the claws of a cat.

'What do you mean by my daughter?' Anger made her purse her lips. 'Are you incapable of calculating ages?'

The Siamese cat's fur was bristling with the static electricity that pervaded the cabin, and it arched its tail as if scenting danger. I muttered something incoherent, but Giovanna Zanon insisted on more explicit amends.

'How old do you think I am? Come on, how old?'

I tried to speak, but could not find my voice at first. Her toenails had ripped through her nylon stockings and were scratching my hands.

'I really don't know. Forty-something . . . But just like that, I couldn't exactly say . . .'

Giovanna Zanon, slightly mollified, did not allow me to finish.

'Forty-something. All right, let's leave it at that.' Maybe she was afraid that someone might have bid her up towards fifty. 'And do you know how old your dearest Chiara is? Thirty-four, if she's a day. She's not a little girl!'

The angels on the façade of the Church of the Jesuits stood out against the grey sky. Venice seemed to float above an opalescent light or the soft tones of a watercolour painting. Giovanna Zanon breathed in so deeply that she exhausted all the oxygen in the cabin. Her breasts nearly burst through her bodice, and the bulges of her nipples were clearly visible. In order to wound me even more she resorted to familiarity.

'I'm sorry, but you're very naïve.'

'Me naïve?' I protested, but I blushed, and that reduced to nothing the little self-possession I still had. 'I don't see why.'

'You poor fellow, you're utterly naïve, that's what you are. You've let yourself be completely taken in by that pair of tricksters.'

The fact that she called Gabetti a trickster did not bother me; but to include Chiara in the same category stirred me to genuine anger, the level of anger and irritation that only the very naïve are capable of feeling. The noise of the engine lessened as the launch slowed down, and the prow fell, as it nosed its way into the canals.

'It doesn't seem fair to me to insult them since they're not here to defend themselves,' I murmured.

'Then it's obvious you don't know them. Let me tell you a few things about the past.'

Giovanna Zanon tried to close her eyes, but she was quick to open them again: the vinegar in them stung her lids. A flock of seagulls was squabbling over some scraps that somebody had thrown into the canal from a window. As the launch passed by, instead of melting away, the seagulls, emboldened by the glut of food, raged against us in their own squawking vernacular, and some of them even attacked our cabin with their curved beaks and their Jurassic-age wings, which made a gentle beating noise against the glass. I was surprised that Giovanna Zanon was prepared to go into so much detail – but lies come over more easily when they are wrapped in a flood of words.

'Gilberto always liked little girls, you know. I think he's a bit of a paedophile. Although possibly paedophilia is just a way of hiding his impotence. When I first met him he was already a mature man, about forty, with that combination of self-confidence and high spirits which is so fascinating to young girls. He was living from hand to mouth, giving professional advice to art collectors, organising exhibitions, and working as a travelling lecturer – always on the same subject, but with some charming touches which made it sound different every time. I attended one of his lectures because a teacher at my school recommended me to do so. Do I have to tell you that I was completely bowled over?' I made a gesture of forgiveness. 'I was a featherbrained adolescent, and Gilberto seemed to me irresistible, with the glamour of an adventurer and that exquisite sensitivity of his. Our engagement was pretty stormy, not because of what you might call tempestuous sexual relations – which were always a bit of a wash-out – but because of my parents' opposition. They went so far as to denounce Gilberto as a seducer of young girls!'

She let rip with a laugh that sounded like the squawking of the seagulls, not a bit like Chiara's deep chuckle. She continued, impudently.

'Some seducer! Gilberto couldn't get it up to save his life. He was useless in bed, but for a girl of sixteen who is romantic and has no ambitions to become a mother, impotence is not a serious obstacle.' She did not mention other carnal inclinations which had probably been satisfied in return for money. 'Do you know how we got my parents' permission to marry? By me pretending to be pregnant. Imagine the irony of that! It was a pregnancy we had to get rid of afterwards by inventing a miscarriage.' One lie hides another, just as snow hides the obscenity of spilled blood, I thought. 'Marriage taught me what an unreal engagement had not even allowed me to guess. I don't understand why you men are so secretive about yourselves, and only let us in on your secrets when the situation can no longer be remedied, and the victim can't get out of it. All the brilliant worldliness that Gilberto displayed in public was poles apart from the self-torture that beset him in private. He knew he had no gift for painting, but even so he wanted to believe he would live on in the memory of his contemporaries with works comparable with those of the great masters, whom he had judged with great critical insight. But critical insight seldom goes together with creative talent.'

Giovanna Zanon had sprawled out on the sofa, and her feet were warming up under the attentions of my hands. They lost their feel of cold marble and their smell of expensive perfume; they were becoming softer, and beginning to perspire, which made them more malleable. What she had not said was that critical insight is the refuge and the alibi of those like me who cannot keep up with the demands and tribulations of real talent, because talent is uncontrollable, and needs the highest

125

imaginable level of courage, the sort of courage possessed only by those who are able to jettison pure intelligence: art is the religion of feeling and emotion.

The launch seemed to be trapped in a maze of canals, like paths between the cluster of palaces the roofs of which left scarcely any gaps for light to penetrate.

'He hoped to cure the sterility that made his life such a misery by having a son who would be at one and the same time his disciple and the inheritor of his teaching, a son who would adore him, and would help him live to a contented old age.' Giovanna Zanon introduced a note of sarcasm into her monologue – the malevolence of one who tries to disguise slander in harmless gossip. 'I placed my fertility at his disposal, but it was no good: natural processes would not do the trick. So we adopted an orphan.'

Up to that point I had listened to her story without expressing surprise or disbelief, just as you would expect from a person of passive temperament. Giovanna Zanon's eyes lost their gleam and became unrelenting, like nightfall.

'Chiara?' I asked, with alarm.

Giovanna Zanon nodded, with calculatedly theatrical emphasis. The launch had tied up against a palace painted blood red, and with a double *loggia*, or porticoed gallery. An ivy, stiff with frost, climbed the façade, and its tendrils reached up as far as the window-sills, as if they were begging to be let in, but somebody had amputated them with shears in a sadistic attempt at pruning. Our helmsman opened the cabin door. Giovanna Zanon put her shoes on to indicate that the massage was over, and threw the mink coat over her shoulders.

'Well, I have told you that we adopted her, but I must correct that, because in fact it was a personal decision by Gilberto,' she went on. The Siamese cat climbed up her coat again, and she admonished it with a slap on the nose. 'All I did was sign the papers – I had already warned Gilberto that that orphan was not going to arouse any maternal feelings in me, far from it in fact. I'm not one to take easily to strangers! Chiara was the mirror in which Gilberto saw himself; he moulded her to his taste, in a process of utter devotion from which I was excluded.'

We entered the palace down one of its sides, walking through a garden which could not be seen from the canal – the Venetians defend their gardens jealously, and tend them for their own exclusive enjoyment. It was a garden with many trees, and with headless alabaster statues hiding in the shrubbery like sentries in their boxes, and a fountain in the Moorish style with a tiled skirting, which provided a constant refrain to the chirping of the birds. It would have been a good place in which to write pastoral poems. Between the latticed branches of the trees could be seen a sky heavy with clouds which threatened a storm at any moment.

'At first I felt I had been passed over, rather in the way the wives of feudal knights must have felt in the Middle Ages after giving birth to the first son, except that in my case I didn't even have the consolation of being a real mother. Chiara grew up and became the apple of Gilberto's eye. Nothing else mattered to him in the whole world. I remember once he compared himself with the figure in that painting by Giorgione. What is it called? *The Tempest.* His only concern was the little girl who was growing up and becoming an adult in accordance with the principles that he had laid down – although it was obvious there were storms on the horizon. On one occasion I couldn't help losing my temper: "But the woman in that picture is suckling her son, possibly the son she has conceived with the help of that man. Neither you nor Chiara will have children to follow you. You're both as sterile as mules."' She swallowed hard. Her mouth was dry, from spite. 'He never forgave me.'

I recalled Gabetti's words when we were in the gondola: 'No, my friend, Giorgione only acted when suddenly gripped by a passion or when tortured by grief, by the bitter aftertaste of lust or the exultation we feel when we succeed at last with the woman we desire. Don't look for symbols or mysticism or complicated mythological meanings in his work.' Gabetti never forgave Giovanna Zanon her ridicule, and he wasn't going to forgive my academic meddling in a picture that belonged so exclusively to him.

'*The Tempest* is the very painting I am here to study,' I said, with an unease that I found hard to conceal.

'Is that so?' Giovanna Zanon turned to me; she was half-amused and half-compassionate. 'Well, I predict that Gilberto will make it as difficult for you as he can, and then some! If there is one thing in this world he considers untouchable, after his little girl, it's that picture. He has never lent it to other art galleries, not even when an exhibition devoted solely to Giorgione was being organised in Vienna. His refusal became notorious, and diplomatic pressure was brought to bear. Gilberto alleged that the painting was in too bad a condition to travel, which convinced nobody. And there have been other art professors here before you to analyse *The Tempest*, but he was merciless with every one of them. He refuted all their arguments publicly, and left them looking ridiculous.' Shrewdly, she suppressed the desire to smile. 'You have to admit that, for sophistry, there's no one to beat Gilberto!'

The door was opened by a Filipino maid who was wiping her hands on her apron in order, no doubt, to remove cooking smells. She greeted her mistress by stooping exaggeratedly low, and relieved her of her coat and gloves before withdrawing.

'We shall be three for lunch,' announced Giovanna Zanon, before the maid could return to her duties. 'I have invited this gentleman.'

Giovanna Zanon walked as if some of her joints were dislocated; she had the spindly grace of storks and skeletons. Her bottom was too flat for my taste – her jeans betrayed the consequences of liposuction – but my tastes do not tally with the fashion of the day, and in fact are directly opposed to them. She crossed the hall, and invited me into a small study which was in half-darkness.

'Come in, come in. Don't stand there as if you'd seen a ghost, I want to show you something.'

The study, which had something of a chapel or monastic cell about it, was lit by a small oil-lamp that inevitably reminded me of the one that Chiara had placed on Tintoretto's tomb the previous morning like a votive offering, the lamp that conceivably still shed some light in the gloom of the church.

'Well, what do you think?'

The flame of the lamp cast its light on a Madonna and Child of modest proportions. Although the austere furnishing of the study and the play of the light seemed to have the effect of lengthening the bodies of the figures, making them look a little like those in a Greek ikon, there were features that confirmed the hand of Bellini: the precise detail, almost that of a miniaturist, in the background landscape; the face of the Virgin, moved by a *pietà* which surpassed and contradicted Mantegna's recommended 'serene harmony'; the petulant pose of the Child who looked as if he was on the point of suffocating or of throwing himself round his Mother's neck as if to strangle her. Bellini's figures of the Christ Child often have prematurely adult features, even ungainly ones at times. Barely an inch separated the hand of the Virgin from the sole of the Child's foot: the inch that separates love from eroticism. That panel had been stolen from the church of the Madonna dell' Orto.

'Is it authentic?' Giovanna Zanon pressed me for an answer.

The fact that it was stolen property did not even shock me.

'Of course it is. It bears the hallmark of Giovanni Bellini, even if the Child suggests a less talented brush – possibly a not very competent apprentice who worked in his studio.' Without hesitation I passed from delivering my opinion to the financial consideration. 'But this must have cost millions!'

In the attenuated light of the study, Giovanna Zanon took on the appearance of a desiccated or dormant snake. Her breasts inside the bodice looked heavy and brimming with milk – but it would be a 'long-life' milk, heavily laced with preservatives.

'When I divorced Gilberto, I swore I would never again marry for love,' she said irrelevantly, or possibly as a round-about way of avoiding the vulgarity of figures. 'But tell me, are you certain it isn't a fake? That fellow Valenzin was capable of imitating Bellini and the whole of his studio put together, if it was suggested to him. And that little slut helped him.'

'What do you mean by slut?' In Italian, the word was short and explicit, totally unambiguous and, to me, highly challenging.

'I've already told you that you're naïve. You've got a lot to learn.'

Maybe I did have a lot to learn, maybe I had to grow up and develop an aptitude for disbelief.

'It is you who are being naïve,' I said. Giovanna Zanon blinked, as if her personal pride was wounded. 'A fake copy of a *cinquecento* painting would not pass a carbon-14 test, nor an ultraviolet test. Ask any technical expert and he'll tell you the same.'

I was salivating from sheer anger as I spoke. Giovanna Zanon closed her eyes with disgust as she felt the drops of my saliva on her face. I readied myself for the insults she would hurl at me, but when she spoke, her voice was oily and artful, reminiscent of a reptile emerging from a long sleep.

'I thought I could trust you,' she said. 'But I can see that you are no different from all the other crooks and con men.'

I was about to protest, but stopped as I felt the gentle pressure of her hand on the front of my trousers: five fingers in all – although they felt like eight at least, like the eight legs of a scorpion, not counting the tail that stings – as they examined the bulge in my underpants.

'What's the matter? Are you keeping yourself for that little slut?'

Once again she used the word that was short and explicit, unambiguous, and challenging; but insults have a way of seeming less serious as one becomes sexually aroused. Giovanna Zanon's fingers resembled dry twigs; they were like those of a drowned man, or the frozen weed that floats on the surface of the water in the canals. The Madonna of Bellini turned aside as if in disapproval of a deed that did not respect the inch of distance which should always be maintained – the distance which makes all the difference between love and brazenness.

'I hope this isn't the way you pay the tricksters you deal with.'

'Kiss me,' she commanded.

Her vinegary eyes grew brighter in the half-light of the room; they acquired a hard gleam. The spots between her breasts looked like blotches where acid has corroded the skin. I began to lick these spots, more bewildered than excited, ignoring the mounds on either side which, strictly speaking, should have been more desirable – although I detest symmetry.

I stroked her shoulder which was also mottled, and I unzipped her jeans. With my peasant hand I felt around the bottom that was too flat for my liking. I kissed her withered neck — a kiss in every furrow — as if I were trying to determine her age by a sort of carbon-14 test. Giovanna Zanon smelled strongly of lavender, but beneath that perfume she smelled the same as me. Nature makes us all equal in spite of skin creams, deodorants, and regular ablutions. Then I asked her:

'What went on between Chiara and Valenzin?'

I recognise that the question was abrupt and its timing bad, or more badly timed than abrupt, because it referred to a past which was over and done with, a time about which I had no right to be jealous. Giovanna Zanon drew away from me as if to re-establish the distance between impudence and abhorrence.

'Are you a complete idiot, or what?' Now it was her turn to spit out at me in her fury. 'What the hell does it matter to me what went on? I just hope she was unfaithful to Gilberto! I just hope Valenzin did fuck her behind his back! I just hope that you get around to fucking her, and that the old fool shoots himself! I only hope you all kill each other for her sake! I shall enjoy going to your funerals!'

She tried to make her rebukes sound severe and also contemptuous, but the circumstances detracted from their dramatic effect: her nipples were still erect from desire, and her jeans had slipped down to her knees, revealing thighs that looked markedly undernourished, almost exposing the bones. Suddenly, a bell rang. This forced her to suppress her anger and put her dress to rights. The flame of the lamp flickered as the Filipino maid opened the street-door.

'Has your mistress got back?' enquired a voice that was offhand with the servant, but suggested an inner lack of confidence.

'Yes, sir. She is in the hall study with a gentleman she has invited.'

There was nothing to betray our amorous antics, apart from the censorious glance of the Madonna. A man appeared in the doorway. He was a feeble-looking man with the face of a gargoyle; he was stylishly dressed, but looked stupid. He had to stoop as he entered the study in order not to bump his cuckolded head on the lintel. He gave a broad toothy smile, like an errand boy or hotel bellhop.

'My dear, I've been to collect our fancy-dress costumes. This year we shall be a sensation, you'll see.'

He was panting a little, like a pet dog begging for the approval of its owner. I could just imagine, with more delight than pity, the humiliations that his wife would inflict upon him when there were no guests present, as if he really were a pet dog or cat.

'Let me introduce you to my husband, Taddeo Rosso, of the famous Rosso family,' said Giovanna Zanon, revelling in her sarcasm. 'This young man is Alejandro Ballesteros, a professor of art. I have invited him to lunch.'

Taddeo Rosso looked closely at my dirty raincoat, its appearance made even worse by the poor light in the room, but quickly switched his smile back on again.

'Giovanna has many foreign friends,' he observed. 'It's a very good thing because it helps us to keep in contact with the rest of the world. Venice is – how shall I put it? – a very inward-looking city.'

He spoke with the quiet imperturbability of those who are used to being ignored, or who are in the habit of spying on others through a keyhole. It appeared that Giovanna Zanon favoured cross-cultural fertilisation, and that Taddeo Rosso was tolerant.

'Naturally, we shall expect to see you at our masked

ball tomorrow night,' she interposed, treating me with more politeness than a few minutes earlier.

'I'm sorry but I don't have a costume, nor the money to hire one.'

Taddeo Rosso blinked, as if he failed to understand. It was only then I noticed he had a little moustache that followed closely the line of his mouth, like an extra lip. It was a mildly fascist type of moustache, divided in the middle by the furrow below his nose.

'But that's not a problem. Giovanna and I always have a spare costume to choose from. Isn't that right, dear?' All he received was a snort by way of reply. 'Come here, Isabella, and show the gentleman the costumes I brought in.'

He went up to the Filipino maid who was waiting in the hall, laden with masks and costumes, every one on a hanger. I looked at Giovanna Zanon with dismay and exasperation, and possibly with a distant regret for the activity we had been unable to consummate, but she looked back, spiteful, and unwilling to be conciliatory.

'What do you think of this one, for example?'

Taddeo Rosso covered his head with a porcelain mask identical to the appalling white face that had appeared at the latticed window after Valenzin had been shot. The apertures at the level of the eyes were also identical with the hollows I had seen, and the nose resembled the beak of a huge bird. I trembled, not so much because of the discovery, as for the fact that I was recapturing a vision which I had believed to be a figment of fantasy. Giovanna Zanon noticed my agitation and gave a sly smile. Once again the network of wrinkles in the corners of her mouth took on the appearance of flaky pastry, and once again her teeth looked threatening like those of a true carnivore. The Filipino maid announced that lunch was served.

SIX

It was an absolutely disastrous meal. Taddeo Rosso did his best to be pleasant, but this was a thankless task because Giovanna Zanon made it as difficult for him as she could, correcting his attempts to be clever with taunts which left the great businessman smarting and on the verge of tears. I could see that their family life was a suffocating one, but as we all know, some relationships are strengthened by a shortage of oxygen. If there was one thing that Taddeo Rosso took pride in and made it possible for him to endure those moments of humiliation heaped on him by his wife, it was talking about the masked ball they were to give the following evening in their palace, to celebrate the start of carnival, a ball that had kept him busy throughout the year and would be attended by the most patrician families of the neighbourhood, as well as his rival tycoons. 'They come to pay their respects to me,' he added, with a pomposity that was incongruous in a man who spent his life grovelling, above all in front of his wife. Taddeo Rosso became quite excited as he recounted the origins of the Venetian Carnival, the mishaps that had sometimes occurred, its splendours, the times when it was suppressed, and its decline from popularity, until he arrived at his closing words: 'What remains of it today is nothing more than a sham, a stunt put on to attract tourists.' He spoke with all the civic pride of a man who considers himself the last custodian of an ancestral tradition. Giovanna Zanon meanwhile played with her silver cutlery, banging her knife against her fork in a sort of private fencing match, which from time to time silenced Taddeo Rosso and his tedious chatter.

I learned from him that the carnival had reached illustrious heights during the most dire and fateful periods in the Republic's history, when epidemics of the plague were at their worst, and the air was poisoned by the deadly vapours given off by the corpses piled up on one or other of the islands, or on neighbourhood dunghills. Healthy members of society, and those still able to mask their bubonic tumours with rice powder, contracted the disease in the orgiastic frenzy that was a euphoric reflection of the other contagion that was due to carry them off. Carnivals lasted for months, until Lent, and to the buboes caused by the plague were added those of syphilis, passed from one to another in the promiscuous behaviour made easy by masked anonymity. In order not to introduce a note of discord into the festive copulating of the multitude, the doctors and surgeons who were responsible for public health at the time dreamed up for their own use a distinctive type of breathing apparatus inside a mask that had a hollow beak filled with disinfectant substances which they inhaled, to protect themselves from the fetid air around. This mask, which, at first, was regarded as intimidating and ill-omened – the Venetians fled from those who wore it in the way we avoid those dismal great birds that feed on carrion – ended up by becoming an acceptable feature of carnival, and took its place in the list of its characters, most of which were derived from the *commedia dell'arte*: Harlequin, Columbine, Pulcinello, and the rest of them.

'You have to get the better of the enemy, that's what we all have to learn,' concluded Taddeo Rosso. He put the mask of the plague doctor on again, and his voice echoed in the nose cavity with a boom that seemed to resound down the ages. 'If you can't beat him, then corrupt him, pervert him, and contaminate him with your own little ways and habits.'

Giovanna Zanon was looking at me with a curiosity that I found disturbing.

'But Mr Ballesteros is not one to allow himself to be corrupted,' she said carefully, assessing how far she could go with me, and probably deploring my cowardice. 'He is one of those who prefer to run away rather than complicate his life. Or am I wrong?'

Seated directly opposite me, she raised her knife and fork as if they were surgical instruments, or weapons with which she would first attack me and then run me through, once she had me completely under her control. The way she spoke was intimidating, but it was Taddeo Rosso who replied.

'Don't exaggerate, my dear. He's just a bit shy, but he'll lose that as he gets to know us better. So, shall I keep the plague doctor's mask for you, for the ball tomorrow?'

I agreed, sheepishly. Taddeo Rosso was about to resume his stupid chatter, but Giovanna Zanon packed him off to his own rooms, on the grounds that there were various private matters she had to discuss with me. It gave me satisfaction, not to say a malign delight, to watch Rosso's embarrassment. With great difficulty, he managed to wipe his moustache with his serviette, and to mutter a brief farewell. There had to be a pathological explanation for that degree of submissiveness. When we were alone, Giovanna Zanon stood up, came round the table, and placed herself directly behind me. I had been searching for an adequate simile to describe her curious, long-legged way of walking, and at last I found it: Giovanna Zanon moved like a praying mantis that rises up in the mating dance that precedes the death of the male.

'You asked me before about Chiara and Fabio Valenzin – what went on between them.'

I did not know whether she was preparing to give me a less irascible answer than the last time, or whether she was about to propose a resumption of our amorous antics at the point where we had left off because of my abrupt and badly-timed question – the later arrival of Taddeo Rosso would not have been an obstacle for Giovanna Zanon, indeed it might even have acted as a stimulus. I trembled as she put her hands on my shoulders with the light touch of a pigeon settling on a cornice. I decided to make a joke of it, as a means of shaking off disturbing thoughts.

'Yes, but I'm not going to ask you again, lest you decide to kill me in a fit of rage.'

She raised her right hand and placed it on my forehead, as if she hoped to be infected by my heightened temperature – because temperatures too are contagious, just like frenzy, syphilis, and the plague. She pulled my head back until it was resting against her stomach, which was as flat as her bottom.

'They were as thick as thieves,' she began. 'Let us say that, for her, Fabio Valenzin represented the outside world with its multiplicity of dangers and temptations, whereas Gilberto wanted to keep her immaculate and for himself alone, just as God wants nuns in convents with unblemished skin and undefiled pudenda.' I tried to move my head away from her stomach as a sign of protest, but Giovanna Zanon pressed it even tighter against the stones sewn on her bodice. 'They had a number of violent quarrels on the subject of Chiara, but not in front of her, obviously. They prided themselves on being gentlemen, so they tried to settle their differences without witnesses. It was assumed that Chiara had artistic gifts, and Valenzin was of the opinion that she should complete her studies abroad; but Gilberto saw no reason for this because there is so much art in Venice, and he instilled in the girl a deep love for this filthy city.'

'One day we shall cease to be a city and become an underwater cemetery, with palaces as mausoleums, and large squares where the dead can walk, but it is our duty to stay here until the cataclysm overtakes us,' Chiara had said to me with the obstinacy of those devotees of fanatical religions, who know themselves to be destined for martyrdom, that enticing form of saintliness. Giovanna Zanon had hardly eaten anything, and her stomach was rumbling loudly beneath her bodice, although possibly the rumbles came from another organ lower down which had not had its fill . . .

'Victories are rarely complete. Chiara remained with Gilberto, but those artistic gifts of hers were not fulfilled.' It seemed to me, judging by the jubilation in her voice, that Chiara's failure relieved Giovanna Zanon of other burdens. 'Fabio Valenzin, on the other hand, was able to enjoy the fruits of this setback to her career; he steered her frustrated vocation in directions that suited him, and used all his technical skill to turn her into a replica of himself.'

Meanwhile, Giovanna Zanon was steering her own sexual vocation with all the skill at her command by sliding the hand she had placed on my shoulder lower and lower, down almost to my crotch, which she had no wish to leave undefiled. I pretended a courage I did not feel.

'What do you mean a replica of himself?'

Through the windows of the dining room I could see the statues in the garden, indifferent to the relentless growth of

139

the shrubs around them. The sky had become full of leaden clouds that suddenly lit up with the first flash of lightning.

'As a counterfeiter.' Giovanna Zanon took great enjoyment in the way she pronounced the word. 'Valenzin got her to do the rough work, in the same way that painters of the *cinquecento* piled the most bothersome bits of work on to their apprentices. Chiara has a good imitative instinct. She's a parasite!'

The storm began its bombardment of the windows, and thunder rolled backwards and forwards across the carpet of clouds, as if it were dicing for the annihilation of Venice.

'Valenzin spent hours and hours with his disciple in the studio that Chiara had fitted up in the garret of the house.' Slowly, the sense of the obscene slander she was hinting at began to dawn on me. 'And I have heard Gilberto crying in his room, while Valenzin was upstairs giving Chiara lessons in the sort of activity at which he was impotent.'

I almost fell for the innuendo, the cunning tactic designed to make her words more subtly effective than a frank accusation would have been; but then I turned round to look at her, and I saw the stream of water that was pouring down the glass of the windows reflected in her face, like a simulacrum of leprosy corrupting her skin and making it crumble away, in spite of all the cosmetic surgery it had received. I was overwhelmed by an unbearable feeling of disgust.

'It is late, and time I went,' I muttered.

I walked away from that place which was too perplexing – or sordid – for my ingenuous nature. The rain was heavy and relentless in the garden of the palace; it fell on the decapitated marble statues, and into the basin of the fountain, splashing so furiously that it drowned out the refrain of the jet. It was raining on the canals, water lashing water, a violent baptism, of which there had been no prior notice, but which, nevertheless, the canals received with unanimity and the same goodwill with which they accepted the water from wash-basins and urinals; it was raining on canals which very soon would again run out of control; it was raining on all the little streets of Venice, and on the suddenly deserted squares under the arcades of which the horrified tourists, with their hats and bells, stood aghast at the sheer weight of water that would ruin the carnival celebrations, or the sham celebrations that the authorities were organising in order to bring foreign exchange into the city. The rain was thunderous and intemperate as it fell on the great houses and palaces of Venice, and their gutters and drainpipes were scarcely able to cope with so much water; and it was raining on the churches, dripping down through the domes and on to the frescoes of Tiepolo. The torrents of water that wore away the edges of the buildings and tried to crack open the stonework goaded me on to ever more chaotic speculations, a jumble of confused impressions that prevented me from thinking methodically. Before coming to Venice, there had always been method in the way I thought things through; the critical insight I had employed as a key tool of my trade had always led me to slow deliberation and logical argument; but Venice had won me over to the religion of feeling and emotion, had dredged out channels in my mind that pure reason is unaware of, had made me useless for the balanced examination of reality, and for calm analysis. It was raining on Venice with forebodings of flood and eternity, and the very air had the texture of sodden ash that until then I had only breathed in my wildest dreams, or during nights of insomnia and distress, when my lungs became the wellsprings of my sobs.

'And there were many nights when I have heard Gilberto

crying. I have seen his blue eyes tinged with hate – his eyes in which co-existed kindness and cruelty – staring fixedly as he lay on his pillow, and becoming livid with fury; his eyes that until then had been trained only for sight were now activated by all the other senses that had not concerned him before: hearing, touch, smell, and taste. All five senses were concentrated in that look, as well as the injuries and weaknesses that afflict each of them: mirages and blindness, excessive sensitivity and failure. And there were many nights when I have heard Gilberto crying, I have seen in his eyes the plans he was making for their punishment, while Chiara and Valenzin's meetings in the attic became longer and longer; I have seen his eyes listening for the slightest rustle of the sheets – so like the sound of trodden snow, so like the violation of a virgin, or the abuse of an innocent person. There were many nights when I have heard Gilberto crying, with those eyes that had become bereft of all trace of kindness, and only retained their look of cruelty, damaged eyes that imagined or foresaw the bloodstain on the sheets. Sheets and snow can recover their whiteness, but the eyes of a man who has been humiliated never recover; there always remains on his retinas a stain that dulls and blinds them, and can only be redeemed by more blood.'

This was the discourse Giovanna Zanon had not quite made, although there is usually no need to be explicit – a suggestive phrase, and sly insinuations, are enough to gratify our attention.

I lost my way at least a dozen times before I was able to make out the house where Chiara and Gabetti lived, near the church of the Madonna dell' Orto. I arrived, my clothes soaked through, and clinging to me: my body would soon cease to have any resistance to rheumatism. Chiara stood there, leaning against a jamb of the main door, as if she was waiting for the rain to stop.

'So you also got caught in the downpour,' she shouted. It was necessary to shout if we were to hear each other above the noise of the deluge.

'I must be jinxed. Since I arrived here I've done nothing but get soaked.'

We stood there without speaking for nearly a minute, hypnotised by the insistent rhythm of the rain, like two tourists who see their holiday ruined. Chiara had a cameo-like profile, or that of a Pre-Raphaelite angel, a perfect tranquillity of expression disturbed only by her aquiline and slightly biased nose. She was applying a salve to prevent her lips from splitting.

'What a nuisance, just as the water was starting to go down.' She wore the same track suit she had worn to climb the scaffolding in the church, the track suit that outlined her well-rounded bottom, and made her apparent slimness misleading. 'I went out jogging, but what made you get so wet when you could have stayed warm and dry in the palace of that old witch?'

I felt a moment of pride as I watched the expression of annoyance crossing her face. Celibacy becomes more bearable when you believe yourself to be the object of imagined rivalries between women.

'Is it true she knows how to get anything she wants from a man?' she asked, by way of tormenting me.

Rain and sweat had matted her hair so that it no longer resembled the frayed strings of a violin. Giovanna Zanon had called her a counterfeiter and a parasite, and also a slut – in fact, she had used another word, equally brief and more explicit, unambiguous and highly challenging – but what Giovanna Zanon had said did not deserve credence, and certainly not respect.

'You mustn't believe I let myself be taken in just like that. I'm quite a tough nut.'

I forced a gentle smile which reduced the credibility of what I had said, apart from leaving me open to attack.

'Well, you know what you're doing; you're old enough to choose your own friends.' Irritation made her sound severe; it was an almost masculine severity. 'But Gilberto was not a bit pleased that you went off with her. That woman has done as much to hurt us as she possibly can. When she lived in this house she was always causing trouble, and now she lives elsewhere, she tells the most terrible lies about us. No, don't apologise. Anyone who listens to her is as guilty as she is: there's no such thing as a lie if there isn't someone there ready to listen to it.'

She was angry out of all proportion, and seemed about to break down under the weight of so much calumny. I raised my hand to her neck, a soothing hand that barely brushed her skin, but the adoration I felt for her travelled down through my fingers.

'Not all the lies or all the dirt in this world can tarnish you or bring shame on you,' I said.

Now that I write these words they seem pompous, but, at the time, I spoke them with a simple conviction that ruled out any hint of rhetoric, and Chiara must have heard them in the way I intended, because she recovered her poise, and no longer needed to lean against the jamb of the door in order to remain upright.

'I'm sorry; you are an angel.'

She put her face close to mine – there was not even an inch between them – and pursed her lips in order to kiss me. I offered her my cheek, but was so overcome with joy – even joy, like astonishment or dismay, can paralyse us – that I did not move fast enough; what I mean is, I did not position my cheek to one side in the conventional way for receiving formal kisses, with the result that the corner of her mouth came into contact with the corner of mine. The contact was brief and almost nonchalant, but it was enough for me to detect the warmth of her lips and their taste of lipsalve. I confess I blushed.

'I'm going to have a shower because I'm very sweaty. Are you coming up, or staying here?'

Unlike me, Chiara was not embarrassed, or if she was she hid it well. She ran up the stairs as a way of continuing the exercise that the downpour had spoiled. The lingering feel of her kiss still quivered in the corner of my mouth, a sensation not unlike a forewarning of measles or a fever. The rain washed away the lies; it sluiced them down the drain of oblivion.

'I'm going up as well. I don't know why I'm standing here like a dummy.'

'Gilberto was planning to show you *The Tempest*, but with this rain, I don't know,' Chiara told me. 'He went on to the Accademia after the funeral, and still isn't back, which means they can't have finished getting rid of the water.'

Whenever she referred to Gabetti she used his first name; she never alluded to any paternal or filial relationship linking them, possibly because these links were various in their nature and included other, secret, forms of love. Chiara kept herself immune from anything shameful, but Giovanna Zanon's wily insinuations continued to fester in my mind; lies may be eradicated like cancer, a kiss may reduce their virulence and even wash them away, but the risk of a new outbreak is always there.

'Will you show me your studio, Chiara?'

'I warn you there's nothing special about it. And it's in a terrible mess.'

I heard her deep chuckle like a spell that banished the final shreds of my suspicion. As we went up the stairs towards her garret, the light lessened until it took on the quality of an aquarium, as if we were penetrating deep inside a grotto bedecked with seaweed. It was a greenish light, almost amphibian in quality. I found the atmosphere in the room almost unbreathable. Chiara, who was used to it, breathed freely.

'It's my private sanctum in this house,' she said, while she turned the key in the lock. 'When I feel in the mood I can spend whole days up here – it's like a religious retreat.'

A large skylight was let into the gabled ceiling, and when the sun was high this would have given good light, but the drumming of the rain on it turned the studio into a sound-box. It really was a mess, with partly-assembled stretchers scattered over the floor, canvases drying on the walls – the humidity level made this a slow process – rags for cleaning brushes that looked like paintings by Jackson Pollock, and squeezed and twisted tubes of paint. There was an easel covered in paint stains, looking like a skeleton decorated with medals, and a stove on which Chiara cooked her frugal meals as long as her spiritual retreat lasted. A door that had come off its hinges communicated with a narrow bathroom, and there was a rickety old bed that did not invite company – or getting to know her better (in the biblical sense). It was little more than a straw mattress covered in crumpled sheets. Above the bed, and fixed to the wall by four drawing pins, was a print of *The Tempest*, actual size, thirty and a quarter by twenty-eight and three-quarter inches, complete in all its detail: the flash of lightning, the naked woman suckling her child with an air of sensual sadness, the pilgrim who witnesses the scene, the city bristling with towers, the trees and the bridge and the stream and the ruins that make up the background to the main figures. The predominant colour of *The Tempest* is green, a green that merges into cobalt blue in the sky with its dense clouds. It is a green that ripples with shifting shadows in the foliage of the trees, is streaked with gold in the water of the stream, and is blended with ochres in the grass in order to give prominence to the woman who is naked, lightly screened by a bush and a piece of cloth that clings to her shoulders like a small cloak. It is green that predominates in *The Tempest*, and it was an almost aquatic green that predominated in the air of the garret, a shifting green like the dense stream of rain running down the glass of the skylight.

'You didn't tell me *The Tempest* was your favourite bedside picture.'

My voice held that note of unease it assumes, from affection rather than disappointment, when we discover that an intimate friend has concealed a detail of their private life from us.

'Go on, don't be silly! You can't be angry about that. I told you *The Tempest* represents the mystery of Venice.'

It was she who represented the mystery of Venice; she had the same wounded beauty, and her own inner world – a sort of private space that tourists would never enter, nor even steal a glimpse of. In my attempt to restore our intimacy I probably made the situation worse.

'Giovanna Zanon told me, among a number of other outrageous things, that Gabetti – Gilberto, I should say – thought of himself as one of the individuals in that painting, the pilgrim who is watching the naked woman. Obviously, you are the naked woman.'

'And the baby? Who would the baby be? The offspring of an incestuous liaison that we are hiding in our castle dungeon?

You have to be really perverted to come up with that sort of nonsense.'

I placed one finger on her lips before she gave way to abuse that would have been unworthy of her.

'Can I have a look at your paintings?' I asked, like someone who brushes away a cobweb he finds irritating.

'Oh, dear. Must you? They're terrible!' Chiara flushed and looked away. Her modesty seemed genuine. 'All right, I'll let you look at them while I'm in the shower, but only on condition you don't make any comment afterwards.'

It was not before she had extracted a nod of agreement from me that she went into the bathroom, the door of which did not fit its frame, leaving gaps through which I could have stolen glimpses of her nakedness, just as the night before I had stolen fragments of her dream; but love cannot live on furtive observations, it needs the consent and participation of the person observed. A picture also needs consent and participation. It does not reveal its meaning to one who has no interest in it, unless it is a bad picture, or has merely been churned out, in which case the merciful thing to do is to look away quickly. That is what I did with Chiara's paintings before their mediocrity damaged the idealistic image of her that I had been constructing. 'Not all the dirt in the world can tarnish you,' I had assured her in a fit of optimism. But although all Giovanna Zanon's insinuations had failed, what would succeed if I lowered my guard were those paintings of hers, because nothing tarnishes an image so much as disillusion. In terms of the quality of their drawing they were irreproachable paintings; they were amazing in the way they caught the play of light, and in their compositions; they displayed a virtuosity that only comes from a deep study of the old masters; but true originality needs to revolt against academic study, and Chiara had allowed herself to be too amenable to its influence. I preferred to think that mimicry – that imitative variant on mediocrity – was not so much a vice of Chiara personally, but one that had been inculcated in her by others, perhaps Gabetti in order to be sure of her dependence on him, or maybe Fabio Valenzin in order to get his revenge, that is to say, to smother in her any attempt to be original. I preferred to believe that this vice of hers was curable, and that I would be the cure.

'That man who was with you in the cemetery. What is his name?'

Her voice reached me from the bathroom, superimposing itself on my ruminations and the tedious litany of the rain. I imagined the gushing water in the shower falling gently over her shoulders, descending in two streams down her breasts, trickling smoothly over her stomach, before plunging like a cataract down her thighs, to run its course around her feet, where it lay submissively quiet. I struggled against my over-indulgent imagination and the force of desire by shutting my eyes.

'You mean Tedeschi, the palace caretaker.'

'Yes, that's the man I mean.' She was soaping the smooth slope of her shoulder, the foreshortened thigh, the curve of her groin. 'He's been like a soul in agony, prowling round here all the blessed day. When I went out jogging he followed a little way behind. I got the impression he was waiting for you to come back. Is there something going on between you?'

I was alarmed to learn that Tedeschi was shirking his duty to look after Valenzin's chest. I had assumed that after the funeral he had spent the day entrenched in the palace, quiet and unsleeping, like those dragons in the old stories that protect hoarded treasure. But the fate of those dragons was always monotonous and inexorable: the insane greed of the stories' heroes led them first to seize the treasure, and then to butcher the dragons with a single chop of their swords.

'Something going on? No, nothing at all,' I lied. But this time, lying that had seemed to me before nothing more than an innocently deceptive game, now made me deeply ashamed. 'It is just that he has suggested he will solve the murder all on his own.'

The rain drumming on the skylight obsessed me; it sounded like the unexpected guest hammering at the door and appealing for shelter. Next to the little stove, there was a rickety cabinet made of some cheap material standing on four feet and with drawers that I began to open out of curiosity – the sort of curiosity that has nothing criminal about it, but which impels us to try to learn more about the person we love by trespassing on their private territory, even at the risk of discovering matters that may damage or cloud our love. The contents of these drawers were in the same disorder as the rest of the garret, a disorder that in any other person would have repelled me, but in Chiara's case seemed blameless, and even comforting, because it brought me close to her. Hidden between some badly folded serviettes and tablecloths I came across an envelope containing photographs. I knew what the contents would be because the negatives protruded through one corner. I hesitated before opening it, not so much out of hypocrisy, or because I had scruples about meddling in someone's past that was no business of mine, but because of the fear of discovering that that past was tainted in a way that nothing could wash clean. I raised the flap of the envelope and took out the photographs, trembling like a gambler who opens a new pack of cards and finds he does not recognise the designs on their faces. They were all taken in the countryside, which in itself made them seem exotic because Venice is a city colonised by stone, where the only grass that is allowed to grow is in private palace gardens. The photographs had been taken towards the end of the day when the slanting rays of the sun lengthen shadows; they were quite small, and not very sharp, or with a sort of spectral sharpness that made them resemble those washed-out portraits that bedeck the epitaphs in the San Michele cemetery.

I was slow to identify the man who appeared in some of them because the closeness of the lens distorted his smiling features as he tried to avoid the camera; in addition to which, he had raised his hand to cover the lens, just as he had pressed the same hand against the mouth of a wound from which his blood was spurting. I was slow to recognise him because his expression was not one of terror — he was smiling; his look was neither motionless nor fixed, but animated with real happiness; and his face was not haggard, or pale like parchment; it was not a face that harboured the vestiges of an unpunished crime — but more precisely that of one who believes himself to be immune to the threat of punishment and fails to perceive the death which, somewhere, lies in wait for him. Fabio Valenzin was not making a serious effort to hide himself from the camera; his gesture more closely resembled the way we reject flattery, or the way we sometimes recoil from a caress, with that sham and ineffectual resistance that is really intended to goad the other person on to more flattery and caresses.

Suddenly, the photographed became the photographer, and it was Chiara who now featured in the rest of the prints; these also were elusive and blurred, but she too was smiling; she offered her profile to the camera, making faces to suggest an annoyance that disguised approval. Her hair was parted and gathered in a ponytail, but a few wisps and locks had escaped and fell in gentle waves over her cheeks and down the line of her jaw. I could not tell the precise point at which these spontaneous pictures stopped, and, under Valenzin's guidance, she began to turn into a model, in a series of different poses. The transition was gradual and there was no suggestion that it was premeditated: just a slow evolution towards passivity, the result of a deliberate process which led to her domination; she became a person who defers, who accedes, and who finally yields. They were close-ups with only imperceptible differences between them, just a slight change in the way she half-closed her eyes, or the angle of her nose, or in the studied arrangement of her hair that framed the look of sensual sadness on her face. Chiara remained passive as the camera spied on her; Valenzin had then stepped back some way in order to get the whole of her body into the frame. She sat naked on the grass, in the same pose as the woman in *The Tempest*, with one leg bent back on which the whole weight of her body rested, with the other one also bent, but slightly raised, her stomach like a hushed guitar, and her breasts like little creatures bewildered by their own maturity. Nearly five centuries had elapsed between the lives of the woman painted by Giorgione and Chiara, nearly five hundred years, with their baggage of death and corruption, but they were both there before my eyes, equidistant and equally alive, like repeated exemplars of the same dream, like victims made to propitiate the same obsession.

'Do you really want to know everything about me?'

Chiara had come out of the bathroom, only a bathrobe hiding her nakedness, but the look she gave me was neither one of censure or complaint: it expressed the heavy heart of one who would have preferred to say nothing, and yet finds herself obliged to reveal the whole truth. I nodded agreement, in a way that conveyed my veneration, and also my agitation.

'Everything.'

She looked like one returned from the grave after five hundred years, enveloped in the steam of the shower, enveloped also in the light of the garret that harmonised all the shades of green.

'Do you think they're indecent?' she asked.

She scattered the photographs over the bed and raised the collar of her robe.

'Who am I to judge things I know nothing about? I'm the one who has behaved indecently by raking through your drawers.'

Nobody deserves to have a moment of innocence stolen from them, and above all when that moment belongs to the past, or to matters that give cause for sorrow. I could see her knees between the folds of her bathrobe and the start of her thighs, giving a hint of the softness of their skin. The rain had stopped, but the garret still had the appearance of a marine grotto.

'You want to know everything, although yesterday you preferred to know nothing,' she began. Her voice sounded strained either from the weight of memories or from remorse. 'Believe me when I say that ignorance is infinitely preferable. However, that is your problem.'

Her feet were bare, and she rubbed one against the other. I looked at her toes that reminded me of tiny seashells clinging to a rock; they were very small toes, and some of them overlapped with others which made them difficult to count. Night was falling on Venice.

'I think I loved Fabio ever since I was a child,' she admitted at last. I nodded as I heard the words that justified my retrospective jealousy. 'I loved him hopelessly and secretly, because I knew that he would never return my love. I knew that Fabio was immune to emotion. His life had been one long preparation for solitude. He was an orphan like me, but he had never had a single person to give him support when he was upset, or to help him through the trauma of loneliness, and this left him dried out internally, and hard on the outside; it left him completely impotent where emotions were concerned. I thought, wrongly, that I could cure that sickness in him, but all my attempts bumped against that impenetrable shell, over and over again. Instead of love, all I got out of him was a sterile substitute for it which made me feel degraded, unhappy, and totally drained. It was like suffering from claustrophobia, but having to live in a tiny space breathing the same old, foul air. I had deluded myself I could help to purify that air – but exactly the opposite happened. Fabio transmitted his sickness to me.'

Perhaps I too was deluding myself when I thought I might dispel the influence that other men had exercised over her.

'What you are saying is terrible,' I said.

'I suppose it is.' The late afternoon hollowed out her face, and made her voice lose its strength, reducing it to a whisper. 'Terrible – but I accepted it and am responsible for it, because I allowed myself to become part of it; I joined in the game and let myself be caught. Fabio was never able to return my love, but instead, he began to profess a sort of morbid devotion; he monopolised me and turned me into something like an object of idolatry.' At this point, inevitably, I blushed, because I too had succumbed to this temptation. 'When he caressed me – and he hardly ever did, because the skin of another person seemed to burn his fingers – it felt as if he was trying to get to recognise the shape of a work of art. He never succeeded in seeing me as I really am, a flesh and blood woman who sometimes burns with desire, and at others is consumed with sadness.'

I was fearful that Valenzin's sterile love might be reincarnated in me, thereby prolonging his accursed influence. I lowered my eyes to the floor and slowly raised them up her legs, admiring that complex curve that goes from the ankle to the calf.

'Then Fabio began to use me as a model for his paintings, or for his fakes. He studied me for hours on end, like a taxidermist who studies the animal he is going to dissect before extracting its internal organs. Maybe he wanted to reify, or depersonalise, me so that his devotion would be more complete, maybe he wanted to shape me to his taste, stylise me, or tone me down, as a Renaissance painter would have done.'

'Just like Giorgione,' I said.

The late afternoon led me also to lower my voice; both of us were talking as if indulging in our own interior monologues.

'Just like Giorgione, for example,' Chiara concurred. 'But you can't keep a one-sided relationship going for ever, however much you persist in it. I used up all my reserves of resistance, I ended up exhausted, and in the end I had to give in.'

This need to give in was echoed in the way she spoke: the words were uttered slowly, like a woman enduring a slow and difficult labour. When she fell silent she seemed torn apart, as if recovering from an operation that had drained her of all past memories. The photographs scattered over the bed lost their aura of obscenity.

'Now you know. That's all there was to it. I warned you ignorance is preferable,' she said.

I decided that her version of events was the honest one, and I could not find a better way of demonstrating this than by taking her in my arms. The soft material of her bathrobe, damp from the recent shower, had a feel like that of moss, which cushioned the hard edges of her shoulder-blades.

'And now Fabio is dead, and he's carried off with him all the efforts I put into trying to save him!'

There was an unassertive appeal for help in her words, although her tone was neither imploring nor anguished.

'Did Gabetti know about all this?' I asked.

'I never made a point of talking to him openly, but neither could I hide it.' Chiara extricated herself from my embrace as if suddenly impelled by a lingering feeling of loyalty towards the dead man. 'Yes, of course he knew. He knew, and he deplored it. Fabio was not the man he would have wanted for me.'

I could not rid myself of the image of Gabetti, his blue eyes livid with fury, while Valenzin gave Chiara lessons in the sort of activity at which he was impotent. I had seen Gabetti watching over Chiara as she slept, with tender rapture, but I resisted the temptation to draw conclusions that were disgusting and unspeakable. The telephone rang, interrupting my speculations.

'I'm coming straight back.'

Her body, inside the bathrobe, had a mobile quality as if made to be fashioned by hands that would shape its grace and its declivities. I spent the few minutes I was alone in the attic looking once again through the photographs that Fabio Valenzin had taken of her, photographs without grace or declivities, or even a tremor of humanity, sad and sterile photographs that rejected the gift of a life. True art reproduces or interprets real life, but spurious art betrays and entombs it, embalms and mummifies it. Night was descending through the skylight, like a menace; I felt I was sinking into a swamp.

'That was Gilberto. He's expecting us at the Accademia in a couple of hours.' Chiara appeared in the doorway to pass this message on to me. 'He's asked me to take a torch because, with the floods, they've had to cut off the electricity in order to prevent short-circuits.'

SEVEN

I had spent so many years refusing to share the experiences and trying to avoid listening to the life stories of people I met, so many years on the defensive, avoiding them when they were about to activate the awful mechanisms of remembrance, keeping my distance from the useless load of confidences to which I was liable to be subjected at any moment – but now all these endeavours were going to ruin. As my own perceptions are not in the least trustworthy and often bear little relation to reality, and my temperament is by nature irresolute, my judgement leaning towards the irrelevant, I had, until then, accepted the opinions of others as being irrefutably true. This credulity of mine had saved me from the need to take difficult decisions, and had kept me out of harm's way in a world only too full of pitfalls for the unwary, but, at the same time, it had turned me into a sort of ship without a compass, at the mercy of helmsmen with fanciful notions of their own. Now, after listening to Chiara and Giovanna Zanon, I discovered that 'truth' depends upon the point of view of the person speaking; I discovered that the private 'truth' of an individual may falsify facts, or fail to understand them, or may even tamper with them for his or her own benefit;

I discovered that nobody is infallible, or omniscient, or even well-intentioned, and this last discovery confirmed me in my suspicion that perhaps this is perfect lucidity, as well as being a condition of constant despair.

While Chiara was dressing, I ran over in my mind the various duties I had put off since arriving in Venice: the visit to the Accademia, the retrieval of the ring, picking up my luggage, and breaking open the chest in which Valenzin may have kept his loot. I felt no sense of urgency as I made this recapitulation – it did not much matter that I was falling behind on my obligations, because Venice postpones events, slows down time, suspends it, and transforms it into a flexible substance, like dreams. I alternated this tally with speculation about the problem facing Chiara as she stood in front of her wardrobe: the careful choice she had to make of certain clothes in preference to others, which would then be left feeling disgruntled or resentful on their hangers, unable to satisfy their own desires or escape their lonely, celibate condition. Like those rejected clothes, I also felt strong desires, but remained celibate.

'I hope you're well and truly ready,' Chiara warned me. At first I did not know if she was referring to the way I was dressed, because my clothes were in a dreadful state. 'Gilberto is going to put you through the third degree.'

'What do you mean, the third degree?'

'He will make you defend your interpretation of *The Tempest*, and when you've done so he'll refute it, point by point, and destroy every one of your arguments. That's his method. He doesn't spare anyone!'

The fact is he had already demolished me once, after our meeting in the police station. I played at feigning impregnability.

'We'll see who laughs last,' I said. 'Whose side are you on?'

Before she could prevent it I pulled her towards me and kissed her on the lips, not in the corner of her mouth, or formally on the cheek, but with a kiss that was much more exploratory, answering the call of her lovely mouth.

'I have to remain neutral.' She gave a laugh that fell to a whisper as her lips lost their neutrality, just as they had lost the taste of lipsalve in the shower. 'I'm only going as a spectator.'

I took her face in my hands; it seemed to burn with all the fires of desire. I kissed her forehead with its incipient furrows, I kissed her temples that beat with a secret fever, I kissed the lids of her peasant-girl eyes, and her slightly biased nose, and her cheeks that had so often been wet with the relentless flow of her tears. I itemised every detail of her face, feeling that in some nebulous way I held the whole world in my hands.

'We mustn't keep him waiting,' she said. 'The later we are, the more obstreperous he'll be.'

While we went down the Grand Canal in the taxi taking us to the Accademia, and as it sliced through the water like a knife, I began to believe myself master of the gentle harmony I had learned only a short time earlier from Chiara's lips, which resounded from the façades of the palaces, under the arch of the Rialto Bridge, and in the outlets of the side-canals, where the cross-currents were at their strongest. Venice seemed to have been saved from inundation for one more year, but it had not recovered fully from the threat of ruin. The city appeared to breathe with that gasping sound that one might expect to hear issuing from the sodden, polyp-filled lungs of a drowning man as he returns to life. Only the bell towers rose to their full height in the midst of such frailty.

'Have you visited the Accademia before?' asked Chiara.

She had put her hand in mine, a gesture which had nothing neutral about it, and her fingers were closely entwined with my fingers, in the way that wax melts into a mould; it was a gesture to give me courage before I faced my dialectical confrontation with Gabetti. I shook my head.

'It will seem a very tiny museum compared with the Prado,' she said. 'The advantage is that being small saves it from hordes of tourists. It was founded by a decree of Napoleon when Venice was ruled by the French and the collection was built up with paintings from the sale of Church properties.'

I observed the profile of its façade, eroded like the rest of Venice by successive invasions of men who had either venerated the city, or morally mutilated it – although, in fact, it remained impervious to domination. Foreigners had thronged to Venice and scarred it with their greedy talons, or they had done their best to deliver it from decadence; but Venice remained loyal to its ultimate destiny, which was to sink grandly into the lagoon, to become an underwater cemetery, with palaces as mausoleums, and large squares where the dead could walk. I should have liked to exclude Chiara from any part in the city's fate, but Venice was an uncompromising rival.

The Accademia had been erected over an ancient Lateran convent, with that self-assurance of secular building in times of unbelief. The façade had been disfigured by a neo-classical porch that clashed with the Gothic style of the church beside it. A line of duck-boards provided access from the landing-stage.

'There's Gilberto all ready to teach you a lesson,' Chiara whispered as the water-taxi drew alongside. She removed her hand from mine as if propelled by a spring. 'I hope you won't let yourself be bullied.'

Gabetti walked towards us across the duck-boards like

an obsequious host receiving guests in the courtyard of his palace – although later he plans to serve them a banquet of poisoned food.

'Good, Ballesteros, the great moment has arrived,' he said by way of greeting. Although he refrained from smiling, his body moved with a detectable swagger inside his elegant suit. 'Did you bring the torch, Chiara?'

A shaft of light dazzled him as he put out his hand to help us disembark; he gave Chiara a look that was midway between affection and a reproach.

'All right, all right,' he protested, but he was not seriously annoyed, as he shielded his face with his forearm. 'Or do you really want to blind me?'

'You blind?' Chiara laughed with delight. 'The day you go blind, all the paintings in Venice will go into mourning.'

Although he said nothing, it was clear that Gabetti was grateful for the compliment, and there was no longer any trace of a reproach in his expression.

'You're very privileged, Ballesteros,' he proclaimed, as we crossed the duck-boards. 'You're going to see *The Tempest* in the museum at a time when there are no visitors, and under cover of perfidious night. *The Tempest*, whose true significance has eluded the greatest experts, will be revealed to you like a virgin in a bridal bed. What more could you ask for?'

'He could ask you to be a little less pedantic,' Chiara admonished him, breaking her promise of neutrality.

There were puddles in the hall of the Accademia, which made it look like the remains of a Roman naumachy. For the past few days, under Gabetti's command, the museum employees had fought a valiant battle against the tides, and had finally won. The air had the narcotic, intoxicating odour that rainwater gives off when it soaks into stonework. In one corner of the hall, like the remains of a brawl, there was a pile of detritus left behind by the flood: weed still oozing a muddy liquid, and other odds and ends that the Venetians were in the habit of emptying into the Grand Canal.

'I've given the caretakers the night off,' said Gabetti, with that casual perfidy of an official who breaks the rules. 'The poor fellows were on their knees, absolutely worn out, and with heavy colds that will take them a long time to get rid of. They're paid a pittance, but when it comes to bailing out the water they really put their backs into it.'

Gabetti had taken the torch, and he lit the way for us past walls covered in fungus. We went up a staircase that led to the art gallery itself, and the sound of our footfalls drummed in the corners like a hushed and guilty echo.

'Does that mean you've left the museum without protection?' I asked, genuinely scandalised. I was a very different man from Gabetti, and utterly punctilious in observing regulations. 'That is irresponsible.'

I looked for Chiara to back me up, but all she did was shrug her shoulders. Gabetti gave a supercilious laugh that held more than a hint of arrogance.

'Over and above the fact that I am granting you the privilege of visiting the museum without other people around . . .' He allowed himself a note of nostalgia: '. . . now that Fabio has gone, there are no thieves of any consequence left in Venice.'

Through a gap in the staircase I could just make out the rectangle of dim light illuminating the shape of the main door — and offering free passage to any passer-by or unwelcome thief. We crossed a room with a moulded ceiling that was reserved for paintings of the *trecento*, solemn virgins reminiscent of Byzantine art, triptychs illustrating scenes from the lives of the saints, with their gilded backgrounds and that elaborate inlay work which distracts attention from the painting and draws it towards the frames. Gabetti flashed the light of the torch backwards and forwards across the multitude of saints, like a dutiful father checking that his offspring are sleeping peacefully. In the nearby rooms, the *quattrocento* was represented by Piero della Francesca, Andrea Mantegna, and Cosmè Tura, amongst others: the faces depicted began to gain in expressiveness and in subtlety, early attempts at perspective began to appear in the compositions, and the backgrounds of the paintings were no longer limited to the monochrome of early icons.

'As you can see, in the Accademia, we respect chronological order in the way the paintings are hung,' Gabetti enlightened me. 'If art experts weren't so dense, and had a bit more commonsense, if they didn't limit themselves to studying just one single artist or one single work of art, and removed their blinkers, they would realise that no new development in painting happens suddenly.'

Gabetti's harangue had no need of a listener, or if it did need one, it was only in order to crush him with the brilliance of his intelligence, but I knew that in reality it was directed at me. He had taken the measure of my weakness in the way a skilled swordsman thrusts forward so that his novice opponent takes up the guard position, leaving his flanks undefended. The building of the Accademia also had its flanks undefended, and any burglar could assault it at will.

'I don't think that is true in my case,' I said.

'Take landscape, for example,' continued Gabetti, who did not even give me a chance to defend myself, working on the ill-mannered principle of simply talking me down. 'Those experts who claim to understand *The Tempest* roll their eyes and exclaim in ecstasy: "In this painting we see the invention of landscape! This is the painting in which nature becomes a major element for the first time!" Drivel! The painting of landscape was not invented at one particular moment, it was the result of a very long drawn out process. Flemish and German artists began to develop a taste for exotic backgrounds, and the fashion was soon imported into Italy. The men who commissioned work from Giotto and Mantegna used to insist that their work should incorporate the latest style, and, little by little, the background, which originally was of secondary importance, was elevated to become the main theme of the picture. Look at this *Pietà* of Giovanni Bellini, for example; it was painted roughly ten years before *The Tempest*, but in it the background landscape has already acquired an importance that, at the time, was almost irreverent.'

Behind the dead and gaunt figure of Christ, behind the aged Virgin who looked down at him with the classic expression of grief, holding him across her lap and raising his head by a few inches – just as I had raised the head of Valenzin so that he should not choke on his own blood – a city of gleaming chromaticism was depicted on the horizon, in the style of Dürer, its pointed spires rising above the surrounding country-side, its walls surmounted by crenellated defence-works, its churches transfixed by the evening light. We were in a small room, the size of a study, like the one in which Giovanna Zanon had cornered me with the excuse of obtaining my authentication of a *Madonna and Child*, also by Bellini; a provisional partition that did not reach the ceiling had been erected in the middle of the room, obstructing the view of *The Tempest*.

'*Voilà*, my dear friend,' announced Gabetti, ushering me through to the other side of the partition with an exaggerated bow. 'Here you behold the cause of all your hard labour.'

I cannot deny that my first impression, made worse by the light of the torch, a light similar to that in an operating theatre which tended to bleach out the colours, was disappointing. The original of *The Tempest* seemed to have lost its subtlety of colour, and appeared much less darkened by time, as if photographs gave it a false *tenebrismo*: the sombre green of the trees had become too even, and the green in the clouds, which in the prints looked as if it was tinged with cobalt, acquired an almost phosphorescent appearance, rather like a neon sign; also, the mother suckling her child had a flesh colour varying between fair and pink and lacking the brownish shade that has persuaded some interpreters of the painting to identify her as a gipsy woman. My disappointment and bewilderment melted away when Chiara said:

'Of course, a direct light of this kind is altogether wrong for examining a picture properly.'

'Any sort of light will do for the sort of examination I am going to put Ballesteros through,' interrupted Gabetti, who was already licking his lips in anticipation of the dressing down he was about to administer. 'Isn't that right, my dear friend? Imagine that you stand before a board of examiners who are about to judge your thesis; imagine that Chiara and I are two professors who are unwilling to accept your conclusions; imagine that, in order to convince us, you have to improvise a dissertation explaining the hidden theme that, in your opinion, Giorgione had decided on.'

At that time of the night, his voice echoed throughout the empty galleries, the labyrinth of corners and the blind passages which made up the Accademia. The torch shone on the canvas of *The Tempest*, distorting its colours, and then it swung round on me in a dizzying, pendular movement.

'I find this an odd way of going about things. Anyway, if

you really want to refute my hypothesis, you will have to work hard,' I challenged him. I guessed that, behind the torch, Gabetti's face took on a discouraged look. 'I am sure you know about the propensity of the gods of Olympus for indulging in incestuous relationships. They knew nothing about the laws of genetics or man-made taboos, and fornicated freely with their daughters, the result of which was a race of defectives. Zeus tried by all possible means to sleep with his daughter Aphrodite, but his sweet words and magic spells were ineffective. Aphrodite would not give in to his attempts at seduction, so Zeus, in order to humiliate her, made her fall in love with a mortal.'

I stopped for a moment, worried that my explanation might be understood by Chiara as a witticism at her expense, but I could not detect any sign of discomfort on her face.

'Go on, go on,' insisted Gabetti.

'Zeus chose as the instrument of his punishment the handsome Anchises, king of the Trojans, who was young and inexperienced – before the Trojan War turned him into an old man who had endured great suffering. One night as Anchises was sleeping in his shepherd's hut up on Mount Ida, Aphrodite came down to earth dressed as a Phrygian princess, and lay with him on his bed of bear and lion skins. When they parted in the morning, Aphrodite revealed to him who she was, and made him swear to keep their encounter a secret. Anchises was horrified when he learned that he had defiled the honour of a goddess, an indiscretion that was punishable by death, and he implored Aphrodite's forgiveness. She assured him he had nothing to fear, provided he never broke his oath. She also predicted that his son would be famous and commemorated by the poets. Anchises, carried away by the urge to boast, was not slow to break his word. A few days later, as he was drinking with friends at a banquet, he felt his tongue loosening. They were being served their wine by a very voluptuous girl who would still have been a virgin if Anchises had not exercised his *droit de seigneur*: although he was a decent fellow he was not one to renounce certain privileges that went with his position. One of his drinking companions spoke warmly of the girl: "Don't you think that girl is even more desirable than Aphrodite herself?" To which Anchises incautiously replied, "Having slept with both of them, the question seems to me absurd, quite apart from being sacrilegious; Zeus's daughter is far superior."'

'Aphrodite's stipulation was very unwise,' said Gabetti, who was leaning against a wall, but still kept the light shining on Giorgione's picture. 'We men love to boast of our triumphs; we can't resist it.'

Chiara's voice broke in through the darkness.

'It would be better for everybody if you all practised a bit more discretion.'

I knew she was asking me to keep quiet about what had happened between us – the very little that had happened.

'Obviously, Zeus was angered by his bragging,' I continued. 'If, until that moment, he had been carried away by spite in making his daughter consort with a mortal, the vanity of Anchises made him furious. He hurled a thunderbolt at the Trojan king with the intention of killing him, but his aim was bad, and it only struck him obliquely across the legs.'

'Even the gods are fallible,' said Gabetti, with the intention of expunging all solemnity and conviction from my discourse.

'Partially fallible. The bolt injured Anchises so severely that from then on he could hold himself up only by leaning on a staff. As for Aphrodite, she gave birth to the baby she had conceived with the man who had broken his promise to her, called him Aeneas, and performed all her maternal duties such as breast-feeding the child, but she refused to have anything more to do with Anchises himself. Although the king of the Trojans wept and wailed, begging her to reinstate him in her affection, Aphrodite simply displayed indifference. She had lost all her previous ardour, and in fact she began to feel an aversion for him. It was only a half-hearted aversion, because the gods cannot permit themselves the luxury of emotions that are too effusive.'

Gabetti nodded appreciatively, but it was left to Chiara to draw the right conclusions from my story.

'The naked woman, then, is Aphrodite suckling Aeneas. Her attitude suggests indifference towards the man who is watching her, and she does not even respond to his look. This could easily be the "half-hearted aversion" to which you alluded.' I thanked her for seeing what I was getting at, with a discreet smile that had nothing boastful in it. 'The pilgrim looking so sadly at her must obviously be Anchises, and his stick or staff must symbolise his punishment. Zeus, meanwhile, is discharging his anger from the heavens. In my opinion, Alejandro's explanation seems very satisfactory. What do you think, Gilberto?'

Gabetti had switched off the torch, as if the objections he was about to make made him feel mean, and in need of the protection of darkness.

'There is nothing satisfactory about it,' he began. 'First of all, it goes against all narrative logic, by which I mean against the natural sequence of events. How can you justify the fact that Anchises is already leaning on a staff when Zeus's punishment hasn't even struck him? The thunderbolt is still suspended in the air.'

'But there is such a thing as iconographic synthesis,' I

protested, and my words resounded loudly through the deserted museum. "To take one example, we have looked time after time at paintings that represent Eve reaching up to pick the forbidden fruit from the tree of knowledge; she has still not yet committed her sin, and yet with her other hand she is trying to hide her nakedness. In other words, we find, all combined in one picture, the fall into temptation and the first consequence of the fall, namely the shame she feels at revealing her naked body. I could give you many other examples; it was a widely used technique, especially in the Renaissance when, in order to meet the requirements of their clients, artists incorporated two complementary scenes – and sometimes more – in one composition.'

Fights between boxers are decided by the weight of blows landed, and I had not flinched under Gabetti's attacks which had been more fanciful than effective. It was now my turn to take the initiative and deliver the knockout. My opponent was slow to react, and his voice was no longer jaunty or over-confident.

'I continue to believe that *The Tempest* does not contain any concrete theme, unless it be a feeling for emotional expression. Its fascination stems from the fact that it defies logic: the curious isolation of the figures, the storm which is brewing but doesn't quite break.' His enumeration of these details was designed to mislead, a defensive mechanism similar to that of a boxer who feints, and skips around the ring, trying to avoid an exchange of punches. 'All right then, if you want to turn it into a puzzle you've got to get all the pieces in somehow. The broken columns, for instance, they are an important element in the painting, but you haven't even mentioned them.'

This time I gave a cruel smile of triumph, which cannot have displeased Chiara, because the darkness that failed to conceal Gabetti's pettiness allowed my triumph to blaze through.

'Please, that really won't do. The broken columns symbolise the love between Aphrodite and Anchises that has been destroyed.'

Chiara intervened at that moment, clearly coming down on my side.

'Or maybe they could be a portent of the destruction of Troy.'

'Quite right. Why not?' I agreed. 'That would strengthen my theory of the existence of iconographic synthesis: there would not be just two but three different events incorporated in the one picture.'

Although I appeared to have won, I was secretly aware that an unsolved mystery is always more enticing than its solution; mystery brings us close to the supernatural, while its solution is merely mechanistic. I was about to vent my spleen on Gabetti, when I thought I heard footsteps above our heads.

'What was that?'

Gabetti switched on the torch and played it across the skylight in the ceiling of the room. Outside, the darkness seemed immutable and primordial.

'Some bird nesting in the rafters. Don't worry.'

A series of clandestine noises also reached us from the hall. Whoever was making them was trying to be stealthy, but unfamiliarity with the building made him trip on the stairs and brush against the walls. We could almost hear his heavy breathing, caused, probably, more by nerves than effort. I held my breath, and Chiara and Gabetti did the same, all three of us sunk in the unfathomable depths of fear. Possibly Gabetti was the least apprehensive, but it was his job to call belatedly on his courage, since it was he who had been negligent with the security of the museum.

'I'm going to see what's happening.'

He left us alone with Giorgione's picture, alone also with the feelings of anxiety that were entering the very marrow of our bones. Chiara huddled against me, gripping me almost fiercely, hanging on to my raincoat, and pressing her face against mine – my unshaven beard must have been painful on her cheeks. Her body was seized by a fit of trembling, and I could feel her legs about to give way. Gabetti had reached the staircase and was shouting at the intruder: 'Who's down there? Who's down there?' – as if he was repeating a chant designed to exorcise a phantom. Again, he repeated the words: 'Who's down—' But he was unable to finish the question. We heard a dull metallic noise as the torch fell down the stairs, before his body collapsed like a dead weight.

'Wait for me here, I'm going to help him,' I said, half-carrying Chiara over to the relative safety of a wall.

Before I could leave her side the glass in the skylight was smashed into a thousand pieces, and a vague shape pounced on me with a force that made me stagger and fall. The Accademia's alarm bells began to ring, like the sirens of a factory on night shift, or church bells announcing the end of the world. A man, much more heavily built than I, grabbed me and pressed me down with all the weight of his body. The broken glass of the skylight gashed my back through my raincoat, pullover, and shirt, and tiny splinters dug into my skin – which had not received any prior training in fakirism. My aggressor held my head in both hands and started to thump the back of it against the floor. He had shapeless arms with bulging muscles and the huge hands of a stevedore, hands hardened from unloading bales of merchandise and in trading punches. I was losing consciousness with every blow. But as much as anything to impress Chiara – love inspires an absurd rashness as well as a ferocious competitive instinct – I made a great effort and thrust my hands up to grasp my assailant's throat in order to strangle him, or at least make it difficult for him to breathe.

The alarm continued to screech, nearly piercing my eardrums, and re-echoing deep inside me like a throbbing tumour every time the back of my head was banged against the floor. With each blow, the splinters of glass from the skylight lacerated my scalp, and I felt as if they were penetrating the bone. Chiara fled, terrified, possibly to call for assistance, or possibly to help Gabetti, or possibly from sheer instinct of self-preservation. If I could have stopped to analyse my state of mind I would have found that it was hatred alone that kept me in possession of my faculties. My aggressor on the other hand gave no sign of distress, and only seemed concerned to finish the job off before the racket of the alarms brought the police in.

'You bastard, I'm going to kill you,' he breathed in my ear, in villainous Italian.

His mouth smelled of eucalyptus lozenges, and his filthy hair, which was slightly wavy, fell about his shoulders making him look like an ancient Assyrian warrior. His ear also was filthy, as far as I could make out as I dug my teeth into it. The lobe was pierced by at least two metal rings, and above these I discerned others the size of wedding rings, or small bangles, which had been inserted through the cartilage. I bit with cannibal voracity, and listened to his howl of an animal caught in a trap, while the warm blood spurted into my mouth, the gristle of his ear crunched between my molars, and the lobe was torn away by my front teeth. The earrings had a taste of iron, but it was difficult to distinguish between the flavour of the metal and the flavour of raw flesh. His blood filled my mouth, overflowed it, stuck in my throat, inflamed my gullet. Maybe it was its high alcohol content that intoxicated me with victory. The thug continued to howl, his shrieks even louder than the museum's alarms, and they only ceased when he resigned himself to the loss of his ear lobe, and broke away from me. He gave a mighty leap which took him up to the skylight, and with a great effort hauled himself on to the roof. It occurred to me that in his flight he would leave a trail of blood that would be slow to disappear, because there was no longer any snow in Venice to absorb it. Still lying on the floor, I breathed in deeply the air stealing through the broken skylight, and spat out the bloody lump of flesh that was caught between my teeth. As I stood up I nearly crashed into *The Tempest*. My fingers actually touched it, but without damaging it, and I breathed in the smell of oil, which, in spite of five centuries having elapsed since it was painted, retained an almost abnormal freshness. The alarm bells ceased ringing.

'Are you hurt?'

My eyes were getting used to the dark and I could make out Chiara's features, which still bore the marks of fear. I felt proud of myself, but was much too weak to have any inclination to show off.

'Just a few bruises,' I said, ignoring the blood which matted my hair. 'And your father?'

The exact relationship between these two was indefinable, but possibly paternity continued to be the appropriate link between them, if only because it encapsulated briefly, and decently, whatever other connections there may have been.

'He's all right. He lost consciousness for a few moments, but it was just a fright.'

'A fright that nearly cost us our lives,' I snorted. 'Have the police arrived?'

I shook splinters of glass from my raincoat. As I walked, the floor emitted a rasping music.

'He's on the phone to them now, telling them not to come.'

An awkward silence reigned. Surprised, I weakly articulated the words: 'What do you mean, telling them not to come? Two individuals break into the Accademia with the clear intention of stealing a picture, they assault us, and cause a lot of damage, and you really believe you can conceal this from the police?'

It was impossible to believe that the lips that justified Gabetti's actions were the same ones I had kissed a few hours earlier.

'Don't you understand? If the press get hold of the news that the Accademia was left unguarded they will build up a huge campaign against Gilberto, and insist on his dismissal. Just imagine the shit they'll throw at him.'

'No more than he deserves,' I pointed out, furiously.

Outside the room that had been the scene of my fight, the museum retained its atmosphere of a temple without worshippers. I could just hear Gabetti speaking in some remote office, that voice of his, skilled in prevarication and geniality, diverting the attention of the police, and advising them not to bother to extend their investigations to the area of the Accademia. 'The alarms went off by accident,' he professed, with that little laugh of his, the laugh of a plausible crook. I sensed in his words that he was dismissing me, that he was throwing me out. I sensed that his laughter was his way of celebrating my departure. I sensed, with growing regret, that I had ceased to exist where he was concerned – and maybe also where Chiara was concerned.

*   *   *

'You can't be trusted on your own. You're a right mess – looks as if they tried to crucify you.'

Tedeschi had ordered me to lie face down on the bed on which he took his rest, that stately bed converted into a pig-sty with its fine linen sheets turned into something resembling sackcloth, and made stiff and filthy with dirt and dried urine. There was not even electricity in that abandoned palace which had been selected as the scenario for Fabio Valenzin's death. The only light Tedeschi had came from an oil lamp that made his features look even coarser than by daylight and shed its oily illumination over the sheets, reducing all the stains to one uniform colour, softening their harshness.

'Right, get your shirt off. Let's have a look at those wounds.'

My shirt, slashed by the pieces of glass, was in tatters; it was nothing more than a rag in which the rips matched the gashes on my back, and stuck to the congealed blood like a second skin. Tedeschi stripped it off me with a not very gentle hand, making some of the wounds bleed again, and then he poured a stream of his fortified wine over my lacerated flesh.

'Hang on, this is going to sting.'

His warning came late because the wine was already running into the gashes, disinfecting them with its high brandy content – not to mention the various germs with which Tedeschi had doctored it, through his saliva. Using a piece of cloth which was undoubtedly innocent of any of the prejudices of preventive medicine, he gave me a stiff rubdown, and with fingers worthy of a market gardener, began to weed out the splinters of glass. I buried my teeth in the pillow, and let him grub around, although I had considerable doubts about the effectiveness of his clinical techniques.

'All the time I thought you were with Giovanna Zanon fucking the hell out of her, and here you are back with me looking like something the cat brought in,' he said.

I still possessed a small reserve of humour.

'And what do you think I'd look like if I really had been screwing that old witch? I'd bet anything she keeps a whip in the closet for beating the shit out of any man she gets into her bedroom.'

'Well, it must be better to have a good hiding while you're on the job, rather than a thrashing and no fuck at all, don't you think? But seriously, Ballesteros, you shouldn't get yourself into so many scrapes. The best thing you can do sometimes is to just sit tight and wait.'

There were pigeons sleeping in the mouldings of the ceiling, all puffed up, and with their heads beneath their wings, like mutilated monsters awaiting the shot that would awake them, and restore them to their full natural shape.

'You haven't done much sitting around either,' I grunted. 'Chiara, Gabetti's daughter, told me you've been spying on her. Do you really think it's right to leave the chest unprotected?'

Tedeschi completed his repairs to my back, and now he dowsed the damage done to the back of my head with another splash of wine.

'I wasn't spying on anybody. The fact is people are very suspicious – that girl must have thought I was a rapist or something of the kind, because she didn't stop running until she'd given me the slip. I also had a snoop round Giovanna Zanon's palace to see if you were giving any sign of life. Nothing at all. As soon as you get hold of a bit of cunt you forget all about your duties.' Tedeschi's coarse accusation made me angry, mainly because the day had not rewarded me with anything of the kind. 'And there's one thing we've got to do

176

together – or did you think I was going to dredge the canal all on my own?' The wine had softened the caked blood, and Tedeschi was searching for the gashes in my scalp. 'Fucking hell, that bastard's made mincemeat of your head. Does it hurt much?'

'Christ, what do you think?' I was beginning to despair of these rhetorical questions. 'But I got my own back – I don't think he'll be wearing earrings any longer!'

I still had the taste in my mouth of the ear I had ripped off. Our voices woke a pigeon which stared at us unblinkingly, with its jet-black eyes.

'Did you recognise him?'

'What do you think? It was difficult to see very much. Gabetti had taken the torch with him.' I spat out a stringy piece of meat which was still caught between two teeth – I did not know whether it was still there from my last meal, or from my brawl in the Accademia. 'What I do know is that character was new to me; I hadn't seen him before in my life. He was a big brute with arms like great hams. His breath smelled of eucalyptus and he wore earrings in both ears, and as for his hair, that made him look like a night-club bouncer. It was combed straight back, thick with haircream, shaved close at the sides of his head, and rather wavy.'

Tedeschi removed a dagger-like sliver of glass from the back of my neck, and showed it to me as if it were a gold nugget.

'Now you'll have to let your hair grow if you want to hide the scars you're going to have on the back of your head,' he maintained, pitilessly. 'I've seen that character. He goes around with another one who is just as tough, except that he has a crew-cut.'

By now he had completed his emergency surgery, which he made clear to me with a playful punch in the face. As I sat up on the bed I had the feeling of having been sewn up, but with sutures that were likely to come apart at any moment.

'The one with the crew-cut must be the one who met Gabetti on the stairs.' Like the invalid who takes comfort in the ailments of the man in the next bed, I was pleased that Gilberto Gabetti had received his share of punches. 'And what do you know about those two?'

The bedroom displayed the same ruined and charmless grandeur that I had had the opportunity of verifying by daylight, the only difference being that the oil lamp added to it the gloom of a wine cellar or a cave. Four or five dead pigeons, blood dripping from their necks, hung from the wall where they were speared on hooks.

'They met up here once with Valenzin to discuss a deal,' recalled Tedeschi. 'Although usually he didn't want me around, he asked me to be there on that occasion, and also asked me to keep my rifle loaded, just in case. Valenzin always had the wind up when he was dealing with thugs. However brave he was in the swindles he carried out, it melted away when he was faced with a mountain of hard muscle. Those types are the hangers-on of some rich bastard – don't think they're working on their own account, they're as thick as two planks. Like Valenzin they used a sort of jargon that was difficult to understand; they talked about a "thingamy" when they referred to whatever it was they were negotiating about, and they only talked clearly when they got down to figures and the fact that payment would be by instalments. The "thingamy" can't have been small beer because the figures they bandied about had a lot of noughts in them – the sort of money that'd take your breath away. When these louts left at last, Valenzin told me: "After this one I'm retiring, Vittorio. I really am going to retire." But he said it without any of the bounce he usually had before one of his big stunts. He also sounded as if he was sorry about what he was up to. I don't know whether this was because of the thought of retirement, or because he had scruples about it. But I don't really believe that – Valenzin didn't bother his head about that sort of thing.'

But I knew that, at least where love was concerned, he did have scruples; I knew that an inner sorrow filled him with a sense of impotence.

'And you never found out what stunt he was working on?' I asked, with the deep despair of someone who holds all the pieces of a jigsaw puzzle but is unable to join them together. 'Did you ever find out if he managed to pull it off?'

'No sodding idea.' Tedeschi bared his rapacious teeth. 'Who can say whether Valenzin was planning some sort of double-cross and the rich bastard sent his heavies to settle accounts. But to tell you the truth, I can't believe Valenzin would be so crazy as to meet up with those characters all on his own, especially if he was planning to con them. You also have to ask yourself what led them to break into the Accademia in that bungling way. There's probably no one like them when it comes to a punch-up, but they don't have the brains to crack a museum. You can't get into places like that by bashing through skylights and creating a racket that's enough to wake the dead. I felt a bit dozy while I was waiting for you, but the alarm bells woke me up all right. The noise even drove the pigeons mad – the poor things'll suffer from insomnia after that.'

In contrast to the pigeons, Valenzin's chest continued to slumber, huddled under the bed, next to the chamberpot in which Tedeschi had again done his business.

'Have you tried to open it? We might possibly find the explanation inside.'

'Of course I've tried.' He clicked his tongue, indicating

irritation. 'With skeleton keys, master keys, jemmies; I've even tried my gas stove, using it like a blowlamp. But nothing works. All I've done is scorch the leather. I decided against using more drastic methods because I didn't want to risk damaging whatever's inside.' He paused for a moment, with an expression of incredulity, or at least suspicion. 'Assuming, of course, that there is anything inside. It's always possible that in the end, Valenzin decided against the stunt that was to pay for his retirement, or he gave it up on moral grounds, which may be why those idiots tried to do it themselves.'

The oil lamp emitted a circle of light over the floorboards, and extended the dim glow of its flame as far as the wall, fouling the air with a thick and eye-stinging smoke. In Venice, crime circulates through underground channels, like molten lava distributing its heat to every individual, although it measures the dosage it bestows on each: from bribery to murder, via theft, all the Venetians I had met shared in its warmth. The realisation left me depressed, and downcast. It filled me with the same feeling of dismay that must have assailed Yahweh when he was unable to find even ten good men in Sodom to merit his forgiveness.

'The problem with you is you're nuts on that girl of Gabetti, and you're all screwed up because she won't come over to your side.' Tedeschi's words were very mortifying. 'What you've got to get into your head, my lad, is the fact that you've only just arrived here, while she and Gabetti are linked together in all sorts of ways.'

'Gabetti is a criminal and a menace to society,' I said, repeating the words I had heard from the lips of Inspector Nicolussi that morning. 'God knows what tricks he's getting up to in order to prevent the police investigating that robbery attempt.'

Tedeschi shrugged his shoulders. The flame from the oil lamp picked out the scars on his face, which might have been seen as an X-ray of his soul.

'If he's working a fiddle, we'll soon hear about it,' he said, with the stubborn impassiveness of countrymen who know from experience that time brings people's misdemeanours to light in the same way that it ripens fruit and harvests crops. 'The important thing is nobody should think they're being watched. Don't be in too much of a hurry; given time they all reveal their hands.'

They had already revealed them to me, at least in part, but what remained most powerfully in my mind in the midst of so much show was the impression that they were all playing with the same rigged pack of cards, making bids and finesses that hid the tricks they were really out to make. Tedeschi was suggesting I should become a passive spectator of the game, but there were certain matters that made it necessary for a spectator to intervene, in order to steal a march on the duplicities of the various contestants. Maybe I was the least suitable person for this job, because the many years I had spent being a docile and obsequious academic had made me insensitive to certain types of lies, or to the ambiguities implicit in people's words. I told Tedeschi of the various discoveries I had made during the day, the uncertainties and contradictions of some of the things that had been said; I told him about the conversation I had overheard between Dina and Nicolussi, about Chiara's sadness, and Giovanna Zanon's malice.

'Those two, Giovanna Zanon and her husband, have invited me to a fancy-dress ball they're giving tomorrow night, to mark the beginning of Carnival.' I repressed a shudder as I thought of myself wearing a plague doctor's costume, similar to the one worn by Valenzin's assassin. In order to ease the strain, I tried to make a joke of it. 'It means I shall be able to find out if she really does keep a whip in her closet.'

Tedeschi knocked back the last dregs of the wine that remained in the bottle after his extravagant use of so much of it to treat my wounds. He also sat on the bed and started unbuttoning his shirt.

'Well, just now we're going to try to find that ring. I always enjoy a good dip.'

His torso was deeply tanned and without an ounce of fat; its lines were broken only by the ripple of powerful muscles. I felt embarrassed by my burden of surplus fat and spare tyres. My paunch was almost as slack and flabby as my understanding of real life. Tedeschi went to the window and scanned the little square, the sole inhabitant of which was the inadequate streetlamp accommodating a whole mortuary of dead insects. The water of the canal lay motionless as it concocted its poisonous brew of sewage.

'Where would you say it fell, more or less?'

'Just below the central balcony, in the middle of the canal.'

I recalled the downward trajectory of the ring; my memory clearly retained the image of its descent and even slowed it down, like the trail of a shooting star, before it was swallowed up in the water. Tedeschi leaned on the window-sill to study the terrain. His skin seemed impervious to the cold, as if it was coated with an invisible layer of whale oil. In my case, however, the damp air worked its way into the gashes in my back like vaporous iodine, and sent shivers down my spine. I pulled my raincoat tightly round me, although after my fight in the Accademia it was fit only for the ragman.

'Let's go down then.'

He took off his fisherman's boots which were thickly

spattered with mud, and also removed his trousers. He did not wear underpants and his phallus swung between his thighs like a pendant. We walked through the *piano nobile*, with its perspective of doors of diminishing size, which the darkness of the night made indistinct and like an interminably long corridor. The mirrors did not reflect us, possibly because they had given up their imaging function as a way of repudiating the crimes that had been plotted and carried out in that palace. How easy and convenient it is to close your eyes, how agreeable to let the wax grow in your ears, how gratifying to turn your back and not to lose your self-control, how pleasant it is to shun other people's quarrels and decline all responsibilities. We went out into the square and, keeping close to the front of the palace, passed along the narrow sidewalk that Fabio Valenzin had followed while the blood poured from the wound in his chest. Before plunging in, Tedeschi stared hard at me.

'You're not going to cry off now, are you?'

I knew that it would have been very wrong to change my mind, or back out, now I had got him involved in this extraordinary task. The windows of the Albergo Cusmano were shuttered — a shuttered window is like an unsilvered mirror, or a man who turns his back on you. I imagined that in one of those closed rooms my luggage lay open, and my clothing stiff with cold. I also imagined Dina lying on her back, on her own bed — with all the darkness of the night centred on her pubis. By then she would certainly have discovered the theft of Valenzin's chest, and her eyes would be huge as she lay there unable to sleep, just as they had been on the night before she murdered her husband — death by suffocation conceals death by poisoning, in the way that snow conceals the obscenity of blood — but then the need to be alert would have given her courage, now the need to be alert would be inspired by a feeling of helplessness, as well as that unavoidable sadness that caged animals suffer from.

'Me cry off? Certainly not.'

The surface of the water came up to Tedeschi's nipples and made them erect. His feet would be sinking into the slime at the bottom of the canal, the revolting consistency of which I had experienced a couple of nights before. He ducked down to get his eyes used to the murky water. When he reappeared to replace the air in his lungs, filthy with mud and weed, he reminded me of those Hindu penitents who bathe in the Ganges as a way of purifying themselves, and then return home with the same sins, and a garnish of shit on top. He dived repeatedly, seven or eight times; each dive was shorter than the last because his lungs were beginning to give out, just like my hopes (or fears) for the recovery of the ring. Perhaps the current had carried it away – except that the canal was not subject to currents; perhaps it had rolled all the way to the Adriatic to contract a symbolic marriage with the waves. Or perhaps it had never even existed.

'I've got it! At last I've got the little bastard,' mumbled Tedeschi, rising suddenly from his speleological exploit.

He held it between his rapacious teeth: it was a gold ring, very heavy, and still shiny in spite of having been buried in the filth of the canal. Tedeschi climbed up the bank, streaming with the jubilation that ancient bronze statues display when archaeologists draw them up from the bottom of the sea, and he spat out the ring at my feet. It was an ostentatious piece of work, ostentatious to the point of vulgarity; the seal was very large, even for a thumb, and was deeply chased. As I was about to bend down to examine it more closely, Tedeschi picked it up in his powerful hands. I noticed that his nails were cracked and split from so much scraping around the bed of the canal. With some difficulty, he read the inscription which ran round the chased surface of the ring:

'*Moriatur anima mea cum philistiim*. Do you know what that means?'

The fact that Tedeschi was naked did not seem in the least indecent, because there was nobody there to stare at him, either lewdly, or accusingly. I dusted off my half-forgotten smattering of Latin, and translated, guided as much by phonetic similarities as by genuine conviction.

'Something like: "May my soul die with the Philistines", but I can't see that the translation tells us much,' I said.

'Why not? Didn't they make you read the Bible at school?' he asked, with the exultation that one would expect from a dedicated student of the Scriptures. 'That was what Samson shouted just before he pegged out. That whore Delilah cut off his hair and handed him over to the Philistines who gouged his eyes out and shackled him to a mill-wheel. Then they hitched him up to the pillars of the palace so that the mob could plague the life out of him, but Samson put his trust in God and he regained his strength. He shook the pillars, and the palace fell down and buried the Philistines. Look at the design on the ring. The reference is obvious.'

He handed me the ring so that I could examine the detail of the design carved in relief which illustrated the inscription: above a masonry wall there were two broken columns, very stylised, and without a base, exactly like the columns that feature in *The Tempest*, behind the pilgrim. I felt myself disturbed by a dark surge of fright, as its significance became clear.

EIGHT

You need the patience of a numismatist to attempt a large jigsaw puzzle, because you have to examine closely the almost infinite number of ways in which you can fit the fretted shapes of all the pieces together. Sometimes, the joins between them are so imperfect they seem to make no sense, and there are times when we realise that a single wrong one would make nonsense of all the others; but we do not allow ourselves to be put off, and we press on with our task, making progress piece by piece, until we come to believe we are endowed with a sort of intellectual heroism. The moment arrives when we have almost got the layout organised, only to discover that it is not enough simply to make the pieces fit together, it is also essential that the final picture should look right and not arbitrary, that the joins, which at first seemed improbable and meaningless, should possess an intrinsic coherence that creates a perfect image. Respect for precise shapes is of no use if, when we finish it off, we find there are distortions in the picture, because then we are in an intolerable position: we have used up a lot of energy, but the muddle is too great for us to work backwards, and we prefer to knock the whole thing to bits because it is built on unsound foundations. Irritation and despair lead us to demolish it – although later we regret having done so, when the floor is littered with pieces of puzzle that have reverted to their primeval state of chaos.

Something similar was happening to me. I had scrupulously observed the rules of academic investigation in order to tease out the meaning of *The Tempest*; I had forced myself to make all the pieces fit, and had devoted five years to the creation of a foolproof explanation, employing all the rules of logic, but two days in Venice had taught me that logic is of little use in life, just as the intellect is of no use in art, because art is the religion of feeling and emotion. Two days in Venice had destroyed five years of work, had trampled my confidence in theorising underfoot, and had reduced me personally to a state of total confusion. *The Tempest*, that picture which I had dissected and put together again with all the patience of a numismatist, was not just an object of aesthetic delight, nor an arena in which experts settled their disagreements, it was also an object of devotion, or tribulation, for those who believed themselves to be its moral owners, or, on the other hand, felt themselves deprived of it – enough to rouse them to fury. It was also a battlefield on which those men and women settled their conflicts, a stage on which their fantasies, desires, and frustrations were exposed.

Finding the ring made it necessary for me to do some rethinking, and although I was by no means certain, it was drawing me towards the view that *The Tempest* was much more than just a network of symbols. Possibly this painting inspired more rapacious material contentions, greeds less metaphorical in nature, and instincts of survival and predation. Possibly, those instincts and greeds and rapacity were so unrestrained and devastating that one or other of the contenders had been prepared to sacrifice himself in order to defeat his adversaries, just as Samson had done: 'May my soul die with the Philistines.'

'Valenzin's killer didn't want to leave any clues,' I reflected aloud, once we were back in the palace. The ring seemed to throb in my hand, like a white-hot stone. 'He's just shot his victim, who is dying in front of him, but instead of finishing him off, he wants to make sure he isn't carrying some object or document that would incriminate him. Then he finds this very large and valuable ring on Valenzin's finger which the police would not have failed to see. The murderer knows it will lead to him, possibly because he was the one who gave it to Valenzin, possibly because the design of the ring refers vaguely to some deal that concerns them both, and in his hurry, he simply looks for a way to get rid of it. It is burning his hand, and so risky to hold on to that he doesn't want to keep it one minute longer. He knows the canals in Venice are a repository of all secrets, so he goes up to the balcony and throws it in from there. Meanwhile, Valenzin manages to stagger a few steps and to get out into the square in order to call for help, but he is unable to speak and his legs won't carry him any further, in fact he is dead on his feet.'

Tedeschi needed a while to take in my reconstruction of events; its shadowy and uncertain nature put him in a bad mood.

'And why should a ring make it so dangerous for him?'

'Here we are dealing in hypotheses, but they are likely to be true,' I replied, trying not to sound too boastful as I produced my explanations. 'As I said, the broken columns correspond exactly with those painted by Giorgione. Add to that coincidence the bungled break-in at the Accademia by those two gorillas – which begins to look like a last desperate hope. It's possible their boss ordered them to do what Valenzin had not done. I think Valenzin had contracted to steal *The Tempest*; I also believe the ring was a present from his client, a mere bagatelle compared with what he was going to receive when he handed it over, but a bagatelle that would always serve as a reminder to Valenzin of his commitment.'

'A commitment he didn't fulfil, and which cost him his life,' concluded Tedeschi, despondently. 'I'm afraid in that case the chest doesn't contain anything. Even so, the murderer took the keys, there's no doubt about that. Valenzin never let them out of his sight. Whenever we agreed to meet here, he used to rattle them to let me know he'd arrived.'

Tedeschi let his eyes wander round the room like someone who has all the facts at his fingertips, but has no idea how to draw the right conclusions from them in order to resolve his perplexity. I assumed the credit for that.

'Possibly the chest contains something else that would be dangerous for those who contracted with him. You can be sure Valenzin got some sort of written undertaking to cover himself.'

The reserve of paraffin in the oil lamp was running low, and it was giving off stupefying fumes that nearly overcame us, and put an end to our discussion. The flame died with a series of gasps and a last guttering sound that slowly diminished in the darkness like the hiss of escaping gas. A fading light entered through the pointed windows of the *piano nobile*, like a series of moonlit daggers stretching across the floor covered with the excrement of pigeons; it rose up the back wall, and lapped against the mirrors which only reflected the dead, and in which possibly Valenzin had had the chance to see himself for the last time, a blurred and spectral image that imprinted itself on his retinas, infused by the rush of blood. Night was falling relentlessly, just as it would have seemed to

Fabio Valenzin, like darkness shrouding the last breath from a shattered lung.

'Where will you sleep tonight?' asked Tedeschi, guessing that I was not going to stay in the palace. 'In Gabetti's house?'

'I don't think I'd be very welcome there.' Sadness, and a need to move on, weighed me down. 'You're never welcome when you know too much. I shall go back to the Albergo Cusmano.'

'We'll be neighbours, then,' said Tedeschi, approvingly. He did not seem daunted by the dark. 'Let me know if the widow tries to corner you.'

'Don't worry, I'll tell you,' I said, without knowing quite what he meant by *corner*.

An alien wind blew around the square, ruffled the surface of the water in the canal and baptised my wounds through the raincoat. The fluorescent sign advertising the existence of the Albergo Cusmano no longer merely droned, it now gave off electric sparks as if finally succumbing to its various short-circuits. The door opened easily when I pushed; there was no need to force it. There was wild disorder in the lobby of the hotel: the furniture was overturned on the carpet, there were chairs with their legs in the air, and the books in which Dina recorded the comings and goings of pretend guests lay scattered all over the place. The lobby had the look of a lumber-room turned upside down. I dodged around the obstacles, suppressing the disagreeable sensation a careful thief must feel when he revisits the scene of his robberies and discovers the havoc caused on a later occasion by a partner in crime who is less fastidious than he is, possibly also more frenetic, and with homicidal tendencies.

'Dina!' I shouted, suddenly feeling very worried.

I ran up the stairs three at a time, urged on by an awful presentiment. Each stair seemed to have the consistency of a quagmire, which made my ascent difficult. On the first landing I glimpsed the corridor with the doors of the rooms either ajar or wide open, indicating that these had been searched as thoroughly as the lobby, but I did not stop to assess the extent of the damage, because I was afraid that Dina might have suffered even more serious damage, and that this most recent thief had unleashed on her all his murderous fury, when he found that somebody else had got there before him.

'Dina, can you hear me?'

I did not expect a reply; I was simply using words as an antidote to fear, words that would delay her death or hasten her resurrection, words that were really prayers or exorcisms to pacify my conscience and banish my feelings of guilt. Only a few hours before I had imagined her lying on her bed, with all the darkness of the night centred on her pubis, her eyes alert, but I had been unable to interpret the fixity of her look. Now, I imagined those eyes petrified in death, acquiring the gleam that develops after a person has been smothered or strangled. I switched on the light, expecting to confirm my forebodings. With relief I discovered that she was alive, that those Byzantine eyes of hers were still able to blink and were emitting a silent lamentation of rage or despair.

'I thought they had done something worse to you. Oh my God, Dina, I'll cut you loose straight away.'

Outside, the wind was making the shutters rattle in their frames and banging them like a pilgrim demanding shelter as an act of mercy. Dina had been gagged with sticking plaster; her wrists and ankles were also held by plaster to the back and the legs of a chair. She had a bump on her right temple and a bruise that extended down towards her eyebrow, but she showed no other signs of violence. The chair was overturned and her skirt was rucked up in a series of creases like an accordion, giving me a glimpse of her very white thighs bulging with cellulite, which probably made them rub against each other in her groin. Her high-heeled shoes had slipped off her feet, but I guessed that it was not the intruder who had removed them, or knocked her over, or raised her skirt. She alone had created this disorder by her efforts to free herself. I pulled the chair upright and caressed her wounded temple. Her weeping continued to be silent because her sobs were trapped in the gag, but she began to cry more copiously, as if the tension that had built up while she was alone had at last been released. Her face was flushed, and her nostrils were dilated like those of a horse, as she struggled to breathe. I ran into the bathroom to look for scissors in order to cut through her bonds.

'Wait just a moment, Dina, you're not alone any longer.'

Her attacker had been thorough and merciless. He had bound her wrists and ankles with so many turns of the sticking plaster that it had constricted the circulation of the blood, and left a number of red circles, the sort of mark left by the shoulder-strap of a brassiere, or a ring on a finger. As soon as she realised she could move, Dina tore off the rest of the plaster as if it were depilation patches. Bruises came up on her skin, but there was no pain in her eyes, because her tears anaesthetised it. She gave me a weak, daughterly hug; her sobs could not break through because of the gag but had their outlet in the movement of her breasts, which trembled with soft and fitful shudders. I felt myself to be not only the recipient but also the cause of those shudders.

'Calm down, the worst is over; I am with you, and you are safe,' I said, and to my soothing words I added the balm of my fingers, which wiped away the sweat from her forehead, and banished the fear from her eyes. 'They can't hurt you any more now.'

Even so I was forced to hurt her a little more, because although her hair was gathered in a chignon which left the back of her neck bare, a few strands had been caught inside the gag. I cut them very carefully, not to leave them too short, and left it to her to pull the plaster off her mouth. Immediately, her cheeks flared up leaving red weals; skin on her lips came away and left them smeared with blood that would be slow to stop flowing.

'I thought I'd suffocate, I didn't think anybody would come and help me.' She spoke with the eagerness, the delight, and the helplessness of one who recovers the faculty of speech after a silence of months or years. 'How can I thank you? It has been so horrible.'

She smoothed the creases in her skirt, looked with dismay at her stockings that were torn to shreds and had fallen round her ankles, but she derived some consolation from seeing that I was in an even worse state. The wind assailed the shutters and whistled through the cracks.

'You can thank me by telling me the truth,' I said, in possibly a rather peremptory tone. 'Who strapped you to the chair? The same one who turned the hotel upside-down?'

I stole a look at the gap left where Valenzin's chest had been, between the wall and the wardrobe, a gap that had something of a burrow about it, and now displayed the desolation of an empty lair.

'Was he looking for the chest?'

Dina looked at me, astonished and bewildered, and without immediately understanding; then her stare gave way to a frown as it changed from docile gratitude to scorn, suggesting that although, because of fatigue, she absolved me of shabby behaviour, she still could not forgive me for it.

'So it was you who took it,' she said with restrained gravity, but in the same resentful tone that I had detected during her conversation with Nicolussi while I was eavesdropping on them from the hotel porch. 'I might have died because of you, and now you want me to tell you the truth!'

'Please, Dina, describe the person who did this.' I tried again to caress her swollen temple, but this time she started back, as if suffering from a spasm of pain. 'Tell me, it is important.'

She looked at me with either utter revulsion or pity; possibly she had conceived a deep hatred for me, or maybe she smelled the effluvia of the wine Tedeschi had used to disinfect my wounds.

'My God, they've also given you a good thrashing.'

I nodded, exaggerating both my own affliction and my sympathy for her. People I had only just got to know had made me the recipient of confidences that were fallacious, or at the very least biased; they had invented stories that were little better than lies, and had exploited my innocence or lack of experience. Now that I understood this, I wanted to find out the truth and eradicate deceit. Truth, I realised at last, is better said when said briefly: garrulity is a kind of embroidery that acts as a defence, and allows us to slip lies through unnoticed. Dina fell back on the bed, overcome by exhaustion or remorse: she too had lied to me, and had attacked me with accusations I should have preferred not to hear. The mattress received the weight of her body with a mildly protesting groan.

'I didn't manage to see his face because he wore a Carnival mask,' she whispered, crossing her arms over her breasts in order to repress the trembling that again began to agitate them.

'The mask of the plague doctor.' I nodded. 'And did you see whether he had filthy hair?'

She remained silent, inscrutably silent, which might possibly have been the prelude to sobs, or an outburst of anger.

'What right do you have to ask me?' The trembling movement of her breasts spread to the rest of her body, as ripples caused by a falling stone spread across the surface of water. 'Now I am going to call the police.'

She tried to get up from the bed, but I held her down by her shoulders, and shook her; I was horrified that my hands too were capable of violence.

'Call the police? And what will you tell them? That you were plotting with Nicolussi, just as you did when you murdered your husband? That you had decided between you to conceal evidence, hoping to keep it up your sleeve until the time was ripe?' I was gripped by an exaltation not far removed from frenzy, and my words were bitter and grating as if spoken out of spite. 'Will you tell them that the Spaniard stole a march on your machinations? I don't believe you're in a position to call anybody.'

Dina shut her Byzantine eyes, either to help her think, or to blot out my presence; she compressed her lips into a firm, straight line, in an endeavour to appear unyielding.

'Let me go, please.'

Her voice was adamantine, as if it arose from some fossil deposit; it was a voice that was both imploring and at the same time faltering. I insisted.

'We must confide in each other, Dina, we have no alternative.' I relaxed the grip of my hands which a moment before had been clenched, and allowed them to become slack, resting lightly on her shoulders in the limp and ritualistic way of quacks and priests. 'I'm sorry for the harm I may have done you; when

I took the chest I didn't think of the consequences. In any case, what I might have done, or not done, wouldn't have saved you from having a rough time. That individual, whoever he may be, would have come here anyway. At least the chest is safe.'

I reflected guiltily that her suffering may have been pointless if, in the event, the chest contained nothing more than crumpled shirts and dirty underwear. I was troubled by the thought that Tedeschi might also be harmed pointlessly because of a great useless, empty object. When Dina began to blink again, I noticed that her eyes were flickering one way and then the other, just as a pigeon's eyes twitch when its neck is wrung.

'And those agonising hours that I've been through – don't they count? Do you know what it's like to be tied to a chair for hour after hour, without being able to call for help? It got to the point where I wanted to die.'

Drops of blood were oozing from every crack in her lips where they had been torn by the sticking plaster, like specks of rust, reminiscent of an ancient and enduring grudge. Her indignation was futile, but it was an indignation she longed to share.

'Of course they count, Dina,' I said. 'And it is because they count that we have to try to ensure they don't occur again. You must tell me what happened in detail.'

She talked and talked, choked with emotion at first from the terror that seizes us all when we recall a recent nightmare, but that gives way to anger and a secret desire for revenge, as the last fragments of the nightmare fade away. After Fabio Valenzin's funeral, and while they were still in the San Michele cemetery, she had agreed with Nicolussi that the 'accidental' discovery of the chest would be put off until the next day. Back in the hotel, Dina switched on the radio in the lobby, and listened to a news bulletin that already included a more or less tedious account of the day's events and a sketchy biography of Fabio Valenzin. At first there were no obvious signs of disorder to lead her to suspect that the chest might have been stolen. Her reaction when she noticed the empty space between the wall and the wardrobe was not one of alarm but more one of surprise, as if somebody had altered the arrangement of the furniture. Little by little, surprise gave way to panic; her first impulse was to run away, but she was paralysed by a feeling of dismay. Nor did she dare telephone Inspector Nicolussi, who by then was probably back in the police station, because the secret nature of the ties between them – even more secret than adultery or an illicit association – made unexpected communications of this kind inadvisable. She was used to bearing the burden of guilt alone and succeeded in calming herself down with arguments that were flimsy but optimistic: after all, the contents of the chest were no concern of hers, and its disappearance relieved her of burdens that she had not taken on of her own free will. Her thoughts were interrupted by the front door bell ringing in the lobby. Her inertia, induced by the belief that everything would come right after all, persuaded her that this would be a new and unexpected guest – as I had been, for example – and that would help to assuage her guilt and helplessness. She got no further than the badly lit corridor when she received the blow on her temple, a very effective blow, dealt possibly by the butt of a pistol, and which knocked her headlong into the pit of unconsciousness. It was a peaceful and painless collapse, and so quick that it left her no time for curiosity, fear, or protest.

'Coming to was less painless,' said Dina. She raised a hand to her bruised temple, and felt the swelling. 'My head was throbbing, and I could scarcely breathe because of the gag; nor could I stand up, but the sensation of drowning and not being able to move were bearable compared with the noises that reached me from the other rooms. I knew then that the individual who had attacked me was looking for the chest, and I foresaw that when his search was unsuccessful, he would take it out on me. It is easier to die than to wait for death, imagining what it will be like, but unable to avoid it, and unable to beg for mercy from the person tormenting you. I lost all sense of time; I didn't know if I'd been unconscious for minutes or hours, nor did I know whether that search was likely to go on forever, but it seemed to me that it would. Finally, it fell quiet, and that horror appeared in front of me: it was wrapped in a cloak topped with a hood through which all I could see was a porcelain mask with the nose of a great bird, and two dark holes that just revealed its eyes. It was a horrible sight.'

She spoke like a sleepwalker, in a neutral tone that seemed to refer to a past so intimidating that it extended its influence into the present. I turned the catch which held the window shut and pushed the shutters closed, so that the wind finally had to give up its claim to admission.

'And what was its voice like?' I asked.

My own voice melted into the night, in the way that a body reduced to ashes seems to melt away when blown by a strong wind.

'If only he had spoken just one word: a swear-word, a curse, or an insult – that would have been preferable to silence,' said Dina. 'He came up to me and pressed the barrel of a pistol against my forehead. I heard him panting and I wanted to plead with him and fall on my knees, I wanted to groan and beg his forgiveness, but all I could do was cry without being able to sob, cry and shake my head backwards and forwards in order to get away from the contact of the metal against my skin. He removed the barrel of the pistol, possibly because, for a moment, he felt magnanimous, and he stared at me through the mask, until he finally seemed to understand that I had no idea either where the chest was. I can still hear his heavy breathing.'

Like a broken bellows, I thought to myself. That same heavy breathing, with its secret, urgent cadence mingled with the soughing of the wind outside, penetrated deeply into my private self. It was the death rattle of a city that had murdered sleep, the heavy combined breathing of Venice echoing quietly along the canals, resounding in the stone vaults, in the colonnades dripping with damp, in the tiny streets like reefs jutting above the water, in the catacombs drowned by neglect and peopled by phantoms, in the grim desolation of palaces without occupants and churches without worshippers. The darkness was assuming many different forms, and was conspiring against me. I was possessed by a terror of almost cosmic proportion, but I realised that terror was the best safeguard against sentimental gloom and physical weakness.

'I can still hear it in my ears,' said Dina, with no hope that it might ever stop.

It would soon be dawn. Although it was still dark, the air had acquired that early morning chill of knives before they strike a blow. By way of atonement, and also out of gratitude to her for telling me everything that had happened, I should have given Dina a brief account of the confusing discoveries I had recently made, but I preferred to break in with a question:

'Does this ring mean anything to you?'

Dina looked at it cursorily, with that heavy indifference experts display as they go about their professional work.

'It's the same one that Valenzin was wearing on the night he was killed, isn't it?'

I had recourse to irony.

'Go on – I had no idea you were clairvoyant.'

'I'm not. Valenzin was here before you arrived.' She tried to smile, but her weary grimace became contorted in a spasm of pain. 'He rented a room here with his own telephone line that he seldom used, except to make or receive occasional calls. There were times when he spent hours and hours waiting for his phone to ring. Sometimes he didn't even pick it up, two rings were all he needed as a signal that it was the moment to act.'

I imagined Fabio Valenzin in that tense wait before going into action, as if he were listening to the unsleeping growth of his beard, hearing the gradual change in his heart-beats before the telephone rang, like a shot or a detonation – although Chiara had assured me he was immune to emotion and was sheathed in a cloak of insensitivity. I imagined him stationary in front of his bathroom mirror searching perhaps in the reflection for signs of a transfiguration that would change him into a new man, one who was skilful at love; but perhaps it merely reaffirmed his cynicism, and made him reject the scruples of conscience that were beginning to weaken him, and also made him reject a nascent sentiment that would have thwarted his plans.

'Did he tell you who had given it to him?'

'We didn't say very much to each other,' replied Dina. Her voice was imbued with a sense of tragedy. 'I took him up a cup of coffee. I think he found coffee comforting, and it made waiting more bearable. He thanked me politely, but not effusively – he always used to say just what needed to be said, and reluctantly at that; but that evening he kept me in his room. He seemed sad or depressed, as if he foresaw his own death, and sadness made him talkative, but in a thoughtful way. He had no interest in anything I might say, he just needed me to listen to his monologue.'

Truth is better said when told briefly: garrulity is a kind

of embroidery that acts as a defence and allows us to slip lies through unnoticed. Possibly it is also a medicine that gives us strength when faced with forebodings of menace.

'He was fiddling with that ring as he spoke, it was tight on his finger and he was trying to loosen it. I remember his macabre comment: "It's a good thing I haven't any heirs. They cut off the fingers of the dead in order to remove their rings!" I was not so much surprised by the horrible things he said as by the conviction with which he spoke. He was like a man condemned to death who senses already what will happen after his execution. "Why should we be so ungrateful towards the dead? Why do we behave like vultures in front of a corpse?" he asked me, but he didn't wait for an answer, it was more as if he was hoping for confirmation or agreement. He told me a legend about the death of Giorgione, the Renaissance artist—'

'It isn't a legend,' I interrupted, pedantically. 'There are letters and documents to prove it. Giorgione caught the plague, and was abandoned by his protectors and patrons, all those who had frequently employed him to liven up their entertainments. When they heard he was dead, they sent their servants to his studio to take away the paintings they had commissioned from him, but not one of them bothered to provide him with a decent burial. It is likely that the remains of Giorgione, mixed up with those of thousands of unknowns, were taken to a distant island and incinerated there. But Valenzin was complaining more than he should have done – Gabetti paid for him to have a decent funeral.'

'Possibly he was referring more to what would happen to his belongings,' objected Dina. 'Now he's dead, we're all behaving like vultures, fighting over that chest of his.'

Although the tone of her voice was neutral and distant, I

sensed a reproach implicit in her words. A tentative dawn was breaking, but the light had a sombre quality, and where it settled on the objects in the room it conferred on them a premature old age, like a sort of presentiment of the future, the same presentiment that had affected Fabio Valenzin in his last moments.

'And what else did he say?'

'Nothing else, because the phone rang at that moment.' Dina was beginning to wilt under the tedium that an official interrogation induces. 'He must have been waiting for a secret sign because he listened to the first two rings without moving, at the third ring he seemed uncertain, and was even more so at the fourth – it was obvious that the last ones were more than he had expected, and they were unplanned. He quickly picked up the receiver with a worried look, as if one of his premonitions was coming true. He spoke in monosyllables that expressed consent, but there was nothing in them of the sort of cool determination we expect to hear from a professional. "I'm coming straight away," he said, before hanging up. He had lost his composure, and he didn't even give me any instructions about what to say if someone called him while he was out. Nor, of course, did he tell me where he was going. But now we know he went over to that palace.'

'And he went to his death,' I said, in the same absorbed tone that Dina had used in her account of the events of that night. 'He went unresistingly, as if he was accepting his fate.'

I sat down beside her on her widow's bed, which took my weight without a single groan.

'I remember I felt sorry for him having to go out on such a horrible night,' continued Dina. 'He had only just left the hotel when there was another call, possibly the signal he had been waiting for: two rings, and then silence.'

'Why didn't you go and tell him?'

'He paid me to look after his chest, and to keep a room reserved for him with its own telephone line. It wasn't part of my job to carry messages,' she hastened to reply. 'Besides which, just a little later, you arrived. I'm not so overwhelmed with guests that I can allow myself the luxury of not looking after them!'

I nodded, with a rather shy pride, but then I spoke sharply:

'Nor should you allow yourself the luxury of frightening them with that story of how you murdered your husband – taking advantage of their credulity.' Dina made a tiny gesture of contrition; it was almost a pout. 'I had enough problems on my hands without other people confessing all their sins to me. I'm not a priest by vocation, you know.'

Dina looked at me with a kind of amused remorse, as if she sympathised with me for not wishing to assume the vocation of a priest. Possibly celibacy leaves its mark.

'Honestly, I didn't want to confuse you even more,' she said. There was both modesty and cajolery in her words, a combination designed to compensate for what she had done. 'Maybe I behaved selfishly, I don't know, but I wanted to keep you with me. I wanted you to hear from my lips what, coming from anybody else, would have been twisted. In Venice, nothing circulates more rapidly than scandal and slander.'

Venice had taught me that slanders grow like a cancer – all that is required is a suggestive phrase augmented by an unctuous tone to butter us up and flatter us as we listen. Venice had also taught me that truth is always biased and refutable, since it depends upon the point of view of the person speaking; each person's version of the truth may falsify the facts, or fail to understand them, or distort them to his advantage.

'Don't you think your version of events wasn't already twisted enough? You left out your complicity with Nicolussi. Who can tell me that the two of you didn't plot the death of Valenzin together? Who can tell me you're not acting out a pantomime in order to lead some poor gullible fool like me up the garden path?'

My anger choked me, but it helped to suppress the shivering caused by an excess of excitement and lack of sleep, combined with the damp chill of the morning. I was frightened by the harshness of my own words when I noticed the genuine signs of outrage on Dina's face, the broken skin that the sticking plaster had produced on her wrists and ankles, the swelling that was growing near her eye, and its bruised lid, looking like an obscene eye-shadow. Words are easy weapons to use and they can cause great suffering; they may seem harmless when we speak them, but once spoken, they are penetrating, like darts, and can deeply wound the person we are talking to.

'You're being very unfair, you shouldn't take it out on me,' said Dina, her voice again broken by sobs.

She sat up on the bed in order not to choke, and put her arms around me, infringing the distance that convention requires of celibacy. The touch of her breasts aroused my desire, but it was desire without passion, the desire of a weak and exhausted man, nothing like the indiscriminate lust that had inflamed me when I saw her for the first time. I caressed Dina through the black sweater that oppressed and mortified her breasts, but I did so without strong territorial ambition.

'You can stay here if you like,' she whispered. 'I shall die of fright on my own, remembering what happened.'

I kissed Dina's wounded brow, her swollen eyelid, and the corner of that eye just at the point where the fine lines of age came together, the tiny wrinkles that time was tracing with irrevocable stealth. I kissed the furrows on her forehead, her bruised cheek-bones, and the cheeks themselves that were beginning to lose their firmness; I kissed her lips which tasted of iron or rusted blood, and they parted with a submissive insouciance – if the contradiction is permitted – as if renouncing their normal severity, and I began to move my hands as I quietly kissed her open mouth. Dina had soft and asymmetric breasts, just I had imagined them, trapped inside the sweater, and her nipples were immature, like seeds that have not yet begun to germinate. In silence, I felt them grow more prominent and assume their full shape until, fully erect, they became hard to my touch, while the flesh that sustained them remained soft. I took Dina's breasts in both my hands, trying to ensure my touch was neither harsh nor vicious, but my hands were clumsy, as they continued their exploration, because they retained the memory of another exploration to which they stayed loyal: my hands retained the illusory feel of another, slimmer body, and other, smaller breasts that they had not even succeeded in touching – or had only done so through a window. I mean Chiara's breasts that had shaped her nightdress like the curled pages of an open book. My lips also resisted promiscuity, they preferred to cling to the memory of other lips with their flavour of lipsalve, and their surrender to 'the inscrutable call' of another mouth, its warmth and its delicate taste. I drew back to restore the distance required by celibacy, with that sense of failure that comes from defeat on a battlefield.

'I'm sorry, Dina, I must go, we shouldn't be doing this,' I apologised.

I also felt a sort of advance nostalgia for the loves that I would never consummate, for the women who would reject me or put me off because of my irresolution, for the nights fated to be numerous that I should have to bear in solitude, crushed by the weight of my unscathed flank from which no god had deigned to extract a rib.

'What's the matter?'

'Nothing. It might just be true that I have the vocation to be a priest.'

The act of moving set up the burning pain in my wounds all over again, adding to the aches in my tired body that were beginning to impose their own tyranny. But my physical pains merely replicated another pain which was, if anything, more humiliating.

'Tomorrow, the police will be here to check over the hotel,' Dina warned me. Words are easy weapons to use, and they can cause great suffering, as hers now did. 'I think I shall tell them it was you who took the chest.'

Dina's skirt had ridden up. Her thighs grew progressively fatter up to the level of her groin, where they rubbed against each other, and I guessed that in that area their texture of warm dough would give way to a more abraded consistency.

'I deserve that for getting involved in matters that are none of my business,' I said, as I left the room.

'In Venice, catastrophes do not actually occur, life hangs by a thread, defying the laws of physics, and it is the threat of what might happen, but doesn't, that makes us anxious and apprehensive,' Chiara had told me, comparing the theme of *The Tempest* with the customs that rule the way the city functions, a city that exists as if estranged from the real world, having turned its back on reason and logic. Anxiety and apprehension were the sensations that assailed me when I pushed open the door of my room, although it would be more appropriate to call it the room Dina had assigned to me, because so far I had not spent a single night in it. I felt anxiety and apprehension on seeing my reflection in the mirror over the wash-basin, the small, blurred mirror that had lost its silvering, and which perhaps only registered the movements of dead men. I felt anxiety and apprehension as I approached the window, confronting once again the palace guarded by Tedeschi and, a little way off, the bell tower of San Stefano, leaning to the right like a lighthouse yielding to the surf breaking round it. I felt anxiety and apprehension as I recognised my luggage on the bed, still unpacked, my clothing meticulously tidy and folded with the care that we unmarried men devote to our belongings. It was the same kind of anxiety and apprehension that we feel when we enter a room where somebody has died, and we discover the immobility of objects lying where their owner had placed them moments before he expired. My clothing had stiffened with the cold, as if starched by the dampness that made it rough to the touch and unpleasant to wear, as if the two nights it had lain there had been enough to make it lose its pliancy, and turn it into funeral shrouds. In order to rid myself of these thoughts I pretended that those nights had not really happened, and were the emanations of a nightmare that had occurred only in my mind. It was a shortlived pretence – although convincing – because in Venice time is suspended, it slows down, and turns into a flexible substance, like dreams.

Even the sheets on the bed had the feel of shrouds, or of snow, an icy harshness that diminished as they gradually absorbed the warmth of my body. The weight of her breasts, which would never be offered to me again, remained on my hands like two palpitating hearts, breasts I had rejected out of a sense of loyalty that now seemed pointless. If there is one thing that typifies the celibate male it is this ascetic attitude towards love – all celibates harbour a delayed adolescence – an attitude that makes us sublimate what should be regarded as a purely physiological experience. It was even more hurtful to realise that this sublimation did not exempt me from physiological urges: I continued to have erections with considerable frequency, and had either to relieve them or repress them, on my own, and this can become a torment after a certain age. I have always envied men who confront love as nothing more than the conjunction of two bodies that compromises no one, and is indulged in with impunity: a mere sequence of incidents that neither impacts on their feelings nor produces lasting pangs of conscience. Possibly because I am excessively sensitive, possibly because I do suffer from conflicts of conscience, I persist in having a guilt-ridden conception of love which leads me to joyless abnegation and perpetual discomfort. I turned to lie face down on the bed, which was at last beginning to lose its feel of a mortuary shroud, in order to repress the advent of possible erections, and also to help the healing process of the cuts decorating my back, which were still bleeding. I gripped Valenzin's ring in my hand, already beginning to attribute to it the virtues of an amulet. *Moriatur anima mea cum philistiim*, pleaded its inscription.

Sounds continued to penetrate through the ceiling: I listened to Dina washing, the squeaking taps, and the thunderous noise of the cistern. I also listened to her comfortless fidgeting on the bed – the mattress betrayed the restlessness caused by her insomnia – and my heightened sense of hearing, bolstered by the silence of the night, increased my sense of abandonment and loneliness, which were not just fleeting impressions but symptoms of a sentence against which there was no appeal. The break-in at the Accademia by the unknown men, my dialectic discussion with Gabetti, Chiara's ambiguous duplicity, Giovanna Zanon's veiled insinuations, the presence everywhere of a murderer lying in wait concealed behind a mask, the possession of a chest that refused to divulge its contents, the accumulation of partial and hideous revelations which had jolted me during the day, now surged around me, weaving a web of deep disquiet. I reckoned that my only hope of salvation lay in unconsciousness, that restful sleep would interpose a beneficent interval and provide protection in the midst of so many uncertainties.

I was wrong. My sleep was racked by incoherent visions that added to my uneasiness – but maybe all dreams suffer from incoherence, and it is only the ramblings of the dreamer that confer on them the impression of intelligibility. I had a chaotic vision of the landscape of *The Tempest*, but deserted by its figures and swept by the storm that broods over it in the picture; I sensed the clean smell of earth that has just been drenched with rain and the arborescent murmur of the undergrowth growing amid the canopy of water, a murmur that had something of a muffled panting or wheezing, a murmur that had the rhythm of a broken bellows, getting louder as I approached the place occupied by the woman in Giorgione's painting, to the right of the stream. There, hidden behind a bush, and crumpled up, lay the piece of linen cloth that had served the woman as a cloak, mitigating the blatant spectacle of her nakedness and serving also as a mat to lessen the scratchiness of the grass beneath her. I bent down to pick up this cloth, which was stiff to the touch, and listened to the small crackling noise it made in my hands, much like the scrunching sound of snow when it is trodden down, much like the violation of a virgin or the abuse of an innocent person. Then I discovered, in the centre of the cloth, a bloodstain of sinuous shape, a stain that was still warm and that soiled my hands and offended my eyes. I emerged from the dream, as if from the viscous mud of a swamp.

'Calm down, Ballesteros, don't be alarmed.'

I recognised Inspector Nicolussi's voice, corroded by nicotine, and far too southern in its accent for a Venetian of pure stock. He must have been watching me secretly as I dreamed, or working out how to wake me, because he had pulled a chair up near the head of the bed, and was lolling back on it while drawing avidly on a cigarette. My eyes were stinging, not so much because of the smoke, as from the crimson stain I had been dreaming of, and that still obscured my vision. I could just hear the sound of the police search being conducted in the adjoining rooms, or more correctly, the sham search. Nicolussi fingered his villainous beard, which he had most probably shaved just a few hours earlier but which had already grown through again.

'Dina has already told me about your exploits,' he said. He lit a new cigarette from the almost extinct tip of the old one, but this activity did not prevent him from continuing his scrutiny: he watched me carefully through the smoke of the cigarette, reluctant even to blink, because this risked stimulating the secretion of his tear-ducts. 'I'll give you five minutes to tell me where you've hidden Fabio Valenzin's chest. Don't even think of playing games with me, because I warn you I'm not in the mood for them.'

As he sat back in his chair, I glimpsed the butt of a pistol tucked under his armpit; his raincoat seemed prematurely aged by late nights, and it deserved early retirement. Nicolussi had spoken with pontifical equanimity; he pronounced his ultimatum as if he was merely commenting on some minor detail to do with the weather, but I knew that his equanimity was false, that Nicolussi was a man worn down by perversions of justice. One of his subordinates came into the room, a recently recruited youngster who would probably have been capable of confusing a police search with a chamois hunt in the mountains.

'We haven't found anything suspicious, sir,' he announced. 'Is there anything else you want us to do?'

'Wait for me downstairs, both of you, I'll join you in a minute,' said Nicolussi. When the youngster had gone, he informed me bluntly: 'Look, Ballesteros, I shouldn't like to spoil your holiday, and I know that tourists like you love the Venetian Carnival, so don't make me lock you up.'

A dim light, slowly growing stronger, came through the window, lapped the walls, and faded as it reached the germ-ridden wash-basin. The sepulchral silence of Venice was broken by a confused babble from the crowds gathered in St Mark's Square, and it even spread through the districts that were most resistant to civilisation. I imagined Valenzin's murderer disguised amongst the multitude of tourists, passing unnoticed in the motley collection of costumes and the fearless anonymity of the masks, mingling his breath with that of others which would involuntarily lend him both complicity and approval. In order to frighten off this vision, I said:

'Do you mean lock me up, and then have to let me out again because there is no evidence against me, as you had to do with Tedeschi? Bear in mind that, legally, that chest does not even exist.'

Nicolussi continued to affect self-assurance, but he began to rock backwards and forwards on his chair.

'I repeat that I am not prepared to put up with your games.'

'Nor are you in a position to insist on anything from anybody,' I replied. I was irritated, and my manner was curt. 'If you want to arrest me, I shall insist on being brought before a judge, and I shall tell him all about your colluding with Dina.'

'You don't know anything,' he muttered. He had, how-ever, changed countenance, and only his villainous beard and the smoke from his cigarette hid his anxiety. 'Don't talk nonsense.'

'I don't know much, and there are certain matters I prefer not to be involved in – everybody has to consider their own conscience – but all the same, I do know some things. You fell in love with Dina and committed various offences that it would be better not to have brought out into the open.' I was scared by the sound of my own voice; it was cold and smug, as if I was in the habit of blackmailing. 'You concealed evidence following the murder of her husband; and for all I know you may have helped her do it.'

Nicolussi expelled a mouthful of smoke from the corners of his mouth, puffing his cheeks out until he looked like a boiler about to explode. The smoke hung in the air, masking the gleam of his eyes. The smoke of a cigarette conceals an infection of the eyes in the way that death by suffocation conceals a death by poisoning, or that snow conceals the obscenity of spilled blood. Dina had come timidly into the room; she was bringing me a breakfast tray that would save me from starvation – the hospitable smell of fried eggs filled me with delight.

'Why did you tell him?' asked Nicolussi, turning to her for an explanation, with a severity that for a moment gave the lie to the power that Dina wielded over him. 'Does a foreigner you hardly know qualify for that sort of confidence?'

Dina had put a dressing on her injured brow; to the discolouration of the swelling were added black rings under her eyes which heightened the sadness of the expression on her face.

'She didn't tell me anything,' I intervened, as Dina looked flustered. 'I overheard a conversation between you two quite by chance. It was yesterday morning before the funeral on San Michele. I had come to pick up my luggage, but curiosity got the better of me, and, instead, I took Valenzin's chest. A thoroughly awkward object it is too, and there's no way of opening it.'

When Dina leaned down to place the tray on my recumbent body, I recognised with mixed feelings of pity, and of loss, the marks which the sticking plaster had left on her wrists, like manacles of an unmerited slavery. I also recognised the softness of her breasts in spite of the sweater constricting them. The sense of loss at that moment became keener, but my pity now changed direction: I felt sorry for myself.

'What you mean is you've not been able to open it,' Nicolussi corrected me, tetchily. He was losing his composure. 'If you hadn't got yourself involved in what doesn't concern you, by this time we should probably know what is in it.'

I wanted to smile, but I found his pigheadedness discouraging, and my smile came over as a sort of tired grimace.

'Please, Nicolussi, don't talk nonsense. If I hadn't got involved with what doesn't concern me, the chest would now be in the hands of that ghastly creature who came here to the hotel. By this time the bird would have flown for ever. Thanks to me we can still get it back.'

The inspector stood up, staggering under the weight of a guilty conscience. The light from the street glanced across his face; it made it shine and become almost transparent.

'You haven't got some kind of dirty trick in mind, have you?'

This time I did smile, with involuntary pride.

'It's funny to hear those words from your mouth. You insist on me being honest, and all you offer in return is hypocrisy. Don't you think you lack the moral authority to be so particular at this stage in the game?' I paused so that he could digest my remonstrance. 'I'm not proposing any dirty trick, although I don't understand why you should have any objection in view of what you've done in the past. All I ask is that my collaboration with you should remain anonymous, I don't want my name to appear in any judicial proceedings, nor do I want to submit to any more interrogations, nor do I want to appear as a witness in a court of law.'

'But it would be highly irregular for me to accept those conditions,' he said.

'You've accepted much more serious irregularities than those, so stop quibbling,' I interrupted. 'You've concealed evidence and covered up crimes. I understand that the motives that have led you to pervert justice are powerful ones, even praiseworthy, I understand that you put your own feelings before your professional obligations, and I understand that you want to keep Dina safely out of it. In your place I would do the same. But don't give me that rubbish and don't play the martyr. I shall hand over the chest to you provided you keep me out of your investigations.'

I stopped speaking, with the slightly shameful feeling of having lied, if only by omission. As time went on I grew more convinced that the contents of Valenzin's chest were trivial and unenlightening, almost certainly dirty shirts and soiled underpants. I was also convinced that the daring shown by the murderer in attempting to recover it was not so much the result of his desire to destroy every clue that might incriminate him, as of that urge to clean things up which comes over criminals after they have committed a crime, and which impels them to go back over the scene in order to eliminate all traces of their presence there, and even the smell of their breath; it is an urge that torments

them, unsettles them, and eventually brings them to justice.

'What Alejandro is asking for is only fair,' said Dina, before
Nicolussi could reply.

She had called me by my first name, to the embarrassment of
the inspector who looked at me with undaunted consternation
– if the contradiction may be permitted – in the way a husband
who has acquiesced in his wife's adultery must look at the lovers
who visit her without making a secret of it in his presence. A
blush suffused my face.

'The best thing would be for you to think it over while I
eat my breakfast and clean myself up a bit,' I said, trying to
ensure that my concession would not sound either overbearing
or peremptory.

'He will think about it,' affirmed Dina, taking Nicolussi by
the arm and leading him to the door of the room.

As soon as I was alone I got down to my breakfast with
a greed that would have looked indecent if I had been eating
in public. I listened to their footsteps as they went along the
corridor and up the stairs. Those of Nicolussi were soft and
stealthy, while the tapping of Dina's heels was decisive and
confident. Although I was unable to catch any of their words,
the different timbres of their voices allowed me to guess at
the sense of what each was saying. Nicolussi soliloquised as
he explained his reluctance; and Dina interrupted him from
time to time with concise comments designed to weaken
that reluctance. Although brief, her comments undermined
his hesitation. As I tried to get out of bed my side pressed
down on Fabio Valenzin's ring, leaving an imprint of its seal.
While the skin quickly recovered its normal smoothness –
hardly a second, just as long as the wind takes to obliterate a
message written in sand – I remembered that Dina knew of its

existence. I was alarmed that she might mention it to Nicolussi, and that this would be enough to excite his curiosity and start further investigations. I felt alarmed that in the course of these investigations he might succeed in worming out of me the links I had established between the ring and Valenzin's murder, links that could only be explained by reference to Giorgione's painting.

I showered in the hotel's communal bathroom with unusual deliberation – the sensual feel of water is at odds with celibacy – and the noise of the water heater almost sent me off to sleep. As I have a propensity for allegories, I was determined to believe that bodily hygiene would wash away more intimate forms of impurity. The steam condensed on the tiled walls of the bathroom like a flowering of improper thoughts. The photographs of Chiara posing in the nude for Fabio Valenzin in the same position as the woman in *The Tempest* still remained in my memory, just as the inscrutable call of her lovely mouth remained on my lips, and the fleeting touch of her shoulder, the mute contact with her stomach, and the nubile feel of her breasts remained on the tips of my fingers. I turned the taps off sharply, before the steam asphyxiated me. As I have a propensity for allegories, I was determined to believe that by switching off the rush of water I would also be fending off the compulsion of desire. But desire does not admit the existence of floodgates.

'It's a deal, Ballesteros. You hand over the chest and I'll leave you in peace.'

Nicolussi's presence there made me jump. He had overcome his hesitations, and now leaned against the bathroom door, as if protecting my chastity. A gust of warm air blew through the passage. I used the towel to cover my back which bore all the scars of my brawl.

'On one condition,' he added, diverting his glance from my private parts, either from modesty or from pity. 'You will leave Venice as soon as possible. It would be very difficult to keep the journalists off your back.'

'Don't worry, there is nothing to keep me in this city.'

It was a lie in the worst possible taste: Venice held me in too many bonds, she had engulfed me in a web of dubious intrigues, the solution to which required my presence, as well as having provided me with the – possibly even more doubtful or pernicious – gift of love, and the stark evidence of my loneliness. I shut myself in my room to complete my washing and dressing, which I did with exasperating slowness, like those actresses who rejoice in perfecting their appearance while a host of admirers prowl outside their dressing rooms, waiting for the opportunity to pounce on them. The mirror over the wash-basin showed me the face of a man back from the dead while my razor removed my beard. Nicolussi protested:

'Hurry up, we haven't got all morning.'

He preceded me down to the lobby, swaying like an Atlas who plans a period of idleness because he is tired of being the bearer of so many sins, both his own and other people's. Dina had descended before us and was helping the young policemen Nicolussi had brought with him, as his acolytes in that pretend search, to pass the time. They were two big lads in uniform, impenetrably thick, and they responded in monosyllables to Dina's vague remarks. The approach of their superior officer triggered an expectant obedience, which Nicolussi took it upon himself to frustrate.

'You two stay here on guard. Ring the station to ask them to relieve you in about six or seven hours.'

No doubt they had joined the police force in order to exercise their active and acrobatic adolescent bodies, and the command that condemned them to a sedentary job produced a drop in morale. Although Nicolussi gave them their instructions in a formal but listless manner, there could be detected in the tone of his voice the anxiety of a man reluctant to delegate, the unrelieved and unremitting affliction of a man secretly in love. Dina and Nicolussi hardly looked at each other, or they did so only quickly – long practice having taught them how to hide their secret. As soon as we were in the little square I raised my eyes and looked at the façade of the palace opposite, hoping to detect the watchful shadow of Tedeschi in one of the windows. I said to Nicolussi:

'Don't be surprised if the chest is empty. I rather think Valenzin was killed for something he failed to do.'

When I jumped over the yellow tape that cordoned off the palace and pushed the door open, Nicolussi clicked his tongue.

'Why didn't I think of this before,' he muttered, reprovingly.

'Don't blame yourself. More or less the same happens to all of us: we lose something and carry on looking for it in the most unlikely places, until in the end it turns up under our very noses.'

The pigeons beat their wings in the silence, and then clustered together near the smooth ceiling, knocking flakes off the frescoes painted by a follower of Tiepolo with their flapping. Nicolussi raised his hand to his armpit where his pistol was concealed.

'And you left the chest all this time without protection?'

The pigeon shit crunched under our feet like ancient flaky pastry.

'Tedeschi made himself responsible for guarding it – he would make a good goalkeeper,' I said with a degree of pomposity so that Nicolussi might appreciate my prudence. 'And he's armed with a carbine that must have belonged to Garibaldi at least, ready for any man who goes near him,' I joked, but Nicolussi refused to make any concession to humour. He held his pistol up in both hands and pointed it at the mirrors that had given up their reflective function.

'Tedeschi, don't be alarmed, it's only me!' My voice resounded in the spiral vault of the staircase, and echoed through the *piano nobile* like a guest trying out the hospitality of each room. Nicolussi resorted to sarcasm.

'It looks to me as if your pal isn't answering.' He cocked his gun and elbowed me aside. 'Let me go first.'

The palace had not lost its air of an abandoned barracks that the darkness instilled. I walked almost on tiptoe, imitating Nicolussi's sideways movement; we breathed in unison, suffering from the same nervousness and the same hoarseness – although I did not smoke. I missed the excremental odours that emanated from Tedeschi.

'The bird has flown,' said Nicolussi, replacing the pistol in its holster. Fury eroded by depression pervaded his face. 'Next time I recommend you be more careful in your choice of friends.'

The room that Tedeschi had been using as his sanctum or headquarters displayed the same air of desolation as a temple bereft of its idols. I was sorry to think that he had betrayed me.

'You don't think they've killed him, as they killed Valenzin?'

'Oh yes, my friend, yes, I do!' he assented, thoroughly irritated. 'And after killing him they cut him up into little pieces, shoved these in the chest, and threw it in the canal. Don't delude yourself, Ballesteros. Tedeschi has made off with the loot!'

NINE

'It is generally assumed that we are guided by notions of impartiality,' said Inspector Nicolussi with weary irony. He spoke as if he were trying to invoke another man, one who had existed before he did, very remote and already extinct, but whose spirit, nevertheless, still lived within his body. I was not sure that I wanted to listen to this exercise in retrospection, but neither could I refuse to do so; besides which, it was too late to get out of it. Nicolussi strung his words together as if articulating a prayer. 'It is generally assumed that in our job we have to keep our personal feelings under strict control, never mind that our baser passions can run riot, our feelings mustn't be allowed to appear. Corrupt practices are permitted provided they don't prejudice the appearance of integrity; the odd negligence is tolerated, provided it doesn't leak out. Occasionally even, negligence and corruption are encouraged by the powers that be in order that the corporate spirit doesn't weaken. But we must never show fear, and vacillation is unacceptable in our code of conduct. If any one of us shows a tendency to pity, he loses face, and suffers forever after the stigma of being soft.' Nicolussi fell silent, a victim of his own introspection, or maybe owing to an attack of amnesia. When he recommenced his monologue, he sounded like an orator bored with his own discourse. 'I cut my teeth as a policeman in Naples; I did well on the promotion ladder because I had the sense to observe impartiality and to indulge my baser passions without ever letting personal feelings get the better of me. That's the only way you can survive in the south. The man who doesn't know how to switch from one side to another ends up mad, or dumped in a ditch with a bullet in his head. Year after year I put in for a transfer to Venice while I stacked up merit awards, and scars. They send you to this city when they think they've squeezed all they can out of you. It's the dubious reward kept for those who need a rest cure or early retirement. It's only when they see you've learned all you can, or you're dropping with fatigue, when they sense you're beginning to lose your touch, that they send you here. Our work in Venice is more ornamental than practical: we shepherd the tourists around, deal with minor complaints, police the more important sites and buildings, deport beggars and vagrants, either refuse or grant visas and resident permits to international crooks, according to how much money their illicit activities are likely to bring in . . .' His voice had become cynical, or sad – or cynically sad – and I allowed myself a smile at what sounded like hyperbole. 'No, I mean it, there are unwritten rules that advise us to go easy with certain criminals, and to turn a blind eye to behaviour which is unorthodox, if that behaviour contributes to the prosperity of Venice. The locals don't usually give us any trouble. Like all species that risk becoming extinct, they make efforts to preserve their way of life, and the preferred way of life of the Venetians is one of prudence and secrecy. They survive inside the last defensive barrier of habits that have not been touched by the floods of tourists; they have dug in against the world outside. It's very different in Mestre, on *terra ferma*, which starts at the other end of the Ponte della Libertà. There, life still goes on in accordance with rules that are much less peaceable. Over there they still kill, rob, and rape each other, but Mestre is outside my jurisdiction. The Venetians have given up crime, at least in its more spontaneous forms; their instinct for self-preservation advises them not to break the laws,' he said. (But only in its more spontaneous forms, I thought to myself. In Venice, crime circulates through underground channels, like molten lava that distributes its heat to every individual, although it measures the dosage it bestows on each.)

'On the other hand, our conduct is always governed by the same principle: it is important to hush up the consequences of crime, it is important not to let scandal upset the vegetable-like pace of life of this city and its inhabitants because, among other reasons, a scandal would frighten the tourists away. I had only recently arrived here when Dina murdered her husband, but I'd had enough time to assimilate the principle. I had to try to ensure that, without going beyond the strict rules of impartiality, my investigations wouldn't cause a fuss – outside the strictly domestic fuss that occurs in Venice when somebody behaves indiscreetly.' Nicolussi must have considered me a receptive listener, because he went on: 'But I hadn't counted on the fact that I'd gone soft. I trusted to my long experience, and the habits I had acquired after many years in the job: impartiality needs a clinical and professional approach with those found guilty, but I broke that rule. Dina's distress disturbed me very much, and I came to believe I shared the motives for her action; I gave in to feelings of pity once I found out about the hellish life she had been living. For the first time in my career I allowed my personal feelings to surface – not neutrality or the baser passions – and I wanted to save her from a punishment she didn't deserve.' There was no longer any trace of cynicism in his admissions, just pain, mixed with spasmodic symptoms of nostalgia. He also had had no difficulty in imagining Dina, her eyes swollen through lack of sleep — to have shut them would have mitigated the intensity of the horror — as she recalled the sordid touch of hands squeezing her breasts, the pain of his teeth biting her nipples, and the slimy feel of a phallus retracting after having injected its poison. 'I began by understanding her misfortune, and then I fell in love with her without any hope that it would lead anywhere or be reciprocated; it was a love that couldn't even be declared — any outside observer would have called it chicanery. I changed the circumstances of the crime, concealed evidence, supplanted the negligence of the judges, and succeeded in having her sentence reduced. I had gone soft.'

He fell silent; the quiet was broken only by his cough. Whenever he stopped smoking, even for a minute, he suffered from discomfort in his chest which reminded him of his dependence on it. He had invited me to lunch in a *trattoria* in the Dorsoduro district, very near the Zattere waterfront, from which Giudecca island could be seen through the banks of fog that had attained the consistency of a fine spider's web. The blurred outline of its shores resembled the silhouette of a hunchback whale drifting on the surface of the water, pestered by seagulls feeding on its flesh. We had penetrated deeply into Dorsoduro, fleeing the bogus farrago that discredits the area round St Mark's and the shoddy artificiality that had taken hold of the city since the beginning of Carnival. I remembered Tedeschi with a twinge of nostalgia, because he loathed tourists and hailed them with derision; but Tedeschi had let me down — he had ceased to be the dragon guarding the treasure in the old stories, and had reverted to being the thief that he really was at heart.

'Don't worry about it, Nicolussi,' I said. I was beginning to feel a shameless desire to reciprocate his confidences and to share with him the secrets that were quietly languishing in the recesses of my soul. 'Who hasn't overstepped the bounds of neutrality from time to time?'

The doctor examining a patient who suddenly finds himself lustfully caressing her oversteps the mark; the priest listening to the confession of one of his women parishioners and who derives a pleasure equal to her own from the account of her sins oversteps the mark; the lecturer who pays particular attention to his girl students and breathes in the enticing odours of their youthful bodies oversteps the mark. I had never overstepped it because I was only an assistant lecturer and did not give tutorials – except when I stood in for Professor Mendoza – or, at least, I had only done so in my imagination.

'How can I not worry about it?' Nicolussi replied, introducing new difficulties. 'For more than five years I have had to live with the same conviction: I love a woman, but my love is forbidden. I ought to get out of this rotten city.'

He stroked his beard with its bristles like porcupine quills, as if he were trying to rub it out, or make it more pliant.

'You should do that, Nicolussi,' I advised him, with the ease that comes from being a stranger. 'Put in for a transfer, or look for other work a long way from here, and take Dina with you.'

He pursed his lips in a way that expressed either depression or resignation. In that moment I felt a strong feeling of solidarity with him, because I understood that he was a coward, that celibacy had eaten away his capacity for resolute action and had tarred him with defeatism.

Half a dozen gondolas paraded in line along the Giudecca Canal. They were packed with Japanese huddled together on the plush seats, and all of them were listening with identical rapture – a rapture as identical as their features – to one of the gondoliers who was singing barcarolles and romantic melodies in a voice like an out of tune gramophone. Mercifully, the fog swallowed them up before this display of bad taste made me sick.

'I think I ought to tell you a few things as well,' I muttered. 'After what has happened I owe you an explanation.'

Tedeschi's desertion had made me feel more vulnerable and had demolished some of my certainties, the very few I had. Inspector Nicolussi had issued an order for his search and apprehension, but not knowing of any abode or residence other than the palace that he was responsible for guarding, the likelihood of recovering the chest was small, and depended upon luck. They were trawling the sordid brothels – in which Tedeschi had given evidence of his sexual feats – and they had enquired amongst those fishing villages that still survived on the islands in the lagoon, but all they discovered about Tedeschi was out of date or contradictory.

'Go ahead, I'm all ears,' he said, encouragingly. 'The only thing I'm sorry about is that you had to choose Tedeschi to confide in. By now, the bastard will have fenced the goods in the chest.'

'The fact is, according to my theory, there aren't any goods of value in the chest.'

The waterfront path of the Zattere was covered with seagulls that stood motionless in the fog like testimonials to a taxidermist. Taking delight in these preliminaries, I gave Nicolussi the ring we had rescued from the canal and related a plausible sequence of events from the time when Valenzin contracted to steal *The Tempest* for a purchaser who sealed the agreement by making him a gift of this item of jewellery, until it culminated with his murder, as a consequence of Valenzin having failed to keep his side of the bargain. Nor did I leave out the later break-in at the Accademia: Valenzin's disappointed client would have sent his hirelings to finish off the job, but they did it clumsily, in spite of the fact that Gabetti had made it easy for them that evening by giving the museum caretakers the night off, in a display of magnanimity.

'Look up the origin of the design and the inscription on the ring in a dictionary of artistic motifs, and you'll have solved the case,' I prophesied, with an optimisim of which I now feel ashamed. 'Alternatively, look for a very muscular individual with filthy hair and one ear with the lobe bitten off. I bet you whatever you like that he, or his pal, is the ghastly creature who hides behind the plague doctor mask, the same man who killed Valenzin and ransacked the Albergo Cusmano looking for the chest.'

Nicolussi turned the ring over in his hand, held it up to the thin light that filtered through the fog, and with difficulty read Samson's posthumous device: *Moriatur anima mea cum philistiim*. Having examined it carefully he threw it contemptuously on to the table, as if it were an object of no value. The scraping of a match added to the harshness of his scepticism:

'What doesn't seem to me to square is that Valenzin, who was such a skilful thief, wasn't able to steal *The Tempest*. You've told me yourself how inadequate the safety measures were at the Accademia.'

'It is probable that he could have stolen it, but didn't want to,' I said. 'Suppose he suddenly developed moral scruples?'

I was certain Valenzin had found a reflection of his own life in *The Tempest* – possibly, like me, he had a propensity for allegories – an artistic representation that reproduced his

227

own anxieties. You cannot maintain an unbalanced relationship indefinitely, however much you persevere in it. Possibly, out of loyalty to Chiara, Fabio Valenzin had given up the idea of the crime.

'Moral scruples?' Nicolussi savoured with intense satisfaction the first puff of his cigarette, as if it were a breathing aid. 'A man like Valenzin who moves on to forgery after failing as an original artist has no moral sense. I see him more likely as a man suffering from feelings of persecution: he saw himself as a true artist, but one who was misunderstood and reviled by an ignorant public that failed to recognise his qualities at the right time, and banished him to an underworld of crime.' The smoke he blew out was permeated and laden with harmful substances after sifting its way through his bronchial tubes. 'Moreover, I don't believe he even realised he was a criminal. Obviously, he knew that what he was doing was against the law, but no more serious than avoiding income tax. Who is going to give up this type of shady work when he knows how to do it and how to take all the necessary precautions? Forging paintings or trafficking in works of art, in his peculiar way of looking at things, were offences from an academic point of view, but not serious ones, given that they didn't harm anybody. Valenzin didn't extort money from the weak, didn't dispossess the poor, and was neither a blackmailer nor a *mafioso*. I very much doubt whether he allowed himself to be distracted by moral scruples.'

Nicolussi rummaged in his wallet, and took out some old, used banknotes that had lost the sinuous indentations of newly engraved paper and would have seemed too honest for Valenzin, who would have rejected them in his transactions. He paid for our meal, and stood up as if suddenly impelled by a decision that allowed no delay.

'I'm going to show you something that will interest you.'

I followed him docilely down to the Zattere landing-stage. The movement of the waters of the canal expired on the steps of the Church of the Gesuati with little splashes that favoured the growth of green scum and the proliferation of mussels on the marble. The façade of the church looked like a gigantic and remarkably symmetrical reef of white coral in the midst of the fog. The landing-stage swayed like a buoy from the waves that dashed against it.

'I was surprised to know you hadn't heard of Fabio Valenzin,' said Nicolussi, his eyes fixed on the western extremity of the Giudecca. There I saw a huge building made of reddish brick, in a style which was halfway between Gothic and that of a factory, and seemed to me daunting. 'An art expert like you should know all the most famous forgers.'

'It's not a subject they teach us in the university,' I said, apologetically. 'I know about the Hungarian Elmyr de Hory from the film Orson Welles made about him, and a Dutchman who forged Vermeers, back in the Forties.'

'Hans van Meegeren.' Nicolussi surprised me with this unexpected display of erudition. 'They caught both of them. They were both clever, but pride led them to make simple mistakes. Hory allowed himself to be ripped off by a couple of blackmailing young lads. They forced him to work like a Stakhanovite, and on one occasion he was so rushed that when he signed a forgery of a Matisse painting, he left out the final "e", and that was his downfall. Van Meegeren was even more audacious: he used the faces of Rudolf Valentino and Greta Garbo as models in his Vermeer forgeries.'

A *vaporetto* drew near, its lights on full, like a nocturnal animal prowling round the coasts of a lost continent.

'You're an expert on the subject.'

'Nonsense,' said Nicolussi, with calculated humility. 'I've read it up, that's all. And do you know why bunglers like Hory and van Meegeren are more famous than Valenzin? It's because they were found out, and the scandal that followed their prosecution exaggerated their talents. But there was no way Valenzin was going to be caught out, in spite of the fact that there are techniques available today that hadn't been invented in the immediate post-war period: the carbon-14 test, infra-red rays, refraction indices, and so on. Anyway, you know all about those.'

'Oh yes, the technical advances,' I agreed, not to appear unworthy of his specialist knowledge, although I was more worried about where we were going. The *vaporetto* stopped at the landing-stage to pick us up. 'Tell me, Nicolussi, what on earth is it you want to show me?'

Facing the Giudecca, which was embalmed in a milky aura, Venice witnessed, as in a mirror, its own decay. Apart from a few churches designed by Andrea Palladio, the character of the island was artisanal and proletarian, with big apartment blocks, their balconies turned into clothes-lines, bedecked with fluttering *blousons*, pinafores, and blue-cotton overalls. There was a reversion to his customary vigour in Nicolussi's expression.

'Don't worry, Ballesteros, you'll soon see. We're going to the Stucky Mill. It used to be a flour mill but went bankrupt many years ago, putting a lot of people out of work – Dina's parents, for instance.' He was silent for a moment, out of respect for them, or, possibly, reminded of the woman he loved. 'Do you see that big building at the end? That's where we're going.'

Left to decay, and besieged by the water like a derelict ship, with its dimensions of a Kafkaesque castle the Stucky Mill was awesome. The red brick was tinged with grey from the fog, making it look even more lugubrious, and it was surmounted by a tower, seven floors high, bristling with broken windows, sombre like a fortress that the Marquis de Sade might well have hired as a place to perpetrate his tortures.

'Interpol was on his track for a few years, but the most they achieved was to prove him guilty of some minor illegality – a false visa or passport, or some such thing.' I was scarcely listening to Nicolussi; I was shaken by that architectural monstrosity. 'There were allegations that he was a forger, but Valenzin and his intermediaries deployed a multiplicity of pseudonyms which enabled him to hide his true identity.'

'You knew who he was, Nicolussi,' I interrupted, with some irritation. 'You knew his identity, and all about his dealings, so you could have brought him to trial.'

The *vaporetto* made several stops before reaching the Sacca Fisola mooring-point at the foot of the Stucky Mill. Local children of the Giudecca were fishing for flounders in the shadow of its façade, as carefree as the birds or the lilies of the field.

'I've already told you that a crook who brings in foreign exchange is untouchable in Venice.' He was leaning against the side of the boat, lost in contemplation of the foam that the *vaporetto* was churning up. 'Besides which, you need witnesses who would have actually seen him working on his forgeries, and handing them over to his clients. And what can you say about those clients? There isn't one who would sacrifice his anonymity by admitting he had bought such and such a picture from Valenzin in order to claim a tax exemption benefit. Not to mention the museums or public institutions that must have paid a fortune for their forgeries. Do you believe they would have the face to admit it? And those rich families who have invested vast sums of money, do you believe they would own up to the swindle, and reveal the fact that their investment was a dead loss? Art forgeries are like share values on the stock market: just as long as the conspiracy of silence is maintained, prices stay high. There are too many interlocking interests at stake to allow the conspiracy to break down. Just imagine Valenzin appearing before a tribunal and offloading his guilt on the dealers who had helped to sell his work, or on the experts who had authenticated his forgeries, or on the museums that had bought them . . . It would have been total chaos.'

The *vaporetto* tied up at last, near the mouth of a canal, which poured out an oily, foul-smelling liquid combining putrefaction with the stench of burned petrol fumes. Stucky Mill had been built towards the end of the nineteenth century by a German businessman in the style of a Neo-gothic vision of hell. Although it now stood empty, the moans of the souls it had ground down still seemed to emanate through its walls. Nicolussi took advantage of a gap in the wire fence that surrounded it to enter a yard thick with rubble and undergrowth. There were rats as big as cats, mating and coupling in the rubbish, giving each other deep bites in the excitement of orgasm. I suppressed my revulsion.

'We were following Valenzin's movements for some months,' said Nicolussi. Less squeamish than I, he kicked the rats aside, disrupting their copulations. 'But it wasn't until after he died that we discovered his laboratory.'

'Laboratory? What laboratory?'

We had reached one of the side walls of the factory, and Nicolussi pushed open a door that gave access to a basement. A very steep staircase, which could have been taken from a painting by Chirico, descended into the darkness below.

'Go down and find out for yourself.'

The low passage leading down to the basement obliged us to bend almost double so that the tops of our heads would not feel the thin breath of the bats hanging from the ceiling above us. They had chosen this place to shelter because it was as hot as an oven. I expressed surprise.

'I would have expected it to be much damper.'

'Valenzin had everything worked out: electric light, and heating whenever he needed it in order to speed up the drying process.'

Nicolussi found a switch, and a series of halogen lights came on, with a brilliance sufficient to light up a stadium. The bats squeaked in unison, and shimmered above our heads in a swarm of papery wings, jostling each other in their attempts to get out. A tank of diesel oil provided the fuel for a number of heaters that gave out a searing heat. In the middle of this crypt there were a couple of easels set up with a board on one and a canvas on the other. I could just make out that they were two not very good paintings of the *cinquecento*, the surfaces of which were smeared with a grease I could not identify. On an aluminium table, like cosmetic concoctions on a dressing table, there was a clutter of pots containing a wide variety of substances: linseed oil, turpentine, a huge range of colours and pigments, balsam of copaiba, pitch, varnishes, alkaline solutions, and many others too tedious to list. There was also a digesting furnace, and other contraptions inherited from the days of the alchemists.

'I don't understand, Nicolussi.'

'Then you should make an effort. Aren't you a professor of art?' snorted the inspector. 'Look: this board and this canvas are authentic. Valenzin, almost certainly with the help of Tedeschi, got hold of them by robbing rural churches. The paintings themselves have no value, but the supports do, because once he has removed the layer of old paint, he can use them for his forgeries. Do you see?' He put his fingers on the greasy substance coating the surface of one of the paintings. 'He would spread an alkaline solution over them, leave them for a few days, and then, very carefully, lift the softened paint with a spatula. That way he could work on canvases and boards of the time so that a carbon-14 test wouldn't give him away. He also found a method for eluding detection by infra-red tests: in the digesting furnace, he cooked the paint dissolved in the alkaline solution in order to separate out its components; by that means he obtained a powder which, mixed with linseed oil, colourants, and soot, gave him an oil paint that was five hundred years old. What do you say to that? He was a bright lad, eh?'

I agreed, in silent awe, even silent horror. Nicolussi also taught me other little tricks of the forgers. To simulate cracking, Valenzin applied directly on to the canvas a layer of varnish widely used by restorers, which gives paintings an unmistakeable golden patina. While the varnish was still fresh, he would paint over it, and as it dried out, this would lead the paint to crack in a multitude of hair-line fissures, resembling a miniature cardiovascular system. For the stretchers and frames he used contemporary wood that he aged with turpentine and pitch, and then exposed to the mercy of woodworm. Nicolussi drew my attention to a corner of the cellar: through a glass panel, enjoying themselves hugely on a bed of wood shavings, there swarmed hundreds of the little grubs.

'The finished work would then be left under these powerful lights, but even so, it could take several months to dry out completely,' he informed me. 'Although it may seem to be dry after a few days, an oil painting can in fact be wet for years — you only need to rub the surface with a piece of cotton-wool soaked in turpentine to lift the pigment. With this process,

Valenzin could be sure of eliminating every trace of moisture before putting his work into circulation.'

The halogen lamps were scorching my skin — not to mention the certainties I had formulated based on very insecure foundations. Leaning against the wall there were canvases of various sizes, all of which looked modern.

'Obviously, before starting on a work of that magnitude, Valenzin made notes and sketches, until he was able to adapt his brushwork to that of the artist he intended imitating. He had learned his craft by copying the Surrealists, so his technique was extremely precise — ideal for imitating the Renaissance painters.'

Just like Chiara's pictures, Fabio Valenzin's sketches were technically perfect, wonderful in the way they caught the play of light, and in their compositions; they displayed a virtuosity that only comes from a deep study of the old masters — but true originality needs to rebel against academic study. I amused myself looking through his sketches: Valenzin made precise imitations of the Madonnas of Bellini, the hieratic multitudes of figures by Carpaccio, and the landscapes of Giorgione. True art reproduces or interprets real life, but spurious art betrays and entombs it, embalms and mummifies it. Among other things I found three or four sketches of the woman pictured in *The Tempest*, with one leg bent back, and the other also bent, but slightly raised, her stomach like a hushed guitar, and her breasts like little creatures bewildered by their own maturity. Valenzin had achieved that smooth impasto effect which makes Giorgione the best painter of naked flesh, but by the time he came to the woman's face he had tired of fidelity to his original subject. I recognised her light brown hair and her ears like shells, or hieroglyphs; I recognised her slightly pointed chin, and her neck looking as if it was made for kisses,

I recognised her contemplative lips, and her nose slightly tilted to one side – although asymmetries do not detract from beauty – I recognised the high cheek-bones and Chiara's peasant-girl eyes, eyes that reflected deep sorrow and stared at me with a sensual sadness. Nicolussi came and stood behind me; he put an arm on my shoulder.

'Do you really believe that an individual like that was capable of moral scruples?'

TEN

By the time we returned to Venice the fog had thickened. Its denseness made it resemble a luxuriant forest, obscuring distances and enveloping the palaces on the Riva degli Schiavoni in a sort of lethal stillness, foreshadowing their disappearance under the water, and habituating them to their future vocation as mausoleums. It was a fog that descended horizontally – if the contradiction may be permitted – like successive layers of ash acquiring a moist opacity on contact with water, like generations of fallen leaves that, on being disturbed, convey the withered caress of death. I did not dare turn my head, so that I should not see the Stucky Mill disappearing far behind us, like a sheer cliff in the grey distance. Night had already fallen, and the *vaporetto* pursued its course with that casual sense of direction possessed by migrating souls as they revisit the landscapes of a previous life, the obliterated scenes of a past that exists only in their memory. Nor did I dare to think about the most recent events; I allowed my meditations to be pervaded by the fog wrapping itself around us, to avoid having to adopt a proper plan of action, and in order to put aside the relentless pursuit of insoluble puzzles. The water smelled of a cortège of corpses, and the light of the streetlamps edging the

Riva degli Schiavoni failed to pierce the skeins of fog. Nicolussi breathed on Valenzin's ring, and rubbed it on the sleeve of his raincoat, as if trying to improve its shine.

'This evening I shall amuse myself by finding out the origins of this ring. What will you be doing? Will you be at the Albergo Cusmano?'

'That's where I'm staying,' I replied. 'Although, now I come to think of it, I'm invited to a masked ball. A very high-class affair. I'd completely forgotten it until now.'

The vibration of the *vaporetto*'s engine was replaced by a smooth tremor, as if a swathe of fog had become entangled in the screws.

'Is that so? You've just arrived in Venice, and already you're hobnobbing with the aristocracy. Who is your host?'

'Hostess, more correctly. Giovanna Zanon, Gabetti's ex. She's married to a man who owns a big chain of hotels.'

I detected a note of amusement in Nicolussi's voice.

'Giovanna Zanon, my God! You don't need to say another word. I saw the way she took you by the arm in the cemetery. She's quite something. So you didn't waste time getting in with her, eh?'

We were bearing down on St Mark's Square, which the fog was converting into a shelter for the tubercular. Its basilica had taken on a rustic appearance, resembling a shed for storing crops, and its golden domes looked like ricks of drying hay.

'Not at all,' I replied. Absurdly, I was irritated. 'She took me to her palace so that I could give her an expert opinion on a painting.'

She had also taken me there to indoctrinate me with her own hatred for Chiara and to create discord between us, but I had held out against her malicious insinuations. It was necessary only not to look back, and to avoid going over the same old ground.

'Well, I'm sorry about that,' Nicolussi sympathised. 'There are scandalmongers who put it about that there isn't a better woman in bed. Apparently, she got plenty of extra-marital practice while she was with Gabetti. What is it about adultery that we indulge in it with greater zest than we do in marriage?'

'Don't ask me, I'm not married – for which I'm grateful.' I was pretending ignorance, but my irritation was undiminished.

The *vaporetto* listed to one side as it neared the landing-stage, like a man reluctantly approaching a marriage bed. There was a large and ill-assorted number of tourists feeding the pigeons in St Mark's Square, and I had a nostalgic recollection of Tedeschi, who preferred to wring their necks. They were also taking photographs of each other – although the fog would present them with a spectral and uninhabited scene when they came to develop their films. Meanwhile, they wearily applauded the strains of an orchestra that sounded rather like a fanfaronade paid for by the municipal government with the money brought in by its liberal attitude to crime. What remained of the Venetian Carnival was, as the hotel magnate Taddeo Rosso had explained to me, hardly more than a sham, a stunt put on to attract tourists. But the most stupefying aspect of it was that they fell for it, drawn by the publicity, and desperately trying to enjoy themselves in a city unprepared for enjoyment of any kind.

'And I'm not married either, my friend, so don't try getting at me,' said Nicolussi. 'But to be serious for a moment, Giovanna Zanon is a woman to be wary of. We've got her listed, down at the station, as one of Valenzin's principal clients.'

'Exactly. She showed me a picture by Bellini for me to authenticate. At first I thought it was the painting missing from the church of the Madonna dell' Orto, but now I've seen Valenzin's laboratory, I wouldn't go to the stake about it.'

Nicolussi's sideways mode of walking passed unnoticed amid the fog and the groups of tourists in their fancy costumes. From time to time among the proliferation of masks, I noticed the predatory silhouette of the plague doctor, like the fleeting memory of a nightmare.

'Giovanna Zanon, like so many *nouveaux riches*, has caught the collecting bug, and her husband pays the bills without a word,' said Nicolussi. 'It wouldn't surprise me if Valenzin put one over her.'

The duck-boards that had welcomed me to St Mark's three days before still lay across the square, although the floodwaters had gone down, granting Venice her umpteenth stay of execution. As a reminder of that amnesty, puddles of brackish water survived in the gaps between the flagstones, contributing to their corrosion. Nicolussi stopped when we arrived at the Mercerie.

'The Albergo Cusmano is on the way to the police station. I'll go with you so that you don't get lost.'

'No, don't worry, Nicolussi, I think I'll go for a stroll.' I rejected his friendly gesture and his company because I did not want to think too deeply, and his conversation fanned my self-awareness – and aroused awareness stimulates the processes of thought. 'Otherwise, I'll leave Venice without having seen anything at this rate. What shall I be able to tell my friends?'

'If you tell them only a third of what's happened to you during your visit, they'll accuse you of making it up, don't you think? Things happen in Venice that common sense wouldn't allow us to take seriously anywhere else in the world.'

I did not see him go off, because the fog swallowed him up when he was scarcely more than a couple of yards away from me. 'In Venice, events happen without quite happening,' I thought, paraphrasing Chiara's oracular statement. 'Threats remain hanging in the air, a flash of lightning doesn't bring on the rain, life hangs by a thread, and time slows down, as it does in *The Tempest*.' Possibly, Valenzin, by portraying Chiara in the same pose that Giorgione had chosen to immortalise the woman in his painting, had been attempting to preserve her intact – an exercise in reverence and admiration, fixing her in a world of suspended unreality. I realised that my mission had to be exactly the opposite. If I wanted to free Chiara, I had to bring her back to real life, I had to negotiate the gulf that looms between the idea and the experience of love, between unspoken adoration and the true expression of feelings; it was a resolution the very idea of which made my shoulders sag with defeatism. I wandered through the little streets that gradually became emptier, and passed a few tourists, their faces covered by masks, as if to conceal their boredom. Before turning each corner, I suffered from the same sinking feeling: behind each wall my tormentor might be waiting to ambush me, disguised in a plague doctor's mask, his gun at the ready – and that would pay me back for meddling. Why not give up? Why not turn round and take the *vaporetto* to Marco Polo airport? Why not renounce the whole impossible venture of love?

I walked aimlessly through the muffled turmoil of the fog, discovering canals that gleamed like liquid asphalt on the point of setting, transforming into fossils the reflections on their surface. I walked aimlessly, but my footsteps were guided by that obscure homing instinct, which leads animals to their byre or stable, that intuitive compass we all carry within ourselves when we want to force an encounter. The district of Cannaregio was populated at that hour by cats of dubious pedigree that retained something about them of princes who have abdicated their thrones: they passed in and out of crumbling palaces, with miauling calls to combat, and they procreated there, ignorant of the notion that it is possible to distinguish between the idea and the experience of love. My vagrancy lasted more than an hour, along narrow walkways that obliged me to perfect my sense of balance by not falling into the water. By contrast, the width of the open space in front of the church of the Madonna dell' Orto surprised me. It is probable that in daylight, or without the fatigue brought on by so much wandering, it would not have seemed so large.

I pushed the door of the church without really expecting to find it open. But it was. At the far end of the central nave, perched on the scaffolding across the apse, Chiara was toiling away at the restoration of the Tintorettos. She was removing flakes of chipped paint with fine tweezers. Fungus was attacking the canvas with a sort of psoriasis that can only be cured with a resinous lacquer. The figures in the *Last Judgement* were contorted in violent foreshortenings which made them look as if Chiara was ridding them of fleas, or tickling them. The floodlight that illuminated her – it was not halogen, I observed to my relief – lessened the *chiaroscuro* effect, and bleached the olive tones that Tintoretto had worked into the skins of the damned.

'You're back at last. We were very worried about you, Gilberto and I,' she said, as I emerged into the ring of light given out by the lamp. 'You go off without saying where you're going, and you leave the two of us up in the air.'

I fell back on sarcasm: 'You could have got the police to

search for me.' Then, with an exaggerated show of feeling, I corrected myself: 'Oh, I'm sorry, I forgot that you don't want the police to go anywhere near the Accademia in case they find out about the robbery attempt. I'm terribly sorry, that was indiscreet of me.'

Chiara looked at me with a mixture of wounded pride and tenderness that disarmed me. The light from the lamp elongated her shadow obliquely across Tintoretto's canvas, and led to her inclusion in the chorus of the blessed who surrounded the figure of Christ, and paraded all their attributes of martyrdom.

'I never expected you to stoop so low, Alejandro.' She spoke in a pitying voice, which made me feel miserable. 'You can't imagine the fuss there would be if certain people found out what happened last night at the Accademia. Gilberto has a lot of enemies among the big shots of Venice.'

'Not without cause,' I murmured.

She bit her lower lip to prevent its angry quivering. I had kissed that lip, and the upper one as well; I had tasted their flavour. Her cheeks reddened, but before I was able to examine the way the blush altered her complexion she turned her back on me. Using a spatula, she blended a syrupy sort of mixture on one of the shelves of the scaffolding, and applied it to the cracks in the painting.

'Of course he has a lot of enemies. The politicos think the Accademia is theirs by right, and they can dispose of its treasures in any way they choose. They have tried more than once to insist on us lending pictures to travelling exhibitions in order to keep in with other European authorities, although they were paintings that couldn't be moved because they were practically in shreds, and needed urgent restoration. Gilberto has had to stand up to public opinion and the politicos all on his own, in order to save more than one picture from total ruin. And then, to get their own back, these same politicos refuse to support him. During the Second World War, the Nazis carried off a number of works from the Accademia, and Gilberto requested that a petition should be sent to the German Government asking for their return, but nobody took any notice of him. The Accademia is the museum with the smallest subsidy of all those in its class. Those vile creatures in the Ministry of Culture hope their negligence will make him resign. But Gilberto puts up with it. Do you understand now why it was important not to disclose that attempted robbery?'

I nodded, with deep humility. I had left the door open, and the fog was creeping in through the side aisles, like those avaricious parishioners who attend mass seated in the pews furthest away from the altar, and never put a penny in the poor-box. Chiara wore her same very baggy, and rather masculine, working jersey that I had got to know in our first meeting.

'We don't have a budget for repairing damage caused by flooding,' she continued. Her voice was that of a woman no longer young; there was a harshness to it, and the suggestion of a break. It was the same voice I had heard on other occasions. 'Nor for the maintenance and restoration of the works of art. Gilberto has had to beg for help from rich private individuals, and I have had to work for nothing restoring paintings that wouldn't have stood up to one more winter. But I don't complain, I do it willingly, it is my duty, and also my life's purpose. Tintoretto, who is my guardian saint, did the same thing: he worked without receiving anything in return, died penniless and unable to pay for a doctor, but he contributed to the greatness of Venice.'

There was a spirit of resignation in her resolve, the same

vocation for self-sacrifice that consumes saints and fanatics, and plunges them into the most altruistic or terrifying of exploits.

'But you should be feeling proud of yourself. You're the one who drove off the thieves from the Accademia. Gilberto ought to take you on as a security guard.'

I felt a growing pride but for different reasons: I had undermined Chiara's resistance, and had secured her neutrality during our visit to the gallery.

'I hope you won't think I'm conceited, but I have to confess I am much more encouraged by the fact that I managed to convince you of my interpretation of *The Tempest*. You saw that Gabetti – I mean Gilberto – was unable to refute my arguments, although he put me through the third degree.'

'He didn't shine, you're right,' she said. 'Possibly he likes you and wanted to be kind, or he sensed that I wouldn't have put up with a humiliating scene, and he didn't dare annoy me.'

She was trying to bring me back to earth, like someone who picks the petals off a flower with a botanist's lightness of touch – but it does not make the mutilation less blameworthy. I protested:

'But you yourself recognised that my explanation was satisfactory. Anchises, Aphrodite, Aeneas, the wrath of Zeus, the premonition of the Trojan War. Or are you going back now on what you said?'

The fog was beginning to assault the side chapels; it was penetrating the stone and attacking its very heart. Chiara's contortions on the scaffolding made the intricate writhings and tortured play of perspectives in Tintoretto's compositions seem very small by comparison.

'It was a satisfactory *intellectual* explanation,' she explained, putting a scornful emphasis on the adjective. 'But there have been other logical, intellectual explanations, so you shouldn't think of yourself as a pioneer. The flash of lightning could symbolise the divine curse that expelled Adam and Eve from the Garden of Eden; Cain is suckling Eve's teats, she having "in sorrow brought forth her child", according to the anathema in the book of Genesis. The pilgrim could be Adam, supporting himself on a staff to symbolise the fatigue and old age by which he is beset, having sampled the forbidden fruit. The two broken columns could be the symbol of death: "for dust thou art, and unto dust shalt thou return". I'm making this up as I go along because there could be fifty different interpretations, all equally plausible.' She plucked the number out of the air to belittle the hypothesis on which I had squandered my youth. 'But art that needs intellectual elucidation for its enjoyment is not true art. A picture that needs explanation is not a good picture. It may be a fine example of virtuosity, a calculated enigma, but not a good picture. Once we understand the keys to it, we can interpret it, but it will fail to excite our emotions. There is no true art without emotion, and *The Tempest*, fortunately, moves us as it is, without our having recourse to guess-work. It may not be an exercise in technical virtuosity, but it excites our emotions.'

I was consumed with despair, exasperation, and disappointment.

'If you take that argument to its logical conclusion, any shoddy piece of work can be called art, so long as it squeezes out a tear.'

'You haven't understood me, Alejandro,' she protested. She was using a spray-gun to apply a sort of lacquer to the cracks that she had previously filled with the syrupy mixture. 'Strength of feeling can make up for what is lacking in a work of art; it can transform and refine it. Look at Tintoretto: he gave himself up to his work with such overwhelming faith that he transfixes us with emotion. He may seem rather crude for our modern sensitivities – or, as you put it, he is very vigorous and luxuriant. There is something elemental, even brutal, about him, but it is the forthrightness of his art that makes him more original than any of his contemporaries. The secret is in his faith. Nowadays, we tend to value those painters who have great technique and a lot of knowledge, those unbelieving painters who have taken academic courses and mastered a number of basic principles. We believe that an artist must demonstrate an almost scientific training in order to satisfy our blessed intelligence. Well then, I prefer an art that is more daring. I have never seen anyone become excited faced with a picture by Leonardo; on the other hand I have seen many women fall on their knees in front of a Virgin by Tintoretto.'

I admired her without reserve, fervently, every atom in my body fused in the bewilderment that her words were producing.

'And I know one who falls on her knees in front of his tomb,' I said pensively.

I admired her even with her contradictions: she was the first to be damaged by her vindication of art as the religion of sentiment and emotion, because her paintings – as I had found when I went up to her attic studio – irreproachable as they were from a technical point of view, suffered from being imitative, that variant on mediocrity. I admired her in spite of her mediocrity as a painter, and because of that mad or fanatic determination that made her sacrifice herself for a city which would not thank her for her dedication. I was beginning to prefer the experience of love to the idea of it.

'That's enough for today,' said Chiara decisively, as she switched off the light that illuminated us. 'Let's go.'

She descended the scaffolding in the dark, and by doing so was able to prevent me spying on her as she came down; it would have been an admiring look, but at the same time lustful, because the trousers of her track suit were, as before, caught between her buttocks, with that easy-going obstinacy – if the contradiction may be permitted – of well-worn clothes. The floodlight had made the flame of a votive lamp illuminating the side altar where the bones of Tintoretto lay pass unnoticed. Now that the obscurity made me awkward and bleary-eyed, the flame acquired the importance of a small conflagration in the centre of the church, making it resemble a waste land razed by the fog. I approached the scaffold to embrace her.

'What are you doing? Don't be so disrespectful.' She tried to break away from me, but without too much of a struggle. The smell of turpentine on her clothes was disturbing. 'Don't you know we're in a church?'

'But it's not open for services. God won't be angry.'

I overcame my usual cowardice, and pulling down the neck of her sweater I kissed her in the place where the collar-bones almost meet, but leave a hollow that cups the lips of the man who worships there. Chiara tried to object, but I silenced her by putting my mouth on hers. My sinuous tongue penetrated her mouth, exploring all its folds and the smooth surface of her teeth. To the pleasure of that deep kiss was added the delight in sacrilege.

'Come on, let's go home, or we'll be excommunicated.'

I noticed how her temperature had risen beneath her sweater and her track suit, I noticed the deep trembling in her thighs, which, misleadingly, seemed more slender than they were, and I noticed also the way her arms fell limply, reminding me of the pigeons after Tedeschi had wrung their necks. She suppressed her own feelings of desire, however, and picked up the basket in which she kept her tools. I still held her close, and persisted in fondling her. I put my arms round her waist, and took her hair between my teeth — love is omnivorous, even a little cannibalistic. The votive lamp we were leaving behind cast a tenuous light on her, just enough to pick her out in the darkness. I trapped her in the side chapel where, as the notice explained, Bellini's *Madonna and Child* had hung before it was stolen. I did not want to put off any longer the attempt to discover the truth.

'Do you know that the painting that has gone from here is in Giovanna Zanon's palace? It was your friend Fabio Valenzin who stole it.'

Water, which came from some subterranean seepage, possibly from the catacombs in the foundations of the church, oozed through the wall of the chapel. It was a rust-laden water that retained the ages-old smell I detected on Chiara's skin. I pushed up her sweater to satisfy my lusting hands, and they moulded themselves to her breasts.

'He didn't steal it. What that old witch has is a forgery,' she whispered. 'Fabio was very skilful.'

'A forgery? So where's the original?'

I spoke very close to her mouth in order to breathe in her breath as it passed between the immaculate whiteness of her teeth. Her nipples were hardening like eruptions of soft metal.

'Do you want me to show you? Do you really have faith in me?'

Instead of replying, I pressed even closer to her, so that she could feel my unscathed ribs that were only too willing to donate one of their number. In the vaulted domes of the Madonna dell' Orto, stone and fog were also fused in an intimate embrace, a mineral osmosis.

'Come back with me.'

She had dispelled my suspicions, and I was no longer troubled by the darkness that earlier had made me jumpy, or by the muffled flurry of phantoms that haunted every turn. Chiara locked the door of the church with a big, heavy key she kept in her basket, inside a chamois pouch. On the Fondamenta della Sensa, next door to Tintoretto's house which Chiara and Gabetti had made their home, a conclave of cats was miauling to a moon that had withdrawn its light from them.

'You'll have noticed that the damp in the Madonna dell' Orto is devastating for the paintings,' said Chiara. 'I personally restored the *Last Judgement* less than ten years ago, and you've seen what a state it is in now. To do the restoration work properly you would have to remove it from the wall and take it somewhere dry to allow the materials to harden but, given its size, that isn't possible. The drying out process can last for months.' It was not necessary for her to tell me this, because in my visit to Valenzin's laboratory I had become acquainted with the problem. 'If the process is interrupted, the defects in the painting come through again even more strongly. In the case of the *Last Judgement*, I have resigned myself to having to repeat the work every so often, but in the case of the *Madonna and Child*, which is much more manageable, I have been able to work on that at home.'

We went up the uneven steps where, on my first visit, I had had to tread barefoot because they were covered by the *acqua alta*. Chiara led the way until we reached the landing of the first floor and the range of rooms that Tintoretto had used as his studios. She looked up the stairwell, and shouted:

'Gilberto! Are you back yet?' While she waited for an answer she bit her contemplative lips, and removed the elastic band that bound her hair in a ponytail. The pressure of the rubber left its mark, a double wave or hollow, which heightened her hair's resemblance to a musical instrument. 'He must be held up in the Accademia, repairing the damage done the other night. Well, as I was telling you, I wanted to bring Bellini's *Madonna* back here, but I hadn't counted on the opposition of the Department of Artistic and Historic Properties, which is where some of Gilberto's most violent detractors get together. They alleged that the picture was in such a terrible condition it was impossible to move it. A distance of barely one hundred yards! But in refusing me permission they were actually getting their own back on a man who had so often ridiculed their ignorance and prevented them from disposing of the treasures belonging to the Accademia to add to their ostentatious exhibitions.'

Tintoretto's studios, which were very bright during the day, still retained a dim light on the whitewashed walls, an indistinct phosphorescence that seemed to hang in the air and materialise in vague forms like ectoplasm from the great beyond. Chiara let me duck through a low door in the far corner of the passage. The floor was made of brick.

'This is the room Tintoretto kept for his studies and his experiments,' said Chiara. 'Nobody was allowed in here other than his closest relations.'

She spoke with the pride of a legal guardian, as if it were her duty to resurrect, or to maintain, strictly controlled entry; I congratulated myself on having passed her test. Chiara switched on a light: Bellini's *Madonna and Child*, separated by barely an inch – the distance between love and eroticism – seemed offended by the sudden brilliance.

'I was furious when I learned they had refused permission – until one night when Fabio turned up with a package under his arm. "Let's see if this present brings a smile to your face," he said as he arrived, rather unexpectedly. I took off the wrapping, and found myself looking at Bellini's painting. With some difficulty I got him to explain. "A client of mine commissioned me to steal it, but I thought I'd rather unload a forgery on her. It's a long time since I did one, and with so little practice I shall begin to lose the knack."' Chiara tried to smile, but her lips trembled with unfathomable grief. 'I still hadn't recovered from my surprise, and he had already turned to go. I asked him: "And when I've restored it, what then?" Fabio shrugged his shoulders – nothing seemed to bother him. "Just let it dry, and I'll take care to put it back where it belongs." "But your client will find out about the swindle," I objected. I wasn't at all sure I wanted to get mixed up in it. "And what will she do? Denounce me? She'll have to swallow her pride and keep quiet. Apart from that who can say where I shall be when it comes out." Fabio was always sparing with his explanations,' she concluded in a gloomy and distant tone, as if she was thinking out loud. 'Now at least we do know where he is.'

I examined the painting very thoroughly, and recognised the hallmarks of Bellini's style which I had seen earlier in the copy owned by Giovanna Zanon when I was still ignorant of Valenzin's fraudulent virtuosity. Chiara did not wait for me to give my opinion.

'Now it will be my job to put it back there.' Her sadness was drifting towards anger, which seemed unjust, given that Valenzin had not deliberately failed to keep his promise. 'He always enjoyed half-doing things.'

'And how do you know that this one is authentic? I warn you, Valenzin didn't overlook the smallest detail.'

Her anger dissolved, giving way to a rather presumptuous merriment.

'Are you trying to teach me? Don't forget I learned my

profession with him.' Again I was assailed by retrospective jealousy. 'It is curious that we forgers and restorers have the same training and use the same techniques. Fabio was unbeatable in his field, but even in his most inspired work there were features that gave him away to the trained eye. You can't just extemporise the natural ageing process of the pigments, because in the course of centuries there are chemical reactions that alter their chromatic tonality. It also happens that colours that were clearly separate from each other five hundred years ago begin to fuse together. You must understand that a slow chemical reaction can't be imitated by a few brush-strokes of linseed oil. The colour in a forgery will always be more even; it is something that will not be noticed by a layman, but I can spot it immediately.'

'You are an expert,' I said, putting my arms round her. 'The next time Giovanna Zanon asks me for an opinion, do you mind if I come out with all this lore?'

'Is that because you want to impress her?'

She tried to duck away, but her not so slender thighs had to accept being imprisoned between mine, while our temperatures mingled in a chemical reaction that did not need the help of centuries.

'If I don't succeed in impressing you I shall have to discover some means of finding consolation.'

For a moment I saw myself as if from far away, like a distant spectator staring in amazement at his own double. The celibacy I had more or less maintained over recent years had prevented me observing the norms of courtship, but now I discovered that their observance did not depend so much on practice as on instinct. There are ways of behaving that are inherited in our genes and carried in the blood – together with the leucocytes. My hand strayed under the elastic of her track suit. It was not the same shy, rustic hand that had felt around Giovanna Zanon's shapeless bottom, but a daring, presumptuous hand, almost as daring and presumptuous as my desires. Chiara's bottom was not one of those uncongenial bottoms that have succumbed to liposuction; the bone could not be felt, the flesh was soft, covering the muscles, and it remained docile as my hand moved lower, beyond the point where her buttocks joined her back like two peninsulas, down to where they acquired their own poise and independence like a pair of islands. I caressed the fine skin of her pelvis and her unexpectedly ample hips, pausing on those soft, tremulous surfaces rounded by cellulite. We refer to this rudely as flab or padding, and Chiara was well endowed in that area.

'Don't touch me there, I'm disgracefully fat.'

'Don't tell me you're fat – you're perfect for my taste.'

Chiara left her basket on the floor, switched off the light, pushed me out into the passage, and closed the door behind her to spare Bellini's Madonna a scene that would have offended her virtue. I put my face between her breasts, and marvelled at the beating of her heart, which resembled that of a frightened bird.

'We'd better go up to my attic. Come on.'

She took me by the hand; it was a pleasure to relinquish responsibility, and allow her to lead me up to her studio at the very top of the house. The air became thicker until it acquired that amphibian consistency that had made me gasp for breath on my previous visit. While she was struggling to put the key in the lock, I began to chew her hair that still held the mark of the rubber band and the indelible odour of turpentine. The night was as black as ink, but an unearthly light, greenish and pulsating, filtered through the skylight. There on the bed, or more exactly the straw mattress, carefully wrapped in a plastic bag, lay a plague doctor's costume. The nose of the mask, facing the ceiling, seemed to be growing longer like the nails of a corpse, with posthumous stealth.

'Christ, what a fright! What's that doing there?' I exclaimed. A shiver ran down my spine.

Chiara gave a laugh that was not just hearty, it was also mischievous.

'One of Giovanna Zanon's servants brought it this afternoon with this note.' She extracted from the plastic bag an envelope made of Japanese paper printed with intricate arabesques. 'You didn't tell me you were going to her masked ball. I'm beginning to discover you are one of those people who insist on openness from others, but don't give anything in return.'

The note contained various flattering flourishes that made me feel deeply embarrassed. Giovanna's Zanon's handwriting was spiky, a sort of mortuary gothic, in keeping with her anatomy. Among the sweet words, she suggested the time when her chauffeur would pick me up in her motor-launch. The poster of *The Tempest* was a shady rectangle on the wall, like the opening into a passage that harboured stormy passions, upsurges of the spirit threatening to break loose.

'What more can I offer you except to say that I am utterly devoted to you,' I managed to stammer out. Sincerity did not prevent me from indulging in the vocabulary of cheap sentiment. 'Please tell me.'

Chiara swept the carnival costume off the bed with the sort of gesture we normally reserve for cockroaches and other disgusting creatures. Then I could see the crumpled, unstarched sheets of well-worn linen, that would feel soft to the skin of anyone lying in them. Sheets and snow recover quickly from blood or from being trampled down, but the eyes of a man who has been humiliated never recover. Chiara sat down on one corner of the mattress, and I sat beside her.

'You tell me nothing about what you do,' she said reproach-fully. 'You wander about all day and then come back looking very pleased with yourself, but you don't tell me why.'

'But what do you want me to tell you?'

I passed my hand over her head without touching it, as if describing a halo; her hair rose up, attracted by the static electricity.

'What it is that you do. You know almost everything about me, so it's only fair if I ask for something in return.'

I turned her head slightly until it was in half-profile. Using my fingers, I parted her hair in several places, and gathering it up between my thumb and forefinger made a sort of topknot from which I allowed a few wisps or locks to escape that fell in gentle waves over her cheeks.

'Fabio Valenzin was killed by those characters who broke into the Accademia last night,' I said, continuing to gaze at the face that Giorgione could have painted. 'He had agreed to hand *The Tempest* over to them, but he gave up the idea, or possibly he decided to foist a forgery on them.'

Overcome by grief, she gave a powerful shudder and caught her breath; her face became distorted as I gave her a succinct account of the facts, based on the rather fragmentary perception I had of them: the finding of the ring, Dina's encounter with the terrifying intruder in her hotel, the loss of the chest and the disappearance of Tedeschi, the discovery of Valenzin's laboratory in the Stucky Mill, all of which added up to a series of disconnected events still needing the necessary cement to weld them together into a solution of the puzzle. As I proceeded with my narrative, I sensed that Chiara was shrinking beside me, and becoming deeply distressed. 'When we talk about a

dead friend,' she had told me, 'we are talking about our own
death, or that part of ourselves that the other has taken with
him, and which dies with him. We don't cry for our friend,
but for that part of ourselves that our friend has taken from
us. The dead feed on the deaths of the living.' There were too
many dead and terminally ill people in her world, dying their
slow deaths. Not only Valenzin, but Gabetti who had imbued
her with that dedication to self-sacrifice, and had tried to isolate
her in a glass capsule, uncontaminated by pathogens from the
outside world; and then there was Venice itself, which would
drag her down in its final collapse.

'You must leave this ghastly city. Come to Spain with me.
A wonderful picture restorer will be very welcome there. You
would even find yourself with too much work.'

I made her lie down on the bed and helped remove her
sweater. Her stomach no longer resembled a mute guitar, but
a violin whose strings are about to break. I placed my ear
on her navel to listen to the workings of her body, her deep,
interior world.

'What you are suggesting is madness,' she murmured. 'My
place is here.'

I caressed her stomach as if it were a sounding board, or
a hemisphere which held within itself the incarnation of the
universe. Chiara's stomach had that sweet convexity with
which nature has endowed women, and which some of them
try to eliminate with abdominal exercises. It had that slightly
swollen smoothness of her most fertile days, the deep and
religious fervour of ovulation.

'Do you still believe that the salvation of Venice depends
on you, as you did when you were a little girl?'

I pulled down the trousers of her track suit and her panties,
which fell about her ankles in an accordion of folds and creases.

Before moving over her, I noticed how thin and fair the hair of her pubis was, like the hair on her head. I remember finding this consistency disconcerting. I had believed that pubic hair was only ever black and dense.

'I can't leave, Alejandro.' She delayed her response as she fitted her body to mine. 'Would you consider coming to live in Venice?'

Her thighs were hairless, and as they parted, they emitted a radiant warmth. I ran my hands down her flanks, which were marked with the dimples and tiny bulges of incipient cellulite.

'That wouldn't help at all,' I said. 'You have to escape from here.'

'Be quiet now, you're putting me off.'

She closed her peasant-girl eyes and pressed her head back into the pillow; her throat curved up revealing a fabric of tendons that my tongue skimmed over, one by one. Her small, barely detectable breasts spread themselves flat over her ribs. I tried to round them out, but in vain. Only her nipples, like eruptions of soft metal, added volume to a body that was much slighter above than below the waist. After vainly persevering, I found that her left nipple was the slower one to become erect – but asymmetry enhances beauty. Possibly it had been damaged by injury, or it suffered from a congenital defect. I entered her clumsily and with some difficulty, but desire acted as my guide and prevailed over my inexperience. Inside, she was as hot as molten lava. It was a powerful sensation. There was nothing gentle or elusive about it. It was fierce, as the moist, membranous tissues drew me into the torrid depths of her. I broke my silence to whisper the endearments normally spoken in those circumstances, and looked unblinking at her face burning like an inferno, and at an inextricable tangle of hair adhering to the sweat on her forehead; but she did not open her eyes, even when she began to sense her orgasm. Her stomach lost its smoothness and became taut with her convulsions – beauty is either convulsive, or it is nothing – and her lips parted to release her gasps. I remember that in that frenzied moment when I was about to expel my seed, I conceived the hope that it would not prove to be sterile. I yearned, absurdly, for it to fuse with her seed, that the two might unite and exist through nine whole months. They were the thoughts of a catechist, and quickly gave way to more sombre ones – which included Gabetti concealed in some corner of the house, his blue eyes tinged with hate, his eyes in which co-existed kindness and cruelty becoming livid with fury. I calmed down, as did Chiara, who at last looked up at me, and smiled. She put her hands over her face, and when she took them away, she was still smiling, as if she could not believe what had just happened to her, but at the same time was overjoyed.

'Come to Spain with me,' I repeated.

'Oh, Alejandro, please don't insist. There are too many things that hold me here.'

I kissed her vulva, which had the appearance of a sleeping sea-anemone, and tasted of seaweed, not so much salty as viscous. I curled up against her, adapting my position to hers, and made her raise her legs into the foetal position. I put my arms round her stomach, which once again resembled a silenced guitar, now that it had received my seed.

'Who holds you here? Gabetti? All children leave their parents sooner or later. It is one of the rules of life.'

Above the skylight, the Venetian sky was fragmenting, perforated by fog and phantasms. That Chiara always referred to Gabetti by his first name, while I persisted in using his surname, made clear the unbridgeable divide between us.

'I shall never abandon Gilberto.' Her tone was unyielding, as if inflected by tragic thoughts. 'I owe everything I am to him.'

'But if he really loves you he shouldn't hold you back.'

She responded proudly.

'No one holds me back. I hold myself back, and I do so happily.'

I loathed that man who had guaranteed a peaceful old age for himself, while my ribs would remain inviolate, very many miles from there. I clung tightly to Chiara, as if I only wanted to exist inside her, within her womb.

'And when you fell in love with Valenzin,' I insisted, 'didn't Gabetti hold you back then?'

'I loved Fabio ever since I was a little girl, I've already told you.' Possibly, her words concealed a deep weariness. 'I fought to cure his sickness and to attract him to me, but I failed. I tried to persuade him to give up his criminal activities and to stay in Venice with Gilberto and me, but I overestimated my own strength: crime was an integral part of his nature, it was too deeply entrenched in him. Fabio was as incapable of distinguishing between right and wrong as he was incapable of distinguishing between art and reality. For him, the two things formed part of the same deception.' She spoke with bitterness, as if she had removed the lid from a funerary urn, and all the dust from the past was choking her. 'I suffered a lot because of him, as I've already told you, so don't trivialise that.'

I realised then that the dust had burned her out internally, and she would need a long convalescence before reviving. I also realised that I had bestowed my seed and my love on a woman who could not be fruitful even if she tried, because she was barren in body and soul, recovering from a pain that was still too vivid. I no longer suffered from retrospective jealousy, but from the overwhelming conviction that I had arrived too late; I felt dispossessed and futile, as well as having a premonition of a future tormented by the relentless memory of Chiara, a perpetual sentence that would make me remember all the details of her face, the patterns of her skin, the ephemeral signs of pleasure on her countenance, and the lasting marks that suffering had engraved deep in those recesses which are inaccessible to healing caresses. I was distressed to realise that I had just lost Chiara after possessing her for the first and only time, and I was depressed by the realisation that this loss would preclude the consolation of forgetfulness. The instants I had spent at her side, as our senses played on each other, would endure tenaciously and frequently in my memory. It is my misfortune to be excessively sensitive.

'If only you had come here earlier, Alejandro,' she said. 'If only I had the courage to begin again.'

I clung even more tightly to her barren stomach which I had hoped to make pregnant; I clung to her with the despair that precedes separations. Although the skylight protected us from the weather, I felt as if the fog were permeating my very body, just as earlier it had permeated the stone of Madonna dell' Orto, in an osmotic process that would end with my death.

'Will you be able to forgive me?' Chiara asked. Her voice was barely audible, and useless for atonement.

'Of course. You are not to blame.'

I was on the brink of tears, and the pain of the wounds in my back, which had been anaesthetised by happiness, reasserted its grip.

'What will you do now?'

'Nicolussi has asked me to leave Venice in return for not

mentioning my name in the judicial proceedings,' I replied. 'I was planning to disobey him, and to stay until the murder of Valenzin was solved and the chest recovered.' I stopped at that point because it was inappropriate to allow my disappointment to sound like cynicism. 'The truth is, I was only putting off my departure because of you. I suppose there's no sense in that now.'

'But you came to complete your studies. You mustn't give up just because—'

I put my hand over her mouth before she offered any other trivial and demoralising reasons to justify extending my stay: that mouth had kissed mine, and I could not bear the idea that she might humiliate me with her pity.

'Give what up?' Disappointment made me bitter – as well as making me feel old. 'I don't give a damn about Giorgione and his wretched painting. My only regret is that I have wasted the best years of my life on stupidities. And what have I got out of it? Nothing. I am a complete failure and a nonentity. I am twenty-nine years old, and I haven't even found a person to share my life. With a bit of luck, and if I put up with my boss's whims, I shall obtain an appointment on the staff of my university. Then I shall be able to do to my subordinates what others have done to me: bully and humiliate them. A fine prospect!'

Chiara snuggled closer to me like an animal looking for warmth. Probably my complaining sounded to her like a reproach.

'If only I could do something for you.'

I kissed her ear, that fibrous labyrinth which held a message in its hieroglyphics.

'If we could both do something for each other there would be an end to our difficulties. But there are things that do not depend upon our will. Now you must rest. I want to see you sleeping before I go off to that wretched ball.'

'Are you really thinking of going?'

'I must say goodbye to Giovanna Zanon and her husband. Courtesy requires it,' I said, with undisguised sarcasm. 'But don't worry, you will be the last person to see me before I leave, so that the memory of you will be the last one I take away with me to Spain.'

I would take that away with me, pristine and perfect, and on my return home I would break it down into small, carefully-measured doses – memory does not allow for imprecision. On one day I would remember her hair resembling the broken strings of a violin; on another, it would be her hearty laughter; on another, the incipient cellulite that blemished her thighs. I would remember, one after another, the photographs and sketches that Fabio Valenzin had made; I would remember her breath mingling with mine, and I would remember her bitter, broken words; I would remember the ever-changing feel of her skin; I would remember those occasions when my eyes had looked adoringly at her, sometimes with her consent, and sometimes without her knowing; and I would recall Gabetti's eyes meeting mine as we each discovered the other's adoration of her. I calculated that this catalogue of recollections would keep my mind occupied until my memory finally gave out, and that cultivating them would make me even more self-absorbed, misanthropic, and inclined to celibacy. I would remember even more exactly, if that is possible, the way she slowly fell asleep, the rhythm of her breathing in time with the pulsing of her blood, and the way she lay upon the shapeless confusion of the bedsheets. I remained still for a long while, holding her stomach, wrapping myself round her back so tightly that her vertebrae made tattoo marks down the middle of my chest, helping her maintain her foetal position, and keeping her soft thighs against mine – those thighs that had seemed misleadingly slender, but which generously covered the bone. I heard the muffled sound of the launch sent by Giovanna Zanon to pick me up, and I drew myself away from Chiara, taking care not to disturb her rest. The mattress seemed to retain my weight for several minutes while I dressed and threw the cape of the plague doctor over my shoulders; the pillow and the sheets took the same number of minutes before they relieved themselves of my thoughts, and recovered from my presence. Before leaving, I anointed her with a kiss at the line of her hair, so that my lips would add the taste of the sweat on her forehead to my collection of other memories: it had a metallic taste, like that of water filtered through the walls of a church, except that it was warm, and reminiscent of tears of sadness.

Giovanna Zanon's chauffeur-cum-servant was getting impatient, and the sound of the launch's horn echoed through the fog. I ran down to meet him before putting on the mask that completed my disguise. I nearly bumped into Gabetti in the doorway. Although his posture was upright, he was leaning against the wall in that irritated manner of people who respect punctuality, and are critical of those who are late.

'Good evening, Ballesteros,' he said, when he saw me. 'It's not right to keep people waiting.'

He made a gesture in the direction of the launch, which was pitching in the water of the canal and emitting an asthmatic put-putting sound, but there was too much spite in his words for him to have been alluding only to Giovanna Zanon's chauffeur: he too had been waiting for me, pretending that we were meeting by accident, and because he wanted the opportunity to gloat over my defeat. We looked at each other defiantly, establishing territorial limits just as we had when we had noticed each other spying on Chiara. Although slim and elegant, his eyes and his papery skin revealed his age. ('And there were many nights when I have heard Gilberto crying while Valenzin was giving Chiara lessons in the sort of activity at which he was impotent,' Giovanna Zanon had told me.)

'It's only been a short wait,' was my way of apologising. 'Apart from which, you've won. Chiara will continue to be the prop of your old age.'

Gabetti smiled. His exultation was despicable.

'Of course, my dear friend. Did you ever imagine she would go off with you, an upstart foreigner?'

Swollen with pride, he seemed to be showing me the door. I ventured out into the fog, to look for the launch before he could add to his verbal victory any further gratuitous expression of delight or malice.

ELEVEN

'I thought you were never going to arrive.' Giovanna Zanon had come down to meet me in the hall. She wore a Domino costume, a vaporous, full-length dress that reached to her ankles, and a sort of black cape or wrap that contrasted with the ringlets of the blonde and powdered wig tumbling about her shoulders. In her capacity as hostess, she had allowed herself the licence of wearing, instead of a full mask, an eye-mask that revealed the flaky-pastry wrinkles at the corners of her mouth, as well as the carnivorous menace of her teeth. 'But do me the favour of covering your face – the delight of a carnival ball lies in anonymity. I hope you will not be as disagreeable as you were the last time you were here; you didn't even leave an address where you could be found.'

There in the hall, voices could be heard coming from the *piano nobile*, and shallow, cynical, jarring laughter, as well as curiously mangled music that sounded like a mass for the dead played to the rhythm of a polka. Giovanna Zanon had had all the chandeliers lit.

'But at least you didn't have much difficulty in finding me.'

'I just had to make a few deductions.' She took my arm.

Her hand was sheathed in a lace mitten, which left visible her fingers with their painted nails. 'Bearing in mind how obsessed you were with that slut, Chiara, it didn't require much effort to guess you would try to be as close to her as possible. I gave orders for the costume to be left at Gilberto's house, and you see how right I was.'

We left behind us the small study that housed the forged Bellini as we went up the staircase leading to the *piano nobile*. They had placed the Filipino maid on the landing like a figurehead, or an obsequious statue. She was dressed as Columbine, with an apron over her flounced skirt that flared out over a bustle. As always, she stooped as her mistress passed by, but now she did so with the stiff bow of an automaton.

'This gentleman is the last of the guests, Isabella,' she instructed her. 'Now you can shut the door and attend to things in the kitchen.'

The servant rushed down the stairs, nearly stumbling over the fullness of her skirt as she went. Giovanna Zanon helped to do up the fastenings of my mask.

'Do you know it suits you very well? You don't look nearly so ingenuous now!'

She attached a fine Moorish veil to her own mask, which hid the drawn skin of her cheeks and the wrinkles in her neck that even her surgeon had been unable to rectify.

'From now on we are two completely unknown people,' she said. Her eyes did not cease however to distil their acid gleam, like vinegar, through her mask. 'Who knows what encounters the night may hold for us.'

'Or collisions,' I replied, discouragingly. I could scarcely recognise my own voice: the concavity of the mask made it sound very grim, matching my state of mind. 'I warn you I'm not in the mood for fun and games.'

Giovanna Zanon roared with libidinous laughter. Her veil was too fine to prevent the smell of her breath passing through; she had drunk some sweet and cloying liqueur, possibly she was already drunk, or possibly in a lascivious haze.

'You poor soul, you're not in the mood for fun and games?' She lifted the front of my cloak and examined what she detected there with apparent approbation. 'Obviously you've been disappointed in love. But I did warn you: the little orphan is Gilberto's exclusive property. However, Carnival makes us forget all our troubles, you'll see.'

Giovanna Zanon started again up the staircase to the *piano nobile*. Her long legs and her panties – excessively ornate for my taste – were visible through her long transparent dress.

'Our guests are of course highly respectable people,' she informed me. 'Today though, they take the opportunity of letting their hair down and becoming much less respectable. Everything is permitted at this party, so don't be surprised if somebody makes improper suggestions to you.' She whirled round abruptly; her panties were also transparent at the front, revealing pubic hair that was black and dense, and this I found vulgar and off-putting. 'I hope you will give me the first dance.'

'I don't think your husband would like that,' I objected, unable to hide my reluctance.

'My husband?' Giovanna Zanon burst out laughing again. It was a laugh that went brazenly on until it collapsed, leaving her weak with mirth. Maybe she had mixed a line of cocaine with her sweet liqueurs. 'Taddeo is a very easy-going and decent man. Don't you know that the only place where decent married couples sleep together is in a box at the opera?' She drew herself up to her full height. 'And not even there now, since they burned down La Fenice!'

The great room in which the party was being held filled me with a somewhat metaphysical depression: the floor was inlaid with squares as on a chess board, and the walls were hung with the same Bordeaux-red velvet as the sofas on the motor-launch that had taken me there – I had no hesitation in attributing the choice of the provocative, brothel-like decorations to Giovanna Zanon. The ceiling frescoes illustrated mythological, mainly bestial copulations: the Rape of Europa, Jupiter's Golden Shower refreshing Danaë, Pasiphaë cuckolding Minos with the bull. They were not out of keeping with the spirit of the evening. A number of musicians dressed as jesters, or *mattaccini*, were playing a melody on stringed instruments that nobody danced to. It was a hotch-potch of discordant notes, somewhere between a requiem and a can-can, that disoriented me at first, and little by little reduced me to a state of dazed unreality. When they finished one piece they jumped up from their stools, left their instruments on the floor and started lobbing eggs in all directions from catapults loaded for the purpose. The eggs were projected at speed, and they shattered on the floor where they deposited their viscous contents, on the velvet-hung walls that quickly began to resemble works by Tàpies or Pollock, over the guests who tried to dodge them by pretending to duck, slithering at times on the mess on the floor. Giovanna Zanon received one on her bosom. The white of the egg soaked through the gossamer dress and made her silicone breasts and the blemishes on her cleavage even more visible, while the yellow dripped on to her stomach like molten wax. One of the guests pounced on her, pressed her against the wall, and raising his mask started to lick all that sticky stuff with the avidity of a farm animal at the trough, until his face was coated in it. Giovanna Zanon laughed and shrieked hysterically, calling for help, but she held her aggressor by the back of his head, just as she had gripped me by the forehead while she was making me listen to her poisonous words. I drew away, repelled, but wherever I looked my eyes fell on similar scenes.

'It's one of our Carnival traditions. The *mattaccini* throw eggs at the crowd who are happy to be daubed with them.'

I recognised the henpecked, ineffectual voice of Taddeo Rosso, the hotel magnate who shared Giovanna Zanon's operatic siestas. His gargoyle profile was accentuated by an eye-mask that included a violet-coloured nose. He had waxed his quasi-fascist moustache in order to emphasise its size, and had smeared rouge on his cheeks. He had made no other concession to colour in his dress: the white ruff contrasting with the black of his doublet, his stockings and wide velvet breeches gave him a funereal look.

'Now we are professional colleagues,' he said. 'You are the plague doctor, and I am the physician.'

He patted his belly which he had padded out with layers of coarse wool, while he extended his hand in effusive greeting. He too had large splashes of egg on his doublet, and he laughed for no apparent reason. It was a ventriloquist's laugh: it ceased as it reached his lips. He spoke slowly and in roundabout phrases, as if he was drugged. His voice was barely audible above the uproar of the orgy, but I deduced from his gestures that he was detailing the pedigrees of his guests. There were both local and international luminaries, an ex-minister, some faded film stars, businessmen with criminal backgrounds, ruined aristocrats, a pair of sodomite couturiers, and groups of pretty young men and second-hand 'virgins' bought in for the occasion who made no objection to having their personal merchandise closely inspected.

'Of course I am paying for all this,' Taddeo Rosso took

care to inform me. 'You can take any one of the girls or boys and do whatever you like with them.'

The orchestra of jesters started up another diabolical tune when they had finally exhausted their supply of eggs. The dilapidated 'virgins' covered their faces with *morette*, oval masks which did not come as low as their chins, but protected their other features. They all wore the same bizarre dress, with the bodice cut very low, leaving their breasts uncovered. Like cigarette girls in night-clubs, they carried trays hanging from round their necks which they proffered to the guests as they passed between them; but instead of tobacco, they offered cocaine and cannabis.

'No thanks, possibly later.' I backed away from one of them to the despair of Taddeo Rosso.

'But my dear friend, this is the ambrosia of the gods!'

From a small bottle, he sprinkled about a gram of cocaine between the girl's breasts that hung like tired twins in the same way that the humps of a camel are distorted when its liquid reserves run out. Instead of inhaling the cocaine, Taddeo bent down, and stained the girl's breasts with the rouge from his cheeks. His moustache became snowy white, and he licked the powder off.

'So what do you think of the party?'

'Marvellous!' The mask made it unnecessary for me to hide my true feelings. 'I congratulate you on your good taste.'

The cocaine induced in him a sense of foolish well-being. Giovanna Zanon was still allowing herself to be pursued by the individual who had wallowed in the mess on her dress, and various other guests were following along behind, blundering about like clumsy elephants debilitated by alcohol and drugs. I heard the sound of someone being sick, and soaking the floor with a cascade of vomit.

'Giovanna is the one you should congratulate,' responded Taddeo Rosso modestly. 'I supply the historical accuracy and certain other fundamentals, but she takes care of the staging. I am very lucky to be married to such a woman, don't you think?'

The spectacle of other people's depravity was producing in me a sensation of total apathy. I was assailed by a compulsion to run away, just as our dreams sometimes persuade us of the need to resolve a problem troubling us.

'Why is that?' I asked.

'Because she has such imagination, that's why.' As he said this he led me to a corner of the room further away from the orchestra, so that he could speak more confidentially. 'You arrive at a certain age when you believe you've tried everything. To get to know somebody like Giovanna at that time in your life is a blessing from Heaven.'

There appeared, just behind a half-open door, a line of six waiters all dressed as Punchinello, the joker of the *commedia dell'arte*. They wore white jackets with false humps on their backs, very broad hats shaped like flattened hoods, and masks with big curved noses. Taddeo Rosso snapped his fingers, and the waiters circulated round the room with trays of canapés and drinks.

'You have to keep their stomachs full so that their energies don't flag,' explained Taddeo Rosso. 'You've no idea how long it took to teach those dimwits. They have no catering experience.'

I noticed that there was in fact something crude about the waiters: they approached people arrogantly, and they disturbed a number of sexual developments and liaisons in the making by their insistence. Not a few of them, either out of ill-will or class resentment, spilled a glass of wine down the front of a woman, or bumped into her from behind so that she might feel the vigour of his proletarian virility between her buttocks.

'I thought they were servants of yours.'

'Not at all, not at all. Giovanna and I get along with very few domestics,' he said, as if the admission diminished his importance. 'I collected this unmannerly bunch from among the dregs of the city: unemployed fishermen and gondoliers. If I'd taken on professional waiters the cost would have been at least double.' I found this meanness extraordinary in a hotel millionaire. 'You can't imagine the incredible demands that every little kitchen-boy makes these days. They've been brainwashed by the trade unions. There's no way the country can prosper today. But we were talking about Giovanna.'

The choice of available pretty boys and stale virgins was diminishing as the evening wore on. Giovanna Zanon had calmed down, and was acting more like a conventional hostess, as she explained to a huddle of guests around her the rules of a game that was both lewd and esoteric.

'You were telling me that you had reached the age when you believed you had tried everything.'

Taddeo Rosso smoothed his moustache, with a decadent smile; grains of cocaine fell out of it like dandruff and lost themselves in the folds of his ruff. I was growing weary of his chatter, and beginning to feel very tired.

'Oh, you are a rogue,' he reprimanded me. 'But I wasn't referring to what you're thinking. Before I got to know Giovanna, I was completely taken up by business; with her, I have discovered there are many other things in life. For example, I used to invest my profits in Swiss bank accounts and properties. Giovanna awakened in me a love of art.'

'I was able to see that the other day. Your Bellini *Madonna* is magnificent,' I replied, trying to ensure that my sarcasm would not give me away.

'And that's just one example! You might like to have a look at my picture gallery. There was no tradition of collecting in my family, but thanks to Giovanna, my descendants will inherit a fortune in works of art.'

He plunged into an embarrassed silence, recalling that as yet he did not have any offspring. Giovanna Zanon, who had finished explaining the rules of the game she was organising, ordered her guests to scatter round the room and into those that led off it. One of the waiters bumped so hard into me from behind with his tray of drinks that some of the glasses broke.

'Clumsy idiot,' Taddeo Rosso reprimanded him. 'Look where you're going.'

A gust of rancid sweat which seemed to emerge from a recent and familiar past assailed my nostrils. I spun round to confirm my hunch: the sinewy hands that awkwardly held the tray and the rapacious teeth I could see behind the Punchinello mask made it easy to identify the waiter. Someone switched off the big chandelier in the middle of the room, and in the ensuing confusion I was able to slip away in the darkness to join Tedeschi.

'I didn't know you were a traitor,' I said accusingly. 'But now I can see nobody's to be trusted. Where have you put the chest? You've got the police very worried.'

To my surprise, Tedeschi seemed angry; he jumped away from me with a sudden movement, almost a contortion.

'The only traitor here is you, you bastard. We agreed we weren't going to tell anybody what we knew. But it's obvious you can't keep your trap shut. I saw you from the palace, gabbing away with that woman who runs the hotel, and I said to myself, "Look out, that fellow's going to sing like a canary." It's a good thing I pushed off!'

After the guests had moved away the room was quiet, except for some stifled laughter and muttering. Giovanna Zanon lit the candles on a candelabra, and moved up and down the room like a sleepwalker. When she pulled one of the curtains aside she revealed the hiding-place of a guest who expressed reluctance to accept the punishment he had to submit to according to the rules of the game.

'That's enough, that's enough, you've got to undress,' Giovanna Zanon interrupted his objections. 'There's no way out.'

The man, possibly some retired dignitary, who was to be made to suffer the rigours of the punishment, was old and frail and disguised as Pantaloon. His false, pointed beard, his Turkish slippers, his red stockings and doublet made him look rather like a satyr shrinking to half his size as he took off his clothes. It was a sickening sight, and I was ashamed for the man as he emerged naked, his legs gnarled with rheumatism, and his weedy chest covered in white hair.

'Underpants as well,' Giovanna Zanon reminded him.

The old man had to lean against the wall, not to lose his balance. His phallus was pendulous and by no means venerable, which gave great amusement to those who had chosen less obvious hiding-places. Giovanna Zanon blew out the candles with one puff, and announced:

'All change!'

There was a flurry of movement and collisions as the guests changed their hiding-places, while the old man, afflicted either by Parkinson's Disease or by lechery, failed to strike the match with which he was supposed to relight the candles on the candelabra so that the game could continue. Tedeschi led me down a corridor that multiplied both shadows and echoes, as far as a *loggia* or porticoed gallery, from which could be seen the palace garden like a place of execution, full of decapitated statues. I could also see the blurred outlines of Venice beneath its pestilence of fog. He gestured towards the lagoon, beyond the San Michele cemetery, beyond the nebulous horizon.

'Look for me on Torcello island. I'll be waiting,' he said. 'But don't even think of bringing anybody with you. I've got something very important to show you.'

I had a dozen questions I wanted to ask, but lacked the strength to formulate them in a logical order; someone, moreover, was coming towards the gallery. I just managed to whisper:

'Torcello island.' I committed that name, which I had never heard before, to my memory. 'And how shall I find you?'

'Don't worry, I shall find you first.'

Tedeschi removed his Punchinello hat and mask, and in one bound leaped over the balustrade; I heard the shrubbery below break his fall. The sound of his departure lessened as he ran off through the muddy alleys: fog, like snow, recovers quickly from footsteps. Only the streetlamps tried, here and there, to pierce the blackness with circles of light that grew smaller with distance, like the edges of a false coin as it circulates from hand to hand. I breathed in the damp Venetian air, in order to blunt lucidity and my memories, and to blunt also an incipient fear that was starting to take hold of me. Chiara would be sleeping not far away; she would have taken advantage of my absence to colonise the whole bed; she loved sleeping diagonally across it, and moving around between the sheets like a puppy stretching. Gabetti would have been surprised not to find her in her room, and would have gone up to her attic; maybe he was watching over her there, intoxicated by his feelings of tenderness. After all, he was the guardian of her repose, not I, the upstart foreigner.

'Why haven't you joined in the game?'

Giovanna Zanon had approached me from behind with the same stealth as Gabetti, as he spied on Chiara. The Domino costume and the wig with ringlets combined with the fog to make her resemble one of those apparitions who used to waylay travellers in ancient times, begging them to pay for a Mass that would release them from Purgatory – or for a quick coupling to compensate them for abstinence in the other world.

'I was looking for your husband,' I lied. 'I lost sight of him when the lights went out. He had promised to show me his picture gallery. According to what he told me, since he married you he has become a great lover of art.'

'Lover is an understatement.' As always, she referred to Taddeo Rosso with a mixture of contempt and pity. 'But I am not responsible for his obsession; I only suggested that he might invest in art because it never loses its value. As Taddeo is a child and wants everything he sees, he started by buying pictures in the way poor people buy cheap prints, purely for prestige reasons. After that, he infected all his friends with the same obsession – you can't imagine the competitive spirit that exists between millionaires. Thanks to Taddeo, Valenzin made a killing!'

The game still going on in the main room was discovering new victims, or winners, and was spreading to other parts of the palace where it was degenerating into casual copulations that the masks made anonymous.

'But Valenzin was a swindler, you know that perfectly well,' I said.

Giovanna Zanon pressed herself against me – she preferred couplings to Masses. Her breath still came drunkenly sweet through her veil, and the egg stains had left a dry crust on her gossamer tunic, like traces of vomit. I stifled my disgust.

'I had already warned Taddeo about that, and I recommended him never to think of buying paintings less than a century old, especially those of the Surrealist school. We insisted that Valenzin should document every picture he sold us.'

The fog was thickening, like lazy smoke, and it was gathering over the city as if trying to embalm it. The Church of the Jesuits which was scarcely fifty yards away from Giovanna Zanon's palace could be made out as if through a misted telescope.

'And how is a painting documented?' I enquired.

'According to where it comes from. If it's bought at auction there's no problem because it is always accompanied by a certificate of authenticity signed by several experts.' At this point I recalled that in the summer of 1962, Gabetti had been dismissed by an auction house because Fabio Valenzin had foisted on him a consignment of false Modiglianis. 'If the picture is bought privately, then it must be authenticated by an expert.'

'And if it is stolen?' I pressed on with growing exultation. 'Because Valenzin was also involved in thefts.'

'There's nothing easier than to document a stolen painting!' Giovanna Zanon laughed with pride. 'The newspapers always make a point of publicising it, and they publish photographs, just in case it falls into the hands of some pure soul who decides to return it. Valenzin backed up his thefts with an exhaustive dossier of press cuttings. He was vain, and loved to keep in touch with the impact of his exploits.' She stood very close to me, her breath penetrated the orifices in my mask, and steamed it up. I imagined that must have been, more or less, the way Venetians of old caught the poisonous vapours of the plague from each other's breath. 'And there's another advantage with stolen paintings: they work out much cheaper than those acquired through legal channels, because the thief has got to get rid of them at all costs, and there are no middlemen.'

The party had attained that point of satiety and inebriation when the guests like to drift apart. A pair of naked girls, possibly two of the second-hand virgins hired by Taddeo Rosso, had pitched their camp on the *loggia*, and were making love to each other, but more drowsily than lustfully.

'Nevertheless, you came to doubt the authenticity of Bellini's *Madonna*,' I said. 'You even brought me here to obtain my expert opinion.'

Giovanna Zanon entwined her fingers round my neck, under the hood of my costume, and more lustfully than drowsily, began to massage the nape of my neck with her varnished fingers. She hurt me when she pulled off one of the scabs on my scalp commemorating my combat in the Accademia.

'But you silly man, all I wanted to do was seduce you,' she purred. 'You seemed so ingenuous and helpless . . .'

I pushed her arms away with some asperity. Possibly celibacy imprints itself on one's character, but the recollection of another woman imprints itself even more effectively.

'Yes, and I suppose all those disgraceful things you said about Chiara were also part of your seduction technique.'

Two men were approaching down the corridor that led to the *loggia*. They were deep in a conversation, of which I only managed to capture fragments because it was carried on in a mixture of innuendo and private codes. Even so, I deduced from a few random words that they were discussing a delicate subject, possibly something illegal, or some bit of chicanery just on the edge of the law. I recognised in one of the voices the servile tones of Taddeo Rosso; the other voice was stentorian, that of a bully, who raised objections to the mellifluous words of his companion and occasionally expressed his irritation with a blasphemy. This voice belonged to a man whose temperament was as arrogant as his costume: a three-cornered hat, an eighteenth-century greatcoat, and a shirt with frilly ruffs, the finishing touch being a severely pale mask. It was evident from his overbearing demeanour that he would have refused to participate in Giovanna Zanon's nudist game.

'You must keep cool,' I heard Taddeo Rosso say. 'And also keep a close rein on those two, they're very obvious.'

The other agreed sulkily. Taddeo Rosso was alluding to a couple of tough individuals who appeared in the *loggia* with that air, somewhere between inquisitive and bad-tempered, required of bodyguards so that their presence in public places does not offend against acceptable conduct, but is at the same time discouraging. They were both dressed as Harlequins, with tight diamond-patterned jerkins, which were nearly bursting from the powerful muscles underneath, and cloth caps complete with bells. Their masks had almost simian features, and included hairy eyebrows. I would have taken them for clones if one of them had not had a crew-cut, whereas the other's hair resembled that of an Assyrian warrior or a night-club bouncer, slightly wavy, and shaved close at the sides of his head. Seeing them I felt the same trepidation I had felt when Tedeschi handed me the ring with the emblem of the two columns. When I noticed the mutilated ear of the hairy Harlequin, my agitation turned into a prickly sensation of the sort that precedes paralysis. I leaned on the balustrade of the balcony while considering the likelihood of escaping unharmed if I jumped over it.

'Is anything wrong?' asked Giovanna Zanon.

The scars on my back, which I had believed to be dry, began to weep.

'No, nothing. What is the name of the man with your husband?'

I spoke to Giovanna Zanon using the familiar '*tu*', which until then I had avoided in our dealings, impelled by the desperate urgency of a man who feels the need for allies, but she took it as a sign that I was weakening and about to give in to her.

'Daniele Sansoni,' she told me. 'He is one of the millionaires competing with Taddeo to see who can accumulate the biggest collection of paintings. He's another one of Valenzin's regular clients.'

I leaned against one of the pillars supporting the gallery. It would not have mattered to me if it had given way at that moment, crushing me underneath, provided that its collapse buried all the others: *Moriatur anima mea cum philistiim*.

'He made his money in the export business, and suffers from delusions of grandeur,' continued Giovanna Zanon. 'He's bought more than twelve noble titles and has had a coat of arms designed for him which he has printed on his visiting cards and embroidered on the pockets of his jackets. Can you imagine it, he's so crazy he believes he's related to Samson, the one in the Bible!'

Sansoni's henchmen or bodyguards were amusing themselves by trying to revive the two naked girls who, after finishing their lesbian love-making, had fallen victim to drunken black-outs, and were now wallowing in their own vomit. The men were reviving them with smacks which sounded like the cracks of a whip.

'Well, I have to go now, it's getting late.'

It seemed to me that the headless statues were descending from their pedestals and surrounding the palace like a police cordon, but the fog was inducing absurd visions, and my senses were functioning badly.

'Just a moment, let me introduce you,' said Giovanna Zanon, before I could leave. 'You ought to see his collection of paintings. The only ones that interest him are those with ruins and broken columns, possibly because they remind him of his fictitious past. Valenzin sold him most of them, and now he's worried they may be forgeries. You could make a tidy sum if you gave him an expert opinion.' I tried to find some excuse, but Giovanna Zanon was already shouting: 'Hey, Taddeo! It would be a good idea if Sansoni met our Spanish friend, he's an art professor, and can tell a forgery a mile off.'

This over-statement of my merits attracted Sansoni's attention as well as that of his two thugs, who looked at each other and gave up trying to revive the girls. Taddeo Rosso was slow to react, but he did so with exaggerated expressions of pleasure that reminded me of our meeting after again being separated when the lights were turned off. His padding had slipped down and now poked through the buttons of his doublet, making him look even more like a scarecrow. A deep dread paralysed me as the introduction was made – Sansoni's bodyguards were not included in this, and they remained at a discreet distance, their thumbs stuck in the girdles round their waists.

'So you specialise in identifying forgeries,' said Sansoni. His voice, besides being stentorian, emerged obliquely from the corner of his mouth, in the way that some men expel their cigarette smoke. One of his eye teeth was crowned with gold – to lend distinction to his appearance.

'Not exactly,' I stammered. 'The truth is, I am a researcher.'

'But he has an infallibly critical eye,' interrupted Taddeo Rosso. 'He has authenticated our Bellini in the little study downstairs.'

Sansoni pulled his hat down over his eyebrows so that it would not fall off. He had a rosette stitched on to the brim which bore the spurious coat of arms based on his surname.

'You know, I could give you quite a bit of work,' he said, testing me out. From the particular way in which he pursed his lips, it was obvious that the 'bit of work' would be exceedingly well paid. 'Provided you're trustworthy, and have time to spare.'

Paralysis made me dumb. Giovanna Zanon made up for my unresponsiveness.

'I can answer for him.' She took me by the arm to emphasise her role of protectress. 'And he's got plenty of time. The poor man has had a useless visit. He came to study that picture by Giorgione, *The Tempest*, but Gabetti has put every obstacle in his way.'

The Harlequin with the filthy hair, who, until then, had remained absorbed in the task of pulling off hangnails from the ends of his fingers, gave a start, which did not go unnoticed by his employer. I assessed that the height of about eighteen feet which separated me from the garden below was likely to leave me with a number of broken bones and many severe bruises, even if I did not fall awkwardly and break my head, but remaining in the *loggia* did not seem to bode any better.

'What's the secret? We all want to be in on it,' said Taddeo Rosso imbecilically, as the hairy Harlequin muttered something in the ear of his employer.

Still in that state of indecision which precedes the most resolute of actions, I was able to contemplate the gashes I had left in the thug's ear. The wound had begun to heal, but it would leave a whitish scar. Sansoni's jaw tightened as he listened to the confidential remarks of his hireling, a movement suggesting that my departure should not be delayed. I clambered on to the balustrade of the balcony — I did not have in my favour the agility of Tedeschi, who had been able to clear it with one leap — and I scrutinised the fog that would serve me either as a couch or a mortuary shroud.

'It's him! I knew it, boss. We've got to get him now.'

For a moment the air took me for a large bird: it inflated my cape, which made my flight easier, and it quickly penetrated the holes in my mask, slowing my rate of fall and abolishing the law of gravity, as often happens in dreams. But then it withdrew its support and let me crash down on a privet hedge. I fell spreadeagled over the branches and stood up before becoming aware of the pain caused by the bruising I had received. As I began to run off I was already harassed by the shadows of the two Harlequins. The diamond shapes on their costumes added an unexpected colouration to the darkness of the night. As I passed near the side of the fountain I snatched off the plague doctor's mask and hurled it into the basin. Bubbles, like hollow tears, escaped through the empty eye holes as the porcelain mask sank slowly into the leaves at the bottom. The wet fog accentuated the outlines of my face. I skirted one of the palace walls, and plunged into a narrow alley that gave barely enough room on either side to pass through; I guessed that Sansoni's thugs would have to go down it sideways if they were not to be trapped by their substantial girths. The light from the streetlamps was sparse, scarcely more than chinks in the all-embracing fog. Every time I came to an intersection, I turned right: ingrained superstition suggested to me that by this means I would distance myself from the centre of the labyrinth. The cape hindered my flight, and it rubbed against every corner as if it wished to take with it the memory of the worn stone. I crossed squares that convoked all the echoes and reverberations of the city in a sort of acoustic phantasmagoria. I passed through porticoes so low that I was forced to stoop, crossed blind bridges that led into darkness like trampolines for would-be suicides. Fatigue was getting the better of me when, at the end of an alley, I glimpsed the Fondamente Nuove quayside. I could no longer hear footsteps behind me, and began to think I had shaken off my pursuers. Then I heard the tinkling of little bells behind my back and felt hot breath on my neck.

'Did you really think you could give us the slip, you poor Spanish sap?'

I recognised the ruffian accent and the bad breath only partially masked by eucalyptus lozenges. Sansoni's bodyguards lifted me off the ground and carried me down to the edge of the quay. They also had rid themselves of their hairy, simian masks, although their true features did not compare favourably with those of the masks, indeed they outdid them in ugliness. I was seized by a blue funk that froze my blood. I guessed they were going to beat me up and treat me with extreme cruelty, but my curiosity about what methods they would use was greater than my terror at the imminent prospect of torture.

'First of all we're going to give you a good soaking,' said the thug with the Assyrian hair.

I had hoped that the first punishment would be relatively mild, bearing in mind that I am an indifferent swimmer. They swung me backwards and then threw me into the lagoon, celebrating my ducking with loud guffaws. The water was so cold it pierced my bones; and it had an acid flavour like industrial waste. I tried to raise my head to take in more air after my first immersion, but found it impossible. Once it was soaked through, the cape weighed as much as a mill-wheel, and it dragged me down as if my presence was urgently required in some cemetery or substratum of the depths. I kicked about in the water while trying to get rid of it, searching for the fastenings that held it tight round my neck, but they were very complicated fastenings that included hooks and double-knotted laces. The laughter of my tormentors standing on the quayside reached me muted, as if distorted by centuries of distance, and the diamond shapes of their costumes fused into a muddle of imprecise colours. The first signs of asphyxiation took the form of a pressure on my temples that grew more intense until my head was splitting; my fingers stiffened and lost their sense of touch, while my lungs absorbed to their very depths the water that was dragging them back to a remote past, antediluvian even, when creatures did not have lungs but gills, and the sea was a sort of womb that propagated the birth of new species. It was terrifying, and yet inviting, to descend very slowly through the levels of animal evolution; it was oppressive, but liberating, to let go and be freed from the eternal penance of remembering, to deny intelligence and the faculty of memory, to yield to the call of the marine depths, and to expel the last reserve of air that remained in my mouth . . .

Hands that were determined either to prolong my agony or to postpone my regression through the evolutionary process brought me back up to the surface, hauled me forcibly on to the quay, and pumped my chest until they had expelled all the water that had flooded my lungs. In my state of semi-consciousness, I was aware of somebody opening my mouth so wide that he nearly dislocated my jaw, and blowing into the cavity air that had been desiccated by nicotine and tar, like a dry desert wind. It got my lungs working again, and freed them of their underwater caprices. With inexpressible fatigue and gratitude I recognised Nicolussi's villainous beard scratching my lips.

'We got here in the nick of time,' he said, and with a gentle slap on my cheek, added: 'Welcome to the land of the living!'

TWELVE

I retain only a hazy recollection of the hours that followed my rescue, an accumulation of scattered, unreliable impressions; Nicolussi's words were disjointed, and they got through to me in the fragmented way that a surgeon's encouraging noises penetrate the consciousness of a still anaesthetised patient who has just left the operating theatre. Their muddled mishmash acted on my soporific state like a sort of chant, a stream of whispered words that I was only occasionally able to piece together in those few moments when my fainting fits granted me intervals of lucidity. I have a vague memory of being carried to a motor-launch and laid down on a wooden bench; I have another vague memory of being wrapped in a blanket and having my face slapped, repeatedly, but not viciously, while the launch moved off, its siren blaring through the night. I also have a vague memory of sicking up a viscous liquid that was a mixture of lagoon water and my gastric juices. Nicolussi took my head in his hands to prevent me choking on my own vomit, in the way I had held Fabio Valenzin's head, supporting his neck while the blood gushed between his teeth. In addition to the din of the siren, the launch had brilliant revolving lights; the two were combining to dazzle and deafen me, and were making me lose consciousness while Nicolussi went on talking, his words all equally unintelligible. Probably he was exhorting me to pull myself together, but I did not even bother to take them in, let alone try to sort them out: they were no more than a buzz in the background lulling me to sleep.

In that dazed condition, I confused the noise of the siren with the crying of a child. I dreamed that once again I was wandering through the landscape of *The Tempest*, which had been deserted by its adult figures; I crossed the bridge over the stream and watched from the bank as a baby was swept down by the current. It was newly born, abandoned in a wicker basket and wrapped in a linen cloth that bore traces of blood, possibly that which its mother had lost during the birth. The current was violent, abnormally so for a stream running through a valley, and the basket had difficulty in staying afloat. The water eddied round the rocks in its path and left ripples of foam between the reeds. I ran in the direction of the stream in order to catch the basket at a point where its course narrowed, without getting my feet wet. The child's cries were loud and urgent; if they did not stop soon he would choke to death. They were the cries of a helpless orphan, possibly sharpened by hunger, possibly because he was calling for his mother who should have been suckling him with her air of sensual sadness. I squatted on the grass and watched the basket as it came near, trying to make out the baby's features, and from them to guess who his parents were. But every feature of his face contained a giddy succession of likenesses; every trait incorporated the patrician features of Chiara, the Jewish features of Gabetti, the emaciated features of Fabio Valenzin, as well as my own, all interwoven, both successively and simultaneously. Urged on by paternal instinct, I extended my arms towards the wicker basket but, as it reached a hollow in the river bed, the waters swallowed the basket, the baby, and its cries; a rosary of bubbles like hollow tears remained the silent witnesses of their destruction. Although I hastened to rake through the dead leaves at the bottom, I found no trace of the child. Quite the opposite: my hands came in contact with a horrible, cold, white, porcelain object, the mask of a plague doctor.

I woke up in a room with no external windows, its walls lined with cork. In front of me, through a pane of glass, I could see what was happening in the next room: all of Taddeo Rosso's and Giovanna Zanon's guests at the fancy-dress ball were lined up on a platform, and were posing one by one in front of Nicolussi's men to be photographed, full-face and profile, to go into the police dossiers, and possibly one day to illustrate their epitaphs. The guests still bore the marks of drunkenness and depravity, aggravated by a perplexity that had not yet attained the level of anger, because the excesses of the party continued to maintain them in a state of nebulous inertia. Nicolussi was taking statements from each one, seated at a plastic table that looked as if it had been designed for surgical operations. The fluorescent tubes in the room gave off an anaemic light that seemed to be tinged with blue as it passed through the pane of glass.

'Don't worry,' said Dina. 'They can't see us. All they can see is a mirror.'

Then I noticed I was naked. Somebody had removed my wet clothes, possibly Dina herself, and had laid me out on a divan made of imitation black leather that the police may have used in their psychoanalytic – or torture – sessions. I covered myself modestly with a blanket that lay rolled up over my feet, but it was too late. Dina would have had time to examine in detail my puny shoulders, my ribs – not one of which had been extracted – and also my weedy sex which had retreated deep inside its foreskin, although a few hours earlier it had betrayed its vocation of celibacy and reneged on its vow of abstinence. Dina smiled sympathetically as I made a move to cover myself.

'I've brought you some clean clothing,' she said. 'And also an infusion. Drink it down, and then you'll feel better.'

She unscrewed the top of a Thermos flask, and poured some of the contents into a plastic cup. The medicinal smell of the infusion took me back for a moment to my childhood when my mother, who had no faith in antibiotics, used to treat my colds with infusions of mallow. I made a space so that Dina could sit next to me. Her bottom was still soft and asymmetrical, although it was severely constricted by her skirt. It no longer excited my desire, just a vaguely filial sentiment.

'Have I been asleep long?' I asked, in an attempt to reconstruct what had happened.

'About five or six hours, I think. Dawn must have broken some time ago.'

It was impossible to tell in that cloistered room how light it was outside. The infusion had a wide range of flavours, as if an infinite number of herbal ingredients had been mixed together. It was sweetened with honey, and, as it slid down my throat, it allayed my feelings of nausea.

'He's gone mad, completely mad,' said Dina, pointing with her chin towards the pane of glass.

Although she was affecting dismay, there was a deep note of pride in her voice.

'Who? Nicolussi?'

Dina nodded slowly, as if lost in thought. The spectacular bruise round her eye had begun to fade, but it still spread up as far as her temple and down her cheek, like a leprous stigma. Nicolussi was interrogating Taddeo Rosso and Giovanna Zanon, who stared at him with resentful insolence, like unblinking automata. The dishevelled state of their costumes could have made them pass for street beggars with an eccentric taste in dress. Giovanna Zanon's face, moreover, was undergoing a process of dissolution, a gradual metamorphosis: both her make-up and its surgical underpinning were collapsing to create a new physiognomy dominated by wrinkles and flabby flesh. Amid the ruin, all that remained was the vintage vinegar of her eyes. On a signal from Nicolussi, one of his subordinates approached carrying the Bellini painting that I knew to be false, the *Madonna and Child* painted by Fabio Valenzin. Giovanna Zanon scarcely reacted, but her husband started to gesture with an exaggerated show of feeling which it clearly gave Nicolussi great pleasure to watch. We could not hear any of the words spoken in the next room, and the scene continued, silent but animated, like a film whose story you know only too well.

'He's gone mad,' repeated Dina, with inexplicable delight. She stood up, and approached very near to the glass, almost touching it. 'Before rescuing you, he ordered the palace to be surrounded, and every living creature in it detained. The police cells are bursting.'

The vapour of her breath condensed on the glass, but quickly vanished, until she breathed on it once again. She pressed her severe lips against the pane, leaving their double impression, streaked with minute furrows. At almost the same moment, Nicolussi rubbed the back of his head. I wondered whether he had become aware of a tickling sensation from that illusion of a kiss, in the same way that, a few nights before, Chiara had been aware of my presence on her balcony, and had responded to my caresses, stirring between the sheets like a puppy stretching.

I recalled the elusive touch of her shoulder, the trusting feel of her thighs, the indefinable sensation of being inside her, in a brief foretaste of the lasting punishment that would be mine . . .

'There were some very influential people at that party,' said Dina. 'And he's arrested all of them without charge.'

'Without charge? Well, he'll pay heavily for this bit of fun. These people won't stop until they've had him removed.'

'I imagine that's what he has in mind.'

The deep note of pride I had noticed in her voice earlier was acquiring a tone of unmistakable joy. I learned from her that, after connecting the design on the ring with Sansoni's noble pretensions, and having found out where the millionaire was, Nicolussi had obtained a search warrant from the duty magistrate and had organised an assault operation on Taddeo Rosso and Giovanna Zanon's palace, which went directly counter to the normal methods of the Venetian police whose activities until then had been characterised by permissiveness and evasion of duty. Dina suddenly seemed to me more graceful, in spite of having left off her high-heeled shoes; inside her sweater, her breasts stood proud, as if endowed with renewed youth.

'Don't you understand?' she said. 'They'll take legal proceedings against him, have him demoted, and sent off to a new job in another city. We shan't have to pretend, or meet in secret any longer.'

I felt a genuine happiness for both of them, but particularly for Nicolussi, who would no longer have to nurse his love in secret. My first feeling of happiness was not slow, however, to subside as I thought about my own future, which was much less benign: nobody would take legal action against me, or have me demoted, and nobody would find me another job that would relieve me of the permanent memory of Chiara – the ghost of her inhabiting my body and my memory like an incurable tumour.

'You've no idea how pleased I am for you, Dina. Really I am,' I said. But my voice sounded dry, and very old, weighed down by the ballast of the past.

'And you're the one who made it happen,' she said affectionately. 'I don't know what you talked about yesterday when you left the hotel, but the fact is he's a changed man.'

It embarrassed me to receive this undeserved praise. All I had done was to listen to Nicolussi's monologue about his and Dina's past, and to show, out of politeness or sympathy, that I was touched by his dilemma, but I had not dared to influence his decisions. Perhaps, however, by making me the repository of his secret, Nicolussi was not looking for a positive response on my part so much as silent acquiescence. Perhaps, when we talk about personal matters to another individual all we are looking for is someone to confide in.

'What's wrong? Why do you look so sad?' asked Dina.

'Sad? Not really. Maybe I'm just a bit down. It looks as if all this is now coming to an end.'

Her Byzantine eyes were studying me without understanding the reasons why I was moping. I was tempted to explain, just to have someone to confide in, but my sense of personal dignity prevented me from exposing my weakness. Celibacy requires an apprenticeship in various forms of vanity, and one of them, perhaps the most difficult to achieve, is to build defences against the pity of others, even at the cost of shutting ourselves away in a sort of autism.

'You can return to Spain today if you like. Aldo asked me to reserve a seat for you on the first flight out.'

'Aldo? Who is Aldo?'

'Who do you think he is? He's got a first name like everybody else, and I don't have to pretend any longer.'

I gave a smile that was cynical in spite of myself.

'I'm sorry. I'm so used to his surname,' I said. I was upset that he had decided to send me away without consulting me first. 'But does he consider the case closed? I don't believe Sansoni and his hirelings will confess as easily as all that. And what has happened to Fabio Valenzin's chest? As far as I know it hasn't turned up yet.' The truth is, I was less concerned by Nicolussi's haste to send me away than by the certainty of the misery I should feel as soon as I left Venice. 'Nicolussi may need me here. There are some very difficult days ahead.'

Dina shook her head to contradict me, but she did it in a kindly way.

'Your presence here would only lead to more complications, Alejandro,' she said, with a hint of censure in her voice. 'What makes you hesitate? Didn't you want to remain outside the main investigation? Well, that is what Aldo is trying to do – keep you out of it. Don't forget he saved your life. You owe him something for that.'

I lowered my eyes, a little cast down by her rebuke. In the next room, Nicolussi had got rid of Taddeo Rosso and Giovanna Zanon after submitting them to an interrogation that I felt sure infringed all their legal rights. He seemed indifferent to fatigue, like those army doctors who move from one wounded man to another, giving immediate aid, without bothering too much about hygienic precautions. While they were bringing up the next batch of detainees, he passed the time rummaging in his raincoat until he found a packet of cigarettes he had not yet exhausted. He took out one that had almost lost its cylindrical form, and lit it with a lighter lent him by one of his subordinates. A cloud of smoke took shape in front of his face like an improvised and fluctuating mask.

'So it was one of those creatures who tied me to the chair and put me through that horrible time,' murmured Dina. 'The bastards.'

Daniele Sansoni entered the interrogation room with a uniformed policeman on either side, looking more like his servants to judge by the respectful way they treated him. Those charged with bringing up his henchmen were less ceremonious. They thrust them forward, and did not provide chairs for them to sit down. Nicolussi spoke at length, but unwillingly. Possibly he was reciting for Sansoni's benefit those legal rights he had violated earlier on. He shook out the cigarette packet on to the plastic table; among the bits of tobacco appeared the ring with the broken columns. Daniele Sansoni listened to the Inspector's accusations without flinching or displaying any less arrogance than usual. Although they had taken away his mask, the paleness of his face resembled the deep pallor of porcelain. He smiled out of the corner of his mouth, revealing his gold-capped tooth as the policeman who had lit Nicolussi's cigarette placed on the table the three-cornered hat Sansoni had chosen for the masked ball, complete with the rosette that flaunted the emblem of his surname, identical to the design on the ring.

'It won't be easy to make them confess, but they'll have to fight hard to refute the evidence that incriminates them, don't you think?'

'Yes, you're probably right.'

Even so, another possible explanation of the recent events was beginning to take shape in a remote corner of my mind, although it was still very shadowy. It contradicted and displaced the one I had so far been working on. I remembered with alarm that Tedeschi had asked me to meet him on Torcello island, where, perhaps, the solution to the puzzle awaited me. Nicolussi had concluded his peroration and was finishing off his cigarette with deep contentment and the pride of a successful detective. There was no longer any trace of sadness in his eyes, nor any sign that he would be deflected from the path he had chosen. Daniele Sansoni and his thugs on the other hand remained silent, like all accused criminals who entrust everything to the skill of their lawyers. Not one of the three would agree to sign the statements put before them, but silence can be eloquent without needing signatures. The accused were already filing back to the cells when Nicolussi turned towards the pane of glass and smiled with that childish excitement of an actor seeking the camera's lens. He was not slow to join us.

'You were marvellous, Aldo.' Dina no longer spoke in the bitter or reproachful way that had cast a cloud over her conversations with Nicolussi when he was still paralysed by moral scruples. 'But you ought to cut down on your smoking!'

She was beginning to display the first signs of that delight in organising others that seizes women who are on the point of getting married, a delight they vent on the habits of others, but which serves only to strengthen their own. They embraced without any sense of shame. Dina's breasts flattened against the Inspector's chest, and he could probably feel them rising and hardening under the black sweater.

'Get dressed, Ballesteros,' he ordered me, without letting go of Dina. He refused even to give me time to express my gratitude for having brought me back to life. 'I want you to go with me to the Accademia.'

I protested nervously.

'You promised you would keep me out of the investigation.'

'And I shall keep my promise. It is precisely because I want to keep it that I need Gabetti, at all costs, to make a statement accusing Sansoni and his men of trying to steal *The Tempest*,' he said. 'This afternoon an investigating magistrate will come to interrogate them, and I can't base my suspicions solely on the evidence of the ring. If only we had been able to get hold of that chest . . .'

There was no direct criticism in his words, but there was a mild rebuke.

'Gabetti will not collaborate,' I said, attempting to dissuade him. 'At the time, he preferred to keep quiet in order to avoid the attentions of the press. His enemies – and I gather he has many – will have his head if it comes out that the museum was unguarded that night.'

Nicolussi gave a sarcastic and condescending smile.

'Don't worry. I'll take care it doesn't come out.' He spoke with an almost schoolmasterly deliberation, as if he was explaining the tricks of his profession. 'But the alarms did go off that evening and Gabetti cannot deny it. He also phoned the police to prevent the squad going out that was already getting ready to go. There's nothing more natural than that I, a diligent police officer, should want to ensure that nothing really did happen. It's just a routine check, and you must help me convince him of that.'

Dina squeezed my arm, begging me to agree. Her proximity was intimidating but also persuasive; it inspired me with courage and submissiveness in equal parts. It wasn't surprising Nicolussi's pulse had quickened when he met her. I continued to put up a feeble resistance.

'But you are not a diligent police officer. And I won't be any use to you. Gabetti can't stand the sight of me.'

'Wasn't he your protector?' Nicolussi lit another cigarette, not yet prepared to cut back on his vices. 'He did his best to help you after Valenzin was murdered.'

'I imagine he did that out of fellow feeling,' I suggested. 'It's normal in the academic world to help a colleague, just in case we need help ourselves one day. But circumstances have changed, and now he would rather not even see me.'

Nicolussi's mouth twisted with suppressed anger.

'In that case we shall have to say that you have reported the robbery attempt,' he said. 'If we do that, he has no alternative other than to collaborate in order to avoid a scandal.'

I gave in, resigning myself to the role of Judas that I would have to play in this farce. Men have a tendency not much studied by psychologists, which consists in acting for no better reason than because we shouldn't, as if the certainty of committing a sin or an error intervenes like an irresistible force obliging us to do so. This unusual tendency, which may not lend itself to analysis, led me to behave shabbily.

'You can count on me, Nicolussi.'

While I was dressing in the clothes Dina had brought me from the hotel – clothing I had not even unfolded, and that was stiff and harsh like funeral garments – I was afflicted by the dejection that casts a shadow over the spirits of traitors once they have committed their crime and become obsessed by the condemnation of their own guilty conscience, in order to avert the condemnation of society. They brood over their guilt, and allow themselves to be oppressed by the incubus of the man at whom they have pointed the finger. And besides dejection, there was condemnation of my own contemptible behaviour: by accusing Gabetti I would not only be abetting his dismissal, I should also be betraying Chiara who could continue to serve as Venice's guardian angel only so long as Gabetti retained his position. Nicolussi was exchanging endearments with Dina in the corridor, to the amazement of his subordinates. The police station had that transitional air of a house before a change of occupants.

'Wait for me in the hotel, Dina,' said Nicolussi.

A cleansing morning sun swept the sky, the first really clear sunshine since my arrival in Venice. A puppet theatre had been set up in the shadow of the bell tower of San Stefano in which the comic love affairs of Pierrot and Columbine were being played out to entertain the tourists. We crossed the Grand Canal by the wooden bridge that, like a memory of Japan – in Venice exoticisms don't clash – links the districts of St Mark's and Dorsoduro. Nicolussi no longer walked crabwise, or in profile; his gait was carefree, even lackadaisical, like that of the passers-by who had nothing better to do than wear out the soles of their shoes. The palaces on the Grand Canal, lined up as if for review, contended with one another to be reflected in the water; these reflections improved their appearance because they stripped them of that sugary, repetitive beauty that typifies certain types of city architecture. The wake of a *vaporetto* reduced the stony mirage to ruins.

'I'm sorry your holiday has worked out so badly for you,' said Nicolussi. 'But you've probably got time to try some other city.'

'It wasn't a holiday, it was a study visit,' I corrected him, feeling slightly irked. 'But don't be sorry, it's not your fault. The fault always lies with the one who makes the journey without stopping to think first of the disruption it will cause to his life. I swear to remain in one place from now on.'

I felt as old as the pyramids, or the desert. Nicolussi clapped me on the shoulder.

'Don't let it get you down, my friend. It isn't worth it. You'll soon get over it.'

I promised myself a peaceful future, with that superficiality of thought common to those who enjoy quiet after a period of convalescence.

Organised tours did not include the Accademia in their itineraries, and only the better informed were entering it, or those who were inclined to wander freely round the city. Even so, an occasional Japanese had smuggled himself in somehow, and was running through the galleries in order not to miss the boat to Murano and Burano, those emporia of cheap mementoes. The main hall of the museum still held its damp, rancid, salty smell, like that of a galleon that has been soaking at the bottom of the sea for centuries until a sudden cataclysm brings it back to the surface. Nicolussi informed the ticket office that he wanted to interview the director, and he identified himself with all due pomposity, making a point of referring to the rank of which he would shortly be stripped. Gilberto Gabetti made us wait nearly a quarter of an hour, but he offered no apology when he came out to meet us. He smoothed his white hair back in an affected gesture that was not natural, and extended a hand blemished by vitiligo. His skin felt to me like that of a toad.

'Ballesteros, what a surprise. I thought you were on your way back to Spain,' he said, with a smile he tried to make courteous but which actually concealed cunning. 'And you, Nicolussi, that's a right hornet's nest you've stirred up. The radio can't talk about anything except your raid last night, and they say you've taken the lid off a whole network of illegal trafficking in works of art.'

Nicolussi shrugged his shoulders to brush aside the flattery; but his modest gesture was affected.

'There are even reports that Fabio Valenzin's murderer may be among those you've arrested. Is it true?'

'That's what I wanted to talk to you about. That, and the failed attempt to steal *The Tempest*.'

Gabetti pursed his lips so hard they disappeared to a narrow line. They were lips wasted by austerity, and barely suitable for making love, but nevertheless gave an impression of licentiousness. With an ambassadorial wave of his arm, he invited us to precede him up the stairs to the galleries. The walls were still covered with fungal growths.

'Frankly, I don't know what you're talking about,' he lied. 'But it would be better if we talk in my office.'

He directed a look of detestation at me, which made me feel I was sinking into an icy abyss. He guided us along a passage that was closed to the public; it had a sad, gloomy, bureaucratic air about it, with a wooden floor that budgetary constraints had prevented from being polished for several decades.

'You know quite well what I'm talking about. Ballesteros witnessed it,' adduced Nicolussi, finally engulfing me in ignominy. 'The night before last, two individuals tried desperately to steal that picture.'

Gabetti's office was as ascetic as its occupant. Not a single hanging discredited the dingy white of the walls, and not a loose paper was to be seen between the folders arranged symmetrically across the desk. He invited us to sit down on two carved upright chairs whose joints were coming apart. Through the window appeared a sky of monastic blue, matching that of Gabetti's eyes.

'Ballesteros has witnessed far too many things; it might be better if he took a little rest,' he said, with apparent frailty, as if every word caused him an internal haemorrhage. 'That's the problem with young people, they believe themselves so bursting with physical and mental energy they want to see everything, try everything, and hear everything, but in the end they understand nothing!'

Once again he smoothed back his white hair with a gesture of self-glorification, as if he feared that so much whiteness might collapse in a gentle avalanche of snow.

'But Ballesteros hasn't made any statement accusing you,' Nicolussi took care to clarify, but his attempt to rehabilitate me came too late. 'All he did was to inform me. And all I am asking you to do is to identify the assailants who almost certainly were the ones who killed Fabio Valenzin. There's no reason why anybody should know whether the museum was, or was not, guarded that evening.'

Gabetti put his fingers together in an attitude of meditation or prayer. He took no notice of Nicolussi; he was just making rhetorical pauses in his monologue.

'All young people are guilty of being opinionated and over-confident,' he continued. But I had left my youth far behind; I had wasted it in sterile researches and arduous academic drudgery. I am a defunct adolescent, or a prematurely aged man. 'I confess that I suffered from the same malady when I was young – but I am talking of a time long before the Punic Wars!'

He gave an affected laugh, but without enthusiasm, before speaking into his interphone to ask for some of his meetings and appointments to be put off. This plea for time led me to guess he was preparing himself for a lengthy harangue – unless Nicolussi dared to cut him short.

'I also cultivated my own self-confidence. Is it surprising? It was drilled into us at university and, as far as I can see, nothing has changed since.' He was wandering off the subject that concerned us; his voice was silky and digressive, but he was only biding his time until the moment when he would attack me directly. 'The night before last I brought Ballesteros here to the Accademia so that he could see *The Tempest*. The lad aroused an irrational sympathy in me, perhaps because he reminded me of the man I once was, and I harboured the hope of being able to correct his delusions.' He half-closed his eyes to suggest that he had been led by magnanimity or by misjudgement, but Gabetti did not misjudge people, nor was he magnanimous. 'The pity is, I found it impossible to convince him; he has been corrupted by the indoctrination he has received. He has considerable knowledge of art, but his capacity for artistic appreciation has been destroyed. A mere knowledge of art is within the reach of anyone of mediocre talent: all that is needed is a little patience, hard work, and a dose of critical discernment. To possess artistic appreciation is another thing entirely, and is a gift given only to a select few. Those who merely know all about it treat a painting like an inert object that they have to research, analyse, and judge; but a painting, assuming it is authentic, doesn't allow for being disembowelled and stuffed, it is a living thing towards which we cannot behave as critics: it calls for an emotional reaction. Responding sympathetically means accepting it without reserve, almost intuitively, but in a way that is unassailable and final. Artistic appreciation is an act of faith, which is why a true perception of art is related to the religious impulse.'

He was breathing with difficulty, as if suffering from emphysema. Nicolussi had had enough by then.

'All this is very interesting and instructive, but it's beside the point.' His daring won him the same look of detestation that Gabetti had earlier directed at me. 'Concentrate on what happened next.'

'I shall concentrate on what I choose. You cannot give me

orders,' replied Gabetti, with marked severity. He loved taking his time, just as he loved causing pain, and he was not going to be rushed. 'Ballesteros likes to analyse and box art in by the use of more or less historicist interpretations. He doesn't realise, the poor fool, that a painting is a mysterious thing that can't be caged in. And he applies his lack of comprehension to *The Tempest*, just as he does to life itself. But real life cannot be spied on, investigated, or understood. Neither life, nor women, Ballesteros!'

I appreciated, or perhaps I merely grasped, the tortuous direction of his strategy and the humiliation he was planning for me. I stood up, propelled out of my chair by what remained of my dignity.

'What are you getting at? Don't you think you've already treated me badly enough?'

I searched his face for a vestige of forbearance, but in vain. I looked for the last time at Gilberto Gabetti; I looked at his snow-white hair, his Jewish features blemished by vitiligo, but still arrogant, his lips wasted by abstinence or malevolence, and his eyes in which co-existed kindness and cruelty but which now wore an expression of beatitude as his victory was finally complete, and I – the upstart foreign intruder – was retreating and withdrawing from the battlefield. As I turned to go I heard his half-smothered laugh.

'Never mind. I'm sorry. Nothing is more wounding than the truth,' he said.

Nicolussi tried to restrain me, but he was more concerned to pump Gabetti for information than to salve my wounded pride. As I went back along the passages leading to the galleries I felt myself on the verge of tears. It is true that nothing wounds more than the truth, and it is true that I am unfit for the real world; it is for this reason that I lose myself in the tangle of my memories and take refuge in passivity and celibacy. But this realisation depressed me less than the notion that the future would never provide me with new landscapes to explore. My loneliness was incurable, and my isolation irretrievable; life would continue, without me, on the other side of the wall, even if it was a glass wall and I would be able to see what was happening through it and could even delude myself I might touch it if I chose. I crossed the room with the moulded ceiling reserved for paintings of the *trecento*, I crossed the next few rooms until I reached the small one that housed *The Tempest*. Possibly, in painting personages who are isolated from the real world around them, Giorgione had tried to represent the terrible malady that afflicted me. A screen obstructed access to the little room, and a notice apologised for its closure, in four languages, on the grounds of unspecified modifications. I ignored the notice, and taking advantage of the fact that no one was looking, slipped behind the screen. The floor of the room had been swept, and the glass in the skylight replaced, although the air still held the smell of fresh putty, a smell somewhere between that of a stable and a chemical laboratory. A direct, almost crude light fell on Giorgione's canvas, highlighting some of the defects I had only been able partially to detect on my last visit. Gabetti had been holding the torch, but its light had been inadequate, and it had not illuminated the whole canvas, leaving parts of it in the dark. Now that I could see *The Tempest* it lacked the refinement of colour and *tenebrismo* that appear in photographic reproductions; it lacked subtlety in its impasto and *sfumato*; it also lacked delicacy in its brushwork, that delicacy which made Giorgione the greatest painter of flesh of his age. I had to get even closer to the picture to verify what at first I had taken to be an optical illusion: the features of the woman suckling the baby as she gazes at the spectator with sensual sadness were identical to Chiara's, her oval chin, her contemplative lips, the nose slightly biased to one side, and her peasant eyes. At that moment, the solution to the mystery came to me in a sudden revelation. I still had to clarify a few details and relevant minor points, but the essence of it had been revealed to me.

THIRTEEN

'I'm sorry you have to leave,' Nicolussi repeated, apologetically. 'But it's better for you, and for me. Things are happening fast – there's a swarm of journalists round the police station, and this afternoon the investigating magistrate is due to take statements from the suspects. Apart from that, my days here are numbered.'

He spoke without rancour, as if he was already dwelling in that future place where he would find happiness, a place that has never figured on any map of my life. He had succeeded in persuading Gilberto Gabetti to volunteer to identify Sansoni's thugs as the men who had tried to steal *The Tempest*, and to the satisfaction he obtained from solving that case was added the powerful, unfettered satisfaction that at last he was settling his own accounts with the past, and had given up being a coward. Dina helped me do my packing: she refolded my shirts and piled them up with the skill of a bride-to-be from olden times, who has been busying herself for many years with the task of organising her trousseau.

'You're not even taking a souvenir of Venice with you,' she said, with commiseration.

But in fact I *was* taking souvenirs with me in the heavier

baggage of my memory, and they were as abundant as the blood in my veins. The presentiments of disaster that had been with me since my arrival in the city continued to gnaw at me with the inexorability of a curse, and had swept away the man I had been – inexperienced, frustrated, and celibate – to replace him with one who, on top of these inadequacies, suffered from the doleful knowledge that he was unable to cure them. A water-taxi was waiting for me by the bank of the canal.

'You've got plenty of time,' Nicolussi reminded me. 'Your flight doesn't leave until five.'

I gazed from the window at the bell tower of the church of San Stefano, leaning to the right like a lighthouse yielding to the surf; I gazed at the green and desolate stretch of water encircling the little square, and the façade of the palace that had been the scene of Fabio Valenzin's final encounter; I gazed at the alabaster balustrades and arches where the pigeons practised their cooing, balancing, and defecating, having quite forgotten the shot that had disturbed their sleep. Perhaps amnesia is the only lasting form of happiness.

'I shall ask the taxi-driver to take me on a tour of the islands in the lagoon,' I lied. 'And what are you going to do from now on?'

Nicolussi replied with that self-contained irony, or remoteness, we assume when we know we are invulnerable to all calamities, however fateful they may seem.

'They'll start disciplinary proceedings against me, I suppose. Several of those I picked up in last night's raid have complained about my abuse of authority.' He cast a yearning glance round the room, until his eyes met Dina's. 'I don't think their complaints will succeed, but they'll send me somewhere else to avoid trouble, and while I'm waiting for them to do that I shall carry on with the Valenzin case. After that, who knows . . .' He stopped, looking to Dina for approval. 'After that, she's the one in charge – possibly until we're married!'

There was a silence that brimmed with the expectation of future happiness that linked them, but excluded me. I felt cast down by the profound melancholy that invisible beings must be afflicted by.

'Well, let's not drag out our goodbyes,' I said.

Dina's reaction was to list a stream of good intentions: meetings that would never take place, promises to write and phone, which we could agree on when parting was imminent, but which would always be put off, because idleness and long distances would prevent us from maintaining these precarious loyalties.

'We'll let you have our news,' she continued. 'Now give me a big hug – and don't be unfriendly.'

I did not even feel the incongruous stab of desire that the proximity of Dina and the austere exuberance of her body had previously caused in me. They both came with me to the door of the hotel, out of an absurd sense of hospitality. Nicolussi avoided all formality.

'Good luck. And don't let things get you down – what Gabetti said was just a load of rubbish.'

I got into the water-taxi that backed until it was able to turn in the direction of the Grand Canal. The screw of the launch caught in the weed and the mud, which made the boat move jerkily forward. Dina and Nicolussi grew smaller in the distance, but before becoming indiscernible, they disappeared from my field of view.

'Where shall I take you?' asked the taxi-driver, without letting go of the rudder.

'To Torcello island,' I said. I still had my appointment with Tedeschi to keep.

The sun was rising quickly to its zenith, and its light flashed over the palaces, sparkling on their tawdry façades. As we went down the Grand Canal, I had the impression I was remaining stationary while that great display of cardboard structures was being carried out of Venice on its way to settling in other city scenarios. The taxi-driver gave me an odd look.

'Are you sure? Torcello is deserted at this time of year.'

He got no reply, and shrugged his shoulders; the promise of money made him respectful. We entered the lagoon through the Arsenal canal. The smell of the harbour water revived the terrors of my recent immersion in it, when I was on the point of drowning. We passed the walled cemetery of San Michele on our right, haloed by a sort of vapour perhaps caused by the dead all exhaling in unison as they rotted away under the earth. A mauvish light with discordant streaks of acidic gold in it sullied the atmosphere as we approached Murano. From there, Venice could be viewed as an immense spit of sand gleaming with mica, like a place apart, anchored in its own unreal world. The launch jolted noisily over the greyish waters of the lagoon, continuing in a straight line towards Torcello whose marshy shores could already be seen in the distance. Seagulls sped through the silent sky, like vultures clothed in baptismal white.

'Where do you want me to leave you?' asked the taxi-driver.

He had stopped the engine and was letting the launch drift towards the reeds that edge the shore. He looked at me with a mixture of distaste and benevolence, just as we look at suicides who have chosen an exotic location in which to do away with themselves.

'Go slowly into the island on one of the waterways.'

We entered through a canal that had pretensions to becoming a river, but whose turbid water was thick with putrefying matter. Many centuries before, Torcello had been rich and fertile, but the salt water had seeped into its soil and turned the land into an inhospitable bog, deserted by most of its population. Only a few fishermen remained there, living in shacks, like lake-huts on stilts, and they appeared in their doorways to watch me go past. The canal stopped suddenly, choked by weed and rubbish, in front of a church that combined elements of Romanesque and Byzantine architecture.

'I can't go any further,' barked the driver. His repugnance was turning to anger. 'Can we go back now?'

'Wait for me here. I'm going to have a look round.'

I had to pay him in advance – and generously at that – in order to allay his lack of confidence. I turned down a path carpeted with dead leaves, their rustle muted by the dampness that had softened them to the point that they blended into the mud. The inhabitants of Torcello – the very few inhabitants of Torcello – had bordered their smallholdings with cypresses that acted both as boundaries and defences. The sun shed a tense and malarial light through the branches and on the surroundings. I walked round the apse of the church, jumping between the thistles, and sinking at times up to my ankles in the boggy ground. I recognised Tedeschi by his uproarious laughter. Seated on a stone bench next to one of those huts on stilts, he was taking delight in the way I slipped and slid.

'I can see you're not a countryman,' was his greeting. 'You've no idea how galumphing you look.'

A fishing net was draped over his knees, and he was mending it with a needle the size of a skewer.

'I can't see what's funny about it, Tedeschi. Nobody can walk properly through all that mud.'

He stood up, and brushed the seat of his trousers before putting out a hand covered with fish scales.

313

'I see you've gone back to your old job,' I said.

'Let's just say I was sick of eating pigeons.' He opened the door of his hut and invited me in; I noticed immediately the sharp and powerful smell of soused fish, and the damp darkness, like a slap in the face. 'I was born here, and my family lived here until they had to move out when they started chucking their chemical rubbish into the lagoon.'

Apart from the nutritious smell of pickled fish, I was aware of the odour of respectable poverty, like a votive relic pining for its devotees. The hut, battered by the weather, had lost its internal dividing walls, and holes in the roof left it open to the sky. Tedeschi had put a rickety old bed in one corner, beside which he had laid out the essential items of his spartan existence: a transistor radio, a paraffin lamp, a gas cooker, and a carbine that was a relic of the wars of Garibaldi. Also, there was Fabio Valenzin's chest, huge and arched, like a Galapagos tortoise. In spite of having changed his residence, Tedeschi was still guarding the treasure, like a dragon in the old stories.

'That's quite a row Nicolussi's whipped up,' he said, revealing his rapacious teeth in his delight. 'You need balls to stir up a hornet's nest with the richest bastards in Venice like he's done. The radio never stops talking about it, and they've even mentioned the ring we got out of the canal as one of the main proofs against whoever committed the murder. But there hasn't been a squeak about you, although you must have helped.'

'Nicolussi and I made a pact: in return for my collaboration, he promised to keep my name out of it.'

Tedeschi crouched down and placed his hands reverentially on Valenzin's chest, as if he were conducting Mass over it.

'But what you don't know is what's inside the chest.'

Tedeschi raised the lid slowly, to draw out the suspense. 'I got it open at last by filing away the locks.'

I approached without pride, even with a sort of weary sadness.

'Of course I know, Tedeschi. The painting of *The Tempest*.'

He looked at me in bewilderment; he found it impossible to understand how I could have worked it out. He stammered:

'You've spoiled my surprise. How did you know?'

'Valenzin was an excellent forger, but there are details that an expert will always notice,' I said, with pride this time – I felt ashamed of pretending to a skill I did not possess. 'The one in the Accademia is a forgery. Somehow or other, Valenzin managed to get in and do a swap.'

The chest, lined with scanner-proof metal plates, was divided horizontally into three compartments, like strata, the contents of which became more felonious the deeper we delved. In the first one, there were piles of dirty shirts and stained underpants; in the second, Valenzin kept the papers recording his transactions, wads of bank-notes, false certificates of authenticity – if the contradiction may be permitted – and a list of his clients with the details of the commissions he had received from them, all meticulously set out as if they provided the material for future blackmail; in the third compartment, wrapped in insulating glass fibre, and inside a plastic bubble bag, was Giorgione's canvas. It was still on its original stretcher, and retained the chromatic subtlety that was lacking in Fabio Valenzin's forgery: the green that predominates in the composition fusing with the cobalt blue of the sky heavy with clouds, rippling with moving shadows in the foliage of the trees, turning iridescent in the water of the stream, mingling with yellow ochre in the grass, and providing the setting for the woman we see naked, barely screened by a shrub, and with a cloth draped over her shoulders like a small cloak. For the first and only time I was confronting the picture whose exegesis had consumed my youth. I had the ominous impression that all my efforts had been vain: my interpretations might perhaps serve to explain the painting, but not to appreciate it as a work of art. Tedeschi, meanwhile, maintained a reverential, almost funereal silence. At last, he said:

'But you were in the Accademia, so didn't you see they'd been swapped over?'

I defended myself without thinking deeply about it.

'It was dark, and I also had to worry about saving my skin.' In that moment too, while answering Tedeschi's question, I was endeavouring to save something more valuable than my skin, something which in fact I had lost for ever. 'You must understand I was in no mood to distinguish subtleties. When I was able to examine it more closely, I immediately realised what had happened.'

From the cabin, I could make out an expanse of marshland that depressed my spirits. Or possibly, the depressing effect lay deeper, and the landscape did no more than embody a display of pantheism. Tedeschi spoke in a voice that was muffled, as if it came through a helmet.

'I thought you'd be interested to discover the truth, but it seems I was wrong.'

'But what is the truth?' I began to feel the despair of a shipwrecked man. 'Truth is made up of prejudice and falsehoods. Do you really believe Fabio Valenzin is worth exposing the truth for? He was a creature devoid of moral scruples. The police have rounded up a few suspects. If they didn't kill him, they might well have done so, and that should be enough for us. We've already proved that neither of us was involved, so what does the rest of it matter?'

Tedeschi nodded slowly, like a man extricating himself from a duty that others have set him, and then rejecting the responsibility when he realises they no longer support him. He guessed that the full truth had been revealed to me, but he also guessed at the reasons that would help me conceal the truth. Deep down, I was grateful for his friendship and discretion.

'Right. And what are we going to do with this blessed chest?'

'Take it to the police. It will help you get into Nicolussi's good books, it contains papers that will support his version of events, and it will help him create an even bigger scandal.' I was quiet for a moment, and then winked as a way of engaging his complicity. 'If you don't mind, I'll take charge of the picture and return it personally to Gabetti. In this area, discretion is essential. I don't want him to lose his job because of us.'

There was no malice in his voice, just a hint of mockery.

'I've got you taped, my lad. Before, you said that Gabetti is an outright enemy of society. Obviously that girl's got something to do with it . . .'

I replaced *The Tempest* in its plastic bag. The paint was beginning to flake off, the joints of the stretcher had become loose with so much carrying about, and the wood was beginning to warp. It needed very careful restoration. Tedeschi gripped my arm with a hand that was almost a claw; his breath, not to mince matters, still smelled foul, but it also gave off the warmth of a hearth in which the most universal human emotions survive.

'It's been a pleasure, Ballesteros. You know you've always got a friend here.'

I left him before any expression of pity or compassion might betray my feelings, and followed the same muddy pathways that had led me there, and had made my shoes filthy. A church bell rang, with a peal like that of a cracked handbell, as if it came from a sacristy beyond the tomb; and the cypresses that bordered the smallholdings seemed to grow taller and more pointed, as if with funereal portent. The taxi-driver did not hide his surprise when he saw me; he had probably taken me for a misanthropist with suicidal tendencies, and had been waiting for the shot that would act as the starting gun for his departure.

'Let's go back to Venice,' I said. 'To the church of the Madonna dell' Orto.'

We returned through the stagnant water of the canal which was covered with a gelatinous green scum that turned into a sort of soup as it was churned up by the screws of the launch. Along the banks, like filthy dunghills, stunted weeds grew out of the skeletons of animals that had come near, and unsuspecting, had drunk of that water and died on the spot. I leaned *The Tempest* against the side of the launch and looked closely at it, just as Gabetti had recommended, without critical pretensions, in the way one looks at a living creature. It was then I realised that Giorgione's painting has no need of biblical or mythological interpretation; it thrills you by its very appearance, and communicates to the spectator the illusion of having been painted for him alone, as if it were an X-ray of his own soul. It was then that it ceased to be a more or less valuable object of study, and became an expression of my own yearnings. In *The Tempest*, as Chiara had pointed out, were to be found fear and anxiety caused by the storm that hangs suspended in the air, and also the sense of loss and mutilation resulting from storms of the spirit when they have become irrevocable. To appreciate *The Tempest* to the full meant plunging into the tangled and difficult terrain of suffering, into the jungle of memories that would begin to besiege me as soon as I left Venice. For the first time there was a tenuous but clean wintry light.

'Anywhere else you want to go?' asked the taxi-driver.

He had moored the launch at the flight of steps leading up to the courtyard of Madonna dell' Orto. As my stay in Venice had cost me very little, I had enough money in hand to allow myself the luxury of being lavish. Once again I paid him generously in advance.

'Wait a bit, and then you can take me to the airport.'

I picked up the painting and entered the church, which seemed to be deserted. The central apse, which on previous occasions had been lit by the lamp that helped Chiara in her work, was deep in shadow, and Tintoretto's paintings were barely visible. Only a smoky, greyish light, as if laden with incense, reached up to them, a light very different from that outside. On the side altar, however, the flame Chiara had lit in memory of Tintoretto was still burning, vigilant, like those oil lamps carried by the Wise Virgins in the parable of the Evangelist, when they went out to meet the groom. At the foot of the scaffolding that enveloped the *Last Judgement*, I found the basket in which Chiara kept her professional gear. I opened the wicker lid and took out the tubes of oil paint and brushes, before discovering the mask of the plague doctor made of porcelain, cold, white, and loathsome. It stared at me through its hollow eyes, and as I held it in my hands it seemed to breathe with a secret urgency that reverberated in the stones of the domed roof.

'I knew you would find out sooner or later,' said Chiara, from somewhere behind me. 'I knew right from the beginning. And I haven't tried hard to conceal it from you.'

It took me a while to make her out, sitting on a bench in the side aisle, that discreet shadowy area normally preferred by the excessively pious for mumbling their prayers once Mass is over. She looked thinner, perhaps because murder, like black mourning garments, slims the figure. She came towards me in the apse, her arms folded over her chest, as if she wanted to conceal the breasts I had tried vainly to round out the night before. The flame of the lamp stamped her profile in bronze.

'Look what I've brought you,' I said, and held up Giorgione's picture.

Chiara threw her arms around me, awkwardly, even despairingly, as if she wanted to reward me, and at the same time find consolation. I felt the soft, smooth convexity of her stomach in which I had deposited my seed – which perhaps was not sterile, perhaps it had linked with hers, and the two would sustain each other for the next nine months. But these were the thoughts of a catechist. I returned her embrace after placing *The Tempest* on the floor, and, as I had done when I first met her, I tried to assuage her tears that would leave traces of salt on the lapels of my raincoat.

'Alejandro, you cannot know how grateful I am. I thought I would never get it back.' She sobbed from pure joy, but it was a selfish joy. 'When I searched through the Albergo Cusmano and didn't find the chest I feared the worst. Then, when you told me that Tedeschi had taken it away, I nearly fainted. I thought he would get rid of it on the black market, and it would already be in the hands of some dealer.'

'Well, you can see you were wrong, because here it is,' I said. 'And you ought to be grateful to Tedeschi. If he hadn't disappeared with the chest, *The Tempest* would be held by the police. Inspector Nicolussi wouldn't have been slow to realise that the one on display in the Accademia is a forgery.'

Chiara knelt down to pick up Giorgione's painting; she removed the plastic bag, exposing it to the incense-laden light filtering through the embrasures of the apse. Her peasant eyes gleamed and she trembled with increasing gratitude.

'You can feel proud of yourself,' I murmured. 'You'll continue to be Venice's guardian angel.'

But she was not even listening to me. The joy she felt in getting the picture back possessed her; it was a sort of alienation setting her apart from this world. Religions, like all manifestations of fanaticism, have that inconvenience.

'Don't you think I deserve an explanation? Or am I just to be made use of and then thrown aside?' I insisted, feeling irritated and resentful.

But my resentment could not be blamed on the retrospective jealousy I felt for Valenzin, nor even on Gabetti's dominance over her. It was, rather, the resentment caused by deceit – taking a Levantine advantage of our better nature. Chiara turned aside, cautiously withdrawing from me. I detected in the corners of her mouth that expression of serenity, or discouragement, that had become a permanent feature of her appearance.

'You have no right to say that.'

'What do you mean, no right?' I was frightened by the sound of my own voice echoing like a blasphemy in the middle of the church. 'Both of you have lied to me, both of you have nearly driven me mad with your tricks, and now you tell me I have no right . . .'

But I knew truth does not exist, it is made up of partial or pious falsehoods; truth depends upon the point of view of the person speaking; nobody is infallible, omniscient, or even well-intentioned. Chiara spoke harshly – perhaps her severity was legitimate.

'Don't say *both* of us – I have never deceived you,' she said. 'I never encouraged you to build false hopes. Right from the beginning I made it clear I would never leave Gilberto and go away with you. Nor did I deceive you when I told you what I used to feel for Fabio.'

'What you felt for Fabio? Nobody kills the person they love.'

She stared at me from that remote place where those who live in a world apart dwell. I could have prevented her from relieving her guilty conscience, but having burdened myself with the confessions and sins of so many other people, what did one additional burden matter?

'We never kill the person we love unless we are moved by an even greater love. Fabio was a frequent guest in our house,' she began. The dim light, or perhaps remorse, drew obscure lines on her face. 'Although he disapproved of his activities, Gilberto felt an affection for him that went back a long way; it was a belligerent and nostalgic affection, like that between two old enemies who grant each other mutual respect. They had had a number of clashes in the past when Gilberto worked as an expert valuer for auction houses. Then there was a period during which they kept apart – Gilberto had various positions of responsibility, and Fabio began to traffic in works of art stolen from countries in America and the Far East. Gilberto moved to Venice, at first as consultant to the Accademia and member of its board of trustees, until later they made him director. His professional difficulties were not balanced by a happy home life. He married Giovanna Zanon, but the marriage was a failure from the start: she refused to have children, probably because she didn't want to spoil her figure. At least Gilberto succeeded in persuading her to agree to an adoption, and that is how I became the person he could turn to, and the one who encouraged him, as well as being an extension of himself. I was to be the one who would live on, and to whom he would bequeath his love of art, his only inheritance. Fabio came to stay with us from time to time, whenever he was shaking off the police.'

She stopped for a moment, intoxicated by her memories. Giovanna Zanon's slanders again began to exude their poison, proof that the person who listens to them is as guilty as the one who utters them. ('Gilberto wanted to keep her immaculate and for himself alone, just as God wants nuns in convents with unblemished skin and undefiled pudenda. Fabio Valenzin represented the outside world with its multiplicity of dangers and temptations.')

'And every one of his visits was an event.'

'An event, or a quarrel.' Chiara was trying to maintain a neutral tone, as if recounting someone else's life. 'I was a young girl, or adolescent, and every time he appeared Fabio disturbed and thrilled me. Through him I discovered worlds very remote from Venice; he talked of cities and peoples whose existence I didn't even suspect. He was also very patient with me. About that time I was taking my first steps in painting, and Fabio taught me the techniques and tricks of the trade. Without realising it I was turning into the most valuable piece in the game of chess that Gilberto and Fabio had been playing for years, the one that justified their opposing strategies: Gilberto, on the defensive, trying to keep me at all costs so that he would live on through me, as if I was the treasure in his castle; Fabio, on the attack, opening a breach in that castle, using me as a battering ram, without worrying too much if I was lost in the process. Gradually, as he obtained a fixed clientele and established his contacts, Fabio travelled less; he set up his base in Venice and his presence ceased to be an event – but still caused altercations.'

Her mouth was dry, and her contemplative lips had turned the colour of parchment, as if corroded by her words.

'You fell in love with him,' I said, to save her having to recount certain passages that I recalled from another occasion.

'I was so ingenuous, or conceited, that I believed myself capable of curing his sickness. But Fabio was impervious to all cures, he was never able to respond to me, although he tried, in his own perverse way.' I was aware of an element of anger in her voice, but she buried it in words of resigned sarcasm. 'For years I persevered in my love for him, for years I sacrificed myself, and I was the battering ram that opened the breach, the captured piece that Fabio could display as a trophy to Gilberto. I also helped him in some of his forgeries – he succeeded in convincing me that there was no crime in deceiving criminals. There was one point on which I refused to give way: "never even think of taking anything out of Venice," I warned him, but what I attempted to forbid gradually became the object of his greed. He had another reason, besides, for ignoring my warning: Venice was Gilberto's spiritual home, and every theft that took place within its jurisdiction was a blow directed at his old adversary.'

'You were the piece captured from the enemy,' I said. 'And you are the queen who has put herself at risk in the end game.'

Tintoretto's figures on the side walls of the apse seemed to be drawing away from us, as if they anticipated their disintegration.

'Fabio had already planned his checkmate, but I still don't understand what made him do something so wicked. A few months before, he had swindled Giovanna Zanon and Taddeo

Rosso out of a vast sum by selling them his forgery of Bellini's *Madonna*. You already know that story. Taddeo Rosso introduced him to another millionaire called Daniele Sansoni, who had developed a strange mania for collecting paintings that incorporated broken pillars in their composition. Fabio immediately palmed him off with a forged Delvaux that featured naked women in a ruined Doric temple, one of the specialities of his youth. But Sansoni was determined to possess works which would outdo the *Madonna* that Taddeo Rosso kept in his study. Inevitably his eye lighted on *The Tempest*, for which he was willing to pay an incredible sum, even surprising Fabio, whose demands were by no means modest or restrained. I learned all this from Fabio himself. He told me about it as a big joke, and showed me the ring Sansoni had given him as a token of their "gentlemen's agreement". I remember he actually used that expression. He also confided in me what he planned to do: he was going to prepare a copy of *The Tempest* and sell it to Sansoni as if it was authentic. Afterwards, he would disappear with the money for a very long time, in order to avoid any reprisals his client might exact when he found out he had been swindled. And to crown it all, Fabio told me he was hoping to make this forgery his final gift to posterity, and he counted on my co-operation. "I want you to pose for me again." It seemed to me a dangerous and inadvisable jest.'

'Then why did you agree to pose?'

She was slow to reply, possibly because she felt ashamed of her weakness, or her collusion in the crime.

'On one hand I was afraid of going against him, and he had a knack for overcoming my reluctance. On the other, as I had been his model on previous occasions, I couldn't easily refuse. After a couple of weeks shut up in his workshop in the Stucky Mill, he had the forgery ready, but he still had to wait for the paint to dry so that the fraud would be credible. One day he phoned to say he had agreed to hand it over to Sansoni at midnight the following day. I was surprised by the excitement in his voice, and his volubility, because he had always been reserved, almost cryptic, when talking about matters like this. It was then he told me he had a room in the Albergo Cusmano that he used as a hiding-place for his thefts. Although his voice was distorted by the phone I knew that that unusual fit of loquacity was not a prelude to leaving me, because he proposed that I should go off with him. I had to make an immense effort to turn him down. I still felt a remnant of my old love for him. He insisted, promising that he would go straight at last, and begged me to give him one more chance. I found it almost impossible to repeat my refusal – I was choked with tears. Before hanging up, and in a much more serious voice, Fabio made me write down a telephone number in case I changed my mind. I couldn't sleep that night, I was torn in all directions.'

Her profile suddenly took on the vulnerable but immutable delicacy of statues that remain on their pedestals even after an earthquake. The poet's words came back to mind:

> I want love or death, I want to die completely
> I want to be you, your blood . . .

'You decided to stay here out of loyalty to Gabetti,' I said.

'For him, and for everything he stands for, maybe from loyalty to an idea, although that may sound stupid to you. My place is here beside Gilberto, surrounded by the things he loves.' Again I admired, and lamented, her vocation for self-sacrifice. 'By dawn the next day, Venice was overwhelmed by the *acqua alta*. One of the buildings most threatened by flooding is the Accademia because it is near the mouth of the Grand Canal. Although the museum employees worked like demons to bail it out as if their lives were at stake, Gilberto had to call on the fire brigade for help. He was busy all day, organising things, and begging for help from other institutions. During one of his absences, and in the middle of the confusion that reigned in the museum, *The Tempest* disappeared. The robbery was carried out through the skylight, not as clumsily as that attempt by Sansoni's underlings, but by a complicated system of pulleys, which made it obvious it was done by a very skilful thief. Gilberto rang me from the Accademia in a state of collapse, and sounding horror-struck. He knew as well as I did who had done it, but he didn't name him, out of a sense of decency. I begged him to calm down, and assured him that in a couple of hours the picture would be back in the Accademia.'

Her breathing had become laboured, loud even, like that of a wounded animal; it was not the breathing of a person who murders casually. Again I thought of the poet's lines:

I die because I am fearless, because I want to die,
because I want to live in the flame, because this alien air
is not mine, but a hot breath
that burns me if I draw near . . .

I would have died or killed for the breath of Chiara, if I had been fearless, but I am a coward.

'I dialled the number Fabio had given me the night before,' she continued. 'He had lost all his excitement and volubility; now he spoke in monosyllables, and evasively, possibly because his guilty conscience prevented him being more explicit. He told me to meet him in the palace opposite the Albergo

Cusmano, but he made no attempt to spare me his insolence – he made it clear it would only be a brief meeting because he had other commitments. I knew then that it would not be easy to get *The Tempest* from him, that he would blackmail me and use me again like a piece on a chessboard. I noticed that I was beginning to feel an implacable hatred for him – nothing like that other type of hate which is more impetuous, but also less lasting. Before going out, I took the pistol Gilberto keeps in his bedside table, a souvenir of his youthful combats, which even today his enemies use to discredit him.'

The mask of the plague doctor stared up at us from the bottom of the basket with that unwavering persistence of corpses abandoned to the elements, when the vultures have devoured their eyeballs.

'Why did you disguise yourself?'

She was leaning against the scaffolding that protected the *Last Judgement*, as if she wanted to submit herself to the divine verdict being dispensed in the upper reaches of the picture.

'It would be an exaggeration to say I was in disguise.' She gave a slow and barely perceptible smile. 'I took an old cloak out of my wardrobe to wrap round *The Tempest*, which I hoped to get back at all costs, and as I was leaving I also picked up the mask. I had a feeling my meeting with Fabio might end violently, and I thought that if I put the mask on I would prevent anybody recognising me as I returned home. It was the eve of Carnival, so my clothes wouldn't attract unnecessary attention. Fabio arrived punctually. His attitude surprised me greatly. He was both insolent and contrite. I asked him to give me back *The Tempest*. He roared with laughter, but there was also a deep sadness in his look. Then he made an obscene remark about Gilberto and my relationship with him. It was a vile thing to say, and until then I had heard it only from

our enemies, a vileness that has a certain currency in Venice.'
I blushed and felt mean, because there had been a time when
I too had given credence to that vileness, although it would
never have passed my lips. But the person who listens is as
guilty as the one who speaks. 'Not only did he say that, he also
mentioned certain absurd circumstances and details that only a
perverted mind could have thought up. When he stopped at
last, he shook his bunch of keys, as if they were a rattle.
"You'll have to kill me first if you want to get hold of these,"
he challenged me. Or perhaps he was asking me to kill him.
I scarcely know how to use a pistol. I fired point-blank at his
chest, but even so I didn't succeed in killing him outright.'

I conjured up the scene: dagger shapes of moonlight would
have been entering through the balcony of the *piano nobile*,
lighting up the wall mirrors in which Fabio Valenzin may
have seen himself for the last time, with that spectral distortion
caused by blood clouding the retina.

'I grabbed the keys and tore off the ring Sansoni had given
him. I was so terrified I couldn't think of a better place to hide
it than the bottom of the canal,' Chiara continued. 'Then, with
a great effort, Fabio made off in the direction of the staircase,
leaving behind a trail of blood that went on pouring out of
him. I wanted to stop him, but I saw you from across the
balcony, at one of the windows of the Albergo Cusmano, and
I was paralysed with fright. I had to leave by a back door,
without the chest. I returned to the hotel the next day, after
the burial on San Michele, but you had got there before me.
I am still sorry for the way I hit the lady who runs the hotel,
but I didn't have time to stand on ceremony.'

I apologised, rather absurdly.

'I'm sorry I've caused you so many problems.'

I caressed her forehead for the last time; for the last time I parted the locks and wisps of hair that covered her ears and viewed that beloved face in which I viewed the world, the face that 'mirrors the flight of graceful birds, who fly to the land of the unforgotten'.

'It was much more difficult concealing the theft of *The Tempest* from you.' Once again she smiled, as if asking for mercy. 'I had to drop some sleeping pills in the glass of milk I warmed up for you, just after we met.' She seemed to be speaking of a very distant time – but Venice slows time down, suspends it, and turns it into a flexible substance, like dreams. 'While you were sleeping, Gilberto and I went to Giudecca, to Fabio's workshop, where his copy of *The Tempest* still remained, and we put it up in the Accademia, in the place of the original. We set up that pantomime of the evening visit to the museum so that you wouldn't notice the change, and to keep you quiet. We couldn't delay the reason for your visit any longer. Obviously, we didn't expect we'd be attacked by those two thugs.'

She had folded her arms again in order to hide her breasts, and was trembling in spite of herself.

'From the moment I met you, the reason for my journey here lost all its meaning,' I said.

I have a tendency to be grandiloquent, possibly because I am celibate, although in that moment I was moved primarily by the memory of the one time with her when I had betrayed my celibacy.

'For me too there were many things that lost their importance. I had constantly to stop and tell myself "come on, Chiara, you can't just let yourself go." But even so, I did occasionally let go, I couldn't be on my guard the whole time.'

She looked up at the paintings, as if seeking a motive for returning to her work of restoration.

'I like you very much, Alejandro. But you came too late.'

She had recovered that determination and spirit of renunciation by which saints are consumed, and which impels them to perform the most altruistic, or fearsome, of tasks. 'And now you must go.'

I succeeded in obtaining one last kiss, I succeeded in undermining her resistance, stealing the saliva from her mouth which had the taste of a rose's thorn. The incense-laden light fell like a deadly sword on my neck.

'Please go away, Alejandro.'

She drew her body away from mine, and climbed the scaffolding, stricken by a sickness for which there was no cure. I obeyed her, although my legs were trembling, just as Anchises' legs must have trembled when Zeus's thunderbolt struck him, leaving him forever after unable to stand erect without the aid of a stick. My footsteps echoed in the stone vaulting; they sounded as old as the world. Before leaving the church, I turned round to look at her one last time, to preserve that final vision in the storehouse of my memories. She had switched on the lamp that lit up Tintoretto's figures, and was preparing to continue with her work of restoration that would only stop when Venice ceased to be a city, and became an underwater cemetery, with palaces as mausoleums, and large squares where the dead would walk.

FOURTEEN

Other faces grow faint and disappear into the common grave of oblivion, but not Chiara's. Time has recovered its normal momentum, the months pass imperceptibly by, the years pass in banal procession, but her features and her voice and the touch of her skin endure, while all the rest becomes a blur. I shall soon cease to be an assistant lecturer. At last Professor Mendoza is satisfied that I have fulfilled the quota of servility that I was duty bound to pay him, and has decided to wangle an examining board packed with influential friends and relations that will sanction my elevation in the university hierarchy. Professor Mendoza has not yet made me a partner in his academic intrigues, but he no longer confines himself to imposing demeaning chores on me; nowadays, he also passes on to me his more dilapidated mistresses (at third or fourth hand), and his more dimwitted female students (those unlikely to achieve better than third or fourth class degrees), so that I can relieve my celibacy with them, and begin to flaunt my virility, an indispensable requisite for obtaining a professorial chair before retirement. They have appointed me to a regular course, in which I teach my pupils the interpretation and analysis of art, but never its appreciation, because it would be inappropriate for our young men to develop a religion of feeling and emotion. They are also preparing a little office for me next to Professor Mendoza's. This is a stroke of luck because now I shall not have to put up with the more boisterous and bumptious of the students – there are candidates lower down the scale who will do that for me. In the university, as in the most needy families, everything is handed down from one generation to the next.

Other faces grow faint and disappear into the common grave of oblivion, but not Chiara's. That is the only way I can survive in the sewer of my present life, the only way I can endure the degrading routine of lectures, tutorials, and departmental council meetings, the only way I can display my gratitude to Professor Mendoza without grinding my teeth, and can listen to his amatory triumphs, which nowadays – since he has decided to promote me – I not only have to listen to with respect, but have to cap with accounts of my own successes. Details like this reveal that he has stopped thinking of me as a subordinate, and accepts me as a colleague. Another sign of the confidence he has placed in me is revealed by the frequency with which he calls me into his office so that I can watch while he lambasts the grant-aided students, usually for the most trivial and arbitrary of reasons, and also so that I can listen to the easy way in which he deals on the phone with other intriguers in the capital who hold key posts in the Ministry of Culture. It is clear he is trying to teach me his own despotic and courtly habits. At times, between lectures, tutorials, departmental council meetings, and the audiences in Professor Mendoza's office, there are intervals of inactivity, and then the stench of the sewer I live in assaults my nostrils. It hits me in the very guts of my dignity, and I almost weep with rage.

Other faces grow faint and disappear into the common grave of oblivion, but not Chiara's. When I finish my work for the day, I shut myself away in my house, and sit there thinking of her. I remember her in minute detail, never in the abstract, but with limitless precision. Today I remember her hair like the frayed strings of a violin, and tomorrow her hearty chuckle, and the next day the fleeting signs of pleasure that passed across her face while I was sharing that pleasure with her. To remember everything of Chiara is both a punishment and an insuperable task, but even were I to succeed I would start all over again; maybe it is a punishment, but I accept its torments and my exhaustion and the prison of those memories, because they keep me alive and cleanse me of my degrading existence. At first, I feared that the eroding effect of time would distort my recollections, or create gaps in them. All my previous experiments in resurrecting the past had succumbed to the corruption of oblivion and to the superimposition of some events on others, but I can state categorically that my fear of forgetting Chiara was unfounded. The images I have of her mount up, not one displaces another, they all persist, awaiting recall and filing, ready to be classified and catalogued. Just as gifts are not received without being reciprocated, I am having to pay for the persistence of these memories with wakeful nights that resist all sleeping pills, and with retreats into introspection, but this penance is worthwhile if, in return, I can relive my sin. I only stop remembering when I am asleep, although I continue to summon up Chiara in my dreams: I do this in a more imaginative way, without adhering strictly to what actually happened. Thus, I can fantasise about the present, making it different and kinder, one in which my memories of Chiara are displaced by Chiara in the flesh, her back sheltered by my stomach and my chest, and by her breathing. But it would be wrong to go too far in what was not, is not, and will not be.

Other faces grow faint and disappear into the common grave of oblivion, but not Chiara's. I have forgotten the features of Daniele Sansoni and his thugs, although I would still recognise one of them by his mutilated ear; I have been able, however, to read in Italian newspapers that they were acquitted of the murder of Fabio Valenzin, due to lack of proof. I am almost incapable of recalling the faces of Taddeo Rosso and Giovanna Zanon, although they did come briefly back to mind when I saw their photographs in the same newspapers, under the headline about the scandal that dominated the front pages. This implicated them in a plot involving the theft and trafficking in works of art, but it died down when it was found that all they had done was to traffic in forgeries. Nor can I recall Nicolussi's face, but I have memories of a tobacco smell and a rapid growth of beard. I rejoice that he gave up being a man paralysed by conflicts of conscience, I rejoice that he escaped from Venice and married Dina in a civil wedding in Naples. I know this because Dina herself kept her promise to write by sending me a brief postcard from that city – more southern and better suited to Nicolussi's accent, and better suited to Dina's buxom exuberance. She will surely have abandoned her severe manner as well as her black sweaters, and her Byzantine eyes will shine more brightly, and her breasts will be more prominent, those soft breasts that I succeeded in squeezing with these hands of mine that turned out to be no good at exploring them because they retained the lingering feel of other, much smaller breasts. However, I have not heard anything about Tedeschi, and his physiognomy has also succumbed to the levelling effect of oblivion, but I almost long for the smell of that vinous breath of his when I compare it with the stench of the sewer that my university gives off, and I continue to rejoice nostalgically in those ancient and universal emotions he was blessed with, emotions that I no longer find anywhere. Of Fabio Valenzin's corpse on San Michele island, all I hope for is that it has rotted away, and that the photograph illustrating the epitaph on his tomb has faded so much that only the healthy teeth in his skull remain visible. I hope Chiara has forgotten him, so that she can revert to being the flesh and blood woman she hides within herself, the woman who at times burns with desire, and at others, is consumed with sadness. Perhaps the one who best outlives the ravages of oblivion is Gilberto Gabetti. Although his snow-white hair and his eyes in which co-exist kindness and cruelty and his hands blotched with vitiligo will have sunk finally into old age, Chiara will be his prop and his pride and his guardian angel. From a distance I admire him, I envy him, and I detest him.

Other faces grow faint and disappear into the common grave of oblivion, but not Chiara's. I have bought a print of *The Tempest*, a full-size poster that I have fixed to the wall of my room with four drawing pins, just in front of the window, so that when it rains, the reflection of the water trickling down the glass appears to fall on it and to melt the face of the woman suckling her child with sensual sadness; in this way I can distinguish through the blur the features of Chiara, her patrician features, with the sole exception of her eyes, which gaze at me like those of a peasant girl. When I contemplate Giorgione's painting, and I do so for many hours towards the end of the day, I cannot avoid putting myself in the place of the pilgrim who also enjoyed her favours, but must be content with watching her from a distance. When I dream of Giorgione's painting, and I do so for many hours of the night, I cannot avoid my catechistic thoughts becoming an illusion or chimera, and then I believe that the baby in the arms of its mother is the son that Chiara and I have produced since my seed lodged in her womb on that one and only occasion, the son who will grow up to follow the same profession as his mother, to safeguard Venice against cataclysms, and have himself ordained a priest of art, which is a religion of feeling and emotion – although I conceal this from my pupils. After these dreams, I awake, and after waking I feel the oppressive certainty that I shall never have children, because my destiny is to be sterile and celibate.

Other faces grow faint and disappear into the common grave of oblivion, but not Chiara's. At times while I am washing and looking at myself in the mirror, I wonder what would become of me if I did not have these consolations, and this punishment. While I am still not quite awake, my face puffy and my eyes bleary, I quickly find the answer: I should be an animal who understands nothing about himself, trapped between a rootless present and a non-existent future. In this way, at least I have a past, and can recall it at will, and dwell in it.

AUTHOR'S NOTE

As gratitude is a rare commodity, and is too often diminished by expressions of disapproval and disparagement, I wish to record here the names of those who have given me so much help. *The Tempest* would have remained 'written in sand' if my father had not worn himself out typing an almost illegible manuscript, to the detriment of his sleep and his health. Moreover, it is his interpretation of Giorgione's painting that Alejandro Ballesteros delivers in chapter seven, an interpretation that is in no way inferior to those put forward by more learned experts. I owe Iñaqui a debt for his unfailing support and company, his consideration, and his search for textual errors: his calm and composure are always a comfort. Silvia eased the writing process by her permanent smile. I owe to Luis García Jambrina, amongst other benefits, the stimulus of friendship; while I was writing this novel, Mercedes was pregnant and I am delighted, and honoured, that the publication of the book has coincided with the birth of their daughter. Blanca always calls me ingenuous when she is angry, but I believe she still derives pleasure from my ingenuousness, as well as from my passionate enthusiasm for literature, which can only be compared with that which I get just from looking at her. She does not, however, approve of my getting drunk in the Balmoral bar. Luis Alberto de Cuenca remains a devoted and reliable friend who is capable of turning the National Library upside down to fulfil my requirements. Also, José Luis García Martín and Antonio Sánchez Zamarreño, who put up with my telephone calls at all hours.

The Tempest is an eclectic book, romantic in the broadest sense of the word, militantly non-realistic, although it employs familiar techniques. A criminal investigation, a love story, and a web of intrigue, often using the methods of pulp fiction and B-movies, have provided me with a framework for expressing my deepest feelings and most intimate anxieties, as well as for vindicating art as the religion of feeling and emotion.

I end by quoting Julien Gracq, a votary like myself of Gothic darkness and oppressive atmospheres: 'May the mighty wonders of the Mysteries of Udolpho, of the Castle of Otranto, and of the House of Usher be mobilised here to communicate to these frail words a little of the magic powers that their chains, their ghosts, and their coffins have preserved: the author can do no less than render homage to them for the enchantment they have never failed to lavish on him'.

Salamanca, October 1997

THE CRIME OF OLGA ARBEYELINA
ANDREÏ MAKINE

Olga Arbyelina, a White Russian princess living quietly with her adolescent son in a small French town, is a relative newcomer to the Russian community there. Intriguingly little is known about her when, in the summer of 1947, she is suspected of murdering a fellow émigre, only for the case to be dropped. As the story unfolds of the preceding year, a picture forms of her upbringing in Russia followed by her exile and marriage in Paris, and the details of a darker, hidden crime begin to emerge, encircling the narrative in an ever-tightening snare.

'The book's fascination, and enormous power, is in the nuanced process by which Olga discovers (and we do with her) what this son, whom she thinks of as a boy in need of protection, has been doing to her ... Monstrous and delicate, convincing and nightmarish, the process challenges your ideas about madness, self-delusion and mother-love in glowing, gauze silk prose'
Ruth Padel in the DAILY TELEGRAPH

'Makine manages plot and atmosphere so cleverly that the reader is desperate to know what happens next ... In his evocation of a golden age long past and his delicate, sensual handling of Olga's relationship with her son, the writing brings Nabokov to mind, but there is no doubt that Makine has his own voice'
Lucy Dallas in THE TIMES LITERARY SUPPLEMENT

'Makine deserves our full attention, he exerts impressive control over [his] themes, hops back and forwards through time with ease, and ultimately never forgets the value of a simple and compelling story'
Lucy Atkins in THE SUNDAY TIMES

'Wonderfully vivid. The descriptions of the terrible, in more ways than one, winter of 1946–7 are glittering'
Allan Massie in the SCOTSMAN

∫

SCEPTRE

THE NANNY AND THE ICEBERG
ARIEL DORFMAN

Conceived the night of Che Guevara's burial in 1967, Gabriel
McKenzie is inextricably bound up in the history and politics
of his native Chile. Twenty-four years on, and still a virgin,
Gabriel returns from Manhattan exile to confront his legacy: a
Don Juan father and a country preparing for the 500th anniversary
of America's 'discovery'. Into Gabriel's quest for manhood and
identity enter one iceberg, a faithful if eccentric nanny and a whole
host of fantastical characters.

'Wonderfully peopled with döppelgangers, metafictional turns and
doses of myth and magic. It affirms Ariel Dorfman's place, alongside
Vargos Llosa and Gabriel Garcia Márquez, as one of the finest
voices in contemporary Latin American storytelling'
Dominic Bradbury in THE TIMES

'A bravura performance, knitted by a suave, hypnotising prose . . .
fascinating' *Llan Stavans* in the INDEPENDENT

'The writing is vital, urgent, energetic, the twists and turns of the
plot ingeniously unpredictable: a magician's box of tricks'
Brian Martin in the FINANCIAL TIMES

SCEPTRE

A selection of bestsellers from Sceptre

The Crime of Olga Arbyelina	by Andreï Makine	0 340 72815 9	£6.99	☐
The Nanny and the Iceberg	by Ariel Dorfman	0 340 71303 8	£6.99	☐
Echoes of War	by William Rivière	0 340 69607 9	£6.99	☐
Casanova	by Andrew Miller	0 340 68210 8	£6.99	☐
Facing Out to Sea	by Peter Adamson	0 340 69565 X	£6.99	☐

All Sceptre books are available at your local bookshop or newsagent, or can be ordered direct from the publisher. Just tick the titles you want and fill in the form below. Prices and availability subject to change without notice.

Hodder & Stoughton Books, Cash Sales Department, Bookpoint, 39 Milton Park, Abingdon, OXON, OX14 4TD, UK. E-mail address: order@bookpoint.co.uk. If you have a credit card you may order by telephone – (01235) 400414.

Please enclose a cheque or postal order made payable to Bookpoint Ltd to the value of the cover price and allow the following for postage and packing:
UK & BFPO – £1.00 for the first book, 50p for the second book, and 30p for each additional book ordered up to a maximum charge of £3.00.
OVERSEAS & EIRE – £2.00 for the first book, £1.00 for the second book, and 50p for each additional book.

Name _____

Address _____

_____

_____

If you would prefer to pay by credit card, please complete:
Please debit my Visa/Access/Diner's Card/American Express (delete as applicable) card no:

Signature _____

Expiry Date _____

If you would NOT like to receive further information on our products please tick the box. ☐